Life of Crime

By the same author

Billie Jo
Born Evil
The Betrayer
The Feud
The Traitor
The Victim
The Schemer
The Trap
Payback
The Wronged
Tainted Love
Backstabber

Kimberley CHAMBERS

Life of Crime

HarperCollins*Publishers*

HarperCollins*Publishers* Ltd
1 London Bridge Street,
London SE1 9GF

www.harpercollins.co.uk

First published by HarperCollins*Publishers* 2018
1

A catalogue record for this book is available from the British Library

ISBN: 978-0-00-814473-9 (HB)
ISBN: 978-0-00-820846-2 (TPB)

Typeset in Sabon LT Std by
Palimpsest Book Production Ltd, Falkirk, Stirlingshire

Printed and bound by CPI Group (UK) Ltd, Croydon CR0 4YY

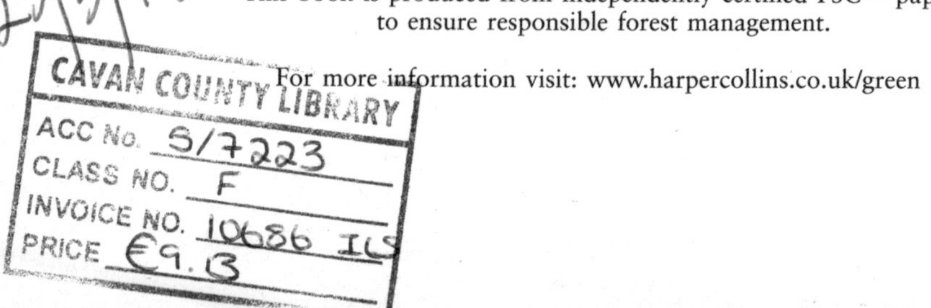

In memory of my dear friend Ronnie's son
Lee John Richardson
1974–2008

ACKNOWLEDGEMENTS

Many thanks to Tim Bates, Kimberley Young, Sue Cox, Pat Fletcher, Felicity Denham, Laura Meyer, Charlie Redmayne, Rosie de Courcy and the whole of the amazing HarperCollins team.

Thanks also to Mauricio Pochettino for making Spurs a joy to watch again. And I can't not mention Harry Kane. Not just one of our own – simply the best!

And last but not least, thanks to all my lovely readers.

'We are all in the gutter,
But some of us are looking at the stars'

Oscar Wilde

PROLOGUE

I was thirteen the first time I ever got arrested and can remember it as though it were yesterday. I was driving a stolen Ford Escort MK 2, my feet barely able to touch the pedals, yet I'd still been able to handle that car like a man.

Cigarettes, I'd been caught with. Illegal ones that'd been brought into the country from Belgium via France. Yet no matter how hard the Old Bill interrogated me, I never admitted to where I'd really got those fags from.

'One of life's losers, that's what you are. You'll never amount to nothing, you stupid little bastard,' my mother bellowed when the Old Bill brought me home.

'Only fools break the law. You're an idiot, boy,' my schoolteacher hissed in my ear the following Monday morning.

Well, I've got news for them. I ain't no loser, neither am I a fool. A bastard perhaps, thanks to my embarrassment of a mother having no idea who my father is. But I'm a winner, and ever since that day I've been determined to prove all the doubters wrong.

I was gifted with charm, good looks, the gift of the gab

and intelligence – all the tools a man needs to make it to the very top. And if I need to trample on a few people's lives and feelings to get there, then so be it.

Well, that's what I used to think, anyway. But I've since learned different.

Sometimes in life – especially when it's a life of crime you're involved in – things don't go to plan.

My name is Jason Rampling and this is my story . . .

PART ONE

CHAPTER ONE

Spring 1994

Johnny Brooks glanced up from his newspaper and looked at his daughter inquisitively over his thin-rimmed reading glasses. 'And where do you think you're off to, young lady?'

'Only to the Sunday market with Trace. I'll be back before dinner.'

'Haven't you forgotten something?' Johnny asked shirtily.

Twenty-one-year-old Melissa sighed. She was running half an hour late as it was; she'd promised to be at Tracey's by eleven. 'What?'

Johnny gestured towards the child who'd caused so many arguments and so much personal heartbreak. 'Your mum isn't well enough to look after your son today. She's gone back to bed with a migraine.'

'Another one? Can't you keep an eye on Donte, Dad? Please. I promise I won't be long,' Melissa asked hopefully.

'No. I bloody well can't. He's your son and you knew your life would change when you decided to have him.

Your mum's run down lately. I don't want you putting her under any more pressure. It isn't fair, swanning off whenever you feel like it.'

Melissa Brooks picked up her son and glared at her father. 'Come on, Donte, let's get away from the old bigot. If you were white, he'd be happy to take you to the Working Men's Club with him. But he hates taking you anywhere because you're mixed-race.'

'That's a lie and you know it, Mel. I like to enjoy a pint on a Sunday and relax. Not baby-bloody-sit a toddler. You made your bed, you lie in it.'

When the front door slammed, Johnny Brooks cursed. He was old school and loathed the fact that she'd got herself knocked up out of wedlock. But that wasn't the reason he was so tetchy of late. His beloved wife was dying – the doctors had found a cancerous tumour on her brain – and nobody else in the family knew, bar him.

'You're late,' Tracey Thompson snapped.

'I know. Sorry.'

'Bloody hell, Mel. I told you to dress up a bit. You could've made more of an effort. And why've you brought Donte with you? You said you'd be leaving him indoors.'

'My mum's not well again so I had to bring him. And it's pouring with rain, case you hadn't noticed, that's why I wore my Timberlands. You're not wearing those high heels, are you? Your feet'll get soaked.'

Tracey studied herself in the hallway mirror. Her long blonde hair wouldn't be blown out of place as she'd used half a can of extra-strong lacquer on it. Determined to impress, she was wearing her ripped faded jeans, short denim jacket, a belly top that showed off her recent piercing and red stiletto sandals. 'How do I look?' she asked, satisfied that she looked incredible.

'Nice. But it's nippy out so you'll probably freeze to death. Never mind. You wanted to stand out, didn't you?'

Tracey chuckled. She had her eye on a lad who worked at Dagenham Sunday Market, hence her getting so dolled up. 'Come on then, bitch, let's go.'

Johnny Brooks sipped his pint while discussing yesterday's football results. Rainham Working Men's Club was his regular Sunday lunchtime haunt. Stepney born and bred, Johnny lived in South Hornchurch now and owned a successful builders' merchants. Everybody knew him in Rainham as that's where his business was. Back in the day, he had been a decent amateur boxer. Although at five foot eight he wasn't the tallest of men, he was sturdy like a bull, and had carved out quite a hard-man reputation for himself over the years. He was forty-eight now and had recently had his ginger hair cropped to cover up the fact his hair had started to recede.

'Your old pal's just walked in, Johnny. I thought he was still in the clink,' said Scottish Paul.

Glancing around, Johnny's expression turned to one of anger. Craig Thurston had been a business associate of his – until they'd fallen out over money. Carol had warned him to steer well clear of the man in future and Johnny hadn't even known he was out of prison.

'He's coming over, Johnny,' Brian the Cabbie added, well aware there was no love lost between his pal and Thurston.

At six foot three, Craig Thurston was a lump. He'd made good use of the gym while in prison and sauntered towards Johnny with a cocksure grin on his face. 'Well, well, well, if it ain't my old mucker, Brooksy. Got that dosh you owe me, have ya? Only I'm collecting my debts now I'm a free man again.'

'Do one, Thurston. I owe you sod-all and you know it,' Johnny spat, even though that wasn't entirely true.

'Not the way I see it, pal. Fifty grand I lost, thanks to you, and I want it back.'

In no mood to part with any money or even discuss what had happened, Johnny stuck to his guns. 'Your own stupidity lost you your dosh, just like it lost you your livelihood. Now, if you don't mind, I'd like to finish my pint in peace.'

Craig grinned, showing the one gold tooth he'd treated himself to before he got ripped off; he knew exactly which buttons to press. 'A little birdy told me your Melissa got herself knocked up. What's your little grandson called again? Shoeshine boy?'

Johnny flew out of his seat and shoved Thurston against the wall. 'You leave my family out of this.' It wasn't Johnny's fault that a mate of his had done a runner with Craig's dosh.

Hearing the barmaid threaten to call the police, Thurston's pal grabbed him by the arm. 'Come on, Craig. Let's sort this another time.'

Craig pointed a finger in Johnny's face. 'I want my dosh, Brooksy – or else. Made sure you got yours, didn't ya, you slippery piece of work.'

'Or else what? You come near my daughter or grandson, I'll fucking kill ya, d'ya hear me?'

'I wonder what your Carol would say if she knew you were shagging your secretary?' Craig tutted, his eyes twinkling with devilment. 'Shirley Stone's her name, isn't it? Blonde, big tits, I can see the attraction. Might have to have a crack at her meself.'

Still able to throw a decent punch, Johnny flew at Craig like a raging bull.

When Craig fought back and Johnny ended up sprawled across the table, smashing their beer glasses, Brian the Cabbie and Scottish Paul intervened. 'Leave it now, Johnny. Can't you see he's trying to wind you up?' Brian urged.

'Craig – your bail conditions, mate. Old Bill are on their way,' Craig's pal warned.

Johnny had winded him, but Craig put on a brave face as he walked backwards towards the entrance. 'See you again soon, Brooksy. Give my love to Carol, won't you? I'll be paying her a visit before long, tell her.'

'Go near Carol and I'll kill ya,' Johnny threatened.

'Ignore him, mate. He's all talk. I'll go up the bar, get us another drink,' Scottish Paul said.

'Don't bother. I'm going home,' Johnny snapped.

'Don't go outside yet in case he's still there. Your face is already cut. You don't want Carol to know you've been scrapping, do you?' Brian the Cabbie warned.

'I'm not fucking scared of him,' Johnny bellowed, storming out the club.

There was no sign outside of Thurston or his pal and as Johnny stomped along the road, he was furious. Not so much at Thurston – he was just a lowlife, chancing his luck. It was himself Johnny was livid with. If he didn't have secrets in the bloody first place, there'd be no cat to let out the bag.

'This is all I bloody well need! That smell is making me feel sick. Whatever you been feeding him?' Tracey wrinkled her nose in disgust. 'You're gonna have to change him, Mel. No way are we going near the shoe stall with him stinking of shit. Put that good-looking bloke off for life, that will.'

'Stop the car then and I'll find a toilet. He's only two, Trace, he can't help it,' Melissa snapped. She and Tracey had first met at school aged eleven and had been best pals ever since. They clashed though, fought like cat and dog at times, but never over anything too serious. Petty things. Tracey was a selfish cow and had no real understanding of children or their needs. A typical spoiled only child, she was.

Tracey pulled over on the corner of Church Elm Lane. 'That pub's open. Sort him in there,' she ordered, holding her nose with one hand while frantically spraying her Angel perfume with the other. Her lovely Ford Fiesta currently smelled like a public toilet.

'Don't cry, darling. Mummy's going to change you now,' Melissa whispered in Donte's ear. He was a good boy, her son. Rarely played up and seemed content and happy in his small world.

Ignoring the glaring barmaid who made a cutting remark about the toilets being for customers' use only, Melissa marched into a cubicle, locked the door and began the none too pleasant task of cleaning her son up. Sometimes she yearned for her old life back. Before she had fallen pregnant, herself and Tracey had been out raving every weekend. They'd even had a girlie holiday in Ibiza, which was amazing.

It had been at a rave that Melissa had met Donte's father. Joel Wright had an immediate effect on Mel that no other lad had before. He'd been eighteen, same age as she was back then, and he was self-assured and handsome. Swept off her feet, she'd slept with Joel the third time they met up and was pregnant within eight weeks of meeting him. Unfortunately, he'd turned out to be a bullshitting user. But even though she sometimes missed her old job, friends, nights out and that free-as-a-bird feeling, she had never regretted the decision to have Donte and bring him up as a single mum. He was part of her, her very own little soldier, and when his smile lit up the room Melissa felt like the luckiest girl alive.

'Drink, Mummy, drink,' Donte mumbled. He had only recently started talking more fluently.

'In a minute, darling. There's a nice clean boy,' Melissa beamed, lifting her son in the air.

When Donte looked at her with his big brown eyes, held her tightly around the neck and whispered the words, 'Love you, Mummy,' Melissa's eyes filled with tears. His scumbag of a father had never even seen him; her beautiful boy deserved better.

Shirley Stone was mopping the kitchen floor when the doorbell rang. She wasn't expecting any visitors, she usually spent Sundays alone. 'Johnny!' she gasped. 'Whatever you done to your face?'

'Had a scrap and fell on some glass. Looks worse than it actually is. We need to talk, love.'

At thirty-eight, Shirley was ten years younger than Johnny. She'd worked for him for the past eight years as his secretary, and when she'd separated from her husband in 1988 their affair had started shortly afterwards.

'You've got blood on your shirt too. Want me to wash it for you?' Shirley offered. 'You've got a couple of clean shirts in my wardrobe.'

'No. Leave it,' Johnny sat on the sofa, urging Shirley to do the same. She was a busty blonde, very pretty, and from the moment she'd started work for him there'd been an instant attraction.

'We're going to have to call it a day, for now at least,' Johnny said, before explaining he'd got into a fight with Craig Thurston, who'd threatened to spill the beans to Carol. Their affair certainly wasn't common knowledge. A couple of colleagues knew, one had even caught them in a compromising position recently, but Johnny had no idea how Thurston had found out. Somebody had betrayed him, that was for sure.

Shirley's eyes welled up. Johnny had been adamant from the very beginning that he loved Carol and would never leave her and Shirley had accepted that. 'OK. If that's what you want.'

Johnny stared into Shirley's pale green eyes and stroked her cheek. 'It isn't what I want, but I have little choice. There's stuff you don't know about Carol's illness and she needs my full attention right now.'

'Did you find out what was causing those migraines?' Shirley enquired. Johnny often spoke about Carol, and Shirley had met her loads of times when she popped into the yard. She was a nice woman and Shirley liked her, but she couldn't help the way she felt about Johnny.

'Yeah, we did. But I can't go into detail, Shirl. I promised Carol I wouldn't say a word to anyone – even the kids don't know yet. I'll have to give up working for a while, so Ken'll be running the yard. Between you and him, I know things'll run smoothly in my absence.'

It didn't take Einstein to work out whatever was wrong with Carol wasn't good, so instead of being narky with Johnny, Shirley hugged him close to her chest. 'You know where I am if you need me.'

Johnny kissed Shirley on the forehead, then stood up. 'Thanks for being so understanding. I'll see myself out.'

*

'So, what's he look like, this bloke? How old is he?' Melissa enquired. Ever since she'd visited the market last week, Tracey had been harping on about some hunk on the shoe stall.

'Does my hair look all right? My lipstick isn't smudged, is it?' Tracey asked, trying her best to walk steadily on the uneven pavement. Her feet were freezing. Five-inch stilettos really were not practical to wear to a market on a chilly, wet day.

'Yeah, you look great.'

'I already told you what he looked like. Don't you listen to anything I say?' Tracey complained. 'He looks a bit older than us, blond hair, curtain-cut, and he's lovely and tall. Wait until you see his eyes – piercing blue, they are. He reminds me a bit of Bros – Luke more than Matt. He's gorgeous. Make sure you say that Donte is yours, won't you? I don't want him to think I've got a kid. Oh, and try on as many shoes as you can. Pretend you can't make your mind up.'

'I'm not taking these boots on and off, Trace. Be easier for you to try the shoes on.'

'No it won't. While you're trying the shoes on, I can talk to him, find out some info. Please, Mel. I'd do it for you.'

Knowing full well that Tracey would sulk if she didn't agree, Melissa reluctantly mumbled, 'OK.'

The distinct smell of fried onions hit Melissa as they neared the burger van. The cold wet weather obviously hadn't put people off shopping, as the market seemed busier than usual.

'We're nearly there,' Tracey announced excitedly. She had no idea what the lad's name was, but he'd definitely seemed interested in her last week. He'd chatted to her and her mum for ages, and as they'd walked away he'd treated Tracey to a lopsided grin and a wink.

'Is that him?' Melissa asked, pointing to a blond guy who had his back turned to them. He was tall and was wearing a tan leather box jacket and faded jeans.

'Don't bloody point. Just act normal,' Tracey hissed, her heart racing.

When the bloke turned around, Mel was rather taken aback. He didn't remind her of Bros – he was far better looking in her opinion. His blue eyes twinkled as he winked at Tracey and said, 'Back again.' He then turned his attention to Donte, who was happily playing with his toy car in his pushchair. 'All right. Is he yours?' the hunk asked Melissa. His eyes were the deepest blue she had ever seen and she could certainly understand why Tracey fancied him.

'Yes. He's two now. Say hello to the man, Donte,' Melissa urged.

'Hello, man,' Donte mumbled, too engrossed with his car to look up.

Jason chuckled, crouched and held out his right hand. 'Hello, Donte. I'm Jason. What ya got there, mate?'

Slightly peeved that Jason was paying far more attention to Donte than her, Tracey held her stomach in, pushed her boobs out and tapped him on the back. 'My mate needs a new pair of shoes, but she's not sure what style she wants. Something with a heel and glamorous, like mine,' she said, waving her left foot under his nose.

Jason stood up and smiled. 'Your wish is my command. You're welcome to try on anything you want. Just gonna serve those other customers and I'll be back. What size are you, darlin'?'

'Five.'

'Give me a minute, then I'll sort out a selection that I think will suit a pretty girl like yourself.'

Melissa blushed. She wasn't by any means ugly, but rarely got called pretty, especially when she was out with Tracey. Unlike her skinny blonde friend, she had shoulder-length brown hair, a size-twelve figure and lacked a decent wardrobe since Donte had been born. Tracey knocked spots off her.

'Pick some shoes out then,' Tracey smirked. She wasn't one bit bothered about Jason calling Melissa pretty. It was obvious he was only being kind.

'I haven't got much money on me,' Melissa hissed in her pal's ear. 'Can't you try some on and buy a pair? He'll get the hump with us otherwise, think we're messers,' she warned.

'OK. But find out where he lives and drinks.'

'Why me? You're the one who fancies him – you ask him. He's gonna think I'm after him otherwise,' Melissa complained.

'No, he won't. Not being funny, Mel, but he's a bit out of your league.'

Carol Brooks had tried to keep herself busy since finding out her fate. A year the doctor had given her, top whack, and instead of wallowing in self-pity, Carol was determined to cherish every moment.

'I'm home, love. You upstairs?' Johnny shouted out.

'Yes. I'll be down in a minute. I'm just sorting through some old photos,' Carol replied, flicking through their wedding album. She was forty-six now, plump with short auburn hair. She'd looked so different on her wedding day; back then, twenty-seven years ago, she'd been blonde and slim. She'd never forget Johnny's words as her father walked her down the aisle: 'Jesus Christ, Carol. You've taken my breath away. What you doing marrying an ugly bugger like me? You look like Lulu, my girl.'

About to remind Johnny of his words, a piercing pain shot through the side of Carol's head and she screamed out in agony.

'Carol! What's a matter?' Johnny yelled, racing up the stairs.

When there was no answer, Johnny pushed open the bedroom door and had never felt so guilty in his life. His beloved wife was lying on the floor, convulsing. Next to her was their wedding album.

Tracey giggled like a silly schoolgirl every time Jason said anything remotely funny. 'You're hilarious,' she gushed, touching the arm of his tan leather jacket.

'Mummy – doggy, doggy,' Donte said loudly, pointing at the toy stall opposite. The stallholder was showing some customers a toy dog that walked and barked.

Jason crouched in front of the pushchair. 'OK to get him out?' he asked Melissa. She'd tried on shoe after shoe and Jason was no fool. He knew her mate was after him and had roped Melissa in to help her out.

'Yeah, sure,' Melissa replied. Watching Jason wander over to the toy stall with Donte in his arms, she turned to Tracey. 'Time you tried some shoes on – I'm not trying on any more, specially since I can't afford to buy a pair. Did you find out where he lives?'

'No. But he's only twenty and drinks at some pub called the Brewery Tap in Barking on Friday nights. He said they have live music in there. We should go down there next week. Can you ask your mum to babysit?'

Jason returned with Donte holding the toy dog before

Melissa had a chance to reply. 'Put that back, Donte. It doesn't belong to you,' Melissa ordered.

'It does now. My treat.' Jason winked.

'Oh no. I can't let you pay for that. Here, I'll give you the money,' Melissa replied, fishing frantically through her handbag for her purse. She hoped she had enough cash on her to cover the cost.

'No, you won't. Listen, Trev on the toy stall owes me plenty of favours, trust me,' Jason insisted.

'Erm, can I try on these black boots in a size four, please?' Tracey asked, pointing to a high-heeled suede ankle boot. She couldn't understand Jason's obsession with Donte. It was odd, to say the least. 'Don't move, Mel. I need to hold on to you,' Tracey ordered, lifting up her left leg to undo the strap on her sandal.

Aware of Jason's blue eyes staring at her, Melissa blushed again.

'I've got a little 'un myself. A four-year-old daughter,' Jason blurted out.

To say Tracey was shocked by this piece of news was an understatement. She promptly lost her balance, toppling over sideways.

'You all right, mate?' Melissa asked, voice full of concern. Part of her wanted to laugh, but she knew how mortified Tracey must be, so held her emotions in check.

Feeling a complete idiot, Tracey quickly put her sandal back on and grabbed Mel's arm. 'Come on. Let's go.'

'Don't you wanna try the boots on now?' Jason smirked. Trev on the toy stall was pissing himself laughing and he was desperately trying not to do the same himself.

'No. I'll try them another time,' Tracey snapped, hobbling off. She'd felt her ankle twist as she'd fallen and it was already throbbing.

'Thanks again for the toy,' Melissa said, walking away.

'Come on, Mel,' Tracey urged, red-faced. The quicker she got away from this market, the better.

'Mel, you forgot something,' Jason shouted after them.

Leaving Donte's pushchair with Tracey, Melissa ran back to the stall. Jason handed her a piece of paper. 'That's my phone number. If you fancy a drink sometime, give us a bell.'

Melissa opened her mouth, but couldn't speak. No words would come out.

'Mel, come on,' Tracey shouted angrily.

Melissa took one last look at Jason, then ran to catch up with her pal.

'What did he want?' Tracey demanded.

'Nothing.'

'Don't lie to me. I saw him hand you something. Did he give you his number for me?'

'No, Trace. Look, I'm sorry, but he gave me his number for me.'

Tracey stared at her friend as though she had gone stark raving mad. This wasn't going to plan at all. 'What did he actually say when he gave it to you? You sure he never meant it for me?'

Melissa felt flushed. 'He said if I fancied going for a drink, I was to call him.'

Tracey was in shock. 'You're not going, are you?'

Mel shook her head. 'Course not. You like him.'

The short journey back to South Hornchurch was awkward, to say the least. Tracey was in no mood for small talk. She was fucking fuming.

CHAPTER TWO

The lifts stank of urine, were covered in graffiti and, as usual, there was a sign on the door saying they were out of order.

'Bollocks,' Jason mumbled. He lived on the tenth floor and had boxes to carry.

The stairs too were daubed in graffiti and reeked of urine, but nevertheless Jason whistled chirpily as he lugged the boxes of knocked-off perfume up ten flights. No way could he leave any downstairs. They'd be thieved within seconds. The type of tower block he lived in, even the door knockers weren't safe.

Jason let himself into the flat that he shared with his mother, brothers, sister and four-year-old daughter. As expected, the kids were fending for themselves.

'Daddy,' four-year-old Shay cried out, holding out her arms for a cuddle. She was filthy, had dirt all over her hands and face, and was still wearing the pyjamas he'd put on her last night.

'Where's Mum?' Jason asked twelve-year-old Barbara. Like himself, Babs, as he fondly called her, had no idea who her father was; the pair of them had been the result of drunken one-night stands. Babs was mixed-race. She was also extremely overweight, thanks to the shit food she ate. It was Babs who looked after their two younger brothers Elton, eight, and Kyle who'd just turned six. A drunken waste of space, his mother was, which was why Jason wanted to find a better home for his daughter. This was no environment for her to be raised in.

'Mum went to get fags, but she never came back. The kids are starving. There's only Weetabix and baked beans in the cupboard, and there's no milk. Can you get us some food, Jason?' Babs asked hopefully. Trapped in the flat looking after three kids, food was the only enjoyment she got in life and she was currently yearning for a Big Mac or a large portion of greasy chips smothered in salt and vinegar. Her stomach felt as if her throat had been cut.

Jason put his daughter down and urged Barbara to make the kids look presentable.

'Why I gotta wash? Where we going?' asked young Kyle.

'McDonald's – I'm treating us. So it's bathtime for all three of ya,' Jason grinned, ruffling Elton's frizzy Afro hair. He and Kyle had the same father. He was no role model though. Known to the locals as 'Rasta Dave', he'd flooded the estate with heroin before getting a ten-stretch. Jason had been dragged to court by his mother, who'd sobbed like a baby as Dave was sentenced. He hadn't acknowledged them, the same way he'd refused to acknowledge that Elton and Kyle were his sons. He wouldn't even put his name on their birth certificates, the loser.

Hearing the kids splash happily about in the bath, Jason's thoughts turned to the girl he'd met on the market today. He'd known her mate had fancied him when she'd come to the stall last week with her mother. And he'd known she'd be back; ditzy airheads like her always were predictable.

Jason lit up a cigarette and took a deep drag. He wasn't looking for a bird to shag senseless. He had plenty of those on the go, including Darlene, the thirty-eight-year-old mother of his old school pal Andy Michaels. What Jason was currently looking for was someone half sensible. A single mum with a council flat or, better still, her own gaff would be ideal.

Hearing a commotion, Jason walked over to the window and stared at the gloomy sight outside. A full-blown punch-up was in progress – par for the course on the Mardyke Estate. Jason loved and loathed the estate in equal measure. It was all he had ever known, and some of the people who lived there were proper. However, lots were not; when you flipped the coin, it was a shithole situated off the busy A13 in Rainham.

Jason's mother wasn't one for adding homely touches. The only thing hanging on the wall in their depressing, threadbare flat was a long mirror in the hallway that Debbie Rampling would preen her fat self in before leaving the premises. Once she was out of the way, the kids would spend hours dancing in front of the mirror while music – reggae and lovers rock, for the most part – blared out the stereo system. None of the kids had many toys, and the ones he brought home always seemed to go missing. Knowing his mother, she was probably flogging them around the estate.

Jason strolled into the hallway and studied himself. Though he had no idea who his father was, he owed the man for his good looks; he certainly hadn't inherited them from his mother. He was handsome and he knew it. He'd also been aware of the power he had over the opposite sex from a very early age and had honed his skills over the years. That was going to be his way out. Living a deprived life was not for Jason Rampling. He was a go-getter and wanted far better. Not only for him, but for Shay too.

'I'm fine, Johnny. For goodness' sake, stop fussing,' Carol said.

Johnny Brooks felt awful. Was God paying him back for his affair? he wondered. Because if so, he wished the big man above would take it out on him instead. Carol didn't deserve to suffer. It was him who was the bastard.

Carol had snapped out of her fit by the time the ambulance had arrived, but he'd forced her to go to hospital regardless. She was petrified of anything to do with the medical profession; even a trip to the GP's brought her out in a cold sweat. Johnny knew she would discharge herself first chance she got.

'You're not going to be able to hide this for ever, you know. We need to think about telling the family, at least. And you should have stayed in overnight, just to be on the safe side. Say you have another fit?'

'Shut up. Melissa must be out of her mind with worry. I can't believe you didn't leave a note. That's the first thing I'd have done. Now call us a cab. Smell of these places reminds me of death. And ring Melissa. Do not say we've been up Oldchurch, 'cause she'll worry. Say we went for dinner round Dick and Yvonne's at short notice. OK?'

Johnny Brooks nodded. Once Carol had made her mind up about something, there was no changing it.

*

Leaving the kids happily stuffing their faces, Jason wandered outside McDonald's to get better reception. He leaned against his pride and joy: a black XR2 with full body kit and shiny alloy wheels. He'd recently treated himself to a Blaupunkt car stereo and 200-watt speakers out of his illegal earnings. He never left them inside an empty car though. Car stereo and speaker theft was rife these days. His motor stood out like a sore thumb on the Mardyke and was like a beacon for the Old Bill; he was forever getting tugged in it. That's why he drove his old white Escort van if he was carrying anything dodgy. Because he owned a mobile phone and decent motor, the police seemed to be under the misapprehension he must be a drug dealer. Nothing could be further from the truth. Having seen so many people on the estate overdose or balls their lives up through drugs, Jason had never touched the stuff in his life. Which was more than could be said for his mother. She smoked weed on a regular basis. Seeing her stoned was enough to put anyone with half a brain off.

Jason liked to think of himself as a younger, better-looking Arthur Daley. *Minder* had been his favourite TV programme growing up and he'd naturally picked up the art of spotting an opportunity and grabbing it with both hands. The one day he worked on the market was the only regular income he had, apart from his fortnightly dole cheque. The rest of his dosh came from selling whatever he could get his hands on, including hardcore porn films. His pal got hold of them from Holland. He'd copy them and Jason would sell the pirate versions, earning two quid per film himself. On a bad week he could sell fifty films, on a good two hundred and fifty. It never failed to amaze Jason how many people watched porn. He even sold loads over the Mardyke, and virtually everybody who lived there professed to be skint.

Knowing his mother's usual habits, Jason rang up the Millhouse Social Club and spoke to the barmaid. She was there, just as he'd known she would be. When she had the cheek to slur, 'What's up?' down the phone, Jason calmly told her he would pick her up in half an hour and she needed to stay at home this evening as he had to go out. There was no point kicking off with her, especially when she was wasted.

His mother reluctantly agreeing, Jason ended the call and thought again about the girl he'd met on the market. Melissa was plain rather than pretty, but if she had her own gaff, she'd do for the time being.

'Where have you been? I've been worried sick,' Melissa Brooks exclaimed. Her parents never went anywhere without leaving a note or telling her beforehand, so their absence today was totally out of character.

'Sorry, love. I asked your dad to leave a note, but you know what he's like – brain like a sieve,' Carol bluffed. 'We went for dinner round Yvonne and Dick's. Last-minute invite,' she added.

Melissa looked suspiciously at her father. 'What you done to your face?'

Carol was quick off the mark. 'Silly old sod walked into the door. I couldn't stop laughing,' she lied. Johnny had told her that Craig Thurston had turned up at the club, kicking off over money.

'You're lying,' Melissa squared up to them.

'Don't start, Mel. Why would we lie?' Johnny spat. Guilt was eating away at him and he'd decided to spend every moment of every day with Carol from now on.

Donte broke the ice. 'Look, Nana. Doggy,' he said, pressing the switch to make the toy walk and bark.

Carol crouched and scooped her grandson into her arms. Johnny's right-wing views had rubbed off on her over the years and she'd been horrified when Melissa had announced Donte's father was black. But a grandmother's instinct had taken over the second the child was born. He'd clung to her little finger at one point and Carol's heart had melted; he was one of the most beautiful babies she had ever seen. 'Who bought you that? Mummy? What's the doggy's name?' she asked.

'A man.'

Confused, Carol said, 'Eamonn?'

'A man, Mum. One of the stallholders bought it for him,' Melissa explained.

'Aww, that was nice. Do you know him?' Carol asked.

'No. And now Tracey has the right hump because she fancied him and he asked me out.'

'Put the kettle on, Johnny, while I have a chat with Mel,' Carol urged. Apart from being a bit tired, she felt fine now.

Carol was a doting mum, always had been, and she missed her son who'd moved up north. Melissa was her world though. They'd had a strong mother–daughter bond from the moment Mel was born. 'Tell me what happened,' Carol said gently. She knew Tracey could be a stroppy, dictatorial mare at times and wished Mel could meet a nicer best friend to hang out with.

Melissa told her the story, concluding: 'She virtually accused me of showing out to him! But I never, I swear. I was dressed like this with my Timberlands on, for Christ's sake, while she was all done up to the nines. It's not my fault he never fancied her, is it?'

'No, it isn't. Tracey's just jealous, love. She'll snap out of it. So what's his name, this lad?'

'Jason.'

'And is he handsome?'

'Very. He's got the bluest eyes I've ever seen and lovely blond hair. And he was so good with Donte. I couldn't believe it when he asked me out. I was in shock. But I can't go. Tracey will never speak to me again if I do.'

'Tracey is boy mad, as you well know. Fancies a different one every week. You go out with Jason if you like him. But don't lie to Tracey; stand up to her for once. She might be angry, but I'd put money on it she'll forget all about Jason in a week or two and move on to her next sodding victim. You mustn't let her rule you – I've told you that before.'

'He gave me his number. It's a mobile. Perhaps it's dodgy and he was taking the mickey out of me?' Melissa suggested.

Carol held her daughter's beautiful face in her hands. She'd never met Donte's father, but the bastard had knocked the stuffing out of Melissa. She'd once been a confident girl, full of life. Now she was insecure and Carol hated seeing her like that. 'Ring him,' she urged. 'Sod Tracey. Remember that time you fancied David Ward? She didn't care when you caught her snogging him behind the bloody bike sheds, did she? Go with your instincts for once.'

'He must be nice to buy Donte that dog,' Melissa said, lost in thought.

'You gotta go for it then, love. My mate Sylvie fancied your father before I snapped him up. Sometimes I wish I'd have let her have him,' Carol laughed. 'Sylv never spoke to me for a month when we started courting, but she soon got over it. True friends are hard to find and not many girls will put up with that madam Tracey Thompson like you do. Trust me on that one.'

Melissa smiled. 'Perhaps I'll ring him. What if it's a dodgy number though?'

'If that's the case, I'll be marching straight down to Dagenham Market next Sunday and whacking him around the head with my handbag,' Carol stated, meaning every word. She was very protective when it came to her children, had once nearly stuck a pair of secateurs into a woman's arm over Melissa while pruning her roses.

Melissa laughed. 'I don't want to seem too keen. But if I do decide to contact him, how long do you reckon I should leave it?'

Carol squeezed her daughter's hands. 'No ifs or buts, ring him on Tuesday. Mummy knows best. She always has.'

'That you, Jason?' shouted sixty-year-old Peggy Rampling. She knew it would be her grandson; he was the only other person with a key to her house.

'All right, Nan,' Jason answered, handing her a box of goodies.

'What ya got for me then?' Peggy asked, delving into the box then looking up at him, disappointed. 'No Guinness?'

'Nah. I couldn't park outside the offie and couldn't be arsed taking the stereo and speakers out the car again. There's perfume in there, some toiletries, a Connie Francis CD and a few packets of them biscuits you like.'

Peggy took the Rive Gauche perfume out of the box and began coughing and spluttering as she sprayed it. 'That ain't the real McCoy. Smells like cat's piss,' she complained.

'It is the real deal, Nan. I bought it off a pal and he wouldn't have me over.'

'Well, he has. Get your money back and buy me some Guinness instead,' Peggy said, lobbing the perfume back at Jason.

'What you been up to? Did you go to bingo last night?'

'Yep! And Friday. Rigged, that bingo hall is. Same faces win every night. Won the regional, that old cow Doris Shipton did. That's the second time she's won it this year and it's only bastard April. Nobody's that lucky. I hope she gets her purse snatched.'

'Some people are just born lucky, Nan. You going again tonight?'

'Nah. I'd like to, of course – gets lonely, sitting in here on me jacks – but I can't afford it.'

Knowing full well his grandmother had money stashed in pots, pans, jars and tins all over the gaff, Jason put his hand in his pocket and handed her a score.

'Thank you, sweetheart. Good boy to your old nan, you are. Don't know how you come out of her, I honestly don't. How is she? As rancid as ever?'

'Same old, same old,' Jason replied truthfully. His nan and mum hadn't spoken since he was eight years old. At five, his mother had decided she didn't want him any more and had palmed him off to live with his nan. Those were the happiest childhood memories Jason had. His nan wasn't perfect – she was a prolific pilferer who'd shoplift anything that wasn't nailed down – but she'd given him love and attention, the two things he never got at home. When Babs was born, his mother insisted he had to live with her again, and his nan hadn't spoken to her since.

'Got yourself a nice girlfriend yet?' Peggy grinned.

'I'm still seeing that one from Harold Hill I told you

about, but I think I'm gonna have to knock her on the head. She's only seventeen. Too young and immature.' Jason told his grandmother most things, but had never mentioned his affair with Darlene. His nan had once lived on the Mardyke and hated her. 'Look at that old slapper. All fur coat and no knickers, that one,' she'd say whenever they crossed paths. The last thing Jason wanted was his gran turning up on Dar's doorstep creating havoc. And he was sure she would if she learned the truth. She was that type of woman.

'You need a mother for Shay, ASAP. Horrible child! Don't bring her round 'ere no more, will ya? Trampled on all me geraniums on purpose last time she visited, and I'd only just planted the bastard things. You need to get her away from that stinking fat excuse of a mother of yours. Because if you don't, she'll only get worse,' Peggy warned.

Jason sighed. His nan wasn't one to mince her words and was usually right. 'I know. Leave it with me. I'm working on it.'

CHAPTER THREE

Melissa Brooks lay on her bed wallowing in self-pity. It hadn't stopped raining all day, so she hadn't been able to take Donte out as she usually did. And her son had a cold, had been whingeing since the moment he'd opened his eyes this morning. Days such as these were the ones she wished for her old life back.

Melissa looked at the time again. Tracey worked on her mother's burger van on an industrial estate and would be home soon. They hadn't spoken since Sunday. When Mel had rung Tracey Sunday evening and last night, her mum had said she'd gone to the pub.

Sighing, Melissa sat up. She'd had lots of friends before she'd had Donte, but had lost touch with most of them now. The girls from work rang her occasionally, but her life seemed so different to theirs it depressed Melissa talking to them. It had only been an office job at the council, but she'd been happy there. She'd left when she was six months pregnant; they'd offered her maternity leave, but instead she took a small redundancy payment. Her father had made it perfectly clear that raising the baby would be her responsibility, so she'd had little choice.

Carol peeked around the bedroom door. 'You hungry yet, love? I finally got Donte off to sleep. Really not himself today, is he?'

When her daughter's eyes welled up, Carol sat next to her on the bed and put an arm round her.

'Tracey's avoiding me, so now I have nobody to go out with. Sometimes I wish I'd taken Dad's advice. It's no fun being a single mum at my age. I miss my old life.'

Realizing a stern talking to was needed, Carol cleared her throat. 'It's too late for regrets, Mel. Donte is part of your life now and always will be. Sod Tracey. She's never been a good friend to you anyway. Ring Jason. Go on. What have you got to lose?'

Melissa fished through her purse and pulled out the number. 'You go out the room then. I need to plan what I'm going to say before I speak to him.'

Carol smiled. 'Just be yourself, love. That's why he liked you in the first place.'

'Elton, stop banging that fucking drum! Doing my head in, you are,' Debbie Rampling bellowed.

Giggling, Elton sang along to Bob Marley's 'Three Little Birds' and banged his drum even harder. He only stopped when his mother yanked him off the carpet by his arm and walloped him repeatedly across the backside.

'Mum, I'm starving,' complained Kyle, tugging at her arm.

'Babs, come and sort these bastard kids out before I strangle 'em,' Debbie ordered.

Jason was having a lie-down in the smallest of the flat's three bedrooms, which he shared with Shay. His mother had the largest and Barbara shared the other with Elton and Kyle.

When his mother decided she couldn't be bothered cooking again and ordered Babs to take the kids round the chippie to give her a break, Jason waited until his sister had left the flat before marching into the lounge. 'I think you and I should have a little chat.'

Lying on the sofa, fag in hand, watching the latest episode of the highly addictive *Jeremy Kyle* show, Debbie asked, 'What about?' in a totally disinterested tone.

Jason picked up the remote and pressed pause. 'About everything. You going out all the time. Babs skipping school at your insistence every time you have a hangover. You refusing to cook for the kids. The list is endless. You gotta sort yourself out, ya know. I'm old enough to fend for myself, but your other three aren't.'

Debbie took a gulp from her plastic bottle of cider, then sneered. 'If you're old enough to fend for yourself, why are you and your daughter living under my roof?' Part of Debbie wanted to tell her son to pack his and Shay's belongings and sling his hook, but Jason was too much of an asset to her financially. He gave her fifty quid a week, helped with the kids and paid for most of the grub they ate.

'Oh, I'm looking for a way out, don't you worry about that. But I'm worried about the kids, especially Babs. You treat that girl like a slave, and it ain't on. You need to start cooking her some healthy food. Poor little mare is becoming obese. You got to be a better parent. I know you're upset Rasta got bird, but it's not as if he ever lived here or helped out with the kids. You weren't exactly mother of the year before he got banged up, and if you don't wake up and smell the coffee, you'll have Social Services on your case. Then you'll have no kids.'

Debbie was well aware that she wasn't 'Mother of the

Year' material, but she loved Elton and Kyle. Rasta Dave had been the love of her life and they were his flesh and blood. 'How dare you speak to me like that? Who do you think you are, you jumped-up little shit! You're hardly Richard Branson your fucking self, are you? Think you're a big-shot 'cause you sell sicko films to nonces round the estate. Well let me tell you something: you're nothing, Jason Rampling. Just a nobody who lives on the Mardyke, same as me. Get that into your thick skull.'

Jason was livid. He hated being spoken down to. 'I'm nothing like you. I'm gonna make it in life whatever it takes. You just fucking watch me.'

Practising her words, Melissa Brooks finally took the plunge and picked up the phone. She'd had nothing to do with lads since Donte's dad had dumped her, and her heart was beating rapidly. She couldn't stop thinking about Jason. She'd even dreamed about him last night.

Silently praying he hadn't given her a dodgy number, Melissa was relieved when the phone was answered on the third ring. He had a distinct voice, gruff and cheeky. 'Erm, hi, Jason. It's Melissa – the girl with the son that—'

'I know exactly who you are. Never forget a pretty face, me,' Jason interrupted. 'How's my little mate, Donte?'

Melissa smiled. Jason seemed so thoughtful compared to lads she'd met in the past. 'Miserable. He's got a cold. How's your daughter? What's her name?'

'Shay. Yeah, she's good. What you doing tonight? Let me take you out for a drink so we can chat properly. Been thinking about you a lot since Sunday, I have.'

Melissa felt a warm glow inside. She was still stunned that a hunk like Jason could be interested in her, but he was obviously very keen. 'OK. I'm sure my mum will look after Donte. I'll ask her in a tick.'

When Mel gave him an address, Jason grinned. He knew that road and it wasn't council, the gaffs were privately owned. Melissa's call couldn't have come at a better time . . .

Carol Brooks was brimming with excitement for her daughter. 'Wow! You look gorgeous. Now go knock him dead. Be confident, Mel. Nothing more off-putting to a man than insecurity, is there, Johnny?'

Johnny looked up from his *Construction News*. 'You do look nice, and your mother's right. Don't put the bloody bloke off. Opportunities like this don't come along every day for someone in your position. I wonder if his kid's half-chat too? Did you ask him?'

'Shut up, Johnny. If you can't be happy Mel's got a date, then sod off upstairs,' Carol ordered. Donte had started picking up on words they used lately and she didn't want him hearing hateful things.

Johnny held his hands aloft. 'All right, I'm sorry. So you gonna bring him in to meet us, this mystery man?'

'No. Last thing I want is you spouting off. He'll run a mile,' Mel snapped. She'd wanted to meet Jason away from the house, but he'd insisted on picking her up from her address.

'Your dad won't say anything bad. Promise her, Johnny,' Carol ordered.

'I won't open me mouth. Honest,' Johnny replied, performing a zip movement across his lips.

'I can hear an engine, love. Did Jason say what car he drives?' Carol asked, peeping through the curtain.

'No. And come away from the window, Mum. Please,'

Melissa begged. She was becoming more flustered by the second.

When the doorbell rang, Melissa felt sick with nerves. 'Right, I'm off now. Do not follow me outside and embarrass me. I mean it.'

Carol turned the TV down and put her ear to the door. 'Hiya, Mel. You look amazing! Where's me little mate? I got him a get well present.'

'Donte's in bed,' Melissa replied, shutting the front door as quickly as possible.

'Did you hear that, Johnny? He brought Donte a get well present!' Carol beamed.

Johnny Brooks leapt out of the armchair and peeked through the curtains. Whoever this Jason was, he sounded too good to be bloody true.

Melissa Brooks smiled as Jason handed her a third Bacardi and Coke. He'd brought her to the Spencer's Arms pub in Ardleigh Green and, although nervous at first, Mel now felt more relaxed. Jason was easy to talk to and they had lots in common.

Jason took a photo out of his pocket and slid it across the table. 'That's my Shay, holding the doll. The other three are my brothers and sister. Taken last Christmas, that photo was. Most recent I have of Shay.'

'Awww. She's really cute, Jase. So, where is her mum? Does she see Shay? You don't mind me asking, do you?'

'Course not. Her mum left us. Walked out when Shay was a few months old and we've not seen her since. Bet you could never leave your Donte, eh, girl?'

'No way. Oh, I'm so sorry, Jason. That's awful. How did you manage? You must have only been young yourself.'

'Case of having to manage. I moved back in with my mum, and my nan used to help out a bit. Shay's too lively for her now though. What about your parents? They good with Donte?' When Jason had found out Melissa didn't have her own accommodation and lived with her mum and dad, he'd felt deflated. Until he'd seen the parents' gaff, that was. They were definitely loaded. And he could tell Melissa was easy-pickings. Plus she was mother material, and that's what Shay needed. His nan was right. Becoming hard to handle of late, his daughter was. Which was no surprise, seeing as his mother was out on the lash all the time and she was left to fend for herself along with Babs and his brothers.

Melissa thought carefully before answering. 'My mum's been great. She's a strong woman who adores Donte. My dad is old school, though. He thinks a girl should be married before she has children. He wanted to kick me out when I fell pregnant, but my mum stood her ground. I take after my mother. I'm a strong woman too,' Mel said, remembering her mum's advice to come across as confident.

Leaning across the table, Jason squeezed Mel's hand. 'I can tell, and that's why I like you. No disrespect to your pal Tracey, but women like her aren't my cup of tea. Too fake. I like real people, like yourself.'

Melissa beamed. 'Tracey isn't talking to me, funnily enough. She copped the hump because you gave me your number.'

'Don't surprise me. Girls like Tracey are ten a penny. Get 'em coming up to me on the stall all the time, and I always give 'em a wide berth. Don't get me wrong; when I was young, before Shay was born, I was partial to the airheads. But if I'm to bother these days, I'm looking for the real deal. A woman I can potentially settle down with.'

Melissa Brooks could not believe her luck. Jason made her heart melt. He also had the potential to be her very own knight in shining armour.

'You on the waiting list for a council gaff?' Jason enquired.

'No. My parents wouldn't want me to live on a council estate. They're not snobs or anything like that, but they worry about me. My dad would rent me somewhere private, I think – if and when I move out.'

'Don't you want your own gaff?'

'Yeah, one day. But not until I'm older,' Melissa replied. She relied on her mother to help her out with Donte on a day-to-day basis, but wasn't about to admit that to Jason.

'Tell me about Donte's father. Does he see the little 'un?'

'No. He dumped me as soon as he found out I was pregnant. He was horrible, wanted me to have an abortion. He's better off out our lives.'

'Is he local?'

'No. We met at a rave. Joel lived over the other side of London, but he came down this way a few times with his pals. I'd meet him up Berwick Manor.' No way was Melissa going to admit she'd chased Joel something rotten and all but laid it on a plate for him. That made her sound like a thick, desperate tart.

'I used to go up the Berwick. Surprised we never met there. Want another drink?' Jason asked.

Melissa took her purse out of her bag. 'Let me get this round. It's not fair, you buying all the drinks.'

Jason stood up. Melissa was pleasant enough, but wasn't much use to him if she didn't have plans to move into her own gaff. Shame, as she'd have been perfect to look after Shay. 'You put your money away. Believe in chivalry, me. If a man asks a lady out, then he foots the bill.'

Melissa smiled when Jason sauntered up the bar. He dressed well. Black suit jacket, white T-shirt, faded jeans and smart leather shoes. She also liked the thick gold chain around his neck and the sovereign- and diamond-studded horseshoe rings he wore. The barmaid had certainly taken a shine to him too. Mel could sense she was flirting because she was acting like Tracey did when she fancied a bloke.

Discreetly making sure Jason was not flirting back, Mel pretended to be engrossed in searching for something in her handbag as her date returned to the table. 'So what's your mum like?' she asked.

'Not the best, to be honest. Men have messed with her head over the years, if you know what I mean. What about your parents? Do they work?'

'Yes. My dad owns a builders' merchants and my mum does all his accounts.'

'A small family-run firm?'

'No. It's a big business. My dad has lots of men working for him. He's got a massive yard just off the A13.'

Jason's ears pricked up. 'I got a pal in the building game. What's your dad's firm called?'

'J J Brooks.'

Jason wanted to laugh out loud, but remained calm. Himself and his pals had stolen stuff from there before the security had been upped. Johnny Brooks was well known in Rainham and it was common knowledge he was loaded. Perhaps Melissa was worth a punt on after all . . .

CHAPTER FOUR

Jason Rampling held on to Darlene Michaels' pert arse cheeks as she rode him in her usual expert fashion. She was the best lay he'd ever had and, considering she was thirty-eight, had a fine figure. Skinny waist, long legs and a pretty face were a rarity in women these days, especially on the Mardyke Estate. She also had a dirty look about her that suggested she was up for anything, which she was. They'd even filmed their romps in the past and had great fun watching themselves in action.

Red-faced, Jason grunted and groaned before finally shooting his load. 'Fucking hell, Dar. Jesus wept!' he mumbled. He then glanced at his watch and leapt out of bed. He couldn't be late, not today.

Darlene lit up a cigarette. 'What's the bloody rush?' she asked, studying Jason's nakedness. He was tall, fit and young, just how she liked them. But unlike others she'd sampled in the past, Jason had a decent-sized penis and knew exactly how to please a woman. She'd taught him that art, and Jason was a keen learner.

'I gotta be somewhere. I'll pop round again tomorrow while Andy's at work,' Jason promised. Andy was his old school pal and had no idea Jason was shafting his mother.

'Where you got to be then?' Darlene enquired, running her hand through her mass of untidy chestnut-coloured hair.

'Just somewhere. Family stuff, dinner. Promised me nan I'd take her to see her friend,' Jason flapped. Darlene hated it if she knew he had a girl on the firm, had refused to see him for a month when her pal had spotted him in a boozer with Tara Shepherd.

Darlene angrily dotted her fag out in the ashtray. 'You better not be dipping your wick in me, then taking some bird out, Jase. Be your hopping pot if you mug me off again, I'm telling ya,' she warned.

Jason buttoned his shirt, sat on the bed and kissed Darlene. 'There's no other birds, only you. Gotta dash now. See ya tomorrow.'

'Erm, I think you've forgotten something.'

Jason glanced at his watch again. 'What? I put the johnny in the bin.'

Darlene opened her legs wide. Her pussy was completely shaved, just the way Jason liked it. 'I haven't come yet.'

Knowing she'd probably refuse to see him for weeks if he didn't oblige, Jason kneeled on the bed and put his head between Darlene's legs. Licking away rapidly, like a child tasting ice cream for the very first time, he prayed she'd come quickly.

'Don't put the bloody jar of mint sauce on the table, Johnny. Put it in this little china pot,' Carol Brooks tutted. Her daughter and Jason had been dating for over two weeks now and today would be the first time she and Johnny would meet Jason properly. They'd said a quick hello to him on the few occasions he'd picked Melissa up from the house, but today he was coming round for lunch and Carol was determined everything would be perfect.

Johnny Brooks sighed. 'Anyone would think Prince Charles was on his way round, not some lad off the bleedin' Mardyke Estate,' he complained. Johnny had been disappointed to find out where Jason lived. Shame the lad didn't come from decent stock, but beggars couldn't be choosers and, given the position his Mel had ended up in, in Johnny's eyes she was a beggar.

'I know you want to find out more about Jason, Johnny, but don't be bombarding him with questions. I know what you're like when you're in interrogation mode and I don't want the lad to think we're nosy, or Melissa to get the hump. She had the right needle when you asked where he lived the first time he stepped foot inside the door.'

'I'm bound to have concerns, love, and so should you. Mel's obviously smitten and if he's gonna be part of this family then we need to know what he's all about. Mel's very vague about his job. I know he works on the market of a Sunday but he doesn't run a motor and take our daughter out on that wage alone, does he? You don't know that Mardyke like I do. Place is full of scallywags.'

'It's not up to you who Mel dates, it's up to her. And I thought Jason was charming the times we met him. If you mess this up for her, you'll have me to deal with – and I mean that, Johnny.'

'Yes, dear.'

Melissa burst into the kitchen. 'Do I look OK?' she asked. She still couldn't believe her luck at having met Jason. He was absolutely gorgeous and entirely different to other lads she'd dated. He hadn't even tried it on with her yet, which showed how much he respected her. He was the perfect gent, and tomorrow his daughter and Donte would be meeting for the first time.

'You look lovely, Mel. But you don't want to lose any more weight; you'll have to buy a whole new wardrobe if you do,' Carol warned. Her daughter was wearing black Lycra leggings and a white baggy top with bold silver print on the front. She'd certainly been hit by the love-bug, had been eating like a sparrow since meeting Jason.

'He's late,' Johnny announced, pointing at the clock on the kitchen wall. He was a sucker for punctuality, lateness infuriated him.

'It's only ten past, Dad, and he has got a daughter to see to,' Melissa snapped.

'Your dad's only winding you up, love. Take no notice,' Carol insisted, glaring at her husband.

Twenty minutes later, Jason finally arrived and, as Melissa ran excitedly to answer the door, Johnny could not help but let a few expletives fly.

'Shut up. I mean it!'

'What time d'ya call this?' Johnny's voice boomed as Jason walked into the kitchen.

'I'm sorry, sir. But my daughter cut herself, was crying, and I also wanted to stop off to bring you these,' Jason said, handing a bouquet to Carol and bottle to Johnny.

'Aww, what beautiful flowers. You shouldn't have, but thank you,' Carol gushed.

'Nice one. Cheers.' Johnny studied the Jim Beam label to make sure it was genuine, before shaking Jason's hand. One of his employees' daughters had recently purchased a cheap bottle of vodka off the Mardyke Estate and ended up in intensive care.

'Sit down, love. Let me take your jacket,' Carol urged. Jason's aftershave smelled gorgeous, and Carol could certainly understand why Melissa was off her food. He had a cheeky lopsided grin and a real sparkle in those deep blue eyes of his. His thick blond hair was an odd style but suited him, and he had charm and a certain aura.

'Thank you, Mrs Brooks,' Jason responded, handing Carol his jacket.

'Call me Carol, love, and my husband's Johnny. We're not formal in this household. A pair of old cockneys, me and Melissa's dad are. Out of Stepney originally. That's where we met.'

Jason had learned the art of being a sweet-talker from an early age. Becoming a market-trader had then helped him polish up his act even more. He asked Carol and Johnny numerous questions, showing genuine interest towards every answer they gave. He was determined to impress.

'So what about you, lad? You said you were off the Mardyke. Always lived there, have you?' Johnny enquired.

'Most of my life. I don't intend to be there much longer, though. Don't get me wrong, there are some decent people live on the estate, but I've always wanted better in life and as a father it's my duty to ensure Shay has the best upbringing possible. I want her to go to a decent school, so I'm working hard to achieve that. Where is Donte? I got him this. I know you said he's mad on anything with a set of wheels,' Jason said, handing Melissa a blue gift bag.

'He's having a nap. Kept me awake half the night. Oh, Jase, he'll love this. Look, Mum, Dad,' Melissa beamed. Jason had brought her son a shiny bright blue truck. It looked expensive, was in a posh box.

Johnny Brooks smiled approvingly, but he wasn't fooled. He could tell Jason was a bit of a wide boy. 'So what d'ya do for a living then, Jason? Melissa said you work on Dagenham Market of a Sunday. That your only job, is it?'

'I duck and dive, Johnny. Work most days of the week. I buy stuff and sell it on for a profit.'

'What sort of stuff?' The lad was obviously fond of throwing his money about and Johnny knew the Mardyke was rife with drug dealers.

'Videos, CDs trainers, jeans – whatever I can lay my hands on really. I have a lot of contacts via the market, so I've got in with a few wholesalers. I don't make a fortune, but I get by. I do plan to up my game one day, mind. My dream is to build my own property. Buy a bit of land. Either that or renovate an old gaff. That's all in the future though, not any time soon. I need to save my pennies first.' Jason had no interest whatsoever in building his own property, but had guessed Johnny would ask such questions so had planned an answer in the hope of impressing the man.

'A client of mine is in that field. Does all his own electrics, plumbing, floor-laying, tiling, to cut back on the costs. You a jack of all trades, are you?'

Jason was slightly taken aback by the reply. He knew Johnny was no man's fool, but was he being sarcastic? Jason held his gaze. 'No. Unfortunately, I'm not. But a man can have dreams, can't he? I would rather be optimistic about my future than settle for a life on the Mardyke. No crime in wanting to better yourself, is there?'

It was at that point Johnny grinned. He remembered saying something similar when he was Jason's age, and he'd gone on to make it in life. The lad certainly seemed like a go-getter. A chirpy, confident bloke who knew what he wanted. Johnny would be proud to take him out for a pint with his pals, might lessen the embarrassment his daughter had caused him.

Clocking the bit of male bonding, Carol nudged her daughter under the table. This was going well, even better than expected.

The roast lamb dinner was delicious. Carol was a decent cook and had pulled out all the stops to impress their guest. She'd even made two pies – banoffee and apple – so Jason could choose a dessert.

'That was amazing! I wish my mum could cook like you, Carol. Best meal I've eaten in years,' Jason enthused.

Carol smiled broadly. Jason was such a polite, charming young man. Her daughter had struck gold, she was sure of that. 'Would you like some cheese and biscuits or a coffee?'

Jason patted his bloated stomach. 'Not at the moment thanks, Carol. I'm full.'

Johnny picked up the bottle of Jim Beam. 'How about a tipple, lad?'

'No. I'd better not. I've already had two beers and I don't want to be over the limit to drive.'

'That's very sensible, love. Isn't it, Johnny?' Carol said.

'Car, Jason. Car,' Donte shouted, bringing a toy into the kitchen to show his new friend.

Jason lifted the lad up and sat him on his lap. He'd always been good with kids; case of having to be, with his mother.

'So, does your mother work, Jason?' Johnny enquired.

'No. She has young children. I'm not going to lie to you, my mum isn't a good role model like Carol is. She's stuck in a rut and has lost her way in life. I help her out as much as I can, but unless somebody wants to help themselves, it's difficult, isn't it?'

'You can lead a horse to water, but you can't make it drink,' Johnny agreed. He liked the lad's honesty. Melissa had already told him and Carol that Jason's mum sounded a nightmare.

'May I use your bathroom, please?' Jason asked.

'Of course. The big bathroom is upstairs, but there's a small one second door on your right in the hallway,' Carol explained.

When Jason left the room, Melissa excitedly asked her parents, 'Well? What do you think?'

'He's lovely, and so good with Donte. I think you make the perfect couple, don't you, Johnny?' Carol gushed.

Johnny nodded, but said nothing. He liked the lad, but couldn't help thinking he was a bit too good to be true. He'd found out his surname earlier, so tomorrow he'd do some digging. If anybody could find out whether Jason Rampling was hiding something, or involved in any skulduggery, then he could.

Jason Rampling cranked the volume up on his car stereo and sang along in tune with Marvin Gaye to 'I Heard It Through the Grapevine'. He was a fan of most music genres, but soul was his ultimate passion.

Today had gone extremely well in Jason's eyes. Carol he already had eating out of his hand, and even though he could sense Johnny was the warier of the two, he knew he'd made a good impression. Johnny had shaken his hand before he'd left, saying, 'Let's go out for a beer soon. Have a man-to-man chat. Can't get a word in edgeways with these women of ours, can we?'

Jason could read people like a book. Johnny had fired many questions at him and Jason knew he would start digging around. That was why he was now on his way to dump Charlotte Rivers. Charlotte was an extremely pretty girl who he'd been dating for the past five months. But she was only seventeen, lived with her parents and her father was unfortunately a builder. He genuinely did like her, but she wasn't his answer to a better life. Her father's company was tinpot in comparison to Johnny Brooks's, which meant she wasn't worth taking a risk on. If he continued seeing her and Johnny found out, it would balls-up all his long-term plans.

She'd recently passed her driving test, so Jason had told Charlotte to meet him in the car park of the Plough at Gallows Corner. She lived nearby, in Harold Hill; they'd originally met in a pub in Romford.

Charlotte smiled as Jason's car pulled up next to hers. She was smitten with him and vice versa. When her parents and brother were out, they'd have rampant sex in her bedroom. When that option wasn't available, they'd drive somewhere secluded and do it in the back of the car. They could not keep their hands off one another. That was a fact.

Jason sat in the passenger seat and kissed Charlotte on the cheek. 'This is a nice surprise,' she said to him. 'I didn't think I was seeing you until Tuesday.'

Jason stroked Charlotte's long blonde hair. She looked stunning this evening. 'I'm really sorry, Char, but we're gonna have to call it a day.'

Flabbergasted, Charlotte's mouth opened wide. 'What do you mean? Call what a day?'

Jason stared at his hands. 'Us. I do like you a lot, you know I do. But I need to concentrate on Shay. It's not easy being a single father. She needs a mum and you're too young to take her on. You're beautiful, you can do far better than me anyway.'

Charlotte's eyes welled up. She had thought things were going so well between her and Jason. 'Have you met someone else? You were fine when I spoke to you yesterday. What the hell has changed?'

Jason squeezed her hand. 'My mum's going through a bad spell; I got a lot on my plate. Course I haven't met anyone else. I wouldn't do that to you. You're a brilliant girlfriend and you've done nothing wrong, believe me. But I have a duty to Shay and I don't wanna bring her up on the Mardyke. She deserves better in life.'

'I don't get what you're trying to say, Jase, Shay needs a mum. What do you mean by that exactly?'

Jason held Charlotte's gaze. He felt sad now, but had to see this through. 'It means rather than being in love myself, I got to look for a woman to love Shay. One day when you have kids, you'll understand.'

'I can help you with Shay. We can take her out for days and . . .'

Jason silenced Charlotte with a passionate kiss. He then opened the car door. 'It's best you don't ring me any more, Char. Be lucky in life, sweetheart. You deserve to be.'

'Jason! Jase!' Charlotte screamed as he got in his own car and started the engine.

Ignoring Charlotte's pleas, Jason drove off into the night. There was always Darlene. He was never seen out in public with her, their relationship was secret; therefore he could keep her on the firm without Johnny finding out.

Turning the volume of his stereo up, Jason sang along with Barrett Strong. 'Money (That's What I Want)' was the song and whoever had written the lyrics must have been clued up like him, he reckoned. Money got you everything and this was his first step to a new life.

CHAPTER FIVE

Jason Rampling glanced at his watch. He'd already called Melissa to explain he was running late, but he hadn't said he'd be this late. 'No. Not that one,' he said, exasperated. 'That's dirty and scruffy. Put on the new pink jacket I bought you,' he ordered his daughter.

'Don't like it.'

'Don't mess me about, Shay. I'm really not in the mood today. Do as you're bloody well told for once.'

'He wants to make a good impression for your new mother, Shay. That's who he's taking you to meet. He's not taking you, Elton, or you, Kyle. You're not important enough to meet her, neither is Barbara,' Debbie Rampling spouted.

Seeing the wounded expressions on his young siblings' faces, Jason glared at his mother. 'Don't say horrible stuff like that to 'em. Of course they'll meet Mel, just not today. Instead of lying there like a beached whale, why don't you get off your arse and cook 'em some grub? Eighty quid I spent in Asda this morning. You got no excuse now the fridge is full.'

Debbie lit a cigarette. 'Getting far too big for your boots

lately, you are, boy. You can fuck off and live with your posh bit of totty, you talk to me like that again.'

'She isn't posh. Mel's just a normal girl, I keep telling you that,' Jason argued.

'Johnny Brooks is cake-o, everyone knows that. Dunno what she's doing with a lowlife like you. Must be desperate.'

'Can I come, Jason?' Elton asked.

'And me. I'm coming,' Kyle insisted.

Jason put his hand in his pocket. 'Not today, lads, but get yourself some sweets,' he replied, handing each a pound coin.

'Have a nice time,' Barbara said.

'Have a nice time,' Debbie mimicked.

Thoroughly annoyed with his nasty bitch of a mother, Jason grabbed his whingeing daughter's hand and dragged her out the door.

Johnny Brooks handed his wife a menu. He'd taken her out for lunch so they could speak about her illness in private. But not only did Carol not want to talk about it, she was still refusing to tell Melissa.

'I wonder how Mel's getting on. So nice to see her so happy, isn't it? He's a cracking lad, is Jason. I do hope they stay together.'

'I wouldn't build your hopes up, love. They've only known one another five minutes and he's a bit of a chancer, by all accounts.'

Johnny had done some asking around. Jason had the reputation of being one for the girls and he sold pornography. He'd learned other stuff about the lad too. His grandmother was a notorious shoplifter and gambler who lived in Dagenham, and his grandfather had been a bookie's runner who'd been bumped off for robbing money.

'Well?' Carol urged.

Not wanting to burst his wife's bubble, Johnny played his findings down. 'I did a bit of digging. Nothing too bad, but he has had lots of girlfriends. Bit of a heartbreaker, by all accounts, so he better not be leading our Mel up the garden path or he'll have me to answer to.'

'I wish you wouldn't poke your nose in, Johnny. Say the lad finds out? And so what if he's had lots of girlfriends? You courted others before you met me, didn't you?'

Johnny felt his face flush. He'd heard nothing from Shirley since ending their relationship. 'Well, yeah. But that's different.'

'No, it isn't. Men will be men and I'm glad he's sowed his wild oats before meeting Mel. She's had boyfriends, hasn't she?'

'Yeah. Wonderful taste our daughter had,' Johnny replied sarcastically.

'Did you find anything else out about him?'

'Not really. Got the impression he has a reputation of being a bit of a wide boy, but I guessed that when I met him.'

'I don't want you asking no more questions about him. Always have to put a spanner in the works, you do. And don't you dare tell Melissa any of this. I don't want that girl's happiness spoilt.'

Johnny squeezed his wife's hand. 'Don't be angry with me. Melissa's my daughter and checking out the latest boyfriend is what decent dads do. Like yourself, I only want her to be happy. She deserves the best in life, the very best.'

*

The girl was a skinny, scruffy little urchin. Her long brown hair looked like it could do with a good brush, and her shoes were tatty and worn. She had a cute face though, even if it was currently sullen, with a sprinkle of freckles across her nose. 'Why don't you play with Donte, Shay? Look, he's enjoying himself and so are all the other children. You don't want to miss out on having fun, do you?' Melissa smiled. The child had so far refused to talk to her, was acting shy and sidling up to Jason.

'Answer Melissa,' Jason urged, prising his daughter's arms from around his waist. It had been his idea to have lunch at a pub with a play area, and he'd driven out to Wickford to do so. He didn't want Darlene to get wind of his relationship with Melissa. Thankfully she had no idea who Johnny Brooks was when he'd casually mentioned his name last week.

'Don't want to. Donte's a baby and I'm a big girl now.'

Jason picked his four-year-old daughter up and swung her around. She was ever so thin, Melissa thought. Definitely underweight for her age. Mel smiled as Jason gently placed Shay in a pit of shiny balls next to a girl of a similar age. Donte was having a whale of a time playing with another little girl.

'Sorted,' Jason grinned as he sat back down. 'She's not usually shy. Probably acting up 'cause she's only used to playing with her brothers and sisters,' he explained.

'Aww, she's lovely, Jase. Who did you tell her I was – a friend?'

'No. I told her you were my girlfriend. Best to be upfront from the beginning, eh?'

Melissa felt a warm glow envelop her. Jason must really be serious about her if he'd told Shay that. He still hadn't tried it on with her. The furthest they'd got was a kiss and cuddle, but they both lived at home, so it was awkward. 'Do you fancy going away for a weekend on our own? My mum mentioned it earlier, said if I wanted a break she'd have Donte for me.'

'Awkward for me 'cause I work Sundays. And, to be honest, I'd rather save up to rent a gaff than waste money on hotels. Be great if one of us got our own place, wouldn't it? We'd have loads of time alone then. So expensive though, what with all the bills and that.'

'Yes, I should imagine it is expensive. My dad's always said when I'm ready to move out, he'll find me a decent place. He wants Donte to go to a nice school in a good area.'

Jason nodded approvingly. This conversation was going exactly the way he'd hoped. 'That's what I want for Shay too. Gotta get her away from the Mardyke soon, preferably before she starts school in September. Call me a dick if you think I'm being presumptuous, but how about we get a gaff together? I know we haven't been seeing one another long, but we get on well, don't we? Be nice to have some independence – what do ya reckon?'

Melissa was stunned. She was sure she was in love with Jason, but it felt a bit too soon to be moving in with him. She felt safe around her parents, even though her dad got on her nerves at times. On the other hand, she fancied Jason something rotten, and the thought of going to bed with him every night and waking up with him every morning sent shivers down her spine.

'Forget I said anything. I can tell you're not interested,' Jason mumbled.

'No. It's not that. Of course I'm interested, I'm just a

bit taken aback as we haven't been together that long. Surely people will think we're rushing into things?'

'Who cares what people think? We both want the same things and we get on well.' Jason leaned across the table and held Melissa's hands. 'You're not average. You're different, Mel. Decent, proper girlfriend material. That's why I really like you.'

Melissa grinned. Those butterflies were doing somersaults in her stomach again. 'I'll speak to my parents, see what they say. But yes, I think you're right. We can make it work. I really like you too, Jason.'

'Mummy, look. Watch me,' Donte shouted out.

When Melissa walked over to her son, Jason smirked. He didn't love her, probably never would, but she was respectable and likeable. And if the gaff Johnny Brooks rented was big enough, she could look after his brothers and sister too. They could stay over at weekends; give them a break from his mother. He was a forward thinker, had it all planned out.

'All right, Nan. I got you some Guinness, look. A whole crate.'

'Me stomach's playing up at the moment, I can't drink 'em. Didn't you get me any fags?' Peggy asked, a disappointed look on her face.

Knowing full well his grandmother wouldn't be satisfied even if he brought her the crown jewels, Jason grinned. 'Nah, but I'll bring some next time. Got something to tell ya. I've met a girl. Family have got a few bob an' all.'

Peggy clapped her hands together like Bill Sykes out of *Oliver Twist*. 'Tell me more. What's her name? How old? Where's she from?'

'Melissa Brooks. She's twenty-one and her father owns

a builders' merchants. Not the small one in Rainham that Andy Michaels used to work for. The other one off the A13 heading towards Aveley.'

'I'm not sure of it, boy. Me memory ain't so great these days. What's she like? Is she pretty?'

Jason shrugged. 'Passable. She's a nice enough girl, though. Mother material for Shay.'

Peggy patted the sofa next to her and when Jason sat down, she squeezed his hand. 'Looks fade in time anyway. A ravishing beauty, I was, when I married your grandfather. Even that mother of yours was a pretty child. It's the ones who are ugly when young that improve with age, you know. Doris Shipton's daughter was forty last week. Looks far better than she did when she was in her early twenties. Same goes for Clara Hedges' girl. Ugly as a pig, that one, when it was born, but she has an attractiveness about her now.'

'So what you trying to say, Nan?' Jason chuckled.

'Ya know. As long as she's got a few bob, just put a bag over her head and hope for the best, lad.'

Melissa Brooks was incredibly excited.

Desperate to tell somebody her breathtaking news, she looked at the clock. Tracey was now speaking to her again and should be home from work by this time. She picked up the phone and was relieved when Tracey answered immediately.

'Trace, you'll never guess what! Jason only wants us to move in together.'

'You what! Why? What exactly did he say?'

Melissa repeated parts of the earlier conversation. 'He doesn't want me to tell my mum and dad it was his idea though, so whatever you do, mate, don't put your foot in it. How's it going with Barry?' Barry was Tracey's new gangster boyfriend. 'I spoke to Jase and he said we should go out in a foursome. We might have to cut down going out a bit now though. Not cheap moving in together, is it?' Melissa gabbled. Her mother had always been a homemaker, had exquisite taste, and she took after her. She could almost picture her and Jason's love nest already. It would have long cream curtains and big chandeliers hanging from the ceiling. The sofa would have to be dark though, because of the kids' mucky paws, and they could buy one of those big four-poster beds. That would be so romantic.

Having had her reservations about Jason since day one, Tracey decided to air them. 'Not being funny, Mel – and please don't think I'm jealous, 'cause I ain't – but something about all this doesn't ring true to me. I find it ever so weird he's not even tried it on with you yet. That isn't normal. Just be careful and don't rush into stuff. I would hate to see you get hurt.'

'The only reason he hasn't tried it on, Trace, is 'cause we've got nowhere to go. We can't do it in my house, or his flat. That's why he wants us to get a place, you muppet. Then we can be together properly, all the time. He's so romantic, Trace. Honest he is.'

Tracey sighed. She still found it hard to believe that Jason had fancied her friend over her. Unless he had problems with his eyesight, it made no sense whatsoever. As for Mel, she wasn't as experienced or streetwise when it came to blokes as she was. She'd made a complete idiot of herself over Donte's father and Tracey didn't want her pal to make the same mistake again. Even though Tracey had a new man she liked, she could not help feeling a tad jealous over this latest news. 'No man is perfect, Mel, always remember that. You don't want to throw yourself in at the deep end like you did with Joel. You have to learn by past mistakes. Once bitten, twice shy.'

'So, you don't think I should move in with him then? Is that what you're trying to say?'

Imagining Melissa and Jason cuddling up together on a shagpile rug in front of a burning log fire, Tracey's lip curled. 'No. Let's be honest, Mel. You hardly know the bloody bloke.'

Johnny Brooks's lip wobbled as he drove along in silence. Carol had finally opened up about her illness, the journey they faced, and it was breaking his heart. He wished he had the tumour instead, would swap places with his wonderful wife if he could. What had Carol ever done to deserve this? She was such a kind, loving, good woman who would fall over backwards to help others. How could life be so cruel?

'I don't want to die in hospital. I want to be at home with you. Can you make sure that happens for me? Even if they have to bring in one of those awful hospital beds and send in carers, I don't mind. As long as I'm at home.'

Johnny bumped his Jaguar up a kerb and held his amazing wife in his arms. 'You'll be at home, my darling, where you belong. I can promise you that faithfully.'

Melissa Brooks paced up and down the lounge. She'd psyched herself up about what she was going to say, but was still dreading the words leaving her mouth. So much so, she'd decided to blurt out the news the second her parents walked through the door. If she didn't and decided to leave it until tomorrow, chances were she wouldn't have the guts to say it at all.

Five minutes later, Melissa heard her father's Jaguar pull up on the drive and she braced herself for the inevitable. Donte was fast asleep. He'd had a wonderful time in the play area at the pub and had literally worn himself out. Melissa sat on the sofa twiddling her fingers as she always did when she was nervous. 'All right? You've been gone ages. Where have you been? I've got something I need to talk to you about.'

'Sit down, love. I need to speak to you about something important. You can tell me your news afterwards,' Carol said. She had finally decided to take Johnny's advice. Melissa had to be told at some point.

'I'll leave you to it,' Johnny muttered, shutting the lounge door. He didn't want to keep breaking down in front of Carol.

Melissa wasn't stupid. Both her parents looked shell-shocked, so something bad had happened. 'Is it Jason?' Mel panicked. 'Has he got another girlfriend?'

Carol sat on the sofa next to her daughter. She held Mel's hands tightly in her own, and bit her lip to stop herself blubbering. She had to be strong now, it was the only way. 'I've got cancer, love. That's why I was getting those headaches.'

Melissa snatched her right hand away and put it over her mouth. The mother of one of her schoolfriends had died of cancer. 'You got to have an operation? You're going to be OK, aren't you?'

This was the hardest part for Carol, so she tried to dress it up as best she could. 'Unfortunately, the cancer is too far advanced for them to operate on me, Mel. But you know me, I'm a fighter.'

Melissa was startled. 'You're not going to die though, are you?'

Carol held her daughter in her arms. 'I'll try my very best not to. But we all die one day, sweetheart. And that's a fact.'

CHAPTER SIX

Jason Rampling was too busy having his penis sucked to answer the phone.

'Who keeps ringing?' Darlene Michaels hissed. Jason brought out a jealous side to her that only her ex-husband had in the past.

'Don't stop. Carry on,' Jason groaned, grabbing the back of Darlene's head.

Darlene waved Jason's phone in the air. 'Who the fuck is Mel?'

Cursing himself for forgetting to turn the poxy phone off, Jason snatched it out of Darlene's hands. 'Mel is short for Melvyn. Mel lives in Barking, buys loads of films off me.'

'I don't believe you. Ring the number back, go on,' Darlene spat.

'Getting sick of you not trusting me, Dar. I ain't seeing no one else, how many times I gotta tell you that?'

Darlene leaned back against the pillow. She tossed her long hair backwards and lit a cigarette. 'I will find out if you're messing me about again, Jase, and I swear, if I do, you'll fucking regret it this time. So will the silly tart you're seeing. I'll have both your guts for garters!'

Melissa was all in a panic. If she wore the low-cut white top, would Jason think she was a slapper offering herself on a plate to him? He'd called her back about an hour ago and said he'd be round by one. Her parents had taken Donte to the seaside and would be out till late. Six outfits she'd tried on and still she could not make her mind up. She'd lost weight, but was nowhere near as skinny as Tracey. Would he think she was fat if she got undressed? Mel hoped not. It wasn't as if she could even turn the lights off.

The sound of the doorbell decided Melissa's outfit and she ran down the stairs in the white top and tight jeans. 'My mum and dad have gone out for the day and taken Donte with 'em, so we have the house to ourselves. I thought we might watch a film or something. Want a glass of wine? I've already opened a bottle. Or do you want a beer? Are you hungry? I can make you a sandwich or something if you like?'

Sensing her nervousness, Jason kissed Melissa politely on the cheek. It was obvious by the top she'd chosen to wear what she was hoping for, but he wasn't particularly in the mood. Darlene had sucked all his energy and sperm. 'Slow down, babe, eh? Let me get in the door. Knackered, I am. Shay wasn't well last night, so I hardly got any sleep,' he lied.

'Oh no. What's wrong with Shay? Is she OK now?'

'Yeah. Seems to be. Just one of them twenty-four-hour bugs, I think. A few of the kids over the Mardyke have had it. That's another reason I need to get Shay off that poxy estate. Full of disease, that place is. The amount of junkies' needles you find in the lifts and on the stairs is horrific. One of the neighbour's kids ended up with HIV. She's only five, poor little mare. You spoken to your parents about moving out yet?' Jason had already decided if Melissa had changed her mind, then he was going to trawl some bars and clubs over the next few weeks to see if he could strike gold elsewhere.

Melissa's eyes welled up. 'You know I said my mum was ill? Well, she's got cancer, and I think she might be dying.'

Jason put his arms around Melissa and soothed her fears. 'I will have a beer after all. Your poor mum. Such a lovely lady. Let's cuddle up on the sofa and you can tell me all about it.'

Melissa nuzzled against Jason's chest. He always smelled of the most gorgeous expensive aftershave. Feeling amorous, she leaned in for another kiss. This was the first time they'd ever been alone in a house together. 'Shall we go to my room?' she suggested.

'I'm a bit knackered to be honest, babe. And say your mum and dad came back early? I would hate them to find us in a compromising position. That's disrespectful in their house.'

Melissa felt humiliated. She could tell when they'd been kissing that Jason's mind was elsewhere. 'You don't fancy me, do you?' she blurted out.

'Of course I fancy ya. You wouldn't be my girlfriend if I didn't. But I also respect your parents, Mel. Your mum's ill. Imagine how bad that would be if they caught us at it.'

'They won't. They're visiting my Uncle David and won't

be back until teatime at least. But if you're tired, forget it. Tracey said it was odd you've never tried it on with me and I'm beginning to think she was right.'

'Tracey's just jealous 'cause she wanted me herself,' Jason said, grabbing hold of Melissa's hand and placing it against his penis. Knowing he had little choice, he led her up the stairs.

'Awww look, Johnny. He's shattered,' Carol said. They'd stopped off on the way to tell her brother David she had terminal cancer and it had been sad and upsetting all round.

'He's a great kid, love. I'm sorry, ya know – for being such an arsehole in the past.'

'You're not an arsehole, just a stubborn old git at times.' They were now having a drink at the Peterboat in Leigh-on-Sea and Donte was snoring while curled up on the seat. 'I've decided I can't tell Mark over the phone, Johnny. I want to visit him and tell him in person,' Carol informed her husband.

Johnny was thoroughly peeved with his son at present. They'd been so close when Mark was growing up. They'd worked together too, until Mark had walked away from everything for a tart he'd met on holiday. They'd argued over that and now Mark rarely contacted him any more. He still rang Carol occasionally, but not as often as he should. 'No way are we driving to Newcastle, love. I will contact Mark, tell him to visit us. Then we can explain the situation together.'

'OK. I feel fine today you know, a bit tired now, but other than that I feel like I'm twenty-one again.'

Johnny stroked his wife's rosy cheeks. She was as

beautiful as the day he'd met her. Kind, mischievous eyes, and that cheeky raucous laugh. 'I love you. Far more than you'll ever know.'

Carol took a deep breath to try to keep her emotions in check. 'Not as much as I love you, Johnny Brooks. You may be a tosser at times, but deep down you got a heart of gold. Promise me when I've gone you'll always look after Donte for me. Knowing you've got his back, I'll be able to rest in peace.'

Tears in his eyes, Johnny's lip wobbled. 'I'll take care of our grandson, don't you worry about that. Always.'

'I'm really sorry, Mel. It isn't you, honest it ain't,' Jason apologized. He wasn't used to suffering from erectile dysfunction and guessed his little problem was down to his romping with Darlene earlier.

Melissa felt humiliated, but tried not to show it. 'Let's go back downstairs, watch TV or a film.'

'I think I'm knackered, babe. Either that or I'm worried about your parents coming home early,' Jason lied. He was actually quite relieved he'd been unable to perform, for the simple reason he didn't want to hurt Melissa. He wasn't a nasty person deep down and if he did find a better prospect and dump Mel, he didn't want her to feel used. She was a nice person and did not deserve that.

'I'm gonna ring my dad, see if they're on the way back. Donte might as well come home if we're just watching TV.'

'Cool. Love spending time with the little man – and you, of course. That's why I can't wait for us to get our own gaff. Be like a proper little family then, won't we?'

'I won't be moving out any time soon, Jase. Not now my mum's ill. No way am I leaving her while she's got cancer.'

Jason sighed as Melissa left the room. Thank God he hadn't given her one. Because if she wasn't prepared to move out and look after his kid, then she was sod-all use to him.

Johnny Brooks picked up Donte's plastic spade. 'Granddad'll show you how to build castles,' he said, chucking some sand inside the bucket and patting it down. Because of the unusually warm weather, the beach was busy and as Johnny played with his grandson and clocked lots of other families doing the same, he could have kicked himself. He'd been such a grafter over the years, had worked six long days a week to build up his thriving business, and it was only now Carol was dying he could see how pointless that was. Why hadn't he spent more time with his own children when they were younger? He and Carol could have had hundreds or even thousands of unforgettable days out if only he hadn't been working all the time. And now it was too late. Well, almost. He was determined to cherish every minute they had left together. Business could wait.

Carol munched on a bag of chips and thought how wonderful the sea air smelled. Since she'd been handed her death sentence she had begun appreciating all the small things in life that she'd once taken for granted.

'Nana, look,' Donte said, excitedly pointing to his sandcastle.

Carol smiled broadly. She might be dying, but watching Johnny and Donte bonding made her feel like the happiest woman alive.

Hours later, Johnny sat Donte in his special chair on the back seat and clipped the seatbelt. His grandson was sleeping, having worn himself out on the beach. 'You getting in the car, love?' he asked Carol.

'Look at that sun going down, Johnny. Doesn't it look spectacular? Can we sit on the wall a minute and watch it.'

Johnny sat on the nearby wall and squeezed his wife's hand. 'I think we should make a list, don't you? Write down all the things you want to do, so we don't forget them.'

'Well, swimming with dolphins won't be one of 'em. Not unless you're planning on buying me a rubber ring!' Carol kept cracking jokes to keep Johnny's spirits high. She was petrified of water, couldn't swim.

'Next nice sunny day we'll definitely go strawberry picking, and I'll give that guest house in Cambridgeshire a bell tomorrow, book us in for a couple of nights. We can go back to that tea shop you loved. I'll treat you to those homemade scones with the cream and jam again,' Johnny smiled. He actually felt like sobbing, but kept a stiff upper lip. He would save his tears for when he was alone, that was the manly thing to do. Johnny stared intently at the sun going down. 'If you had one big wish, you know, something to happen before the cancer wins, what would it be, Carol?'

'To be at those school gates at Donte's first day, but that isn't going to happen, is it? Breaks my heart to think I won't see him grow up. But I'll be looking down on you all, watching from heaven.'

'What else?' Johnny asked. If he could grant his wife her final wish, he was hoping it might ease his own guilt. He rued the day he'd ever met Shirley Stone, he truly bloody did.

'To see our Melissa settled and happy. My biggest dream ever was to see her get married. As you know, I do love a wedding and I would've made a great mother of the bride. I just hope she stays with Jason and he treats her well in life. Not going to see her get hitched now, I know. But I want you to promise me you will give her a wonderful wedding. No expense spared. I want our Mel to have the best.'

'I promise,' Johnny whispered, kissing his wife on the cheek. A plan was forming in his overactive brain, but he wouldn't mention it just yet. He needed to speak to Jason first.

CHAPTER SEVEN

'Dad, Dad, wake up.'

The prodding on the arm finally woke Jason and he sat up, rubbing his bleary eyes. Three nights on the spin he'd been out on a mission to find a suitable mother to raise Shay but none he'd met had fitted the bill. Getting it wrong wasn't an option; he had to get it right or he might as well carry on as he was.

'Nan's got a man in her bed, Dad,' Shay announced.

Jason jumped up. His mother had brought a nonce home last year who'd touched Barbara inappropriately. Jason had gone ballistic when his sister had admitted what happened, and had told his mother if she wanted to get laid in future she should go round the bloke's gaff. In Jason's eyes, putting your kids at risk was an unforgivable act of selfishness.

Elton was sitting on the sofa, eating crisps. 'Mum's having sex,' he said bluntly.

Hearing grunting noises coming from his mother's bedroom, Jason banged on the door. 'Get that geezer out of 'ere now before I fucking sling him out.'

'Mind your own fucking business, you. My flat and I'll do what I like in it,' Debbie yelled.

Jason opened the bedroom door and immediately wanted to vomit. His mother was kneeling on the bed, her arse looking bigger than the moon, with some no-mark giving her one from behind. Jason grabbed hold of the bloke by the neck. 'There's four young kids in this flat. Get dressed and get out, you worthless piece of shit.'

Debbie leapt off the bed and flew at her son. 'You got no right barging in 'ere shouting the odds. Fuck off, go on. I want you outta my home and take your bastard daughter with ya,' she screamed, punching Jason hard.

'Don't you hurt my brother,' Kyle yelled, squaring up to his mother. Babs was sobbing she was so scared. Elton and Shay watched the events unfold in silence.

Jason was laid-back as a rule, rarely lost his temper. But when he did, he completely saw red.

The bloke said nothing as he got dressed and sloped off. He had a wife indoors, didn't want any grief.

Deborah put on her filthy dressing gown. To say she was livid was an understatement. Who did Jason think he was, her keeper? She marched out the bedroom and into her son's. 'Take your shit and go. Go on, I want you out,' she shouted, taking Jason's clothes out the wardrobe and throwing them on his bed. She would miss the money he brought home, but she wasn't being dictated to by anyone. Especially a brat she'd spent ten hours giving birth to.

'You're a disgrace as a human being and a mother. Bringing blokes back 'ere when you're pissed and letting your kids hear all sorts. Have you no bastard shame? It weren't that long ago you dragged a nonce home that mauled Babs while you were comatose in your stinking pit. Them little 'uns deserve far better, and so does Shay.

If Social Services were to find out what you're really like, they'd take 'em away from you, in a flash.'

'That a threat, is it? Gonna grass on me, are ya? Only I'm sure the Old Bill would be interested to know you once robbed the Paki shop at Dagenham East, and now sell snuff and porn films to weirdos and perverts.'

Jason stared at the mess of a woman who had given birth to him. She stank; a mixture of sweat and the stale smell of sex. 'Start packing your toys and stuff, Shay,' he shouted. 'We're outta this dump.'

'That was Jason on the phone. He's on his way over with Shay,' Melissa said, her eyes gleaming with excitement. It was now a whole week since she had last seen her boyfriend and she'd been terribly worried he'd gone off her. He hadn't phoned as much as he usually did either, and she'd wondered if he was avoiding her because of their failed attempt to have sex. Perhaps he felt embarrassed, poor sod.

'See, I told you you'd hear from him soon, didn't I?' Carol smiled. She hadn't been well yesterday, had suffered the migraine from hell, but felt much better today.

'I think Jase has had a few problems at home. He told me he's had a big row with his mum and walked out with Shay. She sounds awful, his mum. Nothing like you.'

Johnny looked over the top of his newspaper. 'Perhaps a man-to-man chat might help. I'll take him out for a couple of pints later.'

'He's coming over to see Melissa, not you,' Carol quipped.

'I won't keep him out long. Just want to make sure the lad's all right.' This was the opportunity Johnny had been waiting for.

'If he hasn't got anywhere else to stay, Dad, can he stay here tonight in one of our spare rooms?' Melissa asked. She had sorely missed Jason and wanted to spend as much time as possible with him.

'I'm not sure about that, love. Your mum's not well enough to have strangers wandering about the house.'

'I don't mind and Jason's hardly a stranger, he's our Melissa's boyfriend,' Carol said. Jason had a happy-go-lucky attitude and Carol would welcome some company. When she and Johnny were alone, the conversation always veered towards her cancer. Telling her son Mark earlier this week that she was dying had been one of the hardest things Carol had ever had to do. She still hadn't mentioned the time frame she'd been given to Melissa, would rather her daughter be kept in the dark.

'OK,' Johnny said. 'I'll speak to the lad alone first, find out the score.'

Jason Rampling felt thoroughly miserable as he drove towards the Brooks's house. He couldn't look after Shay properly all by himself and he had nowhere to go. He had a few pals he might be able to doss with, but they all lived on the Mardyke and their flats were shitholes. His nan would probably suffer them temporarily if push came to shove. But she'd made it clear she was no fan of Shay.

Jason thought about Melissa and was glad he hadn't been too hasty in dumping her. None of the other birds he'd chatted up had a wealthy father like Johnny. Most openly admitted they were skint and their family didn't have a pot to piss in.

He parked on the Brooks's driveway and grinned as Melissa ran out of the house to greet him. 'Had the morning from hell, I have, babe. Sorry I didn't see you all week but I've been having murders indoors and had to look after all the kids,' he lied.

'No, you never. You went out,' Shay stated.

'Get inside the house, you. Little girls your age should be seen and not heard. Don't forget your manners either. You be polite, like how I've taught you to be. Melissa's mum and dad are decent people.'

When the sullen-looking child did as she was told, Melissa put her arms around Jason's neck. 'Missed you, I have. My dad's taking you out for a drink to chat to you, man to man. I think he wants to help you get sorted, Jase. He said you can stay at ours tonight. Unless you have somewhere else to go, of course?'

'Thanks, Mel. No, I haven't got anywhere else to go.' Jason smiled. This was his big chance to impress, worm his way in, and he was determined to grab the opportunity with both hands.

Darlene Michaels was not a happy woman. Jason had promised to come around earlier, then had rung up with some cock-and-bull excuse about his mum slinging him out and him having to look after Shay.

When the doorbell rang, Darlene thought Jason had changed his mind and therefore was gobsmacked to see her ex standing on the doorstep. 'Hello, Craig. I heard you were out. How you doing?' she asked awkwardly. She and Craig Thurston had been an item for a couple of years back in the eighties. He was hardcore, was Craig, the party animals of all party animals and that was the reason she'd dumped him. At thirty-five, he was three years younger than her.

'I'm good, thanks, Dar. You're looking well. Fancy coming out for a drink? Just as pals, like.'

'Not much of a daytime drinker these days, to be honest. But come in and I'll make you a coffee.'

Craig sat on the kitchen stool, laughing and joking about old times. 'Had some good craic, didn't we, girl? I always tell people you were the one I regret letting slip through my fingers. I should've done the right thing and married you.'

Now positive he was trying to hit on her, Darlene quickly changed the subject. 'So, you working, Craig? Still in the building game?'

'Nah, but I will get back into it. Some geezer owes me fifty grand and I need that back to set meself up again. You know how it is.'

'Not someone from the Mardyke, surely?' Darlene asked, wondering if that was the reason for his visit.

'Nah. Johnny Brooks, the cheeky bastard. Been popping down to his yard, but can't seem to catch him there. I will though, and I'll get my dosh back. Took a proper liberty, that bloke.'

Darlene stirred the coffees and handed one to Craig. That name rang a bell and it suddenly occurred to her Jason had mentioned it recently. 'Who is Johnny Brooks? My friend mentioned him last week.'

'Cake-o, Johnny is. Owns J J Brooks, the builders' merchants.'

'Has he got a daughter?'

'Yeah, and a son. He's moved away though, the boy.'

'What's the daughter's name?' Darlene asked, already dreading the answer. She knew Jason like the back of her hand and could tell he'd been asking her if she knew Johnny Brooks for a reason.

'Melissa, why you asking?'

'Because a mate of mine thinks her son is dating Johnny's

daughter. Can you find out for me? She live round this way?' Darlene had that dreadful churning in her stomach that she always got when she suspected Jason of cheating on her. She wasn't stupid and knew one day he would probably meet someone nearer his own age and fall in love. The thought of that happening any time soon made her feel physically sick. Jason Rampling was her addiction, just like heroin was to a junkie. She literally craved him, and when she didn't get to see him for days on end, she'd watch the videos she kept of them making love over and over again while pleasuring herself with a vibrator.

'I'm sure the daughter still lives with Johnny. I'll ask around, see what I can find out for ya – on one condition.'

'What?'

'That you let me take you out for a drink on Friday night?'

Darlene felt so miserable it was an effort to even force a smile. 'OK. Deal. But find out before Friday for me, Craig.'

Johnny Brooks put two pints on the table and sat down opposite Jason. 'So what's been happening?'

Jason explained how awful his home life was, exaggerating for impact. 'That's why I have to get Shay away from there, Johnny. My mother gets so drunk she doesn't know who she's bringing home, and I'm not having my daughter raised in such an environment. Babs was terrified after that nonce tried to rape her. He only stopped when Elton and Kyle started hitting him,' Jason lied. The guy in question hadn't tried to rape his sister, but he had put his hand inside Barbara's knickers while his mother and brothers were asleep. Johnny wasn't to know that though. He needed this man to feel sorry enough for him that he'd want to see to it he got a roof over his head.

'That's bloody awful, lad. Want stringing up, do nonces. So you not got anywhere lined up to stay?'

'No. Only left home today. It'll be difficult for me to work while looking after Shay an' all. She doesn't start school till September, so I suppose in the meantime I'll have to take her to work with me.'

'Things will sort themselves out, they always do. Not been herself, Melissa hasn't, this week. I think she was worried 'cause you went a bit cold on her. Not messing her around, are you? Only she's got enough on her plate with her mum being ill.'

'I'm not a messer. Just had a tough week meself. I had to look after all the kids 'cause my mother went on the missing list. No way was I leaving 'em alone.'

'Are you serious about my daughter?' Johnny had never been one to beat about the bush. 'Because if you aren't, now is the time to say so. I won't be angry, I promise.'

'Well, yeah. I know it's only early days but I think me and Mel can make a go of it. Like a proper little family with the kids, eh?'

Johnny took a sip of his pint and studied Jason carefully. He was a hard lad to read. 'Right, I'm gonna lay my cards on the table. Whatever your reply, I want this conversation to stay between us, you understand that, lad?'

'No worries. You can trust me.'

'Melissa does not know the full extent of her mother's illness. She knows the cancer is terminal, but what she doesn't know is the doctor reckons Carol has between six months to a year to live.'

'Shit! I'm really sorry. Poor Carol. She's such a nice lady.'

'Being the type of protective dad that I am, I did a bit of asking around about you, Jason. I'm sure being a father to a daughter yourself, you can understand that. What I learned wasn't bad, but it wasn't exactly good either. You've got a reputation of being a bit of a ladies' man, and no way am I having my Mel fucked around. Neither am I allowing my daughter to have a boyfriend who sells porn to perverts.'

Jason opened his mouth, then closed it again. He supposed he shouldn't be shocked; a man like Johnny must have connections all over Essex, but he was still a bit taken aback. 'So you want me to dump Mel?'

'No. Quite the opposite. Do you love her?'

'Yeah. Well, I think so. Not really been together long enough to be properly in love, have we?'

'Let me put it another way: do you think you can take good care of her and not break her heart?'

'Well, yeah. I'd like to think so.'

'My Carol's dying wish is to see Melissa settled and happy. She likes you, Jason, sees you as a good match for our daughter. I'm not so sure, to be truthful, but I am willing to give you the benefit of the doubt. Which is why I have an offer for you. My pal owns a big construction firm and has kindly offered to teach you the trade and pay you a decent wage. You said one day your dream was to kind of build your own home, so now's your chance to learn how to. I will buy you and Melissa a house in a nice area that is liveable but needs renovating. That house will be put in your names.'

Jason was gobsmacked. He didn't particularly fancy the job, it sounded like hard graft, but he would show willing for now. The house in a nice area was a dream come bloody true though. 'And in exchange you want me to take care of Melissa and raise Donte as my own. Am I right?'

'Yes, Jason. Just keep your penis in your pants and give up anything dodgy you're doing. I don't mind you keeping the market job and a few sensible little earners. In return, you take care of my daughter, be loyal to her, and I will ensure you all live a life of luxury in comparison to what you're used to.'

Jason held out his right hand. His mother had always said he was a nobody, and he could not wait to prove that fat cow wrong. His teachers in school had been the same. One had even told him: 'It's a waste of time trying to educate council estate kids like you – you'll never amount to anything. You were born on the Mardyke, and you'll end up dying there.'

'So, when can we start house-hunting? Mel's gonna be so excited. Have you mentioned any of this to her yet?' Jason asked. He truly could not believe his luck – and to think he'd been on the verge of dumping Melissa. Thank Christ he hadn't. She was perfect to bring up Shay and he was thrilled he'd now be able to send his daughter to a good school. Perhaps he could even get custody of his brothers and sister, offer them a better life too. He would work on Melissa with that one. Make up loads of stories about how bad things were at home until she felt so worried for the kids she'd agree to let them move in as well.

'I'll find you an appropriate property before you get married. Be good for Carol, that will. A bit of house-hunting will take her mind off the inevitable.'

'Married!' Jason laughed.

'Yes, married, lad.'

'You're joking, right?'

Johnny frowned. 'Nope. I am deadly serious. What did you think I meant when I said Carol wanted to see Melissa happy and settled?'

Jason shrugged. Living with Melissa was one thing, but marrying her was a completely different kettle of fish. 'I dunno. Living together, I suppose. No disrespect, Johnny, but we've not been dating long enough to get married. Can't we give it a bit more time before getting hitched? Say we move in with one another, then argue like cat and dog?'

'Then you'll work at your marriage and stand by your vows. Indians have arranged marriages and they make it bloody work. So can you. It's Carol's dream to be mother of the bride, so if you're not willing to marry Melissa then I'm afraid the deal is off. I'm going to the toilet, so have a little think. Nice home, job, life – or you sod off back to the Mardyke Estate and live with your drunken mother. Your future is up to you, lad.'

CHAPTER EIGHT

Having barely slept a wink, Jason got up at dawn, pocketed the envelope with the five grand in it that Johnny had given him, and drove towards his grandmother's house in Dagenham. He'd agreed to marry Melissa in the end, hadn't had much choice with Johnny's tactics. He really was up the creek without a paddle and all he could do now was pray Melissa knocked him back. They barely knew one another after all.

'That you, boy? What you doing 'ere at this unearthly hour? Not been nicked, have ya?' Peggy Rampling asked, putting on the pretty pink dressing gown she'd pilfered out of Marks and Spencer's the previous day. A doddle to rob, M&S was. They exchanged stuff without a receipt, so all you had to do was shove something small in your handbag, then take it back and get what you wanted. She'd usually flog whatever she got at half the marked-up price to the women down the bingo hall, but now and again would choose something for herself.

Jason paced up and down his nan's front room. 'He wants me to marry her. Given me an address in Hatton Garden of a pal of his and the dosh to buy her a ring today. I don't love her. She ain't even my type. What the hell am I meant to do, Nan?'

'For Christ's sake, boy, calm down. You sound like you've inhaled helium. Who wants you to marry who?'

'That Melissa I told you about. Put it right on me, her father did. He's even got me a job with a mate of his on a building site. A proper job. I can't do that. I don't do proper jobs. Reckons he's gonna buy us a house to do up and put it in mine and Mel's names. But I don't love the girl. I barely know her.'

'Bit hasty, ain't he? Why the rush?'

Jason flopped on to the armchair and put his head in his hands. 'Mel's mother's dying and apparently it's her wish to see her daughter married off. Why me, eh?'

'How much did he give ya to buy the ring?' Peggy enquired.

'Five grand.'

'Well, the way I see it, you got two choices. You either do a runner with the five grand. Or you marry the tart, stay with her a couple of years and cop for half the house. Is she that bleedin' ugly?'

'No. Well, I dunno. More plain than ugly, I suppose.'

'Any brothers or sisters?'

'One brother. But the old man don't get on with him.'

'Sometimes in life, Jason, you gotta look at the bigger picture. If the old girl's on her last legs, you're one death away from a wonderful inheritance.'

Johnny put the mug of tea on his wife's bedside cabinet, smiled and kissed her on the nose. 'How you feeling? I thought I'd cook a fry-up this morning. Bet poor little Shay will think it's Christmas, bless her.'

'Aww, my little mate.'

Desperate to make his wife as happy as possible, Johnny said, 'If I tell you a secret, you got to promise me you'll keep schtum about it. We don't want to spoil the surprise.'

'I won't say anything. What surprise?'

'When we was in the pub last night, Jason asked for my permission to propose to Mel.'

Carol sat up and put her hand over her mouth. 'Really! What did you say? I mean, they haven't known one another long. But it's so romantic. Did you tell him it was a bit too soon?'

'No, love. I gave him my permission. I hadn't been with you that long before I proposed. When you meet the right one, you just know, don't you?'

'I'm so pleased he asked your permission, but it's a bit quick – we were together five months, not weeks. I'm not sure she'll say yes, you know. It's a big step, but oh wouldn't it be wonderful.'

'We will find out soon enough. He's proposing this Friday.'

'Not again. What am I meant to have done now?' Jason asked, as the police ordered him to step out of his XR2. This was the third time he's been pulled over along Dagenham Heathway in the past six months.

'We know it's you peddling filth, Rampling. Only a matter of time until we catch you red-handed,' an officer informed Jason as his colleague searched the car.

Jason looked at his watch. He never argued with the police. It wasn't worth antagonizing them. They'd once planted drugs in Lenny Anderson's car because they couldn't catch him outright. Lenny had given them a load of gyp whenever he got tugged, the silly boy. A three-stretch he'd ended up with because of that.

The van Jason used when carrying anything illegal was kept in a mate's garage and wasn't registered to him. A local headcase, Mickey Two Wives, had sold him the vehicle and it was registered to an address in Wolverhampton. Following Mickey's advice, Jason had never sent off the logbook. It was easy to get a bent MOT and insurance certificate to tax the van. Mickey lived in a caravan just off the A13 in Purfleet and would get his gypsy mates to sort the paperwork for a oner a pop. The van was sign-written, had once belonged to an electrician and still had the company's details plastered down both sides. Jason always wore a dark baseball cap when driving it to cover up his distinct blond hair and not once had he ever been tugged. The Old Bill thought they were so clever, but they weren't. He had always been one step ahead of them.

'All done, guv,' the second officer said, slamming Jason's boot in disgust at finding it empty of anything untoward.

The other officer handed Jason his licence back. 'Watch your back, Rampling.'

Jason smirked. 'Thank you, officers. Have a nice day.'

Darlene Michaels had just returned from the shops when there was a knock at the door.

'Oh, it's you. Got a fucking cheek, turning up 'ere unannounced, seeing as you blank all my calls these days. Fourteen times I rang you yesterday, ya no-good bastard.' Darlene's heart was beating like a drum as it always did when she and Jason argued. She loved him so much it bloody hurt at times.

'I was proper busy yesterday. Sorry. Come 'ere,' Jason

said, holding his arms out. He was dying to get his end away, could feel his penis throbbing with anticipation.

Darlene pushed him away, her eyes glinting angrily. 'I ain't stupid. Been round the block a few times meself, ya know. Who is she? And don't pretend there is no she, 'cause I know there fucking is.'

Knowing this was his chance to come clean, Jason chose his words carefully. 'It's not what you think. I'm in shit-street, Dar. Had a massive bust-up with me mum and I've moved out. I needed help with Shay, so I've got a pal helping me out. She's a bird, but a proper plain Jane. I swear on Shay's life I'm not banging her. I don't look at her in the way I look at you. I'm just sort of using her, to be honest.'

'Do I look simple? Well, do I?' Darlene screamed. 'No way is some tart gonna look after Shay without getting something in return. Got money, has she? You're a slippery snake, Jason, that's what you are. I knew you were up to no good, can always tell. Fuck off, go on. Get out my flat and life.'

'Dar, please don't be like this. You know as well as I do, sometimes in life we gotta put our kids first. That's why me and you can never live together or be seen out, 'cause you don't want Andy finding out. This bird means nothing to me – unlike you, who means the world. You gotta believe me.'

Screaming abuse and throwing punches, Darlene pushed him out the front door. 'And don't come fucking back,' she bellowed.

'Can I have another cuddle?' Shay asked Carol. This woman was nice and Shay hoped she was her new nan.

She was friendly and smelled lovely. She was nothing like her old nan, who swore constantly and smelled nasty.

Carol chuckled. The child had almost a feral look about her. 'Go upstairs and look in the bathroom. There's a black brush on the sink unit, you'll be able to reach it. Go get it and I'll give your hair a good brush for you. Would you like that?'

When Shay nodded and skipped off happily, Melissa shared her concerns with her mother over Shay not liking her.

'She's only a little girl, love, and it's probably strange for her to see her father with a girlfriend. She'll come round in time. You just need to be patient and persevere.'

Johnny entered the room. 'How's my two favourite girls?' he asked, scooping Donte off the floor and lifting his giggling grandson above his head.

'We're fine, Dad,' Melissa beamed. She was so pleased her father had finally accepted her son. 'I don't know what time Jase will be back. He said he had some things to sort out today.'

'I know. We had a little chat last night,' Johnny replied. 'I can't see him and Shay on the streets so I told him they can stay here until he sorts something.'

Melissa leapt off the sofa and hugged her father. 'Thanks! You're the best dad in the world.'

Jason Rampling pulled up on the Mardyke Estate and studied the ring again. It was simple, but nice. A bit like Mel in a way. He wasn't looking forward to putting it on her finger though. The very thought gave him the heebies. Getting married was such a big deal and even though he planned on telling nobody, if Mel did accept the proposal, Darlene was bound to hear it on the grapevine, then chop his bollocks off.

Two years ago, Jason's previous motor had been stolen off the Mardyke, so no way would he chance leaving the ring inside the car. He picked up an empty crisp bag off the floor, put the box inside and shoved it at the bottom of the carrier bag that held the bottle of drink he'd bought from the offie. He dropped his phone in the bag as well, then picked up the second box, the one he'd purchased in a different jeweller's. He had to win Darlene over. His cock was urging him to.

Jason took the stairs two at a time and banged on Darlene's door. He'd been ringing her all afternoon, but she'd been blanking his calls. He knew she would forgive him though. She always did.

Darlene flung open the door. She'd had a good cry earlier before tarting herself up to the nines. She'd known by how many missed calls she'd had that Jason would be back. 'What d'you want? Said all I had to say to you earlier.'

'You look nice. You going out?' Jason knew she always pretended she was going out when they rowed, so decided to play along with her.

'Yes. But where I go and what I do has sod-all to do with you any more. You worry about Plain Jane.'

Jason pulled the box out of his pocket and handed it to Darlene. She wore massive gold hoop earrings and had been vexed when she'd lost one last week. 'An olive branch,' he said.

Darlene glanced at the earrings, then handed them back to him. 'I'm not being bribed, Jase. Neither am I being the other woman. You either knock things on the head with Plain Jane or it's over between us, for good.'

Jason could tell she was warming, so told Darlene what she wanted to hear. 'I can't lose you, Dar, so I'll knock her on the head. I love you, babe. You know that.'

Putting the bolts across the inside of the front door in case her son came home, Darlene grabbed Jason's hand and literally dragged him into the bedroom.

'Jason's phone is still switched off. I hope he's OK. He didn't say he'd be this late,' Melissa stated worriedly.

Carol looked at the clock. It had just gone eight and she was ready for bed. The tiredness and lack of appetite were becoming more difficult to hide from her family, and Carol hated them looking at her with worried eyes. 'I bet he's had a lot of things to sort out, love, and his battery has died. Might even be checking on his brothers and sister. Don't worry. He'll be home soon,' she yawned.

Johnny was none too impressed. Jason had left here at dawn this morning and it didn't take fourteen hours to travel to Hatten poxy Garden and back. Thank God they were looking after Shay, else Johnny would now be thinking his daughter's wide boy of a bloke had run off with his five grand.

'Your mum's right, Mel. Jason told me earlier he had lots to sort out and wouldn't be home until tonight,' Johnny fibbed. He suddenly felt anxious. Had he put his wife's happiness in front of his daughter's?

'Babe, I really do have to go now,' Jason repeated, unclasping Darlene's hands from around his neck.

'So you're definitely gonna tell Suzie tonight you won't be seeing her any more?' Darlene asked again.

'Yes. Already told you that ten times. Same as I told you I rang my nan and she said she'd look after Shay for me.' Suzie Smith was the first name Jason had thought of to blurt out, but his lies were now spiralling out of control. Sex with Darlene was always even more mind-blowing after an argument, but now his ball bags were emptied, he just wanted to leave.

'When you coming round again?' Darlene asked, pure desperation in her voice.

Jason gave her one last peck on the lips. 'Soon. I promise, babe.'

'Where have you been? I was worried about you, Jase. I thought you'd had an accident,' Melissa gabbled, throwing her arms around her boyfriend's neck.

'I'm sorry. My sister rang me earlier, crying her eyes out. Kyle fell over and cut his head open so I had to take him up A and E. Then me phone died,' Jason said, kissing Melissa on the lips. He'd luckily found some Juicy Fruit chewing gum in his car to get rid of the taste of Darlene's vagina.

Johnny was stony-faced when Jason sauntered into the lounge holding his daughter's hand. 'Help your mum up to bed now, love. She can barely keep her eyes open, but was determined to stay awake to make sure you were OK, Jason,' he said, his voice laden with sarcasm.

Donte and Shay were already in bed, so as soon as Carol and Melissa left the room, Johnny stood up and kicked the door shut with his Dealer boot. 'Where's the ring?' he barked.

Jason took the box out of the carrier bag and opened it. He handed Johnny an envelope. 'The receipt and a grand is in there. I looked at dearer rings, but thought Mel would like this one more.'

Johnny stared Jason in the eyes. 'I am warning you one

last time. If you do have other bits of skirt on the go, you need to sack 'em off. Because if I find out you are cheating on my daughter, I will not only cut your cock off, I'll ram it down the back of your throat and get great pleasure in watching you choke to death. Now, do we understand one another?'

Jason Rampling could not sleep. He had got himself into such a predicament and Johnny's threat kept swirling around his brain. He did love Darlene, but they were hardly the next Romeo and Juliet. He supposed, in a way, she was the mother figure he'd never had. He'd always felt safe at her home, loved and wanted. All the things he'd never felt with his own mother.

Sighing, Jason turned on his other side. Darlene was becoming more clingy of late, which was worrying. She didn't seem to give a shit if the neighbours heard them arguing, whereas in the past she'd always turn the music up. And she'd threatened to tell Andy about their affair last time she'd caught him cheating on her. Jason doubted she'd ever carry out that threat, but he'd hate Andy to find out. They weren't as close now as they'd been at school, but Jason would still feel guilty for betraying his one-time best pal in that way.

Juggling a double life was not going to be easy. As Jason twisted and turned the night away, he weighed up his options. Darlene was eighteen years older than him, fast approaching forty. Would he really yearn for her in ten years' time? He doubted it. Women didn't age as well as men. He would always want her in his life though, and that was where the problem lay. Darlene was as much as a drug to him as he was to her. He could not live with her, but living without her seemed almost unthinkable.

But, on the other hand, this was a big opportunity for him. No way was he destined to live the rest of his life on a council estate, he had too much going for him. Melissa might not be Miss World, but she was a path to a better future. Love or money? That was the choice he had to make right now. His heart told him Darlene, but his head told him not to be so stupid.

CHAPTER NINE

'Feast your eyes on these beauties, Jase. Straight off the back of a lorry heading for JJB Sports. A score a pair I want, but you can get forties on 'em all day long.'

Jason glanced at the trainers. The bulk were Nike and Adidas, which always sold well. 'I'll have a think, got other stuff on at the moment.'

Terrence Arnold looked at Jason quizzically. He was ten years older than the lad who ran the shoe stall on a Sunday for him. But they were good mates and he'd never known Jason to look a gift horse in the mouth before. Terrence, or Tel as his pals called him, often received hot property and as a rule Jason was salivating at the mouth to flog it. 'What's up with you?'

'You really don't want to know, mate. Listen. I got to dash. Will bell you about the trainers later.'

'When we having a girlie night out? Don't want to know me now you're all loved up,' Tracey Thompson taunted. She and Mel hadn't had a night out since Melissa had met Jason, and Tracey had no other real friends to hang out with. Tracey had just been dumped by a local villain,

Barry Higgins. She was heartbroken, loved the glamour and attention of being on his arm. Now he was history, no one gave a shit about her.

Melissa picked up the menu. She and Tracey were having lunch in Romford. 'We'll arrange a night out soon, I promise. It's a bit awkward at the moment, with Jase and Shay living at my mum and dad's. I can't just sod off out and expect my mum to look after Shay and Donte.'

'I still can't believe your parents allowed him to stay there. So, have you done it with him yet? He must've tried it on by now, surely?'

'He has tried it on, but just as we were about to do it, my mum and dad came home,' Melissa fibbed. No way was Mel admitting Jason had been unable to perform. Tracey would dine out on that bloody story for years.

'I don't wanna piss on your parade, mate, but something definitely ain't right. Any normal bloke would've shagged you senseless by now. Barry tried it with me on our third date. That's what normal men do. You sure he's not seeing someone else? Is his phone switched on or off when he's with you?' Tracey was still baffled why Jason picked Melissa over her and alarm bells had started to ring. Was he a con man? He obviously had the gift of the gab to worm his way around Johnny Brooks. Mel's father was an ogre when he wanted to be.

'He has his phone switched off most the time. But he does turn it on to call people when I'm with him.'

'Men are men, Mel. They think with their trousers. If he isn't pestering you for sex, then he must be getting it elsewhere. Switching his phone off is well dodgy. I tell you what, next time he plans to go out of a night, ring me beforehand and I'll follow him for ya.'

Melissa suddenly did not feel hungry any more. She'd been in such a bubble since meeting Jason, she'd chosen to ignore his lack of physical interest in her. They hadn't even kissed properly for weeks. A squeeze of the hand or peck on the lips was as intimate as they'd been. And why did he always switch his phone off when he was with her? He said it was because his battery was on the blink. But was that the truth? Or was he lying?

Melissa arrived home with a new outfit, only to be told her mother wasn't well enough to go out tonight. 'She had a headache this morning, love. Was sick and now wants to spend her birthday at home,' Johnny explained.

Jason was in the lounge playing with Donte and Shay, and when he stood up and gave her the briefest of pecks on the cheek, Melissa could not help but think of Tracey's words. Her friend was right, something was definitely amiss.

'I need to pop out for a bit to pick your mum's present up. The kids can come with me. Be nice if they chose a present for her too. She'd like that,' Johnny said.

As soon as her father's car pulled off the drive, Melissa chose to confront Jason. 'You're seeing someone else. I know you are.'

'Don't be daft. Course I'm not. Your mate Tracey been putting silly ideas in your head again, has she? Surely you can see she's jealous.'

'This has got nothing to do with Tracey. I'm not stupid, Jase. You don't even act like you fancy me.'

'Of course I fancy you, ya nutter. What bloke wouldn't? I just want our first time to be special, ya know. We can't be having sex while your mum's ill in bed upstairs. That's disrespectful.'

'Excuses, excuses. I think it's odd how you switch your phone off when we're together an' all. I'm not being taken for a fool, Jase. Perhaps we should call it a day?'

Jason tilted Melissa's chin, forcing her to hold his gaze. 'I'm not mugging you off, ya doughnut. Got a surprise lined up for you. A big surprise. You'll see what you mean to me then.'

'What is it? Tell me.'

Jason silenced Melissa with a passionate kiss. Aware of his erection rubbing against her, all Melissa's worries were temporarily forgotten.

Later that evening, Jason Rampling felt like a lamb being led to the slaughter as he followed Johnny Brooks into the kitchen.

'Ready?' Johnny asked.

'Erm, no. I think it's best I put Shay to bed first in case Mel says no.'

'OK. Get your skates on then.'

Reminding himself that providing a better future for his daughter and siblings was far more important than his own happiness, Jason carried Shay up the stairs.

'Story,' Shay mumbled.

'Once upon a time there was this cute little princess who lived in a nasty tower block in Rainham. Her nan was a fat stinking evil witch who—'

'Like Nanny Debbie?' Shay interrupted.

'Exactly.'

When Shay's eyes closed, Jason continued the story anyway. 'So thanks to the gallantness of her wonderful father, the little princess moved into a posh house with a big garden and lived happily ever after,' he ended.

Jason picked up the ring and with his legs feeling as

though he was trudging through treacle, made his way down the stairs.

'What you doing?' Mel asked as Jason dropped to his knee in front of her.

Jason opened the box. 'Will you marry me?'

'You what! Is this some kind of a joke?' Melissa spat.

Johnny grinned at Carol. 'Put the lad out of his misery then, Mel. He'll get cramp kneeling there,' he chuckled.

Realizing that Jason was actually serious, Melissa put her hand over her mouth. Gobsmacked wasn't the bloody word. 'I don't know what to say. I wasn't expecting this.'

Johnny had told Jason earlier that if Mel thought it was too soon for them to get married but still wanted to live with him, then the offer to find them a property still stood. That option suited Jason down to the ground. No commitment, a nice gaff, and he'd be free to swan off round Darlene's whenever it took his fancy. 'I know it's a bit soon, so I don't mind if you say no,' Jason mumbled, looking into Mel's eyes, willing her to do so.

'I've already given Jason my blessing, love,' Johnny butted in. 'Be lovely for your mum to see you get hitched, wouldn't it? It's always been her dream to see you happy and settled.'

'Shut up, Johnny,' Carol ordered. 'Don't you be worrying about me, Mel. You decide for yourself, love. It's a big step is marriage.'

Not one to be easily shut up, Johnny added, 'I've told Jason I'll buy you a nice house as a wedding present.'

'Leave 'em to it, for goodness' sake,' Carol snapped.

The doorbell brought an end to Jason kneeling in front of Mel like an absolute lemon. He gratefully leapt up. 'I'll get it.'

A tall bloke with dark hair stood on the doorstep. He looked vaguely familiar and Jason wondered where he'd seen him before. 'How can I help you, mate?'

'I'm here to see Johnny. It's urgent.'

'What's your name?'

'What's yours? You Melissa's new bloke?' the man asked, his gold tooth glinting in the dark of the night.

'Why d'ya wanna know who I am? Got nothing to do with you.'

'Just go and get Johnny will ya, mouth almighty. I ain't got all fucking night.'

Jason opened the lounge door. ''Ere a minute, Johnny,' he said, not wanting to alert the women that anything was amiss. The bloke at the door certainly wasn't paying some friendly social call.

'Who is it?' Carol asked.

'Watch your DVD, love,' Johnny replied, releasing the pause button. That had been his surprise present to his wife. The old videos he'd taken of them and the kids over the years he'd had transferred on to a DVD.

Johnny flung open the front door and locked eyes with Craig Thurston. 'Fuck off, else I'm calling the police,' he hissed.

'Nah, you won't. I know too much about ya for you to be involving the Old Bill. I want my money, and I want it sharpish. You've got a week to weigh me out, or I'm telling Carol you've been knobbing Shirley Stone for years. I'm sure she'd also be keen to hear how you got the money to start your business up in the first fucking place an' all,' Craig said quietly.

Jason's ears pricked up. This was an interesting conversation.

Mel poked her head around the door. 'Mum wants to know who it is, Dad.'

'Business,' Johnny barked. 'Make sure the girls stay inside. I won't be a tick,' he told Jason before bundling Craig out the door and down the pathway.

'I mean it, Brooksy. One week you've got – or Carol gets to know what you're really like.'

'Look, it ain't my fault Robbo had you over. I didn't know he was planning a moonlight flit, did I?'

'You roped me in on the job. So it is your fucking problem,' Craig argued. 'Got your cut OK, didn't ya?'

Desperate for Carol not to have her heart broken, Johnny decided to make Thurston an offer. 'I'll give you half of my cut, OK? Twenty-five grand.'

'Fuck off! I want the full fifty I'm owed. Plus interest.'

'I haven't got fifty-plus grand lying around.'

'Don't fucking lie. You're minted now,' Craig spat.

Johnny sighed. He really didn't need this crap. 'Thirty. That's all I can get my hands on. Take it or leave it.'

Craig smirked. 'I'll take it.'

'Was that that bleedin' Craig Thurston?' Carol shouted as the front door slammed.

'No, love. It was a bloke I did a bit of business with recently,' Johnny lied.

Carol eyed her husband suspiciously. She hadn't heard the man's voice, but had looked out the window and seen him walking up the path. 'What business? Only it looked like Craig Thurston to me.'

'OK, it was Craig. But there's no problem. He's got a load of timber he wants to flog me on the cheap, that's all. You got a minute, Jason?' Johnny said, gesturing for the lad to follow him into the kitchen.

'Everything OK?' Jason asked.

'Anything you heard, take no notice. Trying to wangle a few bob out of me, the bastard is. Don't be saying nothing to the girls though. I don't want 'em worrying. Word of advice, lad: never let them indoors know about your business.'

'I didn't hear anything he said to you, Johnny,' Jason lied. He would make some enquiries tomorrow to find out who Shirley Stone was.

Johnny slapped Jason on the back. 'Good lad. Has my daughter given you her answer yet?'

'Erm, no. I think we should leave that for tonight. She didn't look too keen.'

'Nonsense,' Johnny replied, dragging Jason back into the lounge. 'This man's having kittens, Mel, awaiting your answer. You going to keep him waiting all night?'

Melissa grinned at Jason. 'Yes.'

'Yes, what?' Jason mumbled.

'Yes. I will marry you.'

Carol's eyes filled with tears of joy. 'Aww, Johnny. Open a bottle of bubbly. Congratulations to you both. I can't wait to help you look for the perfect dress, Mel.'

Johnny shook Jason's limp hand. 'You got a good 'un there, girl,' he told his daughter.

'Do you want a church wedding?' Carol asked. Even if she died before the actual wedding, it would be lovely to be involved in all the arrangements.

'No need for all that bleedin' church lark, especially when they've both got kids by different partners,' Johnny stated. 'I had a feeling Mel would say yes, so had already set the ball rolling. Luckily there was a cancellation, so I got in there sharpish.'

Jason looked at Johnny in bewilderment. 'Whaddya mean?'

Johnny smiled broadly. 'I mean the wedding's booked. You're getting married three weeks today!'

Unable to stop himself, Jason Rampling dropped his champagne flute in horror.

CHAPTER TEN

The build-up to the wedding flew by and the day before he was due to get married, Jason felt like a trapped budgie in a cage. He hated his new job on the building site. Was constantly knackered and a shadow of his former self. Planning his speech, Jason felt unusually anxious as he rapped on Darlene's front door. She opened it seconds later, eyes blazing with temper. 'Andy's home. Do one,' she hissed.

'I need to talk to you, Dar. It's important,' Jason said quietly.

'I'm done with you. It's over, for good this time.'

Jason stuck his foot out to stop the door being slammed in his face. 'Please, I'm in trouble. That's why I've not been round. My car's downstairs. Just give me five minutes, that's all I ask.'

'OK. But you say what you gotta say, then leave me the hell alone. Got that?'

'Who is it, Mum?' shouted Andy Michaels.

Darlene quickly shut the door. 'Bloody Jehovah's.'

Darlene got in Jason's car, her face like thunder. 'Drive off the estate. We'll be spotted otherwise,' she spat. Barely seeing Jason these past few weeks had driven Darlene doolally and she couldn't keep torturing herself.

Jason pulled up outside some garages and switched off the engine. He turned to Darlene, tried to hold her hands, but she snatched them away. 'Look, I know you're upset with me, but I weren't lying when I told you about that building job I was forced to take. The Social were bang on me case, threatened to stop my dole money and I can't allow that to happen as I need to put a roof over mine and Shay's head,' he lied. 'I have missed you so much, babe, I really have.'

Sick of being taken for a fool, Darlene snarled at him. 'I wasn't born yesterday. You can't do without sex for a couple of days, let alone nearly two fucking weeks. Who is she?'

Jason had perfected the art of looking innocent. His eyes opened wide, a hurtful expression clear to see. 'There is no she. I'll prove it to ya. You let me and Shay stay at yours until I sort us out somewhere decent to live, and I'll give up my job and go on the sick. You get to see me all the time then, don'tcha?'

'Oh, don't talk such bollocks. What about Andy? He isn't stupid, ya know. No way am I breaking my son's heart over you, Jason Rampling. You're not worth it. A compulsive liar and a chancer, that's what you are. Got an ex of mine after me at the moment. Had some good times with him, I did. Got far more to offer me he has than you. The geezer's a go-getter.'

Nobody was more of a go-getter in his eyes than Jason himself. 'Don't talk to me like I'm some fucking idiot, Dar, as you know only too well I ain't. Last chance, sweetheart. Shay and me either move in with you on a temporary basis today, or I move on in life and you won't ever see me again.'

Losing it completely, Darlene smacked him around the face. 'Trying to play emotional blackmail won't work with me, you jumped-up little prick. Virtually brought you up as a lad. You would never have eaten a decent meal if it wasn't for me. Got a very short memory you have, boy. And that's what you are deep down, isn't it? A worthless little boy. Well, more fool me for being sucked in by your charm. Can see right through you now though. You're a nothing, a nobody, Jason, just like your useless fat slapper of a mother.'

Jason had never hit a woman, not properly. But at that very moment he was so tempted to punch Darlene. Somehow he restrained himself. 'Get out. Go on, get the fuck out,' he bellowed, leaning across her to open the passenger door.

'I'm not walking home from 'ere. Drive me back on to the estate,' Darlene ordered.

Jason picked up her handbag and flung it out the door. Keys, make-up, cigarettes and tampons scattered across the filthy pavement.

'You bastard,' Darlene screamed, scrambling around on her knees to retrieve her belongings.

Jason turned the ignition and reversed his XR2. He opened the window. Even in old faded jeans and a white T-shirt with black mascara dripping all down it, Darlene looked as hot as a blazing bonfire. 'You're gonna regret today for the rest of your life, Darlene. Goodbye, sweetheart.'

Sobbing, Darlene yelled, 'No, Jase. Come back. I'm sorry. I love you.'

Jason was debating whether to drive back and drop Darlene home when his phone rang. It was his sister and, such was her anguish, he could barely understand her. 'Slow down, Babs. Try not to cry and tell me again.'

'It's Mum. She went out yesterday morning and never came back. We got no food, or money and now the electric's gone. We're all starving, Jase. Please help us.'

'Don't worry. I'm not far away. I'll be with you in ten.'

Darlene was on her third vodka when she heard a hammering on her front door. Heart fluttering with anticipation it would be Jason, she touched up her hair and lipstick before answering. 'Oh, it's you,' she said, unable to hide her disappointment.

Craig Thurston stepped inside the hallway, delved inside the carrier bag and chucked handfuls of fifty-pound notes up in the air.

'What you done? Robbed a bank?'

'Nope. I got that dosh I was owed – well, thirty grand of it anyway,' Craig grinned. 'Let's book a holiday, be like old times. You choose the destination. We can go anywhere in the world you want.'

'I'm not in a holiday mood,' Darlene said miserably. 'Come from Johnny Brooks that money, did it?'

'Yeah. A bit of blackmail works wonders,' Craig chuckled.

'Did you find out about his daughter like I asked you to?'

'Hell, yeah. Got some proper gossip for you there. Getting married tomorrow, Melissa is. Pal of mine will be there. He's been booked to film it and do other stuff. That your mate's son Mel's marrying, is it? I saw him when I went round Johnny's house recently. Cocksure little bastard with a blond curtain haircut.'

Darlene immediately came over dizzy and leaned against the wall for support. 'What's his name?'

'Who?'

'The groom.'

'I dunno, do I? Want me to ring me mate Tel and find out?'

'Yes,' Darlene replied, her voice no louder than a whisper. Surely it couldn't be Jason? For all his faults, he would never get married without telling her, would he?

'Hello, mate. That wedding you were setting the stuff up at earlier. What's the groom's name?' Craig asked.

'Well?' Darlene mouthed.

'Jason. He's from this estate, by all accounts. Is that your mate's boy?'

'Jason Rampling?'

'Yeah. That's him.'

A watery sensation rose in Darlene's throat. She didn't make the toilet, was sick on the spot all over Craig's fifty-pound notes.

Having forgiven Jason for going on the missing list earlier, Johnny Brooks proudly introduced his future son-in-law to all his pals in Rainham Working Men's Club. For all Jason's faults, he was a good-looking lad who came across as intelligent. A smart talker, who could hold a conversation about most subjects.

Brian the Cabbie nudged Johnny. 'You got a good addition to the family there, mate. Bright as a button, he is. I wish my Wendy would dump that waste of space she's with and find a lad like Jason.'

Johnny Brooks beamed with pride. He still had his reservations about Jason, but in a way the lad had redeemed his own street cred. Melissa getting pregnant by a random black bloke – who'd added insult to injury by promptly dumping her – had been the most humiliating experience of Johnny's life. He'd even stopped going to the Masonic bashes because of it, such was his shame. But he would hold his head up again now, and he'd invited all his fellow Masons to the wedding tomorrow.

Seeing Jason deep in conversation with Scottish Paul, Johnny grinned at him. 'You all right, son? I'll get another round in.'

Jason grinned back. For the first time since this wedding had been arranged, he actually did feel all right. Seeing his brothers and sister in a tearful state of poverty once again had shown him where his priorities lay. They couldn't go on living there with his mother, he had to help them. He'd also popped round to see his nan. She was the only guest he had invited to his wedding and she'd given it to him in her usual sharp-tongued style. 'You can't back out now, you silly bastard. I've chored a new outfit to wear. If it don't work out, boy, just divorce the girl. What the hell have you got to lose?' she'd said.

When Scottish Paul kept rambling on about what a wonderful wife and mother Melissa would be, Jason found himself agreeing. His nan was right. Apart from Darlene, he had nothing to lose – and she was far too old for him anyway.

'He won't do it, Dar. I've already asked him twice,' Craig Thurston said. He'd been stunned when Darlene had spilled her guts to him earlier about Jason; he'd never had her down as a cradle-snatcher.

The shock having now worn off, Darlene was absolutely livid and was pacing up and down her lounge like a woman possessed. 'Fucking little cunt. He deserves this, Craig, believe me. I've got five grand in the bank that my mother left me. Ring your pal back and ask him if he'll do it for that on top of the grand you offered him. No!

Offer him five grand altogether, your grand and my four. That leaves me something for a rainy day.'

'Jesus wept, Dar. You must've really had it bad for this lad.'

'I did. But not any more. Jason Rampling is history, trust me. Go on, ring him back and offer him five. His reputation can't be worth that fucking much. Please, Craig. And I promise you faithfully if he says yes, we'll go and book that holiday first thing tomorrow morning. Perhaps we can go back to Majorca, stay at that resort we did last time. What a laugh that was. Remember Brenda and Stewart who ran that bar? A scream, they were.'

'OK. But this is the last time I'm ringing him, Dar. If the geezer says no, he says no.'

Stomping about with her hands over her ears, Darlene refused to listen to the call. 'What did he say?' she asked when she clocked Craig had stopped moving his mouth.

Craig Thurston grinned. 'Majorca here we come.'

CHAPTER ELEVEN

Jason Rampling woke up at six a.m. In eight hours' time he would be a married man, and for once he had no doubt he was doing the right thing.

Jason sat on the edge of the bed. He and Melissa were yet to find their perfect property, but Johnny owned a few flats that he rented out. The tenants of one had recently done a midnight flit without paying the rent, so he and Mel would be moving into that for the time being. It was a palace in comparison to the Mardyke Estate. There was no doubt that Darlene was going to react like a mad woman when she learned he'd got hitched, but Jason was done with her now. He had given her the option of allowing him and Shay to move in with her, and she'd knocked him back.

Grinning, Jason stood up. This was a new chapter of his life and he was determined to give it a whirl. Melissa was a decent person and tonight he would hold her in his arms and make love to her like a husband should.

'Stunning! Oh, Mel, you really do look beautiful. Your dad and Jason are going to be the proudest men alive when they see you,' Carol Brooks beamed. Mel's wedding dress was traditional white. The bodice had a crochet effect, and the skirt flowed out from the waist downwards with crochet along the bottom. Melissa had chosen to wear her dark hair up, so had a matching crochet head-piece to hold her hair in place. She truly did look stunning, like a princess, Carol thought.

'No. Don't want to put it on,' Shay screamed, knocking the purple bridesmaid dress out of Carol's hands. Shay hated Melissa even more now she was marrying her beloved father.

Carol sat on a chair and urged Shay to sit on her lap. She stroked the child's hair and spoke gently in her ear. Shay could be unruly when she worked up a temper, but was very loving towards her. Carol felt sorry for the poor little mite. She'd rarely left that flat on the Mardyke Estate, by the sounds of it. 'Remember I was telling you all about the seaside last night?'

Bottom lip trembling, Shay shrugged.

'Yes, you do. I told you about sandcastles and explained what the sand and sea look like. And the boats that sail in the water.'

'And chips and sweets,' Shay mumbled.

'That's right. You'll love eating chips on the beach, and as for those sticks of rock, yum yum. So, if you're a good girl for Auntie Carol and you put your dress on, how about me and Johnny take you and Donte to the seaside tomorrow?'

The tiny underfed-looking child's eyes shone as she flung her arms around Carol's neck. 'I love you. Can I call you Nanny?'

*

Jason Rampling studied himself in his pal's full-length mirror. The long-tail tuxedo was a tonic mohair with matching trousers.

Terrence Arnold walked into the room and wolf-whistled. 'Looking good, buddy. If I wasn't married to Susan, I'd half fancy you meself. Any last-minute doubts?'

Jason had only ever owned one suit in the past. A cheap, black one that he wore for funerals. Studying his smart new look once again, Jason knew he could easily get used to the finer things in life. 'No, mate. None whatsoever.'

Johnny Brooks felt extremely proud but also very sad as he laid eyes on his wife and daughter in their wedding regalia. Carol's peach skirt-suit now looked a size too big for her. She still looked beautiful though and Melissa looked absolutely amazing. 'Beautiful, both of you look,' he sighed.

Carol beamed with happiness. She had prayed to God that she wouldn't suffer one of her migraines today of all days, and thankfully he'd listened to her. She didn't even feel tired, considering she'd barely slept last night. Excitement had kept her awake and today she was full of adrenaline. 'You look so handsome, Johnny. Doesn't he look smart, Mel?' Carol gushed. Johnny, Terrence and Donte were wearing the same suits as Jason, bar the bright purple waistcoat the groom had chosen to separate his look from the others.

'I dunno about handsome,' Melissa laughed, giving her father a hug. She couldn't wait to become Mrs Rampling now and the thought of herself and Jason finally sharing a bed later this evening sent tingles down her spine.

'Donte, come and show your mum and nan what a big boy you look in your suit,' Johnny said.

Carol burst into tears at the sight of her beloved grandson looking all grown up.

'Don't cry, Mum. You'll ruin your make-up,' Melissa urged, her own eyes brimming with tears.

'Mel, 'ere a minute,' Tracey shouted out. Melissa had insisted Tracey was to be a bridesmaid, even though Jason was none too keen.

'Wow! You look incredible,' Mel gushed. Shay and Tracey were wearing stunning purple off-the-shoulder dresses, and Melissa couldn't help thinking that Tracey looked far prettier than she did.

'I got something for you,' Tracey smiled, handing Melissa a small box. 'It's that bracelet you loved of mine with the blue stone. Something borrowed, something blue, something old, something new.'

'I thought they were meant to be separate items. Not unlucky if they're all the same, is it?'

'No. Don't think so.'

Unaware that her marriage was doomed anyway, Melissa happily put the bracelet on.

'Answer the door, Babs, and get rid of whoever it is. Not in the mood for visitors,' Debbie Rampling shrieked.

Babs trudged along the hallway. 'It's Dave the Rave, Mum. He's got a present and card for Jason.'

Dave the Rave was the estate's speed and ecstasy dealer. Never one to miss the chance to ponce an illegal substance, Debbie darted towards the front door. 'Jason don't live 'ere no more. What you bought him a present for? It ain't his birthday.'

'It's a wedding present. Ain't nothing special, just a card and bottle of plonk.'

Having already drunk two litres of strong cider, Debbie

wondered if her hearing was playing her up. 'Wedding present! What do you mean?'

Dave the Rave pulled his Nike baseball cap over his eyes. He was on a paranoid one, thanks to the three acid tabs he'd popped last night, and Debbie had always scared the living daylights out of him even when he was straight. He stared downwards at his Diadora trainers. 'I saw Jase in the Working Men's Club last night. He was on his stag do. Look, just give this to him, will ya?' Dave mumbled, shoving the carrier bag in Babs's hand.

Not one to be shaken off easily, especially when two sheets to the wind, Debbie chased Dave towards the lift and grabbed him by his scrawny arm. 'When is he getting married? Where?'

Knowing he was about to have a panic attack, Dave the Rave was desperate to get away. 'Langtons, today at two. Look, I gotta go. Not been a-bed all night.'

'Is Jason really getting married?' Babs asked as her mum stomped back inside the flat.

'Don't ask me, I'm only his bastard mother. Get the boys dressed. And ask old Lil if you can borrow a fiver.'

'Why?'

Debbie glared at her thick daughter. 'Why d'ya fucking think?'

Jason arrived at Langtons Registry Office with Terrence, his best man. 'I don't know a soul here,' he whispered to him, as he made his way to the front of the aisle to await his bride.

'Jason, Jason,' a voice bellowed.

Aware of all eyes on him, Jason walked over to his nan who had bagged herself a seat in the front row.

'You said I could bring someone, so I brought Ted. You

remember Ted, don't ya? It was his grandson Timmy you used to nick the lead off the church roofs with.'

'Yes, I remember, Nan,' Jason hissed, putting a forefinger to his lips in hope she'd get the message. She was only five foot three. A sturdy woman with dyed burgundy-coloured hair. But she literally had a voice like a foghorn, and he could sense all the Brooks's posh friends looking at her. The last thing he needed was for her to tell embarrassing stories about him all day. Johnny Brooks would literally have a heart attack.

'Shake Ted's hand then. Say hello properly,' Peggy ordered.

Jason did as he was told. Ted was a lanky dark-haired Irish bloke who had a dreadful taste in clothes. The cream suit he was wearing looked horrendous. He stood out like a sore thumb.

'The bride's arrived,' somebody shouted.

Jason took his place at the front of the aisle. This was it. Shit or bust.

Johnny Brooks squeezed his wife's hand as the vows were exchanged. Carol was smiling broadly, but crying at the same time.

Jason grinned at his bride. She looked lovely in her dress and he was actually looking forward to ripping it off her later and making love to her for the first time. 'I promise to care for you above all others, to give you my love and friendship, support and comfort, and to respect and cherish you throughout our lives together,' he vowed.

Tracey Thompson was secretly seething. She'd been sure Jason would get cold feet and couldn't believe he'd gone through with it. She didn't believe he loved Mel. He was only marrying her because her father was loaded, she thought bitterly.

'So it is fucking true,' a voice bellowed from the back.

Johnny Brooks looked around in horror.

'You no-good deceitful little cunt. What type of son gets married without telling their own mother, eh?'

'Mum, can we just go?' Babs begged, tears streaming down her face.

Jason wanted the ground to open up and swallow him as his drunken mother marched towards him. The guests looked shell-shocked and he could fully understand why.

'Are you having a party, Jase?' Elton asked.

'Get rid of her, Jase,' Melissa hissed.

'You don't wanna be marrying him, girl. He don't love any bastard other than himself. Only reason he's getting hitched is because your family are cake-o,' Debbie slurred loudly.

'Do something, Johnny,' Carol urged. She couldn't quite believe what was happening.

Johnny Brooks stood up. 'How dare you turn up here uninvited and ruin my daughter's wedding. Get out! Go on, before I physically throw you out.'

'Who d'ya think you are? Rambo? Ya fucking midget,' Debbie retorted.

Peggy Rampling stood up, hands on her hips. She'd never met her other three grandchildren and had no wish to. 'Look at the state of you, ya drunken trollop. No wonder the boy didn't want you at his wedding. You'd break the fucking camera. Barging in 'ere with all your unwanted kids in tow, you should be fucking ashamed of yourself,' she yelled.

As the fiasco continued, Tracey Thompson grinned and said a silent thank you to God. She had been praying that something like this would happen.

CHAPTER TWELVE

'Pass me the salt and pepper, love,' Johnny Brooks said to his wife. He'd hired a professional catering company to cook and serve the hundred and thirty guests.

Carol studied her daughter's face. 'Ruined Mel's day, all that drama did. You know how I hate the C word. Never felt so embarrassed in all my life when she started yelling that out. I could swing for that bloody woman.'

'Me too,' Johnny muttered. The ceremony had finally gone ahead after the police were called to remove Jason's poor excuse of a mother from the premises. Debbie had left before they arrived, dragging her unkempt kids with her. 'What do you think of the décor?'

'Beautiful. But nobody is going to remember that now, are they? The only talking point will be that drunken dragon turning up, spouting all sorts.'

Johnny sighed. He had gone to a lot of expense to ensure his daughter had an unforgettable day. He'd hired an exclusive company to decorate the hall. White drapes covered the walls and ceiling, and a portable white dance floor had been laid with flashing lights that spelled out Melissa and Jason's names. He'd ordered the finest cutlery, glassware and flower arrangements, but it all suddenly seemed like a waste of time and effort. He had seen the looks on the faces of his fellow Masons and their wives when Debbie had yelled her son was only marrying Melissa for money.

'I'm relieved Mark didn't come now,' Carol said miserably. Their son was on holiday in Turkey.

'Granddad. Wee, wee,' Donte said.

Carol patted her husband on the back. 'You see to him while I check on Mel. We'll just have to try to make the most out of the rest of the day. Nothing else can go wrong, surely?'

Darlene Michaels studied herself in the full-length mirror. She rarely wore dresses, but was determined to look the part for her grand entrance later.

'I just spoke to Tony. They're eating at the moment. We'll make a move in a bit; pitch up at that pub nearby. He's gonna ring us when the time's right,' Craig Thurston said.

Adrenaline flowing through her veins, Darlene asked, 'How do I look?'

'Gorgeous. I can't wait for our holiday. Do you good, it will. Rampling's only a boy, you'll soon get over him. Bit of sea and sand is just the tonic you need.'

Darlene picked up her handbag. Jason had hurt her far more than any other man had in the past, and she was determined to return the favour, twice as fucking hard.

Tony handed the microphone to Jason, who cleared his throat before speaking. 'Firstly, I would like to apologize for the terrible behaviour of my mother earlier. Her language and actions were appalling and I am truly sorry if she offended anybody. I would also like to offer a personal apology to Carol and Johnny, who have been so supportive towards me and done everything possible to make this a special day for myself and Melissa.'

Squeezing Carol's hand, Johnny gave his son-in-law a slow nod of approval.

Jason looked down at Melissa and smiled. 'As most of you are probably aware, Melissa and I haven't known one another that long. But I have to say, as she walked down the aisle towards me earlier I truly felt like the luckiest man alive.'

'Pass me the sick bucket. He ain't even shagged her yet,' Tracey Thompson hissed in her new boyfriend's ear. She couldn't believe that the wedding had gone ahead after the earlier fiasco and had been drowning her sorrows ever since, getting louder by the glass.

'Seems a nice enough girl, but she's not his type,' Peggy Rampling whispered to Irish Ted. She rubbed her thumb and fingers together. 'All about the wonga.' Peggy was chuffed to bits that Jason had got himself away from his mother and the Mardyke Estate. It was onwards and upwards for her grandson from now on.

'What Melissa and I have is something special,' Jason continued. 'We both have young children whom we want the best for in life, and together we can be a proper family and raise our kids as brother and sister. As you probably guessed when my mother showed up earlier, my childhood wasn't the greatest. But Donte's and Shay's will be. I intend to work like a Trojan and they will have everything I had to go without.'

'Aww, bless him,' Carol said to Johnny.

Aware of all his fellow Masons clapping his son-in-law, Johnny allowed himself a wry grin and joined in with the applause. The lad was a sweet-talker and had thankfully managed to turn a difficult situation around.

Craig Thurston handed Darlene a double vodka and tonic. The dress she was wearing was jade green. It clung to her curves, showed off her pert breasts and Craig could understand why a young lad like Jason would be interested in her. She had a look of pure filth about her, did Darlene, and when you got her in the sack she'd perform exactly as you'd expect. She was certainly one of the best he'd ever had. 'All right, girl? How ya feeling?'

'Revengeful,' Darlene snapped. 'I bet that old cow of a nan of his is there an' all. Hates me, she does – and the feeling's mutual. My aunt used to run catalogues years ago, Kays and Freemans. Peggy Rampling ordered tons of stuff out of 'em one Christmas, then knocked my aunt. Thieve anything that isn't nailed down, she would.'

'Does Jason's nan know about you and him?' Craig asked.

'No. But she will do soon,' Darlene cackled. 'Serves him right, the lying, cheating, no-good shitbag. After today he can rot in hell for all I care. I never want to see him again.'

Feeling less embarrassed about earlier since Jason's speech, Johnny Brooks took the microphone with confidence. 'Firstly, I would like to thank all of you for coming today. I know it was short notice for some, and Carol and I truly appreciate you making the effort.'

'He bribed my Jason into marrying her,' Peggy Rampling informed Irish Ted. 'Offered to buy him a house.'

'This is so fucking corny.' Tracey Thompson was spitting feathers now. 'Everyone knows the wedding is a sham. He don't love her. The geezer is a fraud.'

'There are similarities about this wedding to mine and Carol's,' Johnny continued. 'We hadn't known one another for very long either when I got down on one knee and popped the question. The finest decision I ever made, that was. When you know, you just know,' Johnny grinned at his daughter, then his wife. 'And if Melissa and Jason turn out to be half as happy as Carol and I have been over the years, then they'll have cracked it.'

Jason Rampling smirked. He'd done a bit of digging and knew all about Johnny's long-term affair with his secretary. He planned to use it to his advantage too. No way was he working on that building site any more. He hated the bastard job.

'You know everything you gotta say and do, don't you, Dar? You wanna be on the ball. Go out with a bang, so to speak,' Craig Thurston urged.

'I won't drop Tony in it, don't worry. And I've memorized how to use the equipment. He must've showed me at least fifty times last night,' Darlene exaggerated.

'Good. I'll be waiting outside for you – and I want to know all the gory details,' Craig laughed. He would probably hear the aftermath from where he'd planned to wait, but unless the back door of the hall was open and he could poke his head around, he wouldn't see the look of shock on people's faces. There was no way he could strut in there. Johnny Brooks would spot him immediately and it wasn't worth starting a war over. The bloke had just given him thirty grand, so Darlene had to deal with this alone.

'Answer it then,' Darlene ordered as Craig's phone rang.

Craig took the call. ''Sup up. It's time to leave.'

*

Tony Trot wasn't too comfortable with what was about to happen. Not only was he a half-decent cameraman and DJ, he'd also built up a good reputation recording messages from loved ones, and playing them back at special occasions. He would edit them with tender care as a rule, adding music that suited the moment.

The Brooks's son Mark was the first to pop up on the huge projector screen. 'So sorry I couldn't be there with you today, Melissa. But by the time you watch this I will be sunning myself on a beach in Turkey. It was late notice, so I couldn't cancel the holiday, but I want you to know I'm there with you in spirit and I hope you and Jason have a brilliant day and a long and happy future together.'

Tony Trot sighed as he popped his phone inside his pocket and went outside for a cigarette. He wouldn't usually get involved in stunts such as this, but he was wary of getting on the wrong side of Craig Thurston and five grand was a hell of a lot of money to knock back.

Tony punched in Craig's number. 'The speeches have started. I'm outside now.'

The Windmill Hall in Upminster had two entrances and it was the rear car park entrance where Darlene was waiting. She knew what order the speeches went in, had the list memorized.

'You all right?' Craig asked her. Tony had left the door ajar so they could hear everything. Auntie Mary who lived in Australia was currently boring the arse off everybody.

'Two more to go,' Darlene hissed.

Craig could see Darlene was nervous. She was jittery, her hands clearly shaking.

'Do I look OK? Has my lipstick smudged?' she gabbled.

'No. You look great, honest. Just say what you gotta say and leave, OK?'

Feeling her heart pounding like never before, Darlene nodded anxiously.

'How boring is this? Can't keep the fixed smile on me face for much longer,' Peggy Rampling complained to Irish Ted. She had never attended a wedding where tons of well-wishes were played on a big screen and it was ever so dull when you didn't know any of the people.

'Most of the messages are from people who are actually here today,' Irish Ted whispered in Peggy's ear.

'I know! What a load of old crap. Why can't they just say it to the bride and groom in person? I want the music to start.'

Winking at his grandmother, Jason took a gulp of champagne. He knew none of these people wishing him well and he too was bored out of his brain.

'Hi, Jason. So sorry I couldn't be at your wedding, but . . .'

Jason stared at the screen in absolute horror. Darlene was sat on the edge of her bed, done up to the nines. The very same bed he'd shagged her senseless on, on hundreds of occasions. 'Shit!' he mumbled.

'Why's that old rotter sending him messages?' Peggy asked Irish Ted, who promptly shrugged.

'Turn this off,' Jason shrieked, looking for Tony, who was nowhere in sight.

'Who is she?' Melissa enquired, totally bemused.

The hall fell so silent you could've heard a pin drop as Darlene added, 'I thought it only right your wife found out what you are really like, Jason, so she can get the marriage annulled.'

'Oh my God! It's a penis! Do something, Johnny,' Carol yelled, putting her hands over Donte's eyes. The camera had now turned away from Darlene and was focused on a large erect member and a woman sucking it.

At first, Peggy thought it was a porn film, but recognizing her grandson, she leapt off her chair. 'If I get my hands on that old slapper, I'll bastard-well kill her.'

Tracey Thompson clapped her hands with glee as a voice from the back of the hall bellowed, 'I'm here, Peggy, you thieving old cow.' She turned around to look at Darlene in the flesh, while most of the guests were still fixated on her giving the groom a blowjob.

'You bastard! Get your hands off me,' Melissa screamed at Jason. She tried to run out of the hall but unfortunately tripped over her dress and fell flat on her face.

Absolutely mortified, Johnny ran over to the mains and ripped the plugs out of the wall.

'Better than *EastEnders* this is,' Tracey Thompson chuckled, nudging her boyfriend. She couldn't believe her eyes, was elated by this latest turn of events. Jason was most certainly well hung.

Tony reappeared via the back entrance. 'What's going on?' he asked, hoping he sounded shocked.

Johnny Brooks lunged at Tony. At the same time, Peggy Rampling flew at Darlene, grabbing her hair and wrestling her to the floor. 'You disgusting old whore. Satisfied now, are ya?' Peggy shrieked.

Jason was utterly dumbstruck, but managed to somehow stagger outside to look for Melissa.

Carol Brooks stood up, tears streaming down her face. 'Stop it! All of you. Stop bloody fighting. Now!'

*

Jason sat on the grass at the back of the Windmill Hall, head in his hands. He couldn't believe what Darlene had done to him. Those videos were private and there was no denying that clear shot of his face that had popped up while she was sucking him off.

Lots of guests had now left, but some were still lingering. 'The wedding is over. Go home everyone,' Johnny had bellowed, his face etched with fury.

'I just wanted to apologize again. I swear she must've got in here and put that on herself. I've never seen the woman before in my life,' Tony Trot said to Peggy Rampling. Johnny had understandably refused to pay him and his microphone had been broken in the scuffle. Other than that, he'd got away rather lightly. Carol most certainly believed him and Darlene hadn't even looked at him as she'd run from the hall. Craig hadn't been mentioned at all, so nobody could link the two of them together, thank God. His reputation was important to him and he didn't want future bookings cancelled.

'So sorry. I really am,' Johnny Brooks apologized, shaking a Masonic pal's hand. He had never felt so humiliated in the whole of his life and would make sure Jason Rampling got his comeuppance. Witnessing his wife in tears was truly heartbreaking, especially as he'd arranged this day solely because he'd wanted to grant her dearest wish.

'Where's Jason?' Carol asked her husband.

'Gone, for good, hopefully. I am chucking all his and Shay's belongings out as soon as we get home,' Johnny snapped. 'Where's Melissa – and the kids?'

'Auntie Clara took Donte and Shay home with her and Mel is in the toilet being comforted by friends. She wants to talk to Jason, so just you butt out of it,' Carol snapped back. After all the build-up to the wedding, she now felt totally deflated. It had been a truly horrendous day, from start to bloody finish.

Spotting Jason outside with his nan, Carol marched over to him. 'What have you got to say for yourself, eh?'

'Don't you be having a go at him. It's that old slapper's fault,' Peggy said, putting a protective arm around her grandson's shoulders. 'He's not been round that Darlene's flat for ages, have you, boy?' She hoped she could salvage something out of this mess. She didn't want him moving back on the Mardyke with his mother, that was for sure.

Jason looked at Carol, his eyes welling up. 'I knocked the affair on the head with Darlene as soon as I met Melissa. I swear I did, you got to believe me.'

'I'm not sure I believe anything you say any more. What the hell was you doing with a woman that age in the first place? She's old enough to be your mother, Jason. It's not normal,' Carol scolded.

'Not everybody is as fortunate as your kids, Carol. Some don't have a loving mother. He spent a lot of his childhood round at Darlene's and the rotten whore took advantage of him. I wish I'd have known earlier, as I'd have put a stop to it. The woman is a paedophile,' Peggy spat.

'Do you honestly love Melissa?' Carol asked Jason.

'Of course I do. I wouldn't have agreed to marry her otherwise,' Jason lied. 'But I can't change my past. We've all got skeletons and all I can say is sorry for mine coming out the closet today. I should've told Darlene I was getting married, been upfront with her. But she threw a tantrum when I ended things, and I didn't want to antagonize her further.'

The lad did have a point, everybody had a past. Was it right to judge him on something that had happened before he'd met Melissa? Carol mused. And even though Darlene looked tarty, she was attractive in a dirty-looking way, so it was easy to see how Jason had fallen under her spell. Young men were easily impressionable. 'I am going to get Mel. You two need to talk in private,' Carol replied.

Having been earwigging, Johnny Brooks appeared and grabbed his wife's arm. 'You will do no such thing. I don't want our daughter anywhere near that filthy bastard. He disgusts me.'

Carol led Johnny away from the Ramplings and towards the hall door. 'Let them talk, sort things out for themselves,' she urged.

'No way,' Johnny barked. 'The marriage is over. He can't be trusted. He's a wrong 'un.'

Carol glared at her husband with hatred in her eyes. 'Don't you start being all virtuous with me, Johnny Brooks. I know all about your bit of fluff, have done for years.'

Johnny felt his blood run cold. Surely Carol wasn't referring to Shirley? 'I don't know what you're talking about,' he bluffed. 'You're losing the plot, woman.'

'I might have a brain tumour, but I haven't lost my marbles just yet,' Carol screamed. 'Shirley Stone! I know all about you and her. You've been knocking her off for years.'

Unfortunately for Johnny and Carol, Melissa had been about to step outside and heard every word. She appeared, tears streaming down her face. 'You BASTARD,' she yelled, lunging at her father, fists flailing. 'You dirty, disgusting old pervert.'

Later that evening, Jason stepped out of the shower in the luxurious hotel room Johnny had paid for as a wedding present. It was opulent, the best gaff he had ever been to, and it made him even more determined to keep hold of Mel and make something of his life.

Melissa had been distraught after learning her father's little secret, had insisted they leave the hall immediately. She was still understandably angry with him too, and they were yet to discuss Darlene in full detail. On the journey here, she'd seemed more upset by her father's behaviour than her wedding being ruined, which gave Jason hope for the future.

Wrapping a soft white towelling bathrobe around himself, Jason strolled out the bathroom. Mel was lying on the bed, flicking through TV channels, her thoughts elsewhere. She'd already showered, was wearing a bathrobe too. 'You OK?' he asked, knowing it was a rather dumb question to be asking. He didn't want her to think he didn't care though.

'I will never forgive him. My poor mum. How must she feel, knowing when she dies that old slag will be hovering, waiting to pounce and take her place?'

Jason sat on the edge of the bed. 'I know. It's terrible. So wrong. Your mum is one of the nicest people I have ever met.'

'Tell me about Darlene. How did you meet her?' Melissa asked, remembering her mother's stern advice as she'd got in the taxi.

Jason lay down next to Melissa on the bed and explained in more detail just how awful his childhood had been and how he'd turned to Darlene for comfort. 'I knew it was wrong, what we were doing. But I was messed up back then,' he lied. He could hardly admit Darlene was the best he'd ever had and he'd enjoyed every second of their wild love-making sessions.

'Do you love her?'

'Don't be daft! She's old enough to be my bloody mother. But I will never forget how kind she was to me as a kid, Mel. Even after today, I can't hate her. What I can promise you though, is that I will never see her again, or betray you like your dad has your mum. When I said our vows, I truly meant 'em. Marriage is the real deal to me.'

'Prove it to me then. Make love to me like you made love to her.'

Jason grinned. 'You sure?' He had thought he might win her round once the initial shock had worn off, but not this quickly.

Needing something positive to come out of this awful day, Melissa draped her arms around her husband's neck. 'Yes, I'm positive.'

Jason dutifully obliged, was up her like a rat up a drainpipe, and as he shot his load, he thought of Darlene.

PART TWO

'A truth that's told with bad intent,
Beats all the lies you can invent'

William Blake

CHAPTER THIRTEEN

1999 – Five Years Later

'Who is it?'

'It's the postman, love.'

'OK. Come in.'

Seconds later, Marianna St Clair recoiled in terror as her regular postman was bundled to the floor by a man dressed in black wearing a balaclava.

'Get down, now! Hands above your head so I can see 'em. Touch any panic buttons and you're both dead,' the man bellowed. His voice sounded gruff, not one to be messed with, and he definitely had a London accent.

Robbery had always been Marianna's biggest fear since her father Pierre had taken over the jeweller's shop in 1976, but thanks to improvements in technology and policing, robberies were virtually unheard of these days. Especially in a high-class area such as Morton Street. 'Take whatever you want. Take it all, but please do not hurt me. It's my father's funeral on Friday,' Marianna wept.

Ordering the postman to stay where he was, Craig Thurston dragged the woman up by her arm and barked at her to fill the bags with her most expensive items. 'Diamonds! Rings, watches, anything with fucking diamonds,' Craig shouted, walloping the postman over the head with his baseball bat to show her he meant business.

Unaware of what was actually happening inside the shop; Jason Rampling was parked nearby on a motorbike. This was the fourteenth robbery he'd accompanied Craig on and by far the most risky, due to the location.

'Go, go,' Craig yelled as he leapt on the back of the bike.

Jason put his foot on the throttle. Seconds later he heard the sirens.

'Hello, Mel. Long time no see. How you doing?' asked Carrie Pritchard.

Melissa Rampling smiled falsely. She hated Carrie. The woman was so up her own arse it was unbelievable. Everything about her was false, including her huge tits that resembled balloons. 'I'm good, thanks. Yourself?'

Beauty salons were now the in thing, especially in wealthier parts of Essex, and as Melissa had her feet expertly pedicured she had to listen to Carrie drone on about how wonderful her life was for a whole hour.

'What are you doing for the Millennium? Ian's booked us on a cruise, but we'll be spending New Year's Eve in the Dominican Republic. The kids are ever so excited. They've excelled since we decided to send them to private school. It's a much better education. You should think about sending Donte and Shay to top schools. Not cheap, but you can't put a price on your children's futures, can you?'

By the time Melissa left the salon she was completely wound up. It had been ages since Jason had taken herself and the kids on holiday. Neither were their children excelling at school. She would have a word with Jason later. If the Pritchards could afford such luxuries, then why couldn't they?

'You OK? Bit of a close shave, eh?' Craig chuckled, as Jason put the motorbike in the back of the van. They'd been chased for a couple of miles by the police and it was only Jason's knowledge of back streets and his expertise of handling a motorbike that had saved them from getting caught.

Jason took the ramp away and slammed the back doors. 'It ain't funny, Craig. We nearly spent tonight in prison.'

'Look on the bright side: gotta be worth three quarters of a mill, our little haul. We'll take it straight down to Mick the Gold, see what he'll give us for it. He's expecting us.'

Mick the Gold dealt solely in stolen watches, gold and diamonds. He had contacts abroad and the stuff would be taken out of the country and sold.

'Let's get rid of the bike first, eh? It's giving me the heebies.'

Craig laughed. 'Chill out, you nutter.'

Melissa Rampling drove towards Upminster Cemetery with a bee in her bonnet. Jason was currently on a bit of work, she knew that much. She could always tell when he was up to something more dodgy than usual, as he became tense and would go out at unusual hours.

Melissa never asked her husband what he was up to. She'd known he was a ducker and diver when she married him and would rather be kept in the dark. As long as the money kept rolling in, Melissa was happy. They lived in a nice area, Chigwell Row, and although she felt their three-bedroomed house was a bit small for them now, she'd furnished it like a palace inside. The chandeliers alone had cost her three grand.

Debating whether to ring Jason, Melissa decided against it. If he was on a bit of work, she didn't want to disturb him. Five years and five months they'd been married now and, considering what a fiasco their wedding day had been, they'd weathered the storm very well.

Their marriage was by no means perfect, but whose was? Jason had his faults. She'd even suspected him of cheating on her a couple of times when he'd come home in the early hours reeking of women's perfume, but she had no proof and he'd denied any wrongdoing. Melissa was a big believer in what she didn't know couldn't hurt her. But she would put her foot down if Jason ever had a dragged-out affair like her bastard of a father had. That would be totally unacceptable.

Melissa would never forget the advice her mother had given her on her wedding day. 'Jason is a decent person with a kind heart, love. He will also be a good provider and father to Donte. I know today has been horrific for you, but you go to that hotel with Jason tonight and give your marriage a go. Forget all about that old scrubber who turned up. Men will be men and she's part of Jason's past. You, my darling, are his future.'

Her mum had been spot on. She'd never had to work. Jason was the breadwinner and also a brilliant father. Donte worshipped the ground he walked on, as did Shay. She could be a stroppy little mare at times, Shay could, and Melissa had never felt she'd accepted her as a mother figure. Donte had called Jason 'Dad' from a young age. But Shay would only ever refer to her as 'Mel'.

The one thing about her mum Melissa had never

understood was the Shirley Stone turnout. They'd had a heart-to-heart about it, soon after her wedding. 'When I went through my early menopause, I never wanted sex, love. Your father is a man and men have needs. Shirley is a decent enough woman and when I die, if your father were to get with her properly, I'd like to think you'll give her a chance. He's no good on his own, your dad. Like a lost sheep, he'll be, without me. That's one of the reasons I never told him I knew about Shirley. Not in a million years would he have ever left me for her, and I don't want him to be lonely. I know you hate him at this moment in time, but you won't always. Never forget what a good father he has been to you, Melissa.'

Well, her mother had been wrong about that. She could never forgive her father for his betrayal, and had been furious when he had moved in with Shirley Stone six months after her mother's death. 'Mum's body ain't even cold!' she'd ranted to Jason. He'd been her rock around that awful time, had soothed, comforted her and wiped away her tears. But it had hardened her, changed her in lots of ways.

Arriving at the cemetery, Melissa lifted the flowers off the front seat. She'd adored her wonderful mum, there wasn't a day went by she didn't think about her and miss her. As for her father and that slapper, Shirley Stone – they could both rot in hell.

As Craig drove towards Mick the Gold's house in Bromley, Jason was deep in thought. That police chase earlier had been a bit too close for comfort and the thought of spending years behind bars, not being there for Shay and Donte, did not appeal to him at all. Melissa didn't have a clue about money. She was good at spending it, that he did know, but she would never survive if he got banged up. Mel spent her days being pampered in salons and having long girlie lunches that cost him an arm and a leg. She'd never get a job. Work was a dirty word to Mel.

It had been roughly six months after his wedding that he'd bumped into Craig Thurston down the Ilford Palais. It was a Monday, Grab-a-Granny night, and he'd gone down there to see a Greek guy he knew about a bit of business. Craig had recognized him and they'd got chatting. They'd then ended up in ChinaTown, the restaurant, had left there around four in the morning and a working friendship had been created. Craig had been straight up with Jason from the start. He'd told him he was the one who'd helped Darlene ruin his wedding and he'd apologized for doing so. 'It weren't aimed at you, mate. But Johnny Brooks is a snidey bastard, he tried to rip me off. Plus Darlene and I go back years,' he'd explained.

Working with Craig was the only way Jason could afford Melissa and the kids' lifestyles. They wanted and expected the best in life and it was up to him to fund it. Melissa in particular was wasteful with money. She seemed to think it grew on trees. He had never told her that it was Craig's doing their wedding was ruined. She knew they were acquaintances now, but would go apeshit if she knew the truth.

'You all right, mate? You're a bit quiet. Like an episode of *The Sweeney* when we was being chased earlier, eh?' Craig chuckled.

'Yeah, I'm OK. Just thinking how much more in front of meself I'd be if Melissa had allowed her father to buy us our first house. She's hard work at times and it's days like today that brings it home to me.'

After learning about her father's affair with Shirley

Stone, Melissa had thrown all her toys out of the pram and obstinately refused his kind offer of buying them their first property as a wedding gift. Carol's death had dug them out of a massive hole. They'd had to rent a shithole flat in Elm Park up until Carol died, but she'd had money stashed away from the death of her own mother that she left the bulk of to Mel. 'I've left your brother ten grand, but I want you to have the other forty. Mark's like your father, he'll always earn a pound note. But you're my little girl. I don't want you living in that flat in Elm Park. Buy a property in a decent area and use that money to secure your mortgage. You won't regret it,' Carol had told Mel on her deathbed.

'I've decided to call it a day with Mandy,' Craig said, referring to his current girlfriend. Things had never worked out with Darlene. They'd had a great holiday but she'd dumped him when they got home. She hadn't been able to get over Jason, and Craig was cool about that now. They were still good mates.

'Why?' Jason asked.

'Too much hard work. Want, want, want all the poxy time. As soon as we get our dosh off Mick the Gold, I'm pissing off to Thailand. Grateful, the birds are out there. Nowhere near as demanding as English women. They make good wives and all of a sudden I fancy having kids.'

'Really?' Craig had never struck Jason as the fatherly type. He was too much of a party animal.

'Yeah, really. Forty now, ain't I? No spring chicken. You and Mel never fancied having a kid? You know, together like.'

Jason sighed. He and Mel weren't exactly at it like rabbits, never had been. But a year after her mum had died she'd stopped taking the pill and had never fallen pregnant. It was a sore subject indoors and it would get on his nerves every month when she'd blub because her period had arrived. 'Mel wants one, but I'm not overly fussed, to be honest. Kids ain't cheap to keep, trust me. Spent over a grand already on their Christmas presents and Shay has now decided she wants a fucking pony.'

Craig grinned. 'Well, with the bit of work we've done today you'll be able to afford it a stable an' all. As I said to you earlier, look on the bright side, my friend.'

'Where's me dad?' asked Shay Rampling, slamming the new mobile phone she'd received only last weekend on the kitchen table.

'Be careful. Cost a lot of money, that did,' Melissa snapped. 'No idea where your father is, but don't be ringing him because I think he's busy.'

'Doing what?'

Melissa stared at the sullen-looking child who had just turned ten. Shay was tall for her age, still had a feral look about her. But she also had the potential to become a stunner. Her eyes were bright blue, her hair long and dark. She reminded Melissa of a young Kate Moss. 'Working, as I said.'

'Yeah, but working doing what? Maisy at school reckons Dad is a gangster.'

'Well, Maisy at school knows nothing. Your father might be a bit of a ducker and diver, but he is certainly no bloody gangster. Donte, I'm ordering a takeaway. Come and choose what you want,' Melissa shouted out.

Dressed in an Arsenal kit, Donte slouched on a kitchen chair. He would be eight next birthday, was a striking boy. 'I want a pizza with extra salami,' he informed his mother.

'I don't want pizza. I want an Indian,' Shay insisted.

Melissa thought of Carrie Pritchard again. She'd been bragging earlier about how well-mannered her children now were. She reckoned private schools instilled politeness into kids, that would set them up for life. Jason was always moaning that Shay in particular never seemed grateful for anything and that had to change. 'To save money and time, can you just pick one takeaway to order from this evening?' Melissa sighed.

'Well, I don't want pizza,' Shay snapped.

'And I don't like Indian,' Donte grunted.

Silently praying that whatever job Jason was on today was a big one, Melissa ordered the children what they wanted. Private school was the answer, she knew that, and the sooner Shay and Donte attended one, the better. They might even learn the art of saying 'Please' and 'Thank you' there.

Mick the Gold studied the last of the haul. He always used a magnifying glass when checking valuables out. 'I'll give you three hundred grand for the lot,' he said.

Craig glanced at Jason, then shook his head. They'd done their homework on the jeweller's in Morton Street, knew what each piece was worth. A lot of time and effort had gone into the job too. They'd watched the shop for the past week, knew exactly what time the postman arrived and when to strike. Craig knew Marianna St Clair's father had passed away and she'd be at the shop alone, but he'd held that particular bit of information away from his partner in crime. Jason was no man's fool, but he could be a bit of a soft touch at times. 'You're taking the fucking piss, Mick. We knew what we were robbing, mate. Well over a million an' a half, the marked-up price. The watches are worth four hundred grand alone. We ain't gonna be ripped off with it.'

The son of a prize-fighting gypsy, Mick the Gold was a stocky man with a bright red face and bulbous nose. His love for whisky had taken its toll over the years and clearly showed in his features. 'Times have changed, Craig. Hot property isn't as easy to get rid of any more, even abroad. This robbery was mentioned on the radio earlier today. A pal of mine heard it on LBC.'

'For fuck's sake,' Jason mumbled. One of their previous robberies when they'd held up a lorry load of electrical goods had ended up on bloody *Crimewatch* and he didn't need that shit again.

'I'll up my offer to three-fifty. But that's it, lads. I can't go to no more,' Mick said.

'I need a minute to talk to Jase alone,' Craig replied.

When Mick the Gold left the room, Jason rolled his eyes in dismay. 'Seven hundred grand at least you said we'd get for this lot. We're nowhere fucking near that,' he said to Craig.

'I know and I'm sorry. But he ain't gonna want this haul to slip through his fingers, trust me. Will you settle for four hundred if I can get him to that?'

Jason shrugged. 'Case of having to, I suppose. But let me tell you something, Craig. No way am I doing another daredevil robbery in Central London that ends up in the fucking news. You ain't got kids, I have. And I intend to see 'em bastard-well grow up.'

'There you are! I was starting to get worried. Everything OK?' Melissa asked, when her husband finally arrived home at nearly midnight.

'So-so. There you go,' Jason replied, handing his wife a sports bag full of cash.

'How much is in there?'

'Fifty grand. Take out whatever you need and put the rest in the safe.' Jason had already hidden the bulk of the money at his nan's house in Dagenham. She had a big cupboard under her stairs and he'd spent ages creating a false back to it. Any cash or valuables he didn't want to keep at home were stashed in tins there, and he very much doubted the Old Bill would find anything were they ever to raid his nan's house. He even stuck a bit of fresh wallpaper over the back of the cupboard each time he used it.

'Well, I need a new car. And I thought I might book us a cruise. Be nice for us to do something special for the Millennium, won't it? And it's been eighteen months since we last had a holiday.'

'Why do you need a new car? There's sod-all wrong with the one you've got.'

'It's five years old, Jason. Kieron has just bought Tracey a brand-new Mercedes. Why can't I have something new for once?'

Kieron Jessop was Tracey Thompson's new bloke and Jason rued the day Tracey had met him. He was a City boy, a high-flyer, and extravagant was his middle name. 'You know full well why you can't be seen swanning about in flashy new motors. Until I find myself a decent accountant and have a legitimate set of books showing I'm earning a bigger wage, we can't be seen to be flashing the cash.'

'But you sell the cars you get from the auctions,' Melissa argued.

Jason's cover for his life of crime was buying cars and

selling them on for a profit. He declared most to the taxman, therefore could legally show certain assets and pay his bills. But what he couldn't do was show more than what he was earning. 'I don't earn enough in the taxman's eyes to be splashing out on brand-new fucking motors, Mel. Told you that before, a thousand times over. Never satisfied, you. Fifty grand I've just given ya and you still want more.'

'I didn't say I wanted more. I just said I wanted to buy a new car and book us a bloody holiday out of it. Those are things that normal couples do, Jason.'

Jason stared at the woman he'd married. She was much prettier now she'd slimmed down a bit and her hair was longer. He walked over to her, put his arms around her waist and pulled her towards him. 'Look, I don't want to argue with you. You just need to play ball for the time being at least. Perhaps I'll look at setting up a new business, one that legally pays more? Leave it with me and I'll have a think.'

Melissa stroked Jason's cheek. He was still a very handsome man. These days his blond hair was swept back and held in place with wax, a far more sophisticated look than the curtains he'd had when she'd first met him. Whenever they were out, Melissa would see other women looking admiringly at Jason and she knew in her heart she was lucky to have him. 'I'm sorry. I came on earlier today.'

The tears came then, so Jason comforted her, reassuring her that one day they would have the baby she seemed to crave so much.

'Do you honestly think so?' Melissa wept.

Jason sighed. He'd had a long stressful day, could really do without this tonight. 'Yeah, course I do. But you got to stop stressing about it, Mel. The doctor has already told us there is no reason why we can't have a baby. We just got to let nature take its course, OK?'

Feeling slightly better, Melissa nodded and smiled. 'OK.'

CHAPTER FOURTEEN

Jason slammed the *Evening Standard* down on the table in front of Craig. The article was on page seven, and clearly stated what they'd stolen was in fact worth over two million quid. It also said the shop owner had died the previous week and his bereft daughter had been looking after the business. There was a photo of the deceased owner, an identical motorbike to the one they'd used and their false registration plate.

'What's up?' Craig asked, glancing at the paper.

'Did you know the old boy who run the shop had died and the daughter would be there alone?' Jason barked.

'Well, yeah. But don't dig me out for it. If she hadn't been there alone, it would've been too risky to rob it.'

'You didn't clump her, did ya?'

'Course not! Whaddya think I am? The press always exaggerate.'

'Says that the haul was worth over two mill. He proper striped us up, Mick the Gold did,' Jason complained. Three hundred and eighty grand they'd walked away with. A hundred and ninety each – and for the risks involved, Jason thought that was paltry.

Craig shrugged. 'No point whingeing now. Still not bad for a morning's work. I think you're right though. We should avoid built-up areas in future. I'll have a scout around Essex, see what I can sniff out.'

Jason plonked himself on the chair opposite. He rarely visited Craig at his home in Langdon Hills and Craig never came to his. They'd sometimes go out for a drink together, but Jason preferred to keep their friendship quiet. Nobody knew that they worked together, and the robberies they'd pulled off were all very different. Even the police didn't seem to have an inkling that any were linked. 'How did you know the old boy had croaked it and his daughter would be there alone? You've not been talking to outsiders, have you?'

'Don't be so daft. Geezer who comes into my car lot let it slip. I just asked a couple of casual questions, then checked it out for meself.' Craig also had a registered business to cover his tracks with the authorities. He owned a second-hand car lot in Basildon. Jason had sold a few motors to him in the past and that explained them being acquaintances if anyone should come sniffing around. 'Look, I know you're pissed off we didn't get as much as we should have, but Mick the Gold has a point. Hot property isn't as easy to shift these days. He's taking a risk getting it out of the country an' all, and at least we know if he did get caught with it, he'd never grass us up.'

'We don't know that though, do we? He's yet to be caught with anything we've sold him. He might sing like a fucking canary for all we know.'

Craig walked over to the kitchen counter and poured two large brandies. He handed one to Jason. 'Get that down your hatch and chill,' he ordered. 'Fancy a night up Stringfellows? We should celebrate properly.'

'Nah, I can't tonight. Mel's invited Tracey Thompson and her latest bloke round for a meal. Be bored to death, I will. Weddings will be the topic of conversation. The silly bastard proposed to Tracey recently. Hired a plane to fly over with the words "Will you marry me my darling, Tracey?" on some big fuck-off banner. She said yes, of course. He's loaded.'

'Do I know him? Sounds a right plum.'

'Kieron Jessop, his name is. Proper City boy, I doubt you know him. He's OK in small doses. Must have a screw loose to want to marry Tracey though. She's high-maintenance, her.'

'Is that the bird we bumped into at the Epping Forest Country Club? Blonde, big tits. Looks like a glamour model.'

'Yeah, that's her. She watched us like a hawk and that's why we left early. Always been jealous of mine and Mel's marriage, she has. Got a habit of sticking her oar in when it ain't needed. Perhaps she'll mellow a bit now she's met the one. I dread to think what the wedding'll be like, mind. I can picture her and him sat on thrones like the Beckhams.'

Craig laughed. 'Well, she was certainly a sort. I'd have given her one, had she asked nicely.'

Jason stood up. 'You'd give anything one. I better make a move now, mate. I promised I'd pick me sister and brothers up from school and take 'em out for something to eat. Have fun tonight and I'll bell ya tomorrow.'

'Sweet. Laters, pal.'

'I've not seen you around here before. Are you new to the area?' Melissa asked the woman she was chatting to in the hairdresser's. Mel was a regular at the salon, knew most of the locals.

'Yes. My husband and I moved here last month.'

'Where did you live before?' Melissa enquired. The woman had a posh accent and oozed class.

'Twickenham. We had to move because of our careers. The commuting would have been too much. We've bought a house on the old Claybury Hospital land. Do you know it?'

Melissa's eyes opened wide. She most certainly did know it. Repton Park was an extremely sought after area and it cost an arm and a leg to buy even a flat there. 'Yes. It's lovely on Repton Park, isn't it? My husband and I are hoping to move there soon,' Melissa lied. 'We are currently in Chigwell Row, but I feel we're outgrowing the property a little now.'

'I'm Eleanor, by the way,' the lady said warmly. She was very attractive. Her hair was long, a chestnut colour, and Mel guessed she was mid to late thirties.

'I'm Melissa. Melissa Rampling.'

'Oops. Your baby has woken up,' said Sonia, one of the stylists.

Melissa was amazed when Eleanor stood up, walked over to the corner of the salon and lifted a stunning little girl out of her pram. 'Wow! Is she your daughter? I didn't even see her as I came in.'

'Yes. This is Ruby, the whole reason our lives have been turned upside down,' Eleanor replied, walking over to Melissa with the child in her arms.

'She is truly beautiful. Aren't you, sweetheart,' Melissa smiled, tickling the child's chin. She had that terrible pang of envy she always felt when seeing a pretty baby. It was so unfair God hadn't blessed herself and Jason with a child of their own.

Eleanor stroked Ruby's face and the little girl gurgled

happily. 'She has made our lives complete. My husband and I tried years for a baby with no success and then we tried IVF. My husband is a doctor and he booked an appointment with a friend of his, a specialist in Harley Street. Dr Kazim is a miracle worker.'

'That's amazing! I am so pleased for you.'

Melissa watched in the mirror as Eleanor fed her child, gently winded her then laid her back in the pram. Her brain was whirling with all the questions she wanted to ask.

'Do you have children?' Eleanor asked, as she sat down next to Melissa.

'Yes, two. But my husband and I would love another.' Melissa lowered her tone. 'We have been trying for ages.'

'Oh, it's so frustrating, isn't it? I used to cry to my husband at that trying time of the month, without fail.'

'Me too.'

'I'm a counsellor now. That's the main reason we moved from Twickenham. I'm opening my own practice in Buckhurst Hill.'

'That's great! What an amazing woman you are,' Melissa gushed, truly meaning it. 'Please don't think I'm being forward, but would you like to go for lunch one day? I could talk to you for hours.'

'That would be lovely. But I get very little spare time, so please be patient with me.' Eleanor delved into her handbag. 'That's my card and the other is Dr Kazim's. You should visit him in Harley Street. He's a very busy man though, so you might have to wait a couple of weeks for an appointment.'

Melissa was bemused. 'But do I need IVF if I've already had a baby?'

'Dr Kazim doesn't just do IVF. He's an expert in all

areas of fertility. Be warned, he isn't cheap. But he is brilliant and I am sure he will be able to help you.'

Melissa clutched the cards close to her chest. This was fate, it had to be.

'Hmmm, so who's got room left for dessert, I wonder?' Jason grinned.

'I have!' three voices said in unison, just like he knew they would. Once a week Jason would pick his brothers and sister up and take them out for a meal. The Harvester was their current favourite, but sometimes they'd ask to go for a pizza instead.

'Can I have a Rocky Horror?' Barbara asked, licking her lips.

'I'll have that too,' Elton said.

'And me,' Kyle added.

Jason chuckled. He'd had sod-all to do with his mother since his wedding. She'd rung him a few times, on his earhole for dosh, but he'd told her where to go and every time she got hold of his new phone number, he'd change it again. He loved his brothers and sister though, found it hard to believe at times they'd come out of his mother's stinking body. Unlike her, they had a heart. 'I suppose I can stretch to three. You better eat 'em all up though,' Jason winked.

'Why are you not having one?' Barbara asked her big brother. She weighed over fourteen stone now. But she loved her food and could not understand why anyone would turn a Rocky Horror down.

'Mel's cooking later. We've got friends coming over for dinner,' Jason replied.

'When are we coming over again, Jase?' asked thirteen-year-old Elton.

Jason sighed. When his brothers were younger he'd had them and Babs stay with him and Mel every other weekend. All three had loved it. It had been something for them to look forward to in their shitty lives.

It wasn't Babs who'd brought that particular arrangement to an end. Bar eating them out of house and home, she'd been as good as gold. It was the boys Melissa had got fed up with. She felt they were leading Donte astray, making him insolent. They'd broken things as well. Mirrors, garden ornaments, and Donte's toys. But it was Kyle who'd put the final nail in the coffin. Melissa kept a treasured glass jewellery box in their bedroom that had belonged to her mother, and Kyle had somehow smashed it to pieces. 'That's it, Jason!' Melissa had screamed at him. 'Your brothers and sister are your fucking problem, not mine. I don't care how often you see them or what money you give them, but I will not put up with 'em wrecking my beautiful home any more. And that is my final word on the matter.' Jason could understand where she was coming from. Elton and Kyle were typical rough council estate boys, but they couldn't help it. Not with a mother like theirs. Jason often wondered how he'd ended up so sane and cool. It had to be his father's genes. There was no other explanation.

'Yeah, why don't we come to yours any more, Jase? Is it 'cause I smashed that thing that time? 'Cause it was an accident ya know. I never meant to break it.'

Jason stroked his youngest brother's cropped hair. 'I know you didn't, and that isn't the reason you don't stay over any more.'

'What is the reason then?' Kyle enquired.

Jason looked into Kyle's sorrowful brown eyes and felt sad. Melissa had no right to ban his siblings from their home and it was about time he stood his ground. 'You are coming over, at Christmas. It was meant to be a surprise.'

'Really?' Babs asked, clapping her hands with glee. Last Christmas had been awful. Her mum had gone to the pub at lunchtime, had come home drunk and she'd had to try and cook the dinner herself. The turkey had been raw in the middle and she and her brothers had a bout of food poisoning the following day. Kyle was the worst. He'd been admitted to hospital for two days.

'Yeah, really,' Jason laughed. The look of excitement on all three faces was worth an argument with Mel. Christmas was all about family and if his wife didn't like this particular arrangement, then she could lump it.

'This is wonderful prawn curry, Mel. You must give me the recipe so I can cook it for my husband-to-be,' Tracey Thompson grinned, looking adoringly at Kieron Jessop.

Kieron raised his eyebrows. It was a standing joke between himself and Tracey that she couldn't cook. She'd struggle with the simplest of tasks such as preparing beans on toast or boiling an egg. 'Only if you promise not to poison me.'

Giggling, Tracey stroked her fiancé's thigh. She had almost given up on finding Mr Right until that fateful evening she'd literally bumped into Kieron in Faces nightclub and dropped her drink all down his shirt. He'd been with a couple of footballers who played for West Ham and the girls were all over him and his pals like a rash. But Kieron only had eyes for her and had taken her out for a wonderful candlelit meal in a restaurant in Soho the following evening. They'd been a couple ever since and Tracey could scarcely believe her luck. Not only was

Kieron blond, handsome, funny and charming, he was also incredibly wealthy and generous. For years Tracey had thought Melissa was the lucky one for snaring Jason, but not any more. Good things come to those who wait and Kieron was living proof of that. He had far more going for him than Jason bloody Rampling and Tracey could not wait to become Mrs Jessop.

'More wine, Jason?' Melissa asked, grinning like a Cheshire cat.

Jason eyed his wife suspiciously. She'd been bouncing off the walls ever since he'd arrived home earlier and he knew something must have happened. 'Spill the beans then,' he urged. 'Won the lottery, have we?'

'No. I don't know what you mean,' Melissa chuckled. She had never been good at keeping good news to herself, especially if the wine was flowing.

'Did I tell you, we think we've found the perfect wedding venue?' Tracey asked.

'Yes, you did. Is it the stately home in Hertfordshire?' Melissa replied.

'No. We viewed that and wasn't exactly keen. Looked much nicer in the photos than it did in the flesh.' Tracey squeezed Kieron's hand. 'Shall you tell them, or shall I?'

'You tell 'em, babe.'

Producing photographs from an envelope, Tracey proudly laid them on the table. 'The Seychelles! Isn't it stunning? We're having a beach wedding and reception. But don't worry if you can't afford it. As you are going to be my only bridesmaid, Kieron has kindly offered to foot the bill for you and Jason. All expenses paid, that is.'

'And why wouldn't we be able to afford it?' Jason snapped. He could not think of anything worse than having to travel thousands of miles to watch a woman he did not like get hitched.

'I'm sorry. I didn't mean it like that. But Kieron insists on paying for you anyway.' Tracey held Mel's hand across the table. 'Please say you'll come. With everything that's going on with my mum, you're the only one I can truly rely on.'

'Of course we will! I was only saying to Jason the other day, we're long overdue a holiday. We'll have to bring the kids with us, but we'll pay for them.'

'We'll pay for the lot, Mel. We're not a fucking charity case,' Jason barked. He didn't dislike Kieron. But he was a proud man and no way would he let another bloke pay for his holiday. He was no pauper.

Melissa had planned to tell Jason tomorrow about her chance meeting with Eleanor at the hairdresser's, but judgement clouded by the three glasses of wine she'd drunk, she now decided she could not wait until then. She produced Eleanor and Dr Kazim's cards from her purse and slid them across the table.

Jason picked the cards up. 'Who're Eleanor Collins-Hythe and Dr Kazim when they're at home?'

'Look, don't be angry with me, but Tracey knows all about our fertility problems, Jase. I had to confide in someone. Anyway, today I walk into the hairdresser's and there's this glamorous, posh lady sat in the next chair to me. We got talking and it turns out her husband is a doctor. She and her husband tried for years to conceive and she went to see one of her husband's friends in Harley Street. Dr Kazim is a fertility expert – the best in the country, by all accounts. I rang his secretary when I got home and I've booked us an appointment for Thursday week. I'm so excited. I really cannot wait to be pregnant again.'

'Good luck the pair of you,' Kieron said awkwardly. Jason wasn't amused, he could tell.

Seeing Tracey Thompson smirk was the final straw for Jason. He snatched hold of the cards, screwed them up and chucked them in the bin. 'Fuck you and your baby obsession, Mel. I'm done with it.'

When Jason stomped out of the room and grabbed his leather jacket, Mel chased after him. 'Where you going? You can't go out. We've got guests.'

'Yeah, *your* guests,' Jason hissed. 'How dare you discuss our private business with them or randoms in the hairdresser's? Do you know how that makes me look? There was sod-all wrong with my sperm count when you dragged me to our quack, so best you tell 'em that.'

As Jason went to open the front door, Melissa grabbed his arm. 'I'm sorry, OK. I'll tell 'em. Please don't go out.'

'Go fuck yourself. Oh, and by the way, my brothers and sister are coming to us on Christmas Day. Sick of you wearing the trousers in this house. I pay all the bills. Laters, sweetheart. And don't be waiting up 'cause I won't be coming home.'

Tracey Thompson had never quite got over the fact that Jason had chosen Melissa ahead of her. It had grated on her for years, though since meeting Kieron her anger had diminished. However, when handed a golden opportunity for a bit of shit-stirring, she wasn't about to pass it up. 'I don't know how you suffer his behaviour, Mel, I really don't. I mean, you were understandably excited about your news, so why wasn't he? Are you sure he really wants another child?'

'Are you OK, Mum?' Donte asked, poking his head around the kitchen door.

'Where's my dad?' Shay enquired. Both she and Donte had been woken by what sounded like an argument and the front door slamming, so had come downstairs to be nosy.

'Go back to bed. I'm fine. Your father had to pop out on business,' Melissa lied, wiping her eyes. Perhaps Tracey was right? Jason had never seemed as keen on them having a child as she was.

Draping her arms around Kieron's neck, Tracey kissed him on the lips and thought how lucky she was. For years she'd been jealous of Jason and Mel's relationship, but not any more. It had taken a long time to find a better man than Jason Rampling, but finally she had and she was determined never to let him go.

'Another bottle of your finest champagne, sweet cheeks. And get whatever you want for yourself,' Craig Thurston grinned, shoving a handful of notes down the scantily dressed waitress's top.

'Rein it in a bit, Craig. We don't exactly look like bankers,' Jason warned.

'Money is for spending and life is for living, mate. You worry too much,' Craig laughed. 'I booked me holiday today. Flying out on the sixth of Jan for a month. Be getting fresh jiggy-jiggy every day over there. But in the meantime, I shall have some fun with these lap-dancers. She's hot, that bird there, look.'

Unlike a lot of lap-dancing clubs, the girls in Stringfellows oozed class and Jason couldn't take his eyes off one in particular. She turned around, looked at him and that's when the recognition hit home. 'Jesus Christ! That's Charlotte!' He nudged Craig. 'My ex.'

CHAPTER FIFTEEN

'Fucking hell, babe. Jesus wept!' Jason panted, his rhythm quickening.

'Harder! Faster!' Charlotte Rivers ordered lustfully.

Jason duly obliged and felt the wetness of her pussy as she finally orgasmed. 'You're so beautiful, you are. I never forgot you,' he said in earnest as he shot his load shortly afterwards.

Charlotte propped herself on her elbow and grinned. She'd known the second they had locked eyes earlier that they'd end up in bed together and she'd been right. The sexual attraction between them was electrifying. She'd had goosebumps on the way home in the taxi at the thought of it. No man she had met since had matched up to him in the sack and she doubted they ever would. Jason Rampling was a very special man indeed. 'Want a cigarette?' Charlotte asked, lighting one for herself.

'Nah, thanks. Given 'em up. So tell me about yourself. I meant what I said, you know. I never forgot about you. You're even more beautiful now than I remember,' Jason said, stroking her cheek. 'How long is it since we last saw one another? Over five years, ain't it?'

'How long is it since you dumped me for no apparent

reason in the car park of the Plough pub, you mean?' Charlotte chuckled. 'Broke my bloody heart, you did. But time's a healer, eh? I never forgot about you either, though. You're a tough act to follow.'

'I'm sorry about the way I treated you. You didn't deserve it, but I was on me uppers at the time and couldn't have offered you much. You were always destined for greater things.'

'Bullshit!' Charlotte laughed. 'If I remember rightly, you dumped me because you were looking for a mother for your daughter and you thought I was too young. How is Shay? She must be a big girl now.'

'She's ten going on twenty. Proper little character, she is. A chip off the old block.'

'Why doesn't that surprise me?' Charlotte grinned. Jason was even more handsome than she remembered and she couldn't take her eyes off him. He'd been a boy when she'd first met him and now he was a man. A fine specimen of one too. 'So did you find her a mum?'

'Yeah. Case of having to. I had to get Shay away from the Mardyke.'

Charlotte touched Jason's wedding ring. 'How long you been married?'

'A few years,' Jason lied. He couldn't tell Charlotte the truth as she would know he'd dumped her for Mel. 'What about you? You with anyone?'

'Not any more. I got engaged a couple of years ago, but that never worked out.'

'Nice gaff you got, by the way.' The flat was a new-build and was beautifully furnished. It was trendy-looking and homely at the same time.

'I started work at Stringfellows eighteen months ago and moved into this place shortly afterwards. I used to flat-share with another dancer, but Kim now lives with her boyfriend. I only rent at present, but I'm saving up to buy a place. The tips are very good at Stringfellows. I make a lot of money there.'

'Good for you, girl. Better to be independent than have to rely on others.'

'Does your wife work?' Charlotte enquired.

'You've gotta be kidding! Work's a dirty word to my old woman. Spends all day wasting my hard-earned dosh.'

'What do you do now? Still a Del Boy?' Charlotte laughed.

'Yeah. Leopards like me don't change their spots. I still duck and dive but I got a legitimate business too. I buy and sell cars – keeps the missus happy.'

Charlotte grinned. 'You don't sound too happy.'

Ready for round two, Jason inserted his middle finger inside Charlotte's tight pussy. He felt no guilt towards Melissa whatsoever, and why should he? She sucked him dry financially, like a leech. 'If I was happy, I wouldn't be 'ere with you, would I?'

When Charlotte took Jason's penis in her mouth and began expertly sucking him off, he groaned with ultimate pleasure. He'd had the odd fling since getting married, but never a full-blown affair. That was all about to change though, and Jason knew it.

'Why you crying? Has my dad left you?' Shay Rampling asked hopefully. She had always resented Melissa acting like her mother and often thought how much more fun life would be if she and her dad lived alone.

'No. Your dad's working,' Melissa snapped. She had been crying ever since she'd woken up alone in bed this morning. Jason never stayed out all night, not unless he was on a bit of work, and the thought of him being with another woman was too much for Mel to bear. For all his faults, she loved her husband and would be totally lost without him.

'Why you crying then?' Donte pried.

'Because I've got bellyache. Now go in the other room and watch your film,' Melissa ordered.

When the doorbell rang minutes later, Melissa dashed into the hallway hoping Jason had forgotten his key. 'Oh, it's you,' she said dismally.

Tracey Thompson fell into her best friend's arms.

'Whatever's wrong?' Melissa asked, wondering when the drama in her house would ever end.

'My mum's moving to Turkey to live with her toyboy. How can she leave me, her only daughter? I hate her, Mel, and him.'

'So, will we be seeing one another again?' Charlotte Rivers enquired.

Jason put his hand inside Charlotte's bathrobe and squeezed her buttocks. Watching her gyrating in that club last night had done wonders for his libido. Her hair was messy, brunette, and she'd reminded him of a young Darlene from a distance. 'What do you think?'

'I don't know. You tell me.'

'Well, put it this way. I am gonna take up golf and invest in a set of clubs. It's about time I had a hobby where I can get away at weekends, don't you think?'

'I think that's an excellent idea, Mr Rampling. You look like a golfer with that slicked-back hair. Not sure your curtains would've suited the course though.'

Jason laughed. 'You leave my curtains alone. That haircut was the bollocks. What you doing on Thursday?'

'I have nothing planned.'

'Good. Be ready by noon. I'll pick you up here.'

'Where you taking me?'

Jason tapped the side of his nose. 'That's for me to know and you to find out.'

To say Charlotte Rivers was over the moon was an understatement. She had her first and only true love back in her clutches and no way was she letting him go again. She loved Jason, always had done and always would.

'Hello, stranger. You hungry?' Melissa casually asked when Jason finally arrived home. Her heart was beating rapidly, had been all day, and she kept having visions of him with another woman, but she was determined to act normal, would hate him to think she was bothered.

Shay ran into the kitchen and hugged her father's legs. 'Where you been? Mel's been crying all day.'

'Don't lie, Shay. Tracey was the one who couldn't stop crying in the kitchen earlier, not me.'

'Stayed round a mate's,' Jason told his daughter.

'What's in that big bag, Dad?' Donte enquired, wondering if it was a present for him.

'Golf clubs. I had a game this morning with Craig and I've been bitten by the bug. About time I found meself a hobby,' Jason lied, surreptitiously looking at Mel for a reaction.

'Go in the lounge you two. I need to talk to your dad a minute,' Mel ordered.

'She been round again then, Tracey? What's up with her now? Kieron seen the light and binned her, has he?' Jason asked. He was determined to act as casual as he possibly could.

Melissa shut the kitchen door. 'So is that where you stayed, at Craig's?'

'Yeah. I was determined not to come home after you showed me up spectacularly in public.'

Melissa draped her arms around her husband's neck. 'I'm sorry. I just got over-excited. I should never have said anything in front of Tracey. I know how much you dislike her.'

'Too right you shouldn't. So why's she been round 'ere bawling today?'

'Her mum is moving to Turkey to live with the twenty-five-year-old toyboy she met in Marmaris. Tracey's distraught, as you can well imagine. She reckons he's only after a visa.'

'There's no fool like an old fool, eh?'

'Am I forgiven?' Melissa asked.

Jason pecked his wife on the lips. 'I suppose so.'

'Please can we go to that appointment with Dr Kazim though, Jase? There must be a reason why I'm not getting pregnant.'

Knowing if he agreed to Melissa's demands it would make it easier for him to get out and see Charlotte, Jason reluctantly nodded. 'Just the once, though. I got better things to do than be trotting up Harley Street every five minutes.'

Melissa smiled. 'Thank you.'

Later that evening, Melissa's suspicions were aroused again. Jason had been acting weird all day and she could tell his mind was elsewhere. The more she thought about it, the stranger she found it that he'd arrived home with a set of golf clubs. He had never shown any interest in golf before. He wasn't a sporty person, only ever watched the boxing on TV. 'So where did you buy your clubs from?' Melissa enquired.

'Bought 'em off Craig. He's got a new set. No point me investing in brand-new ones just yet,' Jason lied. Craig knew he'd gone home with Charlotte last night and had told him golfing was the best excuse to cover up an affair. 'Pop round and pick up my clubs. That'll cover your back,' he'd said before they'd left Stringfellows.

'I never even knew you liked golf.'

'I didn't. Never played it properly until this morning. Very therapeutic, it is. I got the same chilled buzz from it as you probably get with all those spa trips and massages I shell out for.' Jason had fully expected an inquisition and had his answers well prepared. He couldn't stop thinking about Charlotte and the fantastic sex they'd had. Thursday could not come quick enough.

Knowing when to shut up, Melissa tried a different tactic. 'Shall we watch a film?'

'Yeah, if you want,' Jason muttered. He was sprawled out on the sofa. Last night had worn him out, but was worth sapping his energy for.

Melissa was surreptitiously watching her husband in case he showed signs of guilt once he realized she'd put on *Fatal Attraction*, but he was distracted by his phone ringing.

'Slow down, Babs. I can't understand what you're saying, love,' Jason urged.

'What's up? Where you going?' Melissa asked as Jason ended the call, then leapt off the sofa.

'My mum's fallen down the stairs. She's in a bad way, not moving. Babs has had to call an ambulance.'

Melissa spent the next couple of hours knocking back the red wine and wondering if it had really been Babs on the phone. Call it feminine intuition, but she was positive Jason had spent last night with another woman.

'Mum – Dad's home. Elton and Kyle are with him,' Donte yelled excitedly as he ran to answer the door.

Melissa was almost as relieved as she was horrified to see Jason's three siblings walk inside her beautiful home. But at least she now knew he'd been telling the truth.

'Go upstairs, kids. Shay, Donte, let 'em play with your toys,' Jason urged.

Wanting to get back in her husband's good books, Melissa feigned concern. 'Is your mum OK? What's happened?'

Ashen-faced, Jason puffed his cheeks out and shook his head. 'It ain't looking good, Mel. Mum's in a bad way. They think she might've broken her back.'

CHAPTER SIXTEEN

'All right, boy? Take your shoes off. Just had me new shagpile carpet laid out of that two grand you gave me and I don't want it bleedin' ruined,' yelled Peggy Rampling.

Jason obeyed her orders and walked into the lounge.

'You've got a face like a smacked arse. What's a matter?' Peggy asked.

Jason sat on the sofa next to his nan and squeezed her hand. 'I've got some bad news. Mum fell down the stairs in her block on Saturday and got rushed to hospital. I didn't want to tell you over the phone. I was hoping she'd be OK. She isn't though. I've just come from Oldchurch after speaking with the doctors and they reckon she's done her spine in. The vertebrae or something. They don't think she'll ever walk again.'

Remembering her Debbie as an innocent ponytailed child, Peggy's eyes momentarily welled up. They soon dried though as Peggy reminded herself of what an embarrassing humungous beast her daughter had become. 'Pissed, was she?'

'Yeah.'

'Oh, well. Not as if she hasn't asked for it over the

years, is it? Your mother's lifestyle was always going to end in tears. Where are the little 'uns?' Peggy asked. She never referred to Barbara, Elton or Kyle as her grandchildren, and had only laid eyes on them once, at Jason's wedding.

'They're staying with me and Mel for the time being. It's only temporary, though. Mel won't have 'em live with us and, to be honest, we haven't really got the room. I've booked a meeting with Social Services next week. Mum's gonna need twenty-four-hour care by the looks of it and no way am I allowing Babs to be her carer. That poor little cow has been Mum's drudge for years as it is, and she deserves to have a life of her own. I'm hoping the authorities will let Babs look after the boys and keep the flat on, though. She'll be eighteen next birthday and is certainly mature enough. She's brought them up virtually all their lives anyway, and I don't want 'em going into care.'

'Well, I hope it all works out, Jason. I know how you worry about those kids.'

'Will you do me a favour, Nan?'

'Don't be asking me to look after 'em, boy, because the answer is most certainly no.'

'I know that and I wouldn't ask you anyway. Will you come round mine for dinner to meet 'em though? They're at a low ebb at the moment, Babs especially. It will do 'em good to meet you, I know it will.'

Peggy squeezed her grandson's hand. She loved Jason very much and was extremely proud of the man he'd become. 'OK. But I'm only doing this for you. I'll go out thieving, chore 'em some presents. Don't arrange it for a weekend though. That's when the big money's up for grabs at the bingo. How about Christmas Day? That'll suit me.

Don't want your old nan spending Christmas on her own, do ya, boy?'

Melissa Rampling flung open her son's bedroom door. He immediately stopped dancing, so did Elton and Kyle. 'Turn that racket down, now! I can't hear my bloody self think.'

'Always moaning, you are. You told us to amuse ourselves in the bedroom and we did as we were told,' Donte answered back. He loved having Elton and Kyle around. They were exciting and far more fun than Shay.

'I never told you to play loud music and jump up and down till you come through the floorboards, did I? You sound like a horde of elephants from downstairs.'

When Elton and Kyle started to giggle, Donte decided to answer back again: 'Thought you were going out anyway. Why you still here?'

Melissa grabbed her son by the arm and marched him out of his room and into hers.

'Get off me. You're a loony,' Donte complained.

'I'll give you loony in a minute, you keep giving me cheek.' She hated the change in her son's behaviour whenever Jason's brothers were around. He acted far older than his years and cocky, one of the very reasons she'd banned Elton and Kyle from her house in the first place.

'What we done wrong? We was only dancing.'

Melissa pointed a warning finger in her son's face. 'Skating on very thin ice, you are lately, which is why I've decided to send you to a private school. You'll have to learn some manners then, won't you? They don't put up with rude little boys.'

Praying that Elton and Kyle were not earwigging, Donte put his hands on his hips. 'I'm eight, not two. And I don't wanna change schools.'

'Tough. You are not growing up like those other two. I will not allow it.'

'Frank, Gary, this is my pal, Jason Rampling. It's his first time at the club today and I am sure you will view him as a worthy member. Jason's a car dealer like myself, which is how we first met,' Craig lied.

Jason shook hands and chatted amiably to the men. 'They seem all right,' he said when they walked away.

Craig grinned deviously. 'Regional Crime Squad, Gary is. I've often wondered if he's bent, seein' as he drinks with a few faces down 'ere. He might come in handy one day if we need a favour. You never know.'

Apart from thieving, drinking and shagging, golf was Craig's only other real passion in life and it had been his idea that Jason join the club. 'You can never cover your backside enough, mate. Ian's the man you wanna have a word with. He'd cover for me all the time when I was out shagging behind Mandy's back. She was always ringing or turning up 'ere. Just bung Ian an occasional drink and he'll put Mel off the scent if she starts prying. He's a damn good liar an' all.'

Jason nodded. He liked the club; it had a good feel to it. He'd played his first round earlier and enjoyed that too. 'So, what do you reckon? Is it possible I could be the next Tiger Woods?'

'You got a good swing, I'm telling ya. Get a few lessons under your belt and you'll be able to give me a run for me money.'

Jason chuckled. 'I don't think so, mate. I couldn't hit a barn door, let alone a hole in one. So what's occurring with Randy Mandy? You dumped her yet?'

'Nah. I'll wait till I get to Thailand and do the honours

over the phone. She's bound to go psycho, so that'll give her time to cool down. I ain't taking no chances though. I'm hiding me motors and Darlene is house-sitting for me, so she can't trash that.'

Jason raised his eyebrows. He knew Craig kept in occasional contact with Darlene, but last he'd heard she had sub-let her flat on the Mardyke and moved in with a bloke in Grays. 'How's Dar doing? Not told her we're working together, have you?'

Craig shook his head. 'My word is my bond. Don't think it's working out with Dar and that geezer. She rang out the blue the other day asking if there was anywhere she could rent near me. Told her I was sodding off on holiday for a month. Give her a bit of time to sort herself out, won't it? She still asks if I've seen or heard anything of you. You and her should bury the hatchet now. Time's a good healer.'

Jason shook his head. 'Some things are best left in the past. I'd rather stick with the memories. I can't wait to see that Charlotte again though. She's hot with a capital H, her.'

'Good-looking bird, I'll give you that much.'

'Booked a restaurant and hotel up town earlier today. I won't be able to stay out all night again, mind. Mel won't suffer that twice in a week.'

Craig nudged Jason. 'See that geezer just walked in, got a blue Pringle jumper on. If you're ever thinking of getting yourself a top accountant, then he's your man. You remember when Billy Jacobs got off that gold bullion charge? Well, he was his accountant and he backed Billy in court. Had every answer going. He also gave him an alibi for the robbery.'

Jason studied the bloke in question. He was a tad

overweight, tall, and wore glasses. 'Looks like a vicar in golf clobber. What's his name?'

'Simon. Simon Champion.'

'You look like I feel. I had another row with my delusional mother this morning. That's her lot now. Let the toyboy rob her blind, the silly old slapper,' Tracey Thompson moaned as she plonked herself opposite Melissa. The Bluebell Restaurant in Chigwell was a regular haunt of theirs.

'Thanks for meeting me at such short notice. Been pulling my hair out all morning. I had to get out the house before I punched someone.'

'His brothers and sister driving you mad again?'

'They do my head in. My home doesn't feel like my home while they're stopping with us. It's like a bomb's hit it and I'm a bundle of nerves waiting for 'em to break things. I rung the cleaner up and asked her to do four hours while I'm out. She'll keep an eye on Donte for me an' all.'

'Donte not at school?'

'No. Shay's off with tonsillitis, so Donte woke up this morning telling me he had a sore throat too. There's nothing bloody wrong with him and he's going to school tomorrow. I just want the other three out. Babs is harmless enough, all she does is eat. I looked in my cupboard this morning and it was virtually bare.'

Tracey burst out laughing. 'On that note, I think we'll order. Shame Jason's brothers aren't a few years older. They could've moved in with my mother.'

Jason looked at Simon Champion's card, then put it back in his pocket. 'Cheers for that introduction, Craig. I'm gonna call him tomorrow to arrange lunch. I got to get my finances and paperwork sorted properly. He was telling me he can invest money for me in Jersey, hide it, like. What a nice guy. Funny bastard too.'

'Yeah. He's a good bloke. But be warned, he isn't cheap and whatever he does for you, he'll want a cut for himself.'

Jason felt relieved more than anything. Hiding cash in his nan's cupboard had started to worry him since they'd nearly got caught on this latest robbery. The story had now died down in the press, and they'd set fire to the bike. Both he and Craig had strong alibis lined up for the day in question if needed.

'Where we going now?' Jason asked. The golf club was in Brentwood and he knew they were travelling in the opposite direction to the way they'd come.

'You'll see. I want to show you something. Your paperwork and finances aren't the only thing you need to get in order. I am gonna show you a new way we can earn money. Lots of it.'

Over at the Bluebell, the wine was flowing nicely and Melissa had finally admitted to Tracey that Jason hadn't come home last Friday night.

'Where do you reckon he stayed? I bet he wasn't at Craig's and I find it really fishy he turned up in the morning with a set of golf clubs. Sign of wrongdoing that is, trust me.'

Melissa shrugged. 'He's gone golfing again today. Wherever he stayed, I can't prove anything. He has been acting a bit distant, but that might be because of his mum. Even though he can't stand her, he was upset she might never walk again.'

'Well, I would never put up with Kieron staying out all

night and he knows it. When men stay out it's usually for one thing and one thing only.'

'I agree. But I did piss him off and I think he wanted to prove a point. I won't be happy if it happens again though, believe me. And I'll tell you something now, Trace. If he ever did to me what that arsehole of a father of mine did to my poor mum, I would kill him, stone dead.'

'We visiting someone?' Jason asked, bemused. It had started to get dark now and they'd just turned off a rural road and were approaching a massive mansion.

Craig put his foot on the brake. 'I don't want to go no further in case the security lights come on. But I want you to take a good look at that gaff.'

'It's special, I'll give you that. You haven't bought it, have you?'

'You've come straight to the point with that question, Jase. No. Of course I haven't bought it. I wouldn't be able to afford it with the measly cash we earn. But we could both be living in gaffs like this if we moved with the times.'

'What the hell you on about, mate?'

'Tommy Beezley recently bought this gaff. I was in nick with him. He was treading the same path as us, the hold-ups, the blaggings. Did a five-stretch for armed robbery and gave me a valuable piece of advice. "Blagging is a thing of the past now. DNA and technology have seen to that. When I get out this shithole I am going to earn myself a fortune." Those were Tommy's exact words to me the day before his release. And now he lives here.'

Jason was interested now. The gaff was lit up like a palace and obviously had many acres surrounding it. 'So what does Tommy do?'

'OK, this is where I know you are gonna balk, but think

before you do. Last week was a bit of a close shave for me too, pal, and I'm too old to go back inside.' Craig lowered his voice, even though it was just the two of them in the car: 'Tommy supplies drugs. He brings 'em over from Holland. Cocaine, to be precise. I had a long chat with him the other day and he's offered to set us up. You in or out?'

Jason held his hands up. 'Count me out. Not my scene at all. I have seen too many people's lives ruined where I grew up.'

Even though he'd expected this reaction, Craig wasn't about to give up. Jason was top drawer and he didn't want to lose him as his partner in crime. 'Just think about it. Promise me that much at least.'

Remembering the time he had seen one of his mother's friends convulse then die in their home at a young age, Jason shook his head. 'Nah, mate. You're on your own with this one. But I wish you all the luck in the world with it, I truly do.'

As Elton, Kyle, Donte and Shay all rushed towards him talking nineteen to the dozen, Jason held his hands up. 'Whoa! Slow down, one at a time.'

'The boys broke the TV in the lounge, Jason. They were mucking about and it fell off its stand and smashed. It was an accident, but Melissa says we have to leave tonight,' Barbara explained.

'We hardly touched it. It just fell,' Elton lied.

Jason poked his head around the lounge door and winced. No wonder his wife was peeved. The weight of the TV had cracked their new laminated flooring too. 'Where is Mel?'

'She popped to the shop. Shall we pack our things?' Barbara asked.

'No. Accidents happen. Please try and be more careful in future though, and stay out of Mel's way for a bit. I'll talk to her. You go upstairs. I'll give you a shout when we order some food.' Melissa had flatly refused to cook while his siblings were staying there, so they were currently living on takeaways.

Melissa arrived home minutes later with a face like thunder. 'Seen the damage, have you? I want them out, Jason. Tonight! Had it up to here, I have,' she yelled, raising her arm.

'I can't just kick 'em out, Mel. Not after what's happened with their mum.'

'Why can't they stay at their own flat? Barbara's an adult, can take care of the other two. Your mother was never bloody in anyway.'

'Just let 'em stay until I've spoken with Social Services. Please, Mel. I'm all they've got.'

'No. Enough is enough, Jason. Those boys are a dreadful influence on Donte, and my son is my priority from now on. I want 'em gone before any more damage is done. Bad enough I got to suffer 'em at Christmas, along with your nan. Best you book a restaurant because no way am I cooking.'

Jason's lip curled. 'You leave my nan out of this. I ain't taking 'em home tonight and that's final. I pay the fucking mortgage 'ere, not you.'

'Fine! Enjoy looking after them then,' Melissa screamed, stomping up the stairs.

Jason was amazed when his wife reappeared minutes later with Donte and a suitcase. 'What you doing?'

'Booking into a hotel with my son. Let me know when they're gone.'

Donte was crying. 'I don't want to go to a hotel. I want to stay here, Dad.'

About to tell Melissa what a selfish cow she was, Charlotte flashed through Jason's mind. If his wife wasn't around, he could spend the whole night with her at the hotel on Thursday. He stroked Donte's head. 'Do as your mum says, boy.'

CHAPTER SEVENTEEN

As Christmas beckoned, Jason felt as though he had the weight of the world on his shoulders. Craig was still adamant he was embarking on a new career and Jason had no idea where his next bit of work would come from. Having a wife and mistress wasn't cheap and he was spending money like water.

'Oh, Jason. Look at that. Isn't it exquisite?' Charlotte Rivers said, pointing at a necklace in the window of a jeweller's in Bond Street.

It had been Jason's idea they spend the day up town so Charlotte could choose her own Christmas present. Now he wished he hadn't as he clocked the price. 'Do you want to try it on?' he asked.

Charlotte beamed and squeezed Jason's hand. The necklace was white gold with a diamond-studded heart. 'Three grand is a lot of money. I really don't expect you to spend that much. I do love it though. Beautiful, those diamonds. Look how they sparkle.'

Yet to tell Charlotte he would have to cancel their plans over the Christmas period, Jason hoped the necklace would act as a sweetener. 'You're worth every penny. Go try it on.'

'Are you ready to order, Melissa?' asked Eleanor Collins-Hythe. When Melissa had called her, it was her husband who'd insisted she go out with the woman. This was the first time they'd seen each other since they'd met at the hairdresser's.'You'll never guess what,' Melissa beamed.

'Go on.'

'I'm four days late and I'm never late.'

'Wow! How exciting. Did you visit Dr Kazim?'

'No. I booked an appointment, but had to cancel it. My husband and I had a bit of a falling out. I rebooked the appointment, but I might not need it now, fingers crossed.'

'Wouldn't it be wonderful, Melissa? What a fabulous Christmas present for you and hubby. When will you take a test?'

In a hotel room in Mayfair, Jason was performing cunnilingus on Charlotte Rivers.

'Oh, Jase. Jesus fucking Christ! You're the best,' Charlotte groaned as she was brought to a shuddering orgasm by her lover's expert tongue.

Deciding this might be as good a time as any to break the bad news, Jason slithered up the bed and stroked Charlotte's hair. 'We're gonna have to cancel our day out on the twenty-eighth, babe. I'm sorry. Mel has gone behind my back and arranged for us to visit her brother, and there's nothing I can do to get out of it.'

Charlotte propped herself on her elbow, a stony expression on her usually pretty face. 'But I thought you and your wife were no longer a proper couple.'

'We're not. I still have to play the family man at times

though, for the sake of the kids. I wouldn't be with her if it wasn't for them, trust me.'

'You have one daughter, Jason, and you're a man of substance now. There must be some connection between yourself and Melissa otherwise you'd leave her.'

Jason felt uncomfortable. Charlotte had hardly mentioned Melissa until now and he didn't know how to respond. 'It's awkward. I worked my bollocks off to buy my gaff and Mel's the type to bleed me dry if I ever left her.'

'But I don't see how she can bleed you dry. You haven't got any children together, therefore Donte isn't your responsibility.'

'She'd want half the house though, wouldn't she? Which means I'd have to sell it.'

'Do you love her?' Charlotte asked.

'No. You know I don't.'

'Do you still sleep together?'

Jason flopped on his back and put his hands behind his head. 'We share a bed but we don't really have sex.'

'What do you mean by you don't really have sex? You either do or you don't.'

Having enjoyed every second of the time he'd spent with Charlotte up until now, Jason was taken aback by the endless questions. He didn't need her grilling him, he got enough of that at home. 'We ain't had sex for months,' he lied. 'Way before I bumped into you again.'

'I'm not that naïve girl you met years ago, Jase. I'm all grown up now and to be honest I'm not cut out to be someone's bit on the side. You need to think about what you really want over Christmas. I do love you, but I won't wait around for you for ever.'

*

'I'd better be making a move soon. Ruby will wonder where her mummy's got to.'

Melissa stood up. They'd eaten lunch in Ye Olde Kings Head in Chigwell and it was the usual buoyant Christmas Eve atmosphere. People in Santa hats, laughing too loudly and drinking too much.

Eleanor Collins-Hythe hugged her new friend. 'Well, it's been fabulous seeing you, Melissa. I hope you, your handsome hubby and beautiful children have a wonderful Christmas.'

'You too.'

'And don't forget to let me know as soon as you do the test. I wish you all the luck in the world, I truly do.'

'Thank you.'

'Oh, and you must bring hubby round to meet David. Or we can come to you. Let me know when you're free and we'll pop something in the diary,' Eleanor grinned.

When Eleanor got into her car, tooted then waved, Melissa smiled politely and waved back. She doubted she'd be seeing her any more. Eleanor was far too nosy and asked too many questions. Jason had always warned her not to talk about business or finances with anyone. It was hard to make friends with new people when you had to keep so much quiet, and Melissa didn't trust her.

Having told Melissa he had a bit of work on and wouldn't be home until late this evening, Jason was now at a loose end. He was meant to be having dinner with Charlotte at the hotel but after she stormed off in a huff, it was pointless him staying up town alone.

Yesterday, Jason had received a call from Oldchurch Hospital asking to speak to him in person about his mother, so Jason decided to head up there. He had no wish to see her, but knew she'd been on Babs's case about becoming her full-time carer and over his dead body was he allowing that. Babs was living back on the Mardyke Estate with his brothers now and she had enough on her plate taking care of them. He'd been helping out financially, checking up on them regularly, and a lady from Social Services was monitoring the situation too. It was a big ask for a seventeen-year-old, but Babs had always had a mothering instinct and seemed to be coping OK so far.

Jason introduced himself to the ward sister and was none too surprised by what she had to say. 'What has happened to your mother is a terrible thing and understandably tough for her to digest. However, she is being extremely difficult and I will not allow my staff to be physically or verbally abused.'

'I'm very sorry. She's always been a difficult woman. How much longer is she going to be in hospital for?'

'There isn't much more we as medical staff can do for her. Your mother isn't in pain as she has no feeling from the waist down. She will never walk again – the spinal cord is too severely damaged – however, with extensive physiotherapy treatment, she can learn to adjust to her condition. There is no reason why one day she cannot live independently again. But she will need to work hard, put in the effort.'

'The words work and effort aren't in my mother's vocabulary I'm afraid. She never lifted a finger when she had the use of her legs, so I doubt that'll change.'

'I'm sorry to hear that. Your sister will be caring for her, is this correct? Only we will need to start the ball rolling on getting her discharged.'

'Not on your nelly! Take no notice of anything my mother says. Barbara, my sister, has no wish to be her carer. Neither does anybody else in the family. Set the ball rolling by all means, but she'll have to go in a home, a place that can cope with her needs.'

'I fully understand. Would you mind having a word with her while you're here though, please? She had a visitor yesterday who brought alcohol into the hospital. Vodka, to be precise. The empty bottle was found inside your mother's bed after she'd spent the night being loud and abusive. It really isn't fair on the other patients, or the staff.'

'I'll have a word, but she rarely listens to anything I say. Your best bet is to contact the appropriate authorities and get her out of here ASAP.'

With a heavy heart, Jason entered his mother's little side ward.

Instead of kicking off like he'd fully expected her to, tears of self-pity poured down Debbie's face. 'What am I gonna do, boy? You have to help me. Please.'

Jason had not seen her properly since his wedding and she looked even worse than he remembered. Her hair was lanky, she was fatter than ever and her face was red and blotchy. 'If I could wave a magic wand that enabled you to walk again, then I would. The only person who can help you now is you. The sister said you can be independent again one day if you're willing to adapt to a new life.'

'And what does that silly Irish whore know? My spinal cord's fucked, so how the hell can I be independent? You have to help me, son. You're the only one who can. Speak to Social Services and see if they can find me a nice bungalow. Babs will look after me. She's a good girl.'

'Nah. That ain't happening. Babs has her hands full looking after the boys.'

'But kids are meant to look after their mothers when they get ill. It's their duty.'

'Not mothers like you. You never looked after us when we were ill. I remember having a sickness bug once and you still went out on the piss. Tied me to the bed like you usually did. Did it not occur to you that I might've choked on my own vomit? I could've fucking died.'

'I don't remember that. Still here to tell the tale though, ain't ya?' Debbie spat. 'I'm not going into a home. Nobody can force me,' she shrieked, fire in her eyes.

'Keep your voice down. You're already on the verge of being slung out as it is. There's people who are dying in 'ere. Show some respect.'

'I'll die too if I have to go in a home. Please, son. Help me. I'll kill meself otherwise. I swear I will.'

'Emotional blackmail won't work. And don't keep upsetting Babs, because if you do, I swear I'll stop her visiting you.'

'Get out! Go on, get out before I scream the fucking place down!' Debbie was practically foaming at the mouth, spit was flying out of her gob as she screeched at him. 'You're no son of mine. You're evil, pure evil, and I hope you die a truly painful death. You are nothing more than a nasty, money-grabbing little shyster. I wish I'd have smothered you at birth.'

Any empathy he had felt now vanished; Jason looked at his mother in total disgust. 'Unlike you, I am not a nasty person. Therefore, I hope you somehow find peace in life. You'll never see me again though, Mum. We're done – for good.'

As Jason left the room the last word he ever heard his mother say to him was 'Shitcunt.'

*

'Well, you've changed your tune. I thought she was your new bestie. Whatever went wrong?' Tracey Thompson was secretly pleased and relieved. She had felt jealous when Mel kept rambling on about how bloody wonderful Eleanor was.

'I can't put my finger on it, there's just something about her. She wants to know the ins and outs of a duck's arse for a start, and I can sense she sees me as a bit thick.'

'You're not thick,' Tracey lied. Melissa could be very thick, especially when it came to Jason.

'I think I was in awe of her when I met her in the hairdresser's, and I have no idea why. Perhaps because she's an older woman with a great career and a baby? I feel silly now. I even put on my posh voice to impress her. I also clocked the shock on her face when I showed her a photo of Donte today. She's very middle class and I could tell she never expected him to be mixed-race. She'd only had a couple glasses of champagne but sounded plastered.' Melissa put on a lah-di-dah accent and gushed, '"Oh my God! How handsome. He looks like a young Denzel Washington!" I mean, come on! How the hell does she know what Denzel looked like as a kid?'

Tracey was nearly wetting herself. 'You crack me up, mate,' she said, hugging her pal. 'Sod Eleanor and all the other randoms that come along. We're besties for life, me and you. We don't need anyone else.'

'She answer?' Craig Thurston asked, lining up another row of Sambucas.

Jason downed a shot and slammed the glass against the bar. 'No. Why is it women feel the need to play mind games? I've not even done anything wrong.'

Having been out on the lash since lunchtime, Craig was not only pissed, but was also in a piss-taking mood. 'Perhaps she wanted a ten-grand necklace, ya tight bastard?' he chuckled.

Overhearing the conversation, Simon Champion slapped both Jason and Craig on the back. 'Don't talk to me about bloody women. My fiancée of nine months dumped me last week because she met a professional footballer. I wouldn't mind if he played for Manchester United or Liverpool. But – wait for it – he plays for . . . Brentford. I mean, come on, the geezer's got to be a loser.'

Craig Thurston burst out laughing. 'Not as much of a loser as my mucker Jason. He just spent three grand on a necklace for a lap-dancer, and now she won't answer the phone to him.'

'Shut up, you tosser,' Jason laughed.

'And on that note I will bid you lads goodbye. Have a good Christmas. Our lunch is in the diary, Jason. See you then, if I don't see you beforehand.'

'What you doing for the Millennium?' Jason asked Simon.

'Going to Dubai. My ex booked it and I paid for it, so rather than waste the holiday I'm taking a pal with me. I'll have a better time there than she will in, erm, Brentford!'

Melissa checked that Shay and Donte were both asleep, then took the test out of her drawer. She opened the box and read the instructions.

Should she take it now? Or leave it until after Christmas? It would be a wonderful present to give Jason tomorrow if it was positive. But on the downside, it would totally spoil her day if negative.

Melissa put the test on her bedside cabinet and stared at it. Decisions, decisions . . .

'I'm slaughtered, mate. Gonna order a cab soon,' Jason Rampling told Craig. He wasn't the biggest drinker in the world, but had hammered it today. His mother was enough to put a sane person off drink for life.

'Shut up, you lightweight. Listen, I got an idea that will solve all your problems.'

Jason stared at the phone. He'd left Charlotte loads of texts, but she was still blanking him. 'I think I'm in love with her, ya know,' he slurred. 'Those tits, and that arse . . . she's just so fucking pretty. What am I gonna do?'

Craig downed another shot. 'You're gonna shut the hell up and listen to me. Birds come and go, mate, and if Charlotte truly does love you, then she'll wait. But firstly, you need to secure your future. She ain't going to want you if you're skint, is she?'

Jason held his hands up. 'No way am I flogging cocaine, Craig.'

'I wasn't even gonna suggest that again. Just listen, will ya? Johnny Brooks is worth millions and you are married to his daughter.'

'So? Hasn't exactly made me happy, has it?'

Craig tapped the side of his head. 'You're not stupid. Use your brain.'

'I don't understand what you're trying to say.'

Craig rolled his eyes and pointed the middle and forefinger of his left hand at the side of his forehead. 'You take him out, then half of Melissa's inheritance is yours.'

Jason's eyes widened. 'Are you for real?'

'Sure am. I can get you a shooter an' all. And, for a price, I'll even do the deed for you. I've always hated that cunt.'

As Jason burst out laughing, mocked his pal and called him a 'mad bastard' he had no idea that one day things would become so bad, he would actually take Craig up on the offer. No idea at all.

CHAPTER EIGHTEEN

On Christmas morning, Jason was woken up by a rarity: breakfast in bed. He sat up, squinting. 'What time did I get in? Sorry I was steaming. I had a tough day.'

'You got home about eleven and you told me all about the terrible things your mum said. No wonder you needed to let off steam after visiting that horrible cow. What time you picking your family up? I'll change Donte's bed in case your nan wants to stay over too. He can sleep with us.'

Jason eyed his wife suspiciously. She'd been dreading spending Christmas with his family, had not stopped whingeing about it. 'You've changed your tune. And what's with the breakfast in bed?'

Melissa grinned. 'You work hard all year round and deserve to be spoiled on occasions. Is there any money from yesterday you want me to put away?'

Remembering his lie, Jason shook his sore head. 'The job didn't go ahead, babe. Sorry.'

'No worries. I know I don't say it much, but I do love you, Jase.'

Thinking how weird she was acting, Jason rammed a sausage in his mouth. 'Ditto,' he mumbled.

'All right, boy? All those dustbin bags are to go in the car. Been on a roll recently. Nearly got caught in Woolworths the other day, mind. Didn't even know they had store detectives until I spotted this hooked-nose ugly prat clocking me. So I darted round another aisle and put the stuff back.'

Jason shook his head. 'You'll be the death of me, Nan. What am I going to do with you?'

'You should have seen her face when she stopped me on the way out. "I believe you have some items in your shopping trolley that haven't been paid for," she says, all hoity-toity. Course them nosy bastards you get in Romford were lappin' it up, staring for all they was worth, so I told her to search the bleedin' trolley. Right there in the doorway she starts pullin' out me bag of pick'n'mix sweets, a bit of skate, two lumps of haddock and me jellied eels. There was sod-all else in there!' Peggy cackled.

'Great story. But please don't repeat it in front of Mel, will ya? She wouldn't get it, if you know what I mean.'

'Oh, I know exactly what you mean, love. She looked a right stuck-up cow the day you married her.'

'Who wants another sausage roll?' Melissa asked.

Babs licked her lips. 'Yes, please.'

Elton nudged Donte. 'Why is your mum being so nice to us?'

Donte shrugged.

Melissa put a plate of sausage rolls on the coffee table.

'Your brother will be back soon. Are you excited you're finally going to meet your nan?'

'Will she bring us presents?' Kyle asked.

'I'm excited,' Barbara replied.

'She isn't very nice. I don't like her,' Shay piped up.

'She'd old and loud,' Donte added.

'Is she thin or is she fat like our other nan?' Elton enquired.

'And Barbara,' Kyle giggled.

'Don't be nasty now,' Melissa urged, giving the boys a warning look.

'It's OK, Mel. I don't take any notice,' Babs smiled. She'd got thoroughly used to jibes about her weight, had been on the receiving end of them for years and no longer let the subject bother her now she'd left the school bullies behind.

'She's here!' Kyle shouted.

'She's a midget. How did she give birth to our massive mum?' Elton chuckled, pressing his nose against the window.

Melissa plastered a smile on her face and opened the front door. 'Merry Christmas, Peggy. They're all in there waiting for you.'

Peggy pursed her lips. 'I bet they bleedin'-well are. Probably guessed I'd bring presents with me.'

'Hello, Nan,' Barbara Rampling beamed, hugging the woman she had never met close to her chest.

'Mind, dear. You'll crush me ribs. Nice to meet you, and you two,' Peggy said, removing herself from Barbara's sumo-wrestler grasp and forcing a smile for Elton and Kyle. She had no interest in them whatsoever, truth be known, was only doing this for Jason's sake.

'Is there presents in there for us?' Kyle asked, pointing at the dustbin liners.

'Yes. Help yourselves,' Peggy said. She turned to Melissa. 'See, I told you so.'

'I can't believe you bought us a PlayStation and games, Jason. I can't wait to beat Elton at Crash Team Racing,' Kyle beamed, clapping his hands with delight.

'I wanna play Tomb Raider first,' Elton insisted. 'This is like our best present ever.'

Jason got both his brothers in a playful headlock. 'Best you don't play Barbara up no more then, else the PlayStation will have to be sold. You be good boys from now on, OK?'

'We will,' Kyle said.

Barbara was near to tears as she laid eyes on her posh Nokia phone. 'Does it work?' she asked dumbly.

'It sure does. I've already registered it and charged it up for you,' Jason smiled. 'And it ain't just any old mobile, Babs. It's the new 7110 that you can access the internet with.'

Babs's eyes opened wide. 'Really! What can I look up then?'

'Anything you want. I thought we'd take a look together; see if we can find you a job. The boys are getting older now and you need to think about your future.'

'But I can't work. I have to look after Mum.'

'Not every day, you don't. You can still see her at weekends. She'll be in a care home soon, so she won't be lonely.'

'What's this?' Peggy enquired.

'A pure silk scarf. I hope you like it. I chose that,' Melissa said.

'Well, it's pretty. But where do I go to wear a bleedin' silk scarf? Chop me head off on the way out the bingo for that, the robbing bastards. Poor old Doris got mugged as she left there a couple of weeks ago. Broke her wrist an' all.'

'Mel's got the gift receipt, so you can change it for something else if you want. I thought you might wear it when you go out dancing with Irish Ted.' Jason winked at Melissa.

'Ted's got gout. Can't walk any more, let alone bleedin' dance.' Peggy studied the scarf some more. 'I'll keep it, I think. You can put it round me neck in me coffin, Jason. It matches that green dress I told you to cremate me in.'

'Are you dying, Nan?' Elton asked.

'Soon, probably, yeah. I am knocking on a bit.'

Kyle perched himself on the edge of Peggy's armchair. 'Can I give you a hug?'

Jason burst out laughing. 'Happy Christmas, everybody.'

'What time did you call the cab for, Mel?' Jason asked. She was being unbelievably nice to his family and seemed in a thoroughly buoyant mood.

'I didn't. I'll drive your car. It's big enough for all of us to squeeze in.'

Never having been one to hold back her words, Peggy pointed at Barbara. 'You sure? She'll have to sit in the front then.'

Giving his nan a warning look, Jason turned to Melissa. 'Don't drive. Have a drink.'

'I really don't fancy drinking, Jase, honest. I'll have a glass of bubbly later though, I promise. And thank you so much again for my beautiful earrings and all my other gifts. I love them,' Melissa gushed, studying her diamond studs in her compact mirror once more.

'Had a result when you met my Jason, didn't ya? Beautiful home you have and he's such a thoughtful lad,' Peggy said to Melissa.

As happy as she felt, Melissa's patience had already started to wear thin with Jason's grandmother. Mel had never liked her since the day she'd met her and could sense the feeling was mutual. 'He hasn't always done me proud, Peggy. Don't you remember what happened at our wedding?'

'Do you mean when Mum turned up swearing?' Barbara enquired.

'Amongst other things,' Melissa snapped, deciding now was as good a time as any to spring her big surprise on Jason.

Jason opened the envelope. 'Disney World, Florida! What's this then?'

'I booked us a holiday. The kids will love it.'

'Jesus, Mel. You could've asked me first. How much this set you back? I've only just paid the balance on the Seychelles for your mate's poxy wedding.'

Peggy pursed her lips. 'I think you mean, how much did it set you back, boy.'

Having left it late to book anywhere, Jason had been unable to find a pub or restaurant with availability in Chigwell, but had managed to get them into one in Brentwood, thanks to Simon Champion, who'd recommended it and pulled a few strings as he knew someone who worked there.

The Bull was situated on Brook Street and as Jason opened the door to allow Melissa and the kids inside he grabbed his nan's arm. 'I know you don't like Mel. But don't keep winding her up. Please, for my sake.'

Peggy looked surprised. 'What am I meant to have said that's so wrong? Only stating facts. She bought you a holiday out of your own money.'

'I just want a peaceful Christmas, OK?' Jason warned.

'Whatever!'

'Put your paper hat on. Shay's got hers on,' Melissa urged her son.

Aware that Elton and Kyle had screwed their hats up and thrown them on the floor, Donte did the same.

'Pick that up,' Melissa ordered.

When Elton and Kyle giggled, Donte did the same. 'No.'

'Make him pick that up, Jason,' Melissa hissed. It infuriated her how her son always played up in front of Jason's brothers.

'Do as your mum says, boy,' Jason said.

Peggy bent down and picked the hat up.

'Put it back. Let him do it,' Melissa shrieked.

'Keep your hair on. It's only a bit of bloody paper,' Peggy retaliated.

Desperate to keep the peace, Jason marched his nan up the bar. She had never seen eye to eye with Melissa, which was why she rarely visited the house. 'Stop pushing her buttons. I'll get the brunt of it if you carry on,' Jason said.

'Her fault for making a mountain out of a molehill. It was a bit of bleedin' paper. Sitting there like Lady Dunnabunk, full of airs and graces. Wants to get off her lazy arse and get a job, help you out a bit. And that beauty salon she was harping on about wants shutting down, robbing bastards. Done nothing for her looks, has it? She's still as ugly as the day you bastard-well married her.'

'Enough, Nan. Let's change the subject, please. So, what do you think of your grandchildren?'

'They're all right.'

'That all you've got to say?'

'Babs needs to lose some weight, poor thing. She'll never get a boyfriend looking like that, ya know.'

About to defend his sister, Jason decided not to bother. His nan was the most outspoken person he'd ever met and she was far too long in the tooth to change now.

Melissa had just eaten the last of her prawn cocktail when she saw them. 'Oh my God! I don't bloody believe it!' She grabbed Jason's arm. 'I am not staying here. Look,' she urged.

A short, sturdy man with ginger cropped hair, Johnny Brooks was easily recognizable even from the back. The woman standing next to him was taller, glamorous with blonde hair and Jason guessed immediately that it was Shirley Stone.

'Who is it?' Donte asked. He'd only been young when his mum had fallen out with his granddad, therefore had no recollection of him whatsoever.

'We need to leave. Now,' Melissa hissed.

Peggy rolled her eyes. 'Here we go,' she mumbled.

'We can't leave. We haven't had our dinner yet. He won't come over, and if he does, I'll sort it,' Jason promised.

'Who we meant to be looking at?' Barbara piped up.

'No way am I breathing the same air as that scrubber,' Melissa insisted. Her heart was beating incredibly fast, but she was frozen to her seat.

'Drama queen,' Peggy muttered.

When Johnny turned around, Shay recognized him. 'It's Granddad,' she exclaimed, running towards him. Johnny and Carol had been so kind to her she had never forgotten either. Even though they were not her real grandparents, she would always regard them as such and remembered crying for days after Carol died.

When Donte stood up, Melissa leapt out of her seat and grabbed her son. 'You don't go anywhere near him, do you hear me?' she screamed.

By now, lots of other diners were looking their way and Jason felt embarrassed. 'Stop creating a scene. You're making the situation worse,' he told Melissa.

Johnny hugged Shay, then walked over to his daughter. 'Melissa, Jason, long time no see. Hasn't this one got big? And I take it this is Donte?' he asked, stroking Donte's head.

Melissa leapt out of her chair like a Jack in the Box. 'Get your hands off him, you dirty old pervert.'

'Mel, tone it down, for Christ's sake,' Jason pleaded. They had the whole bloody pub looking their way now.

A bloke on the next table stood up. 'Has that man touched your child?' he asked.

'Better than *EastEnders*, this,' Peggy muttered.

Jason stood up. 'Nah. Everything is fine, mate. Family issues, that's all.'

When a woman piped up asking if Johnny was a paedophile, Shirley Stone felt it was time to intervene and marched over to the table. She pointed at Johnny. 'He is my partner of many years and I can assure you he isn't a pervert. That' – Shirley pointed to Melissa – 'is his daughter, who hates him for no good reason.'

'Leave it, Shirl,' Johnny urged. He was red-faced enough as it was.

Melissa picked up Peggy's glass of port and threw it in Shirley's face. 'No good reason! You old slag. Shagging my dad behind my mother's back. Well, this is from her,' Mel screamed, throwing a punch.

'Mum, stop it,' Donte pleaded, tears streaming down his face.

'That's me port gone for a burton,' Peggy mumbled.

'Leave Granddad alone,' Shay yelled.

A man appeared from behind the bar. 'I'm afraid I must ask you all to leave.'

Jason grabbed hold of his wife. 'No worries, mate. We're going.'

'Would've been better fed going to a homeless shelter. Bastard-well starving, I am,' Peggy Rampling moaned as Jason neared her house.

'I'm so sorry about today, Nan. I'll make it up to you. I'll take you out somewhere nice, just me and you. You got anything indoors you can cook?' Melissa had been hysterical on the journey home, so he'd driven the car. Seeing her father with Shirley Stone had triggered something within her and when she'd ordered him to take his nan home at once, Jason hadn't bothered to put up a fight.

'Nope! Got nothing in the cupboards or the fridge,' Peggy lied. 'I mean, Irish Ted invited me to spend Christmas with his sister in Dundalk. Next year I will bloody well go. Never known such a drama queen as your old woman. Mind you, it was hilarious when the whole pub thought Johnny Brooks was a child molester,' Peggy cackled. 'Can't wait to tell 'em that story down the bingo hall. It'll go down a treat.'

'I'm not visiting her poxy brother now. I'm going to tell her I'm spending time with you instead. Back me up if she rings you,' Jason urged. He had told his nan all about Charlotte and the predicament he was currently in. She might be a wind-up merchant, but anything he told his nan in secret would never be repeated.

'Yeah, no probs. When you gonna bring Charlotte round to meet me, by the way?'

'Soon.'

'You not coming in?' Peggy asked, when Jason pulled up outside her house and kept the engine running.

'No. Best I shoot straight off, the mood she's in. I need to make sure the kids are all right. Will you see Babs, Elton and Kyle again if I arrange something? Mel won't be involved, just us.'

'I don't know, love. Maybe. But take a word of advice from me. She ain't the full shilling, that Mel. Get rid of her ASAP.'

On his way home, Jason stopped in the car park of the Maypole pub. Up until yesterday, Charlotte hadn't had his number and he'd been too scared to turn the bloody phone on all day in case she rang up in front of Mel.

With a heavy heart, Jason pressed the on button. He remembered sending her loads of drunken texts, cringe-worthy ones.

'Oh, bloody hell,' he mumbled.

> It's you I want! I'll leave Mel in the new year, I promise xxx

Jason winced as he read similar sloppy shit, then smiled as he clocked Charlotte's reply sent this morning.

> I am so sorry I was such a cow – was just upset that I wouldn't be seeing you again soon. I love my necklace and I love you. You are worth waiting for!
>
> Merry Christmas
>
> C xxx

Jason deleted all the messages and started the ignition. He had a big decision to make soon, that was for sure.

*

'I'm so sorry, Jase. I truly am. The kids are fine. I cooked them pizzas and garlic bread. I couldn't help myself though. I lost it when she came over. How must my mum have felt, knowing she was dying and he was knocking off Shirley? It must've been torture for her.'

'In fairness, your mum did tell you she didn't want your dad to be lonely and you were to give Shirley a chance, Mel. She was dealing with it in her own way and perhaps you should now take her advice.'

'Never! I wish my dad was dead. I really do.'

'Oh well! Where are the kids now?'

'Upstairs, on their PlayStations. I apologized to them too. They're fine, honest.'

Jason walked over to the fridge, took out a can of lager, flopped on the sofa and switched the TV on.

A minute later, Melissa plonked a bottle of champagne in front of him and poured two glasses.

'I'm not in the mood for bubbly, love. It's been the Christmas from hell. There is sod-all to celebrate,' Jason said bluntly.

'But it's not over yet. This is your main present,' Melissa replied, handing Jason an envelope.

'Oh, for fuck's sake, Mel. Not more extravagance. You're going to have to rein it in a bit from now on, love. I ain't Baron Rockefeller, ya know.'

'It cost nothing. Well, less than a tenner. Just open it.'

Jason's jaw dropped as he laid eyes on the pregnancy test. 'Nah. You can't be. You winding me up?'

Melissa pointed to the positive sign and grinned. 'No joke. I am having your baby. We did it, Jase. We finally did it!'

PART THREE

'One may outwit another,
but not all the others'

François de La Rochefoucauld

CHAPTER NINETEEN

2001 – Two Years Later

'Absolutely taters, I am. The things I let you talk me into, Rampling,' Craig Thurston said. The November air was crisp and it had just started to drizzle again.

'Never forget, this was your idea in the first place,' Jason retaliated. He then went quiet, his body filled with fear at what lay ahead.

How had things come to this? Jason mused, even though he knew all the answers. It was an accumulation of unavoidable things, events and rash decisions that had brought him to his knees. Money made the world go round and when it started to run out, you were doomed.

Back in the day, he and Craig would do approximately three robberies a year. Most involved jewels and diamonds, but the more DNA forensics improved and CCTV cameras were installed, the harder it became. That's why Craig had bailed out, and on a personal level, he'd made the right choice. Craig was earning bundles now, had even lent Jason twenty grand recently.

Jason, on the other hand, had collateral now, thanks to the flats he'd bought in Jersey. But readies wise, he was struggling. Even the cars from the auctions didn't bring in the dosh they once did. People wanted to pay for everything on the never-never these days and with some dealers offering 0 per cent finance deals, they bought from them instead.

'I'm starving. I hope he hasn't gone on an all-day bender,' Craig moaned. For the past three Sundays they had watched Johnny Brooks's movements and he seemed to be a creature of habit.

Feeling a wave of unease wash over him, Jason decided to air his concerns. 'I don't know if this is a good idea, you know. I got a bad feeling about it.'

Craig turned around. Both men were dressed in black leathers and balaclavas. They'd had to take their helmets off to hear each other clearly. 'You're joking, right?'

'Something don't feel right, not with you riding the bike and him being late.' Jason had managed to get hold of another Kawasaki, similar to the one they'd used in their last robbery. It was a ZZR1100, a beast, and Craig was no biker.

'We've got a van parked three miles down the poxy road! I've ridden it the last three Sundays, haven't I? Don't go cold on me now, Jase. Not after freezing me bollocks off four Sundays on the spin.'

Jason fell silent again. He'd managed to pull off two robberies alone since he and Craig had parted company. They'd both netted him a decent amount of cash, but on the last he'd slipped running out of the shop and had very nearly got caught. A bystander had tried to apprehend him and Jason had panicked. He'd been forced to spray CS gas in the have-a-go hero's eyes and literally escaped by the skin of his teeth. He wasn't like Craig, who thrived on threats and violence. He hated seeing the terrified look on innocent people's faces, which was why he'd made a better getaway driver.

Melissa Rampling leaned over her son's wooden cot and switched on the musical mobile.

'Hush-a-bye baby on a treetop. When the winds blows, the cradle will rock. When the bough breaks, the cradle will fall. Down tumbles baby, cradle and all,' Melissa sang softly while staring at her son's handsome face.

Tearing her eyes away from Bobby, Melissa glanced at her watch. She had no idea where Jason was, but guessed he was playing golf again. He spent little time at home these days, had probably told her this morning where he was going. But she'd been so hungover she couldn't remember.

'Mel, Donte's starving and so am I. What we having for dinner?' Shay shouted out.

'I'll be down in a tick,' Melissa yelled back. Walking around the cot, Mel planted a kiss on her son's cute little button nose. 'I'll be back later, boy. Sleep tight,' she whispered.

But it wasn't Bobby's actual face Melissa was kissing. It was the image of him she had insisted they have enlarged and hung above his cot. Unlike other mothers, she would never hear her son's first words or watch him take his first steps.

Bobby Rampling was dead.

'I'd better be off now, lads. See you same time next week,' Johnny Brooks said.

'Oh, don't be a bore, have one more. Rhymed that,

didn't it?' Scottish Paul laughed at the words he hadn't actually meant to be funny.

'Paul's right. While the cat's away, the mice will play,' Brian the Cabbie added, knowing full well Shirley was visiting her sister down in Kent and wasn't due back until tomorrow.

Johnny stood up. 'Nope. I've already had two pints over my usual quota. Not like the old days where the drink-driving laws were relaxed. Pulling you up left, right and centre these days,' Johnny insisted, not realizing that if he did get a tug he'd be way over the limit with the seven pints he'd had already.

Johnny was old school. Would never dream of booking a cab to and from his weekly session in the Rainham Working Men's Club. Real men could handle themselves after a few bevvies.

Starting his ignition, Johnny flicked through the CDs. He decided on a bit of Patsy Cline. His Carol had loved Patsy and even though he was very happy with Shirley now, he'd never forgotten his wonderful wife. She'd been the making of him and would always have a special place in his heart.

Having no idea that two men were waiting to shoot him near his home in North Ockendon, Johnny swung his Jaguar out of the car park and jovially sang along to 'Crazy'.

'I think we should go. He's obviously gone somewhere else,' Jason said. The weather was dismal and the fact things hadn't gone exactly to plan told Jason it wasn't meant to be.

'Nah. Let's give it another hour. Shirley's car's not on the drive, so I reckon he's stayed out a bit later because she's away or something.'

Jason fell silent again. He wasn't the type to take another man's life, but he was bloody desperate.

Thinking of Charlotte, he sighed deeply. She'd been on his case big time lately, but he couldn't leave Melissa at present. Aside from the fact he was in no position financially to make the break, she hadn't coped at all well with Bobby's death and, for all her faults, Jason felt something for her. He'd even ended his affair during Melissa's pregnancy, had done the right thing, and for a while they'd been happy.

The move to Repton Park had been costly. Melissa had been four months gone when she'd insisted their house wasn't going to be big enough for a baby as well and they needed a new one. Then there were the private school fees. Jason had stuck firm on that one for a while, but as per usual Melissa had got her own way in the end. Donte had been the first to go to one. Melissa had actually taken him out of his primary school and done the deed without a word to Jason. Not wanting his own daughter to miss out, he had waited until Shay was ready to move to secondary school before taking her to view one. Shay had liked the look of it, so now he was paying well over thirty grand a year in school fees.

'Jase, this is him, I think,' Craig hissed.

Jason clutched his helmet – the one protecting his head; he doubted he could find the other one right now, it was so shrunken with fright. He suddenly felt ill and was trembling all over.

'You ready?' Craig asked. Johnny had a big house in the lanes out in Ockendon and the spot where they were lying in ambush was hidden and roughly half a mile from his gaff. The plan was to follow him, then strike as he leaned out of the window to swipe his key against the electric gates.

Singing away with Patsy to 'Three Cigarettes in an Ashtray', Johnny didn't notice the motorbike behind him. He was thinking about Shirley. Her sister was recovering from an operation, which was why Shirley had gone to stay with her for the weekend. They'd moved into their current abode six months after Carol died and this was the longest they'd spent apart. Johnny couldn't wait for her to return tomorrow. He'd really missed her.

When the bike screeched to a sickening halt next to him, Johnny's initial reaction was to shut his window and lock the doors.

Jason felt the bile rise in his throat as he raised the gun.

'Go. Now!' Craig bellowed.

Spotting the gun, Johnny's eyes bulged with terror. He ducked down, instinct telling him to cover his head with his hands. Shirley flashed through his mind. He couldn't die, not like this, she'd be devastated.

Jason couldn't move, was like a frozen statue.

Absolutely livid, Craig snatched the shooter out of his pal's hand.

'Noooo,' Jason yelled, trying to knock Craig's hand away from its target.

As the sound of gunshot filled the air, the last thing Jason saw as the motorbike toppled over was blood spattering against Johnny's window.

'I hate seeing you like this, Char. You deserve better. If men are going to leave their wives for their mistress, they usually do it within the first six months of the affair. I read that in an article in *Cosmopolitan* recently.'

Charlotte Rivers took a gulp of her piña colada. Jilly

Barker was her best friend, one of the only people she could really trust. 'I know he loves me. If I thought otherwise, I wouldn't be with him. There is something he is not letting me know though, and I'm determined to find out what it bloody well is.'

'Does Melissa use a gym? Only that's how I found out the low-down on Richie. I took out a membership where his ex trained. Asked a few questions.'

'I do know what gym Melissa uses, actually. Jason let it slip once. Oh my God! That's a great idea.'

Ordering his young pregnant Thai wife to cook him something to eat, Craig Thurston marched Jason out the back and into the garage. He locked the door.

'I know I fucked up and I'm sorry, Craig, all right.'

'All right? All fucking right!' Craig shrieked, slamming Jason against the brick wall. He paced the garage with his head in his hands. 'I got a wife and my first kid on the way. A favour, you asked me for, a fucking favour. Then you freeze like a cunt before knocking the bike over.'

'It was an accident. I'm sorry.'

'Let's just hope he's dead, you numpty. Otherwise we might both be hauled in for questioning. What the hell was you thinking, eh?'

Jason lowered his head. He felt stupid, weak and bad for letting Craig down. 'I dunno, mate. I suppose I'm not cut out to kill. I'll make it up to you though, I promise.'

'Damn right you will.'

Melissa slurped the last of her wine, lay back on her pillow and closed her eyes. Alcohol eased the pain, temporarily at least.

Bobby had been such a wanted and incredibly beautiful

baby. Blond hair, blue eyes, perfect features, just like his daddy.

Nobody could tell Melissa what had gone wrong. Apart from suffering severe sickness bouts, she'd sailed through her pregnancy. It had honestly been the happiest time of her life. She could remember the weekend clearly. She and Jason had painted the nursery. They'd listened to soul music while working, planning their son's future throughout.

'Problems with the placenta are thought to be the most common cause of stillborn babies,' one doctor told Melissa.

'Sometimes a genetic or chromosomal defect is the reason a baby does not survive,' said the midwife.

But nobody could put their finger on the reason. Bobby weighed eight pounds two ounces at birth, so he'd obviously been feeding from her useless body at some point. Melissa could just not get her head around losing him. She was due to be admitted six days later to be induced. Why was life so cruel and unfair?

Tears rolling down her cheeks, she thought back to that fateful day. She'd felt a bit strange the evening before but put it down to the curry she'd eaten. On the Sunday morning, Jason had gone off early to play golf and she'd had a lie in. When she woke up just before midday, she knew instantly something was wrong. Bobby had been a little wriggler and kicker throughout the latter months of her pregnancy and that awful day he wasn't moving at all.

Melissa got up and wandered into Bobby's nursery. They'd had everything in place for his homecoming. Even his little wardrobe and chest of drawers were full of babygros and clothes for when he got a bit older.

Staring at Bobby's photo, Melissa pressed the button on his musical mobile.

'Hush, little baby, don't say a word, Papa's gonna buy you a mocking bird. And if that mocking bird won't sing, Papa's gonna buy you a diamond ring . . .'

Jason stopped at the Crown and Crooked Billet on the way home, on Craig's advice. 'Pick up your motor and make sure you get flashed by a fucking speed camera as close to your nan's house as humanly possible. Then go in your local, laugh, bastard-well joke and act normal,' were Craig's exact words.

Peggy, as per usual, was Jason's alibi. He hadn't gone into detail about what he was up to today – he never did. His nan was the one person he knew he could rely on if anything came on top, and if need be, Irish Ted would back up his story too.

The Crown and Crooked Billet wasn't exactly Jason's local, but since Bobby had died he did pop in there from time to time. Anything was better than being indoors with Melissa getting bladdered and singing nursery rhymes like a nutter.

Feeling less like socializing than he could remember in a long time, Jason pushed open the door of the pub. He spotted Glyn Hopkin. Unlike himself, Glyn was the car dealer of all car dealers. Jason bowled over to him and slapped him on the back. 'All right, Glyn? How's it going, mate?'

Within the hour, Jason pulled up outside the house. He wasn't the biggest fan of Repton Park. A lot of the people who lived there were too up themselves for his liking. His neighbours were all right. A Spurs footballer lived one side, an *EastEnders* soap star the other. They were both fairly down-to-earth, unlike most of the locals.

With a heavy heart, Jason turned his ignition off. Had Melissa heard the news yet, he wondered. She'd told him loads of times she wished her father was dead. It was because he knew how much Melissa hated Johnny that Jason had gone ahead with this stupid idea. Melissa wouldn't grieve, she'd be relieved. And then there'd be the inheritance to look forward to.

About a month after that embarrassing Christmas Day in the Bull in Brentwood, when they'd bumped into Shirley and Johnny and it had all kicked off, Melissa had received a lengthy heartfelt letter from her father. Johnny had told Mel how much he loved and missed her, and how it had broken his heart to see his grandchildren again, knowing he could never be part of their lives. The interesting paragraph for Jason though was the one in which Johnny told her that he'd made a will, and even if she never spoke to him again, 50 per cent of everything he owned would be hers. He'd insisted that's what Carol would have wanted.

Spotting his father's Mercedes, Donte bolted out of the house. 'All right, Dad. Where you been? I've been calling you.'

Jason got out the car and ruffled Donte's short dark hair. He'd left his phone at his nan's this morning, for obvious reasons.

'Sorry, boy. I was over at your nan's, then I popped to the pub. The battery's dead. I forgot to charge it up last night. You OK? Where's Mum?'

'I'm OK, but I'm bored. Shay's gone out with her friend and I wanted to go round Calvin's, but Mum's crying and drunk again, so I thought I'd better stay indoors. Do you think she will get better soon?'

Donte was nine now, a handsome boy with big sad eyes and a beautiful smile. He would certainly break some hearts one day, but it was Jason's he was currently breaking. If his grandfather was dead, the boy would be terribly upset, and he had enough on his plate at the moment as it was. 'Your mum will get better one day. Let's go indoors and get on that PlayStation, eh? What game d'ya fancy?'

'Extermination!'

Later that evening, after he'd put the kids to bed, Jason poured himself a much-needed brandy and sat at the kitchen table. There had been no phone call regarding Johnny and Jason wondered whether he had been found yet. His driveway was surrounded by trees and big bushes, but his car would be spotted tomorrow in daylight.

Jason put his head in his hands. He wanted to call Craig, but daren't. 'Best you and I steer clear of one another until this blows over. Don't be ringing me either, unless it's urgent.'

Jason thought of Johnny. He had to be worth two million at the very least. It wouldn't surprise Jason if it were closer to four, once all his assets were thrown into the equation. He still owned his builders' merchants, though he didn't run it any more. And he owned loads of properties, mainly flats, that he rented out. If Jason was to go through with his plan and leave Melissa, then he wanted her to be financially secure. They could have a clean break then. He wouldn't fight her for any of her father's inheritance, providing she supported herself in future and gave him half of what their home was worth. After the money he'd spent on her over the years, he couldn't be fairer than that. Her wants and whims were enough to drive most men insane.

Having put on a CD of his absolute idol, Stevie Wonder, Jason did not hear Melissa pad down the stairs in her slippers. She made him jump.

'What's up? What time did you get in?' Mel asked.

'Hours ago.'

'Where you been, golf?'

'No. I told you yesterday, my nan hasn't been well. I was visiting her and cooking her dinner today. I popped in the Billet on the way home, and I've been on the PlayStation with Donte. He was bored and alone. Shay had gone out with her mate and I doubt you even knew. What type of a mother are you? Only, this can't continue. It'll soon be eighteen months since Bobby died. Time you snapped out of the drinking and mourning. You got two other children who rely on you, need you. Bobby is dead, Mel. No amount of grieving is going to bring him back. End of.'

'End of what?' Melissa shrieked. 'You are so callous, Jason. Heartless, in fact.'

Unable to stop himself, Jason grabbed Melissa and marched her over to the mirror in their bathroom. 'Take a look at yourself, Mel. What happened to that attractive woman that used to take pride in herself? You're a mess. Look at the state of your hair and nails. You barely go out the door any more and I doubt you've even showered today – look, you're still wearing the same pyjamas you had on last night. I can't take much more of this. Our children, the two living ones, deserve better.'

When his wife stifled a sob and bolted back up the stairs, Jason poured himself another brandy.

What he had done today was actually for Melissa, little did she know it.

Jason put his head in his hands and thought of Charlotte. He wanted to be with her. But he couldn't leave Melissa in the state she was in. They'd been through a lot together and he wasn't that much of a bastard. Or was he?

CHAPTER TWENTY

The following morning the phone call Jason had dreaded finally arrived. He rarely slept in Melissa's bed any more, had all but moved into the spare room, and he snatched at the receiver before his wife could. 'Hello.'

'Is Melissa there please?'

'Who is it?' Jason asked, knowing full well it was Shirley Stone.

'It's Shirley. Melissa's dad's partner.'

'Oh, hi, Shirley. This is Jason. I think Melissa's still asleep. Can I take a message?'

When the woman dissolved into tears, Jason felt his heart pounding against his chest. Trying to keep his voice normal wasn't easy. 'Has something happened, Shirley?'

'Yes,' Shirley sobbed. 'It's Johnny. Someone shot him.'

'Oh Jesus, no! Where? When? Is he OK?'

'It happened yesterday, outside our house. I was in Kent, visiting my sister. Who would do such a thing, Jason?'

Jason's voice quivered. 'But he's alive, right?'

'Yes. But only just.'

*

'Hello,' Charlotte Rivers smiled at the receptionist. 'I wonder if you can help me. I'm new to the area and want to join a gym. I was wondering if I could take out a monthly pass? To sample this one, so to speak. Obviously, all being well, I will then sign up for a year.'

The receptionist smiled back. 'Of course. What's your name, love? Have you got any ID with you?'

Thrusting her friend's borrowed driving licence towards the lady, Charlotte replied, 'My name's Jilly. Jilly Barker.'

Melissa sat bolt upright in bed. 'Shot! What do you mean, shot?'

'I mean shot, love, with a gun. He's OK though. Shirley was upset, understandably. Your dad has been operated on and the doctors are hopeful he'll be fine.'

'Fuck Shirley,' Melissa hissed. 'I bet this has something to do with her. I mean, why would anybody want to shoot my dad?'

Jason's emotions were all over the place. Part of him was relieved Johnny had survived, the other half of him wasn't. He and Craig had been clad from head to foot in leathers with crash helmets on, but say Johnny had somehow recognized them or overheard their voices? There'd been a few words shouted when the bike had taken a tumble.

'Say something then,' Melissa ordered. 'What else did that slag have to say?'

'That your dad's in Oldchurch and he'd want you to visit him. He lost a lot of blood and it was touch and go for a while, she reckons.'

Melissa's lip curled into a snarl. 'Over my dead body! What, with her there? I wonder if my mum is looking down. What goes around comes around.'

Outside the bedroom door, there were two very interested listeners.

'We should visit him,' Donte whispered in Shay's ear.

Shay grinned. 'OK.'

Charlotte Rivers was disappointed. There weren't many in the step class and the few women she'd tried to strike up a conversation with weren't exactly friendly. 'Do you fancy a coffee?' she asked a bimbo with fake hair and breasts.

'No. Got to pick Bill and Ben up from the crèche,' the woman giggled.

Charlotte smiled politely. She might be a lap-dancer, but had class and a brain. 'OK. Maybe another time then.'

As Charlotte went off to freshen up, the mousy girl who'd trained alone in the corner tapped her on the shoulder. 'Hi. I'm Sue. I'll have a coffee with you, if you like?'

'Who was that? Not Shirley again, was it?' Melissa asked Jason.

'No. Babs. My mum's been playing up again. She's told Babs if I don't get her her own place, she's going to kill herself.'

'You're not going to help her, are you?'

'Nope. She's made her own bed, let her lie in it,' Jason snapped. He hadn't seen his mother since visiting her in Oldchurch Hospital and had no wish to ever lay eyes on her again. According to Babs, she lived in a decent enough council-run home that had been specially adapted to cope with people who needed round-the-clock assistance. There were staff on duty twenty-four hours a day, and his mother had her own room. But she hated it there. Probably because she couldn't pour alcohol down her fat neck, morning, noon and night, was Jason's guess.

'I thought about what you said yesterday and you're right. I have let myself go recently and I'm going to do something about it.'

Jason smiled. 'Good.'

Charlotte Rivers had struck gold. Sue Cable was the ultimate gossip and the ideal person to glean information from. Charlotte already knew what Melissa looked like as she'd sneaked a look in Jason's wallet while he was taking a bath recently. There had been a photo of Mel and the kids inside, and she'd also made a note of the address on his driving licence.

'Where have you moved to round here? I have a flat near the Crown and Crooked Billet,' Sue informed her.

'I actually live in Wanstead, but my friend trains here and she recommended this gym to me.'

'Who's your friend? I'm down here most days so I'm bound to know her.'

'Melissa.'

'Melissa Carrington?'

Charlotte's heart beat wildly. 'No. Rampling.'

'Oh, I see. She doesn't come down here any more, does she?'

'To be honest, I haven't seen Melissa in ages. But the last time I bumped into her, I mentioned I was moving to Wanstead and she recommended this gym.'

'Nobody's seen her. Not since she lost Bobby. I see her husband driving about in his big Mercedes from time to time. Rumour has it, he's a villain. The girls down here reckon that, anyway. Nobody seems to know what he does for a living and Melissa was always vague. Do you know what he does?'

'Yes. Jason deals in cars. Who is Bobby? Their dog?'

'No. Their baby.'

Coffee shot out of Charlotte's mouth and landed on Sue's Pineapple sweatshirt. 'Baby! What baby?'

'They had a baby and he was stillborn. They called him Bobby. A few of the girls from here went to his funeral, but I didn't get asked. I'm not really one of their gang.'

Feeling as though she was about to have a heart attack, Charlotte's face turned a deathly white. She put the cup down, her hands trembling.

'Are you OK?' Sue asked.

'No. Not really. When did all this happen? When was Bobby born?'

'Erm, let me think. It was last year in the summer. I'm sure it was August, but it might have been July.'

Feeling sick as a dog, Charlotte snatched her keys off the table. 'I gotta go.'

'When will you be down here again?' Sue shouted out.

Charlotte did not reply.

Switching on his other phone, the one Melissa thought he solely used for work, Jason was thoroughly disappointed when he read Charlotte's text.

> Can't do tonight. My nan's not well. Going up hospital.
>
> Speak soon,
>
> Cx

'Bollocks,' Jason mumbled, switching the phone off and chucking it across the bed. He'd not seen Charlotte for almost a week now, was missing her terribly. He was also concerned she'd had enough of the situation, as she'd been acting odd lately. She still worked at Stringfellows and his biggest fear was that she'd meet another bloke there and dump him. He wouldn't blame her if she did. She'd waited long enough for him to leave Mel, but there never seemed to be a right time to do so.

'Where you going? I'm cooking shepherd's pie, your favourite,' Melissa informed Jason as he walked into the kitchen with his jacket on. She could sense he was slipping away from her recently and would hate to push him into another woman's arms.

'Popping up the golf club for a couple of hours. I'll have my dinner when I get back. Do you want me to bring anything home? I'll stop and pick up some wine.'

Determined to show she was making an effort, Melissa smiled falsely. 'I don't want any wine. I rang the doctor's earlier and booked an emergency appointment for tomorrow morning. I'm going to ask for anti-depressants, Jase, and have some counselling. It's time to sort myself out once and for all.' Jason's blunt words had been the wake-up call Melissa had needed yesterday when he'd forced her to look at the state of herself in the mirror.

Jason walked towards his wife and kissed her on the cheek, the way he would his nan. He would always have feelings for her, but not like he had for Darlene, or Charlotte. They were his only true loves. 'Good girl. I won't be long.'

Melissa waited until Jason's car pulled away, then darted up the stairs. The kids would be home from school in an hour or so and she needed to spend some time with Bobby. She would hate her son to think she'd forgotten all about him.

To say Charlotte Rivers was fuming was an understatement. She'd never been more livid in her life. 'I must have mug stamped on my head, me. How could I have been so fucking stupid? I hate him, Jilly. No way is he getting away with this. Let's go round his house, now! Poor Melissa needs to know what a lying, cheating, no-good arsehole she married.'

Jason had once bought her a stunning ornament that spelled out the word 'LOVE'. It occupied pride of place on the floor in Charlotte's lounge. She picked it up, managed to hurl it a few feet. It smashed in half. 'Bastard,' she shrieked, before bursting into tears.

Jilly leapt up and held her sobbing friend in her arms. She had tried to warn Charlotte that Jason was playing her, but love is blind, as the old saying goes. 'He's not worth smashing your lovely home up for, Char. Tell you what, I'll make you a black coffee, sober you up a bit. Come on, let's go in the kitchen,' Jilly said softly.

'I don't want a coffee. I want to talk to his wife. And I cannot wait to see his smarmy face when he realizes it's me at the front door. How could he do this to me? Well, more fool me for taking him back, twice. I am such an idiot. I thought it odd when he ended it last year and was determined never to take him back again. It's as though he has some hold over me – and I'm not exactly thick or ugly, am I?'

'No, Char. You are brainy and beautiful. You deserve so much better. But let's not be rash about confronting him. Have a think overnight about what you want to do. If you still want to pay his wife a visit tomorrow, I'll come with you, drive you there. You don't want to turn up drunk. You'll look like a fool.'

'How could I make myself look any more of a fool than I already have? And I am a fool. He told me he never slept with Melissa, and I actually believed him. I don't just hate him; I hate my bloody self for being so stupid.'

Jilly stroked her friend's hair. 'You're not stupid, my love. You just made the mistake of falling in love with a man who happens to be a very good liar.'

'All right, mate?' Jason said, slapping Simon Champion on the back. In addition to being his accountant, Simon had become a very good friend.

'The wanderer returns. Where you been?' Simon grinned.

Craig had ordered him to show his face in places he usually would and act normal. 'Been busy,' he said, leading Simon away from the men he was drinking with.

'What's up?' Simon asked.

'The usual. Mel's still not good.' Jason had first introduced Simon to Melissa when she was pregnant and they'd got on well. That was why he'd never told Si about Charlotte. His friend was old school in a lot of ways and Jason doubted he would approve of his cheating.

'You seen Craig?' Simon enquired.

'No, mate. Not recently,' Jason lied.

'Rumour has it, he's been arrested.'

Jason felt his stomach lurch. As far as Simon knew, he and Craig were just pals. He knew nothing about any work they'd done together. 'Shit! Really? What the hell for?'

Simon raised his eyebrows. He knew Jason must know more about what Craig got up to than anybody. That's why he'd issued a gentle warning the last time they'd taken a trip to Jersey together. 'Rumour has it Craig's involved in some heavy shit now, Jase. Just watch your back, eh,' he'd told his pal.

'Ringing motors?' Jason bluffed. Craig still owned his car lot in Basildon.

Admiring Jason's loyalty, Simon shrugged. 'Your guess is as good as mine, but if the gossip is true, my money would be on drugs. The Old Bill turned up at his house this morning by all accounts, raided the gaff.'

Feeling his bowels loosening, Jason excused himself to go to the toilet. This was too much of a coincidence. No way had Craig been arrested for drugs; he was too far up the chain to be caught. He must've been hauled in for shooting Johnny.

'You all right, mate?' Danny Jackson asked, shaking his penis at the urinal.

Jason didn't reply as he slammed the door of a cubicle. He was shitting himself, literally.

CHAPTER TWENTY-ONE

Dean Swan was Craig Thurston's new right-hand man and when he knocked on Jason's door minutes after Melissa left for her doctor's appointment, Jason felt his gut churn.

'Got a message from the boss. He wants to see you ASAP. He said to meet him at the Camelot – in the car park opposite.'

Relieved that Craig was no longer in police custody, but worried that Deano might have been followed, Jason glanced up and down the street. He'd known of Deano for years. He was a Rainham lad and even though he was Craig's new sidekick, Jason guessed Craig would not have spilled the beans to him. Deano was no main player.

'Don't worry. The boss told me to make sure I wasn't being followed and not to knock while your wife was at home. I've been parked at the end of the road for the past hour. He never said what it was about. Just said he needed to talk to you.'

Heart pumping rapidly, Jason glanced at his watch. 'OK. Tell him I'll be there in half an hour.'

Deano grinned. 'Will do.'

*

'How does this outfit look? Not OTT, is it?' Charlotte asked Jilly.

'You look fine. Casual, but glam. You always look lovely, whatever you wear.'

Charlotte studied herself in the mirror. Black short leather jacket, white T-shirt, faded jeans and high-heeled black knee-length boots. Choosing an outfit to meet your lover's wife for the first time wasn't easy.

'What time do you want to leave?'

'Soon. I'm hoping to catch Mel home alone. Shay and Donte should be at school if we leave soon, and I doubt that bastard hangs around indoors in the daytime. He might even have other women on the go, for all I know.'

'I very much doubt that, Char,' Jilly said honestly.

'If he's there, he'll try and shut me up and talk his way out of it. Can't do that if he isn't there, can he? Melissa needs to know the truth. I bet she doesn't have a clue what he's really like. All those weekends he told her he was away playing golf, when really he was with me.'

'Please remember it's not his wife's fault. He's the liar, not her. Don't be too harsh with her, will you? She has lost a baby.'

'You know I'm not a nasty person. Unfortunately, there is no easy way to break the news to her, but I'll break it as gently as I can. With a bit of luck she'll agree we've both been duped. It all makes sense now, you know. May, last year, he dumped me for no reason. Then he came back with his tail between his legs end of September, begging for another chance. Those months I didn't see him coincided with the latter part of Melissa's pregnancy and when they lost the baby. I bet if Bobby had lived I would never have seen him again. He'd have been too busy playing happy families to give me a second thought, the selfish no-good pig. Come on, let's go.'

Satisfied that nobody had followed him, Jason swung into the car park opposite the Camelot pub. It was on the verge of Hainault Forest and mainly used by dog walkers.

Craig was parked up in a car Jason did not recognize, a small Golf GTI. He usually drove a big BMW and Jason guessed he'd swapped vehicles to throw off anybody trying to follow him.

'You all right, mate?' Jason asked, dreading the answer.

'No, I ain't. Walk,' Craig barked, strutting into the undergrowth.

Jason felt his nerves jangling as they walked deep into the forest in silence. 'Where we going?' he asked.

Craig glanced around to be sure the coast was clear, then grabbed Jason by the neck and slammed his body hard into a thick tree trunk.

Jason's eyes bulged with fear. He had never been scared of Craig in the past, even though he knew many who were. But deep in the forest, with Craig's gold tooth glinting through a crack of sunlight shining in between the trees, Jason was scared all right.

'You fucking idiot,' Craig bellowed, punching Jason hard in the stomach. 'Do you know what you've just put me through? You stupid fucking coward.'

Deciding to play dumb, Jason clutched his stomach and crouched on his haunches to get his breath back. 'Jesus, mate. That bloody hurt. Whatever's happened?'

'Hurt! You're lucky I ain't brought a gun with me and blown your thick brains out. I'm fuming. Fucking livid.'

'Why?'

'Because I've just spent twenty-four hours down the cop

shop on suspicion of shooting Johnny fucking Brooks. The cunt's still alive, thanks to you ballsing things up.'

'I knew he was alive. Shirley rung the house. Why did they arrest you? No way could he have recognized you in those leathers and crash helmet.'

'Well, he obviously fucking did, because someone's put my name forward. I never told a soul about what we planned to do, did you?'

'No. Course not.'

'I'm six foot three, Jase. Muscular, thickset. He must've recognized me when the bike toppled over, or heard my voice when I shouted at you. A favour, you asked for, a fucking favour, and this is the shit you land me in. Good job I got rid of the shooter. Natchaya was terrified when they burst in and raided the joint. She's five months pregnant, for Christ's sake.'

Jason felt dreadful. 'I'm so sorry, Craig. I truly am. So what happened down at the station? Did they mention me?'

'No. They mentioned Deano. As luck would have it, he was at a christening all day on Sunday, so that could be proved.'

'Deano said he didn't know why you wanted to see me when he knocked. Did they arrest him as well then?'

'Deano knows jack-shit. They just went round his house and said they were investigating an incident that happened on Sunday and could he confirm his whereabouts that afternoon. He could, so I suppose they checked out his story.'

'And you?'

'Darlene was my alibi. Good job she's clued up – unlike you, ya tosser. Thank Christ I had the brains to leave me car outside her gaff an' all. My old next-door neighbour backed up the story, saying I'd been there all afternoon.'

'So they just let you go?'

'After twenty-four long fucking hours, yes, Jason. The last thing I need with what I'm involved in is the Old Bill sniffing around. I still can't believe what you did. It baffles me.'

Feeling like a complete and utter dickhead, Jason stared at his shoes. 'I know. I honestly can't apologize enough, mate. Anything I can do to make it up to you, just say the word.'

'Actually, there is something . . .'

'Jason's car's not there. That has to be Melissa's, surely?' Charlotte said to Jilly. She could feel the adrenaline kicking in now.

The car in question was a white Mercedes.

'He never even told me he moved here you know. As far as I was aware, he still lived at Chigwell Row. I only found out when I looked on his driving licence. I hate him, Jilly. He is a complete fraud.'

'Shall we get this over with?' Jilly asked.

Charlotte touched her lipstick up. 'Just give me five minutes. I want to think about what I'm going to say first.'

It had been a big step for Melissa to go to the doctor and admit she wasn't coping with life. She'd broken down in the surgery when Dr Parrish was kind to her, but now she was home she felt better for going.

Prozac, she'd been prescribed. She'd been told it might take a while for her medication to work and that counselling would also benefit her immensely.

Melissa stared at Eleanor Collins-Hythe's business card. She hadn't really kept in touch with the woman after she'd gone out for lunch with her that time. But she'd bumped into her a couple of times since moving to Repton Park, which had resulted in them having a coffee together once.

When Bobby had died, Eleanor had obviously heard through the grapevine and had called Melissa, then attended her son's funeral. At the time, Melissa had told Tracey that Eleanor only turned up to be bloody nosy, but in fairness, she doubted that now.

Melissa sighed. She didn't fancy seeing a male counsellor. They wouldn't understand what she had been through. Even Jason didn't. Neither did she really want to pour her guts out to a complete stranger.

About to ring Eleanor to arrange an emergency appointment, Melissa was disturbed by the doorbell. Two women were standing outside. One attractive, the other absolutely stunning. 'Hello. Can I help you?'

It was the stunning one who replied. 'Hello, Melissa. I think we need to talk. My name is Charlotte and I am your husband's mistress. Or ex-mistress, I should say.'

Melissa's complexion turned a chalky white colour. 'Is this some kind of joke?'

'I'm afraid not,' Charlotte replied sadly. 'It seems Jason has been stringing us both along for some time now.'

Melissa was dumbfounded. She couldn't speak, neither could she move. 'How long?' she managed to mutter.

'How long have I been seeing Jason?'

Melissa nodded.

'It's a long story. I first dated Jason before you met him, but he dumped me when he met you.'

'Recently?' Melissa croaked.

'It's been off and on for years. He told me he was only with you because of the kids. He swore he didn't love you and told me you never slept together. I only found out about Bobby yesterday. I'm so sorry, Melissa, I truly am. If I had thought you were still a couple, I would never have entertained him.'

'It might be easier if we speak inside,' Jilly suggested.

'No. I don't want you in my home,' Melissa hissed. She turned to Charlotte again. 'When? When did you see him?'

'All those weekends he said he was playing golf, he was actually with me. He promised me he would leave you this June. But then he turned up at mine and said he couldn't leave yet. He told me you'd had a nervous breakdown.'

Melissa clung on to the door frame for support. She could not quite believe her ears. How dare Jason tell his bit of fluff details of their home life? And she hadn't had a nervous breakdown, the lying arsehole, she'd been grieving the loss of their son. 'I think you should go now,' Melissa said, stony-faced.

'I'm very sorry for turning up like this. I just thought you deserved to know the truth. I can also assure you that if you decide to stay with Jason, I will not interfere in your marriage any more. It's over between us for good.'

Melissa slammed the front door, sank to the floor, put her head in her hands and sobbed her heart out.

Jason Rampling was in a bit of a pickle. Thanks to his weakness at not being able to pull that trigger, he was now unable to say no to Craig's request.

'OK. I'll talk to Paul and sort it,' he promised.

'He is trustworthy, this Paul, isn't he? Obviously, don't tell him what the properties are for. But make sure he doesn't go blabbing.'

'He won't. He's sound,' Jason insisted. His pal owned

an estate agency in Dagenham and Craig wanted him to rent a property where a major cocaine haul would be taken to, cut up, then distributed from.

Craig pushed an envelope towards Jason. They were sitting in his car now, chatting amicably. 'False documentation in there. I don't want you renting the slaughter under your name, just in case it comes on top.'

'Slaughter?'

'Just a figure of speech in my game. Look, I would usually pay you a fair whack for this. But seeing as you owe me twenty grand, you'll be helping to clear your debt. Give your mate a good drink, a few grand or something, keep him sweet. I also want you to get hold of six unregistered mobile phones for me.'

'And how am I meant to do that?'

'Use your fucking brain. Your brothers are thieves, ask them to chore some.' Craig fixed him with a penetrating look. 'You don't just owe me twenty grand, remember, Jase. You owe me big time.'

'Mum, stop it. Why are you ripping up all of Dad's clothes? Please stop. You're drunk,' Donte cried.

'He's not your father, Donte. He's a no-good, womanizing, lying shitbag,' Melissa screamed as she hacked at the sleeve of Jason's favourite leather jacket with a large pair of scissors.

Having just arrived home from school, Shay ran up the stairs to find out what all the shouting was about. She knew Melissa wasn't the full shilling these days, but as she stared at all her dad's lovely clothes cut up in a pile in the middle of the bedroom, even she was shocked. 'Oh my God! My dad is going to kill you. You've completely lost the plot.'

'Go and pack your stuff, Shay. You're leaving with your father,' Melissa spat.

'Leaving! Why? What have I done? Or Dad?' Shay argued.

Chucking the scissors across the room, Melissa put her hands over her face and cried. 'Your dad has cheated on me for years with a tart called Charlotte. Even when I was pregnant. She turned up here today and told me everything.'

Donte burst into tears. Though the man he called 'Dad' wasn't his real father, he'd always looked up to him as such. 'No. It can't be true, Mum,' he sobbed.

'I'm afraid it is, Donte. Now go and get me some dustbin liners. He can take his clothes with him – what's left of 'em, anyway.'

Aware that Melissa had been drinking, Shay put her hands on her hips. 'You're mad. I don't know how my dad puts up with you.'

Melissa glared at the child. 'And you, go pack your stuff and wait for your bastard of a father outside my house. Now!'

Bursting into tears, Shay ran from the room.

With a heavy heart, Jason drove towards home. Charlotte still had her phone switched off and he was so hoping to see her tonight. He needed a release from the shit day he'd had and being with her always cheered him up no end.

As he pulled up outside his house, Jason blinked in astonishment. Shay was sitting outside crying, surrounded by neighbours and bin bags. He slammed the handbrake on and leapt out the car. Had the doctor advised Melissa to chuck Bobby's stuff away? But why now? The dustmen didn't come until Thursday.

'Dad,' Shay cried, running towards him and hugging him tight.

'Whatever's wrong, sweetheart?'

At that precise moment, an object flew out of the upstairs window and narrowly missed Jason's head. He looked down. It was his and Melissa's framed wedding photo. He looked up. 'What the hell is going on?' By now they were surrounded by a crowd, including the *EastEnders* actress who lived next door.

'Your tart's been round here, Jason,' Melissa yelled. 'You know the one: Charlotte – unless you've got more, you lying, despicable cunt. Get out of my life, for good. You're dead to me now, just like my father.'

Feeling totally humiliated in front of the neighbours and at the same time realizing Melissa was inebriated, Jason started picking up the dustbin liners. 'Come on, Shay. Melissa's obviously having a bad day.'

'No point taking your clothes with you, Dad. She cut them all up,' Shay said loudly.

Determined to save face, Jason grinned at his neighbours. 'Shit happens, eh? Show's over now, guys.'

'Where we going to live, Dad?' Shay asked tearfully.

Jason led his daughter away from the onlookers. 'Just shut up and get in the bastard car.'

Peggy Rampling huffed and puffed as she climbed the stepladder. Irish Ted had invited his family over to England for Christmas and she had offered to cook them Christmas dinner. She'd never met them, so seeing as the weather was dry and bright this morning, she'd decided to take the net curtains down, wash them and hang them on the line. They were spotless now, but she was struggling to hang them back up. So it came as a relief to see her grandson pull up outside. Until she spotted he had Shay with him, that was.

'You all right, boy?'

'No. I'm not.'

'Whassa matter?'

'Go upstairs for a minute, Shay, while I talk to your nan,' Jason ordered.

'No,' Shay spat.

'Don't mess me about, girl. I'm not in the mood,' Jason retaliated.

'She ain't staying here,' Peggy said bluntly.

'Don't want to stay here. I hate it here and I hate you,' Shay bellowed, before running up the stairs in tears.

'Charming!' Peggy retorted.

'She's just upset, Nan. Melissa's thrown us both out. She found out about Charlotte.'

'Oh dear. How?'

'Charlotte went round the house earlier. Listen, I need to go and see Charlotte, sort this mess out. Can you look after Shay for me until I get back?'

'No. I'm going bingo.'

'Please, Nan. We need somewhere to kip tonight. Can we stay here?'

'You can. Can't you ask someone else to look after her though? You know I can't stand kids around me.'

'It'll only be for one night. Please?'

Peggy screwed her nose up. 'All right. But put my nets up before you go off gallivanting.'

'Can't I do it when I get back?'

'No. I don't want that filthy old bastard across the road bogging in here. I swear he's a pervert. Do it now.'

*

'Are you OK, Mum?' Donte asked worriedly. He had seen his mother cry before, but never like this.

Melissa rolled over on her bed and hugged her son tightly to her chest. 'As long as I have you by my side, I will always be OK.'

Donte smiled and hugged his mum back. He was the man of the house now, needed to look after her.

'We'll be fine, you know. Us Brooks are made of strong stuff. I know you will miss your dad, but he is never coming back, son. You OK about that?'

Appalled by what Jason had done, Donte's lip curled. 'I hate him, Mum. I'm glad he isn't my real dad and if you ever take him back I will hate you too.'

Thrilled by her son's loyalty, Melissa kissed him on the forehead. 'Don't worry, I won't. Jason is history.'

CHAPTER TWENTY-TWO

Six Months Later

'We therefore commit the body of Deborah Jane Rampling to the ground. Earth to earth, ashes to ashes, dust to dust. Looking for the blessed hope and the glorious appearing of the great God in our Saviour Jesus Christ who will change the body of our humiliation and . . .'

Turning away from the vicar, Peggy Rampling poked her grandson in the arm. 'If Jesus is going to change her body of humiliation, he's got a job on his hands. Come on. Let's go. I've heard enough religious old bollocks for one day.'

Jason put an arm around his nan's shoulders. She was in her late sixties now and not as heartless as she liked to make out. He'd known she'd been crying this morning before he picked her up, could tell by her puffy red eyes. And he'd seen the tears roll down her face during the actual service, even though she'd fiercely wiped them away. 'It's nearly finished now,' he whispered.

'About bleedin' time. Not sure I fancy the wake. Might get you to drop me straight home.'

'Please come, even if you only stay for an hour. I won't be hanging about for long myself. I thought you said Irish Ted was meeting you there?'

'He is. Tight old bastard will go anywhere if the booze is free. That's probably why half these ponces turned up. She wasn't that popular, your mother.'

'Is that it? Can we go now?' asked Elton.

'No. We got to throw earth in the hole first,' Babs wept.

Jason put both arms around his sister and hugged her tightly. The poor cow hadn't stopped crying all day; she blamed herself for what had happened. Elton and Kyle had not shed a tear between them and instead of wearing the black suits Jason had shelled out for, had worn black hooded Adidas tracksuits. 'We don't like suits. If you don't let us wear our tracksuits, then we ain't coming,' Kyle had bluntly told him this morning.

'You going to throw some dirt, Nan?' Jason asked.

'No. I'll walk back to the car. My arthritis is playing up, so it'll take me ages anyway.'

Jason picked up a bit of dirt and chucked it on top of his mother's coffin. After months of threatening to kill herself, she'd finally done so. An empty container of high-strength co-codamol was found next to her body. Along with a paracetamol packet and a couple of extra-strong cider bottles.

One letter she'd left, addressed to him. It blamed him for her death and everything else that had been wrong in her life.

Jason took one last look at the coffin before leading Barbara away from the graveside. He wouldn't grieve. Far as he was concerned, his mother had been dead for many years.

*

The wake was held in Millhouse Social Club. It was situated along the busy A13, within spitting distance of the Mardyke Estate. It was also the only local drinking establishment that Debbie Rampling hadn't been barred from. Most of the mourners lived on the Mardyke and Jason had laid on a free bar and buffet for them.

Peggy nudged Irish Ted. 'Look at that bloke over there, the skinny one with the moustache. The greedy bastard's pissed already.'

'No, he isn't. That's Phil. He's got multiple sclerosis. I'm going over to say hello to him.'

Peggy turned to Jason. 'How much has it set you back, this funeral, boy? That didn't look a cheap coffin.'

'It wasn't,' Jason replied. He might not have liked his mother much, but neither was he going to give her a pauper's funeral. Being tight wasn't in his nature. 'Not sure. But with the wake on top, I reckon about five grand.'

'You must have more money than sense,' Peggy spat.

'I'm absolutely boracic, if you want the truth. I'm going to have a word with Melissa tonight. She called me yesterday. If our marriage is over, then we're going to have to sell the house. I can't afford to keep paying her mortgage and my rent. The lease is up on my flat next week and I've told the landlord I won't be renewing it.' Jason had taken out a six-month lease on a flat in Buckhurst Hill. Shay lived there with him.

'Well, you know my feelings on the subject of that wife of yours. The woman's a loony, cutting up all your lovely clothes like she did. You should demand to move back into the house. What's she ever put towards it? Wouldn't know what a job was if one fell out the sky and hit her on the bonce.'

'I'm gonna call her later. We've barely spoken since she booted me out.'

'What about the other one?'

'Who, Charlotte?'

'Yes.'

'Dead in the water,' Jason mumbled. He couldn't be bothered going into detail, but not only had he begged Charlotte for forgiveness at the time, he'd also gone up to Stringfellows a couple of months ago to beg her again. A colleague of hers had informed him that not only had Charlotte left the club, she'd left the country. Turned out she'd met some rich American and moved to the States to be with him.

Learning Charlotte was engaged was a kick in the teeth at the time, but Jason was over it now. At the end of the day, she was a lap-dancer and therefore not the ideal mother figure to help him raise his daughter.

'Why you so skint then? I thought your new business was doing well.'

'It is. But I have a lot to lay out for. The kids' school fees aren't cheap and the mortgage is an arm-and-a-leg job.'

It had been Terrence, Jason's old boss and best man, who had advised him to open a shop. Terrence was clearing storage units on a regular basis and would often unearth gems. Jason often joked he'd swapped porn for pawn, as that's what he now was: a pawnbroker. He bought and sold second-hand stuff too. Electronics, gold, antiques and even art. The shop was in Barking, which wasn't the most affluent of areas. But the more upmarket stuff he would advertise on the internet and people would travel from far and wide for it.

The shop had only been open four months, and was

ticking over more than nicely. Unfortunately, though, it wasn't yet turning over enough to pay for Melissa and Donte's opulent lifestyle. The house in Repton Park was mortgaged up the hilt and that was the biggest drain on his finances. The bills there were extortionate too.

'What about the money you got from flogging those two flats in Jersey?' Simon had advised Jason to invest in property a while back. But he'd since had to sell.

'That's tied up.'

'In what?'

Babs walking over saved Jason from answering. Nobody knew what he had used that money for, only him.

'Elton and Kyle have gone. They were bored.'

'Whatever,' Jason muttered. His brothers' bolshie attitude had been getting on his nerves lately.

'Is that all for you, that food?' Peggy asked Barbara.

'Yes, Nan. I'm starving.'

'Don't speak with your mouth full, you'll choke. Go and sit down and eat it properly with a knife and fork.'

'OK.'

When Babs waddled off, Peggy turned to Jason. 'Did you see what she had piled on that plate? It was that heaped up it was falling off the bastard edge!'

'She loves her grub, does Babs. Always has done.'

Peggy pursed her lips. 'Yes. It shows.'

Melissa Rampling studied her appearance in the full-length mirror and was none too impressed by the bloated reflection staring back at her. Unlike most women who had suffered the humiliation of being cheated on, she hadn't lost weight. She had turned to comfort eating, scoffing herself silly on chocolate and cakes in the hope it would make her feel better. Not forgetting the wine. She must have downed gallons of the stuff, trying to stave off the boredom of another lonely night. Alcohol and crap food had unfortunately become her rock, but Melissa was ready to end that particular relationship now. She needed to get her act together if she was going to take him back. Otherwise, he was bound to stray again. Six months was a long time to spend alone. It had given her food for thought, and she now knew what she wanted and needed. Another baby.

Donte poked his head around the bedroom door. 'Getting glammed up 'cause he's coming round, are you?' he asked accusingly.

'No. I am making an effort because I've let myself go recently. It's about time I did something about it.'

'You always look nice to me, Mum.'

Touched by the compliment even though she knew it was a blatant lie, Melissa gave her ten-year-old pride and joy a hug. The break-up had hit him as hard as anybody and she'd recently been called in to speak to his head at the posh private school he attended in Chigwell. They had concerns that he was falling behind.

'Are you looking forward to seeing Shay later?'

'Suppose so. I'm not looking forward to seeing him again though.'

Melissa stroked her son's face. 'Please, let's just have an argument-free day. Whatever you think of your dad, you have to remember he's still very generous to us. We wouldn't be living in this lovely house if it wasn't for him, neither would you be going to the best school in the area.'

'Don't call him that. How many times do I have to tell you, he isn't my dad any more? He's Jason to me now, OK?'

'I understand the way you feel, darling. But be civil. Not for his sake, for mine. It is my birthday, after all.'

'Happy birthday, mate,' Tracey Thompson grinned, thrusting a gift bag in Melissa's direction.

Melissa hugged her best mate. 'What you bought me? Not another vibrator, I hope,' Mel chuckled, remembering her Christmas gift.

'Nope. It's a sensible present, for once. I hope you like it. Got some gossip for you, so I brought this too,' Tracey said, waving a bottle of champagne in the air. 'I thought we'd have a little tipple, before I enlighten you on my latest disaster.'

Melissa led Tracey into the kitchen. Although she and Jason were currently not living together, they'd been happy until that fateful day. Tracey, on the other hand, had never been lucky in love. After a whirlwind romance, she'd married Kieron Jessop. Mel had never seen her pal so blissfully contented, but her happiness wasn't to last. A keen biker in his spare time, Kieron had been out on his Harley-Davidson when he was hit by a lorry travelling at speed. He'd died instantly. Tracey had been inconsolable. To Melissa, it had sounded like a gift from God when her friend broke the news that she was carrying Kieron's baby. Tracey didn't think so though. Unable to face the thought of bringing up a child alone, she'd opted for an abortion. Then she wiped Kieron completely from her memory, by changing her name back to Thompson.

'Get the glasses out then,' Tracey ordered, popping the cork.

'Just a small one for me. It's a bit early.'

'It's never too early on your birthday, girlie. Bottoms up,' Tracey urged.

'So, what's this latest disaster, then?'

'They say things come in threes, don't they? Well, I got up yesterday and there was a leak in the ceiling, so I rang that old boy I have doing odd jobs for me and he came straight round. I got the ladder out, 'cause he needed to get up in the loft, then I hear crash, bang, wallop. He's fallen off and knocked himself out. I can't wake him, so I had to call an ambulance. They wheeled him out on a stretcher with one of those neck braces on. Christ knows what the neighbours must've thought.'

Melissa chuckled. Nothing ever seemed to go smoothly for Tracey. 'Did you hear if he was OK?'

'Nope. Then I decided to go out with that bloke last night. The one on that dating site. The car dealer.'

'The nice-looking dark-haired one?' Melissa asked. Since Kieron died, Tracey'd had lots of casual relationships, but seemed to shy away the moment a man became serious about her. Mel guessed that deep down she had a phobia of getting her heart broken again.

'Yep, only he looked like the bloke in the photo's granddad. Honestly, Mel, I swear that photo weren't of him. And as for the outfit – I have never been so embarrassed to be seen out in public with someone.'

'What was he wearing?'

'White jeans and a bastard Hawaiian shirt, I kid you not! The silly old sod thought he was the bollocks too. He sat next to me, put his hand on my knee and had the cheek to say, "You wasn't quite what I was expecting, but you'll do for me, baby. You'll do for me." I couldn't get away from him quick enough.'

Laughing, Melissa asked, 'How did you make your escape?'

'When he went to the toilet, I bolted. He's sent me loads

of messages via the site today. Thank God I have the brains never to tell these blokes where I live or give them my phone number. I'd have weirdos ringing constantly and queuing up outside if I did.'

'You know what they say, Trace: you've got to kiss a lot of frogs to find your prince. There is another Mr Right out there somewhere for you, I'm sure of it.'

Tracey raised her eyebrows. 'Not on that dating site there isn't. So, what you up to tonight? I thought we'd go up Faces, celebrate your birthday in style. It's been ages since we've been out clubbing together.'

Melissa felt awkward. Tracey would blow a fuse if she knew Jason was coming round, which was why she hadn't mentioned it. If she did decide to take him back, she would then break the news gently to her friend. 'Nah. I'm too bloody fat to fit in any of my dresses at the moment, mate. You should go, though. Ask one of your other friends to go with you.'

'Open your pressie,' Tracey urged.

Melissa put her hand inside the gift bag and ripped open the tissue paper. The dress was beautiful. Long, slinky and black. It was expensive too, Mel could tell by the French label. 'Oh Trace, I love it. I doubt it'll fit me at present, but I'm starting a diet Monday, so fitting into this will be an incentive.'

'It'll fit you now. Try it on. It's ever so stretchy.'

Donte poked his head around the door. He had never been overly keen on his mum's best pal, so kept out the way whenever she visited. 'I'm bored, so I'm popping round Calvin's to play Grand Theft Auto. What time is that man I no longer call my father coming round?'

Aware that Tracey was glaring at her, Melissa cringed. Trust Donte to open his big mouth.

'Seven, so make sure you're home by quarter to.'

Tracey was both furious and astounded. 'No wonder you didn't fancy Faces. Did it slip your mind to tell me you were spending the evening with that no-good arsehole? I can't believe you're letting him back in the house. How could you, after what he did?'

'The house belongs to him, Trace. It's in his name, remember? And I was going to tell you afterwards. I knew you'd kick off and I couldn't be doing with your reaction today. We're getting a takeaway, that's all. The kids miss one another and it really isn't fair on them to keep up this silly not-speaking scenario.'

'You've softened towards him, haven't you? I can hear it in your voice,' Tracey snapped.

'What Jason did was awful and I will never truly forgive him. But I'm hardly blameless myself. After Bobby died, I completely fell to pieces. Jason did everything he could to help and comfort me, but I took my anger out on him and pushed him away. I'm not making excuses for what he did, but I can see where I was in the wrong too.'

Tracey's lip curled with anger. 'But he was knocking Charlotte off way before you got pregnant. Conveniently forgotten that, have you? The man has no morals.'

'Don't be mad at me, mate. It is my birthday.'

Absolutely seething, Tracey slammed her glass against the kitchen table. 'Remember your wedding reception? Then this slag Charlotte turns up at your door and Jason admits to a full-blown affair with her. If you take him back, you want your brains tested, Mel. Jason is a player and he'll only break your heart all over again. Once a womanizer, always a womanizer. Leopards like him don't change their spots, mate.'

*

Glancing at his Rolex, Jason Rampling picked up his phone. 'Where the hell are you, Shay? I told you to get your butt back here by six thirty at the latest.'

'You did, and I told you I didn't want to spend the evening with Mental Melissa. I'm at Natasha's and that's where I'm staying.'

Jason was furious. His twelve-year-old daughter was the bane of his life just lately. As if he didn't have enough on his bloody plate. 'If you don't come, I swear to fucking God I will take you out that posh school where all your muckers are and you can go to the local comp instead. Oh, and you can forget your summer holiday in Marbella with Natasha and her parents. You won't be going there either.'

'All right. I'm leaving now.'

'Mum, they're here,' Donte shouted. He was literally dreading the evening ahead; he would never forgive Jason for what he had done to his mother.

Melissa's heart was beating wildly. 'Open the door then,' she ordered, trying to keep her voice calm. It was six months since she'd seen him. They'd spoken on the phone, but Mel had refused all offers of meeting face to face.

'Happy birthday, Mel,' Jason said, handing her the huge arrangement of flowers.

Melissa smiled. 'Thank you, Jason. Go sit in the kitchen, make yourself comfortable.'

CHAPTER TWENTY-THREE

Jason waited until the kids had gone upstairs before squeezing Melissa's hands. 'Thanks for inviting me and Shay round. I am truly sorry for cheating on you, ya know. I was bang out of order.'

Melissa promptly snatched her hands away. 'Have you seen her since? Charlotte.'

'No. She's engaged to another bloke now.'

'How d'ya know that?'

'Bumped into a pal of hers.'

'She was very pretty.'

Jason smiled. 'So are you.'

Melissa looked at her husband with steely eyes. He had hurt her so much, she was determined he would never do so again. 'A lot of changes need to be made if you're going to move back in.'

'Like what? Just name 'em.'

'No way are you swanning off to Jersey, on golf trips, or anywhere else for that matter. Now I know what you get up to behind my back, I can never trust you again.'

'OK.'

'I don't want any of your family round here either, and that includes your nan.'

'Fair dos.' Jason knew full well his nan wouldn't come round anyway.

'I also want us to try for another baby.'

Jason opened his mouth, then closed it again. This was the last request he'd been expecting.

'Say something then,' Melissa urged. 'I know what a good dad you are, so I would never stop you seeing our child if we were to split up again, if that's what you're thinking.'

Jason was searching for the right words. He didn't particularly want another child, but he did want to come back home.

'When can I move back in?' he asked.

'That all depends if we're in agreement on what we want out of life, Jason.'

Jason shifted uncomfortably in the chair. 'OK. If you want a baby, we'll have a baby.'

'I can still visualize her you know, Charlotte, standing on my doorstep. I can even remember the perfume she was wearing. Tracey sometimes wears the same. Trace was round here earlier and Donte let slip you were coming by. She thinks I'm off my head even allowing you across the bloody doorstep.'

'Good old Tracey. Still stirring up shit, I see. Some things never change. And in fairness to me, I do pay the bloody mortgage on this house. The extortionate amount it costs comes out of my bank account, bleeding me dry every month. Look, Mel, I know how much I hurt you and I've got to live with that. But I am willing to do whatever to make our marriage work again. So, yes, I see no reason why we shouldn't try for another baby. But let's not rush into things. We need to get back on track first.'

Melissa stared at the man she had married. He was so bloody handsome, still gave her butterflies. She squeezed his hand. 'Tell me about your mum's funeral. How did it go?'

'Shall we go downstairs? Check they haven't murdered one another,' Shay suggested to Donte.

'No. Leave 'em to it. Do you think your dad loves my mum?'

Shay shrugged. 'He doesn't say much, but I think he's missed her.'

'It was horrible when you left, you know. My mum was a wreck, drinking wine all the time and crying.'

'Your mum was drinking wine all the time and bloody crying before we left. I think she drove my dad to do what he did by keeping on about Bobby all the time.'

'That's no excuse for him cheating on her,' Donte spat.

'Not saying it is.'

'Do you reckon they will get back together?'

Shay sighed. 'Dunno. But can we talk about something else now? I'm bored with discussing them.'

'Has there been anyone else, Jason? You know, since her.'

'There's been no one else, I swear,' Jason lied. He was a man – of course he'd indulged in a few flings. He wasn't about to admit that to Melissa though. 'What about you?'

'I slept with our mechanic,' Melissa replied casually.

'You slept with Steve!'

Pleased by the look of horror on Jason's face, Melissa nodded. She wanted him to know how it felt, how much it hurt. That's the only reason she had gone on a couple of dates with Steve. The sex had been awful and she'd hated every second of it. But it had been worth it for revenge.

Jason paced the room and punched the wall. 'I don't believe you, Mel. Why Steve? Couldn't you have humped a stranger? I took my car to that cunt only last week.'

'No point you getting sanctimonious with me. You started all this. At least Steve wasn't a full-blown affair.'

'Steve. Fucking Steve,' Jason mumbled.

Thoroughly chuffed her husband was so upset, Melissa said, 'Sit down. I think we both need a drink, don't you?'

'Well? Any sign of blood?' Donte asked as Shay returned to the bedroom carrying crisps and two cans of Coke. All his pals at school were in awe of him having Shay as a sister. They rated her 'cool' and 'well fit'.

'No visible sign of blood or gore, but neither of 'em looks too happy. I think they were arguing about something, but shut up as soon as I opened the door.'

Donte propped himself on his elbow. 'If they don't get back together, can we still keep in touch and hang out occasionally?'

'And why would I want to hang out with a little squirt like you?' Shay mocked.

'Because I'm the closest thing you'll ever have to a little brother.'

Shay grabbed Donte in a headlock. They might not be blood relations, but they'd always referred to themselves as brother and sister. 'I suppose we might keep in touch. If you're lucky.'

Jason Rampling was still reeling. Melissa sleeping with another bloke was something he hadn't prepared himself for and the fact it was his bloody mechanic just made the situation ten times worse. 'I'm paying that liberty-taking bastard a visit tomorrow. I'll give him what for!

I bet you was pissed, weren't you? Ply you with booze first, did he?'

'No. I wasn't pissed,' Melissa lied. 'And don't you dare pay him a visit. We weren't together at the time, Jason. I was a free woman.'

'Loose woman, more like. And what do you mean, "not together"? Have I missed something here? You divorced me without me knowing? Only, as far as I'm aware, we are still married. You might not be wearing your ring, but I am,' Jason said, thrusting his hand towards her. That hurt too. The fact she had taken her ring off. He hadn't, not once.

'If it makes you feel any better, I only slept with Steve the one time. It didn't feel right, so I ended things immediately afterwards.'

'Was you dating him then? Or just bending over car bonnets?'

'Neither, and I seriously do not have to justify myself to you, Jason Rampling. You even ruined our wedding reception, remember? What a hideous old slapper she was. Most humiliating moment of my life. Do you honestly think I believe you have gone this past year without having sex once? I wasn't born bloody yesterday, you know.'

Jason put his head in his hands. All this was far more difficult than he'd anticipated. Melissa had changed, seemed stronger and more bullish. 'I had a couple of one-night stands, OK. But I swear they meant nothing. It's you I want to be with.'

Melissa forced a smile. This was difficult for her too, but she knew deep down what she wanted. 'We can make this work you know.'

Jason clenched his wife's hand. 'I hope so.'

*

'How are Elton and Kyle doing? And Barbara?' Donte asked Shay.

'The boys are doing well. They go to some recording studio along the A13 to practise their music now. They're MCs. Babs has got a job now too, but she's fatter than ever, poor cow.'

Donte's eyes opened wide. Jason's younger brothers were mixed-race like him, but always acted, spoke and dressed like proper black boys. That impressed Donte. He'd learned lots of slang words from them and they'd taught him plenty about music. 'Are they recording an actual track?'

Shay scrolled through her phone. 'Why don't you ask them yourself?'

Melissa knocked back her wine. It had been a tough evening, but she was proud of the way she'd held herself together and was sure they were getting somewhere. 'Who were the other couple?' she asked Jason.

'What other couple?'

'The couple of flings you admitted to.'

Jason held his hands up. 'I don't even remember their names, and that's God's honest truth. One I met on a stag weekend. I was that drunk I couldn't even perform properly. And the other I met up town in some bar. It was just sex, babe. Nothing more, nothing less.'

'I bet you never used anything, did you? That's another thing we better add to our "To Do" list. You'll need to get a test done at the STD clinic.'

'I'm not bloody stupid, Mel. There's sod-all wrong with me. How do I know you haven't got a dose? Make Steve bag up, did ya?'

'Yes, I did actually, Jason. I'm not quite as irresponsible

as you. You get tested before you come home, or you don't come home at all. Entirely up to you.'

'OK, I'll get tested, for Christ's sake. But I need you to do something for me too.'

'What?'

'Let me put all Bobby's stuff away somewhere and redecorate the nursery. I find it depressing, and if we're going to make a fresh start we need to look to the future, not the past.'

Melissa's eyes welled up. She still sat in the nursery some days, but not every day. Eleanor, her counsellor, had suggested the very same thing as Jason, so Melissa nodded sadly. 'OK. But I want to keep the photo on the wall. We can't forget about him completely.'

'He'll never be forgotten, babe. He's our little boy.'

Feeling emotional, Melissa quickly changed the subject. 'Did you know my dad moved to Spain?'

Jason's eyes opened wide. 'No. When?'

'A couple of months back. He sold the house and the business. The old slapper's gone with him. I don't think he felt safe here any more after being shot. Good riddance to the pair of 'em, if you ask me.'

'Did they ever arrest anyone for shooting him?'

'Not as far as I know. My dad reckons it was Craig Thurston who shot him. I think the police arrested him but then let him go. Didn't you used to do business with him?'

'That was ages ago. I haven't seen Craig for Christ knows how long,' Jason lied.

'Well, don't be having no more to do with him, will you? Looks really bad, you hanging out with him, if he tried to murder my dad.'

'Nah, course not. I don't think it was Craig though. I

know your dad owed him money once, but he got that back. Why would he want your dad dead?'

'Don't know. But my dad reckons he heard his voice.'

'How do you know all this? You talked to your dad?'

'No way! I will never speak to him again after what he did to Mum. I bumped into my dad's cousin and he told me all the gossip. He reckons Craig is a proper wrong 'un and is involved in drugs now.'

'Really?'

'Yes, really. Steer clear of him, Jason. I mean that.'

'Will do. I need to use the bathroom.'

'It's the first door on the right,' Melissa joked. 'I'll pour us both another drink.'

Jason ran the tap and switched his phone on. Four abusive text messages threatening all sorts flashed up.

He ran his fingers through his hair, face etched with worry. He would have to pay that bitch a visit. She needed silencing, quickly.

CHAPTER TWENTY-FOUR

Cringing as his phone rang, clocking it was her, Jason snatched at it. 'What now?' he hissed.

'I just wanted to say sorry for all those horrible things I said. I didn't mean them.'

'You can say that a-fucking-gain. Had you been drinking?'

'No. I was angry. Got every right to be, haven't I?'

Jason rolled his eyes. She had no right to be anything, the nut job. 'Is that all?'

'Yes.'

'Apology accepted. But don't ring or text me no more.'

'Got no intention of.'

'Good.'

'Oh, do you know what? I'm not sorry after all. Go fuck yourself, Jason.'

'I got a bad feeling about this. Like my mum is going to kill us both,' Donte said, chewing at his fingernails.

'Stop worrying and chill. The school must've read the letter yesterday. They would've rung your mum immediately if they were suspicious,' Shay replied. She'd been the one who had written the letter explaining Donte would not be in school on Thursday as he had to attend his uncle's funeral. She had also written one for herself.

'So, what are we going to say again if we get caught? My mum usually calls the school if I'm ill, you know.'

'That you really missed seeing Elton and Kyle and I arranged the meet because you got emotional after speaking to them on the phone. Both your mum and my dad'll buy that story. They'll also be happy we've got one another's backs. We're not going to get caught though, so just relax. Train's here now, come on.'

'You sounded stressed when I called, so I thought this might come in handy,' Tracey said, waving a bottle of red wine.

'Come in, mate. Meant to be being good, but I could do with a drink.'

'So how did it go with Jason?' Tracey asked. She was dying to know all the gossip.

'We got on OK. Although he did say some hurtful things.'

'Like what? He's got some front, saying hurtful things after what he did.'

'He said I bleed him dry at times. I don't agree. Apart from my new car, I've asked him for nothing in over eighteen months. The Cartier watch was a birthday present. He reckons we live above our means and I need to be more careful with money in future.'

'He's trying to turn the tables, Mel. You know what he's like – anything to dig himself out of a hole. There you are. Drink that, and calm yourself down,' Tracey said, handing Melissa a glass.

'My mother never paid for a thing when she was married

to that bastard who I no longer call my father. I thought that's what real men did, Trace. You know, kept their wives. Did you pay for anything when you was with Kieron?'

'No. But I did used to treat him to stuff when I went shopping. I'd buy him a nice shirt for work, or something more trendy to wear at weekends.'

'But where did you get the money to do that?'

'Erm, Kieron's bank account.'

Melissa waved her hands in the air, chuckling. 'I seriously rest my case.'

Donte Brooks was having a very exciting day. Even though Shay was sort of his sister, they'd never done much stuff without their parents being involved, and Donte was finding the whole experience enlightening. First they'd got on a Central Line train to Mile End. Then they'd hopped off, changed out of their school uniforms and into the casual clothes they'd brought with them. Now they were on the District Line to Dagenham Heathway and were waiting to be picked up.

Shay grinned at Donte. 'You seem more chilled now. Enjoying yourself?'

'Yes, I am actually. Thanks for arranging this, Shay. It's cool.'

When Donte squeezed her hand, Shay felt the first pang of guilt. He wasn't a bad lad and did not deserve what she was about to do to him. However, she had the life of Riley living alone with her father in Buckhurst Hill, could come and go as she pleased, and Shay had no desire to move back to Repton Park and live with that nutter Melissa again.

*

'So, did you end up going clubbing the other night?' Melissa asked Tracey.

'Nah. Couldn't be arsed, in the end. I wasn't well after I left here, was sick on the way home all over myself in the bloody car.'

'Not pregnant, are you?' Melissa joked.

'Chance would be a fine thing. I haven't slept with anybody since Simple Simon.'

'Aw, don't call him that. I think he's lovely and he certainly isn't bloody simple. Jason reckons Simon's the best accountant he's ever had.' It had been Melissa's idea to fix Tracey and Simon Champion up in the first place. Jason hadn't been keen, had said Tracey was a gold digger and Simon deserved better. Simon was a jolly chap who was fun to be around, but Tracey was hard to please when it came to men. She'd dumped him after a few months when they'd first dated in 2001, then done the same when they'd got back together briefly earlier this year.

'If the spark isn't there, it isn't there, Mel. I know Si's a nice guy, but looks-wise he's not my type. Too square.'

'So why did you let him shell out for that expensive cruise earlier this year? You must have known you didn't fancy him then.'

'Because I'd never been on a cruise and he offered to take me on one. I didn't ask, or beg him, did I? Anyway, enough about Simon – let's talk about you instead. Decided if you're taking Jason back yet, have you?'

'No. But I'll have to make my mind up soon,' Melissa lied. She had already arranged a date for Jason to move back in. 'His contract runs out on the flat end of next week and his landlord wants to know if he's staying.'

'That's not your problem, Mel. Let him rent somewhere else if you're not ready.'

'Between you and me, I think he's got a bit of a cash-flow problem. We're mortgaged up to the hilt here and both our cars are on the never-never. The kids' school fees cost a fortune, and no way do I want Donte changing schools.'

'I thought Jason's pawn shop was doing really well. Has something gone wrong?'

'Not as far as I know. Jason says it's a temporary problem and that he has something big in the pipeline. I suppose it makes sense financially to allow him to move back in. It'll be a long time before I allow him in my bedroom though.'

'I thought you wanting another baby was the reason you were thinking of taking him back. Gonna be a bit difficult to conceive if you're sleeping in separate rooms, isn't it?'

'That's before I found out he'd slept with two more tarts other than Charlotte. Both one-night stands and both slags. He doesn't even remember their names, said they meant nothing to him.'

Tracey put her hand over her mouth. 'Oh my God! You so can't take him back. You'll never be able to trust him. He's a fucking wrong 'un.'

In a recording studio that was actually a big shed at the bottom of somebody's back garden, Donte was having his first taste of MCing and alcohol.

Elton was fifteen now, Kyle thirteen. Both were good-looking lads who kept up with the latest fashion by stealing whatever they desired. They looked alike, had the same number three haircut with three shaved lines on the right-hand side. All the Invincibles did. That was the name of the gang they'd recently joined. Most of the members were from Barking, so if they weren't in the recording studio these days, they tended to hang out there.

'Have a puff on Elton's joint,' Shay urged Donte.

'No. I better not.'

'Wimp,' Shay laughed.

Elton took Shay to one side. 'He's only a baby. Leave him be. You'll get the boy into trouble.'

'It won't hurt him and I have my reasons. Melissa hates you and Kyle and she hates me. No way am I living with her again.'

'They back together?' Elton enquired.

'Not if we do things my way, they won't be.'

Elton chuckled and walked over to Donte. 'Wanna try some? It'll make you feel good.'

Not wanting to seem like a stupid kid in front of the three people he looked up to the most, Donte took the joint, put it to his lips and puffed. Seconds later, he nearly choked to death.

'All right, Jase?' Deano grinned, picking up an old Atari games console off the shelf. 'How much for this? I used to have one of these but it broke.'

Jason's heart sank, as it always did when Craig's sidekick paid him a visit. There was only one reason he was here. 'Price is on it, thirty quid. But if you want it, just give me a tenner. That's what I paid for it.'

'Cheers, pal,' Deano grinned, slapping a tenner on the counter. 'I'm a true wizard at Pac-Man.'

'What can I do for you?' Jason asked.

'In a nutshell, two slaughters, one in Dagenham and one in Barking. Six clean mobile phones and a van. Transit kind of size. Nothing old or pikey-looking. Low mileage too. We don't want it breaking down.'

'When do you need all this by?'

'End of next week at the latest. Oh, and the boss says to give your estate agent mate eight grand this time. I think he wants to keep him sweet,' Deano said, pulling a large envelope out of the inside of his jacket. 'There's fifty grand in there. Pay for everything out of that and the boss says keep the change.'

Jason mentally did some maths. He could get a proper van at the auctions for four grand, eight to his pal Paul, so that made twelve. And the mobile phones, deposits and a month up front on the slaughters was peanuts. 'Leave it with me. I'll be in touch next week.'

'Sweet. Oh, and the boss says he'll be in touch soon. I think he wants you to meet his son, Harry. Cute little baby he is, Jase. Half Chinky, ain't he?'

Jason smiled politely. Deano wasn't the brightest of lads and he couldn't be bothered to tell him that the child's mother actually came from Thailand. 'OK, mate. Tell the boss, I'll see him soon.'

When Deano left the shop, Jason sat on the chair he kept behind the counter and put his head in his hands. He hated being involved in this set-up, but how could he say no? Not only did he owe Craig big time, with the current state of his finances, the thirty-five grand he'd be left with was a hell of a lot of dosh.

'No more, Shay. That boy gonna be proper ill,' Elton warned as Shay handed Donte another joint. After his initial choking session, the lad had been puffing away like a sailor and the poor little sod's eyes had started rolling in his head. Kyle thought it was hilarious to see 'Posh Boy' pissed and stoned, but Elton didn't find it amusing. Donte was only ten and making him ill wasn't part of the plan.

When Donte began to MC again, slurring his words, Kyle put his hands inside his bright red Adidas tracksuit bottoms. 'Go, Posh Boy, go,' he roared, trying not to wet himself.

Sensing they were all going to be in big trouble, Elton walked over to the deck and took the needle off the record. 'Enough. We need to straighten him up, then get him home. My mate Tyler will drive us. I'll give him a call.'

'You OK?' a concerned Melissa asked, tapping on the bathroom door.

Tracey wiped her mouth with a tissue and flushed the toilet. She opened the door. 'I think I must have a bug. Sorry, mate.'

'You sure you're not pregnant?' Melissa asked, in earnest this time. She'd been extremely sick all the way through her pregnancy with Donte. So much so, her racist of a father had insisted it was because different races did not mix and she was ill because she had got up the duff by a black man.

Tracey was about to joke that, if she was, she hoped the child didn't look like Simon, when the doorbell chimed. 'You get that. I'm fine now, honest.'

Melissa was shocked to see her son and Shay on her doorstep. Both were wearing shorts and T-shirts instead of their school uniforms.

'I'm sorry, Mum,' Donte mumbled, putting his hand over his mouth and bolting to the safety of his en-suite bathroom. He had never felt so ill in his entire life.

'What's wrong with him? Why aren't the pair of you at school? Where are your uniforms?' Melissa was gobsmacked. They didn't even go to the same schools. Donte's was in Chigwell and Shay's in Wanstead.

Shay rarely cried, but knew how to turn on the waterworks when it suited her. She did feel a bit bad. Donte had trusted her and she'd betrayed him. 'I'm so sorry, Mel, I really am. Blame me, not Donte. It's not his fault.'

Alarmed now, Melissa grabbed Shay by the arm. 'Just tell me what has happened,' she shrieked.

'When we were upstairs playing music the other day, Donte said how much he had missed Elton and Kyle. I put him on the phone to them and they invited us to go to a music studio today where they were recording a track. Donte was really upset because he hadn't seen them, so I wrote him a letter getting him out of school for the day.'

'You did what!'

'I'm sorry. But I didn't know there'd be loads of other lads there. He picked up a couple of drinks and I think they must've had vodka in them. We thought we were drinking Coke.'

'My boy is drunk! That what you're telling me, is it?'

'Well, yeah. But he'll be OK. I made him eat a Big Mac.'

Grabbing Shay by her skinny shoulders, Melissa literally pushed her out the door. 'You stupid little mare. Get out, go on, get out! And you're not welcome back, not ever!'

Shay couldn't help but smirk as she walked around the corner to where Elton's pal Tyrone had promised to wait. Mission accomplished, she thought smugly. Her dad was bound to be pissed off with her, but she was sure she could win him round – she always did.

Shay's smirk was swiftly wiped off her face when she turned the corner and discovered they'd left her stranded. She had spent all her money on kitchen roll, detergent and air freshener for the car after Donte had puked up in it, so what the hell was she meant to do now? Buckhurst Hill was miles away.

*

Always happy to be of assistance and get away from the small two-bedroomed house she'd purchased in Collier Row with what was left of Kieron's money after she'd spunked the rest, Tracey Thompson topped Melissa's drink up. It grated on her immensely that Mel lived in such a beautiful property and she lived where she did. Why was life so unfair? She would've lived in a mansion by now and been treated like a queen had Kieron not died. She still had her looks. Men would wolf-whistle at her on a daily basis, even more so since she'd had her breasts enlarged. So how was it that plain, overweight Mel had ended up with Jason and a luxury property in Repton Park? 'No way can you take him back after this, mate. Scum – the whole family are, and you have to put your Donte first.'

Tears streamed down Melissa's face. She'd been checking on Donte every ten minutes to make sure he was still breathing. She'd even contemplated taking him to the hospital to get his stomach pumped, but what sort of mother would that make her look? If they involved Social Services, she would die of shame. 'That's Jason ringing again. I can't speak to him again tonight, Trace, I really can't. He's livid though. I can tell by all the messages he's left. He reckons he's taking Shay out of her private school. Bet he don't though.'

'Not the school's fault, is it? Jason, Shay, the lot of 'em are from that bloody shithole. Told you you should have never married him, Mel. You can take the family off the Mardyke Estate, but you can't take the Mardyke Estate out of the family.'

Jason strolled inside the Crown and Crooked Billet. It was Steve the mechanic's local. He spotted him immediately.

Steve was playing pool with another bloke. 'You got a minute, mate?' Jason asked, gesticulating for him to follow him outside.

Reluctantly, Steve did as he was asked. Jason didn't seem angry, and Melissa had sworn to him when she'd dumped him that she would never admit to their fling.

Steve's worst fears were confirmed when Jason grabbed him by the throat. 'Mel said you and she were dead in the water, mate. I'm sorry, OK? But I'd never have gone there otherwise,' Steve gabbled.

The day from hell had taken its toll on Jason. He grabbed Steve's jaw and smashed the back of his head repeatedly against the wall. 'I ain't your mate, and you ever go near my old woman again, I swear I will break every single fucking bone in your body. Got that?'

CHAPTER TWENTY-FIVE

Shay Rampling was bored. She was also furious that her father had cancelled the holiday she'd so been looking forward to in Marbella. 'Dad, can we talk please?' she pleaded. It had been two days since Donte had got drunk and she knew he was OK as she'd heard her father talking to Melissa on the phone.

'Get dressed. We're going out,' Jason snapped.

'Where we going?' Shay asked. She hadn't been allowed out the door these past couple of days, not even to go to school.

'We're paying Melissa a visit and you are going to beg for her forgiveness.'

Shay shook her head. 'No. Not doing that.'

Jason grabbed his daughter by the arm. 'Yes, you fucking are.'

'No. I don't want to live with her again.'

'Why?'

Shay burst into tears. 'Because she isn't my real mother.'

Tracey arrived at Melissa's house with a big box of chocolates. She handed them to her friend.

'Thanks, mate. But I'm meant to be on a bloody diet.'

'I know, but I also know how much you love Thorntons. How is Donte now?'

'A bit shaken still, not his usual bubbly self, but he's not ill as such. I let him have the week off school so his body recovers properly. He's currently in his room playing computer games. How about you? Are you over that bug?'

'Yes. I'm feeling much better, thanks. Jason still stalking you, is he?'

'He paid Steve the mechanic a visit and threatened him the other night. I was annoyed at first when he told me, but then he explained why. I truly believe he's sorry for what he has done, and that he loves me. He's told me as much.'

Lip curling, Tracey clapped her hands slowly. 'Your very own knight in shining armour. Lucky you, mate.'

'If the mountain won't come to Muhammad, and all that cobblers,' a familiar voice chuckled.

Serving a customer, Jason spun around in horror. Craig was standing by the door with his baby in his arms. 'All right, mate. Be with you in a tick,' Jason spluttered. Since their falling out, he'd avoided Craig like the plague and had even stopped going to the golf club. Not because he was scared of him or anything like that. Jason just felt he was a small part of Craig's firm now, therefore if anything came on top, he didn't want to be associated with Craig. That's why he'd decided to keep his distance.

The customer was a messer and when he left the shop without buying anything, Jason turned the open sign around to closed and locked the door.

'Meet Harry,' Craig said, thrusting his baby into Jason's arms.

'A belter, ain't he, mate. I was gonna visit you at some point. I've just been so busy with this gaff, you know how it is. Where you parked?'

'Round the corner. Natchaya's in the car. She's gonna look after Harry while I take you for a drink.'

'I haven't got time to go for a drink today, mate. I've got shit-loads to do.'

'That can wait. We need to wet the baby's head. And you're going to need a drink when you hear what I've got to say, trust me.'

Jason's heart sank. Whatever now? he thought. 'OK. Reckon I can spare you five minutes.'

Melissa sat on the edge of her son's bed. 'How you feeling, love?' She wasn't angry with Donte for what had happened, but was still furious with Shay, even though she'd apologized earlier. How dare that little madam write Donte a note to get him out of school? Jason had promised he'd punished her and nothing like this would ever happen again, but Melissa needed to ensure it didn't.

'I'm OK, thanks. What are we having for dinner?'

'I thought we might go out for a pizza. What do you think?'

'Jason's not coming, is he?'

'No. But we do need to talk about Jason, love.'

'You getting back together?'

'We're not rushing into anything. But we had a long chat on the phone last night and decided for financial reasons it's probably best if Jason moves back in. His lease runs out on his flat next week, so a decision has to be made soon. He won't be sleeping in my bedroom. We will just see how we all get on and go from there.'

'Will Shay be moving back in too?'

'Yes, unfortunately. Look, I am still livid with Shay for leading you astray. Nothing like that must ever happen again, Donte, do you hear me? If she suggests anything of the sort in the future, I want you to come straight to me. She's older than you, so are Elton and Kyle, and I don't want you socializing with any of them outside this house. Elton and Kyle aren't welcome here any more, so you won't be seeing them again. You need to mix with Calvin and other lads and girls your own age.'

'OK.'

Aware that her handsome son looked near to tears, Melissa wrapped her arms around him and held him close to her chest. 'For all Jason's faults, he loves you very much, you know.'

'Don't love him. I hate him.'

Jason Rampling forced a half smile as Craig Thurston returned from the bar.

'How's Melissa? I heard she cut all your clothes up,' Craig chuckled.

'We're about to give it another go. Look, Craig, I will help you out on this next job, but then I'm afraid I'm going to have to bow out. It's too much of a risk for me if I'm back with Mel. I can't bring trouble home, gotta think of the kids. She also thinks it's you who shot her father.'

Craig's steely green eyes bore into Jason's. He glanced around to check there were no earwiggers, before leaning forward. 'You're going nowhere, Jason. You're indebted to me, unfortunately. And I need your help. Now tell me a bit more about this estate agent pal of yours. How well do you know him?'

*

It had been Melissa's idea that she and Donte visit her mum's grave before eating. Today would've been her mum and dad's anniversary, and Melissa could not help despising her father even more than usual.

'Are we going to eat at my favourite pizza restaurant in Woodford, Mum?' Donte enquired.

'No, love. We don't want to bump into anybody from school, do we?' Melissa said sensibly. She'd told the school Donte had tonsillitis. Her mum was laid to rest in Upminster Cemetery and Melissa knew there were pizza restaurants in Upminster or nearby Hornchurch.

'I'll get the flowers out the boot,' Donte said. He didn't remember his nan at all, had been too young. She looked a nice lady in all her photos though, had a kind face.

'Bloody hell! You're going to be taller than me soon,' Melissa joked as Donte linked arms with her. He had really shot up this past year and was already up to her shoulder.

'Was my real dad tall?'

'He was taller than me, but nowhere near as tall as Jason. Shush now, love, as people are visiting their loved ones.' Melissa hated talking about Donte's real father. He had treated her despicably on learning she was pregnant and not once had he ever tried to make contact with his son.

'Nan's already got flowers,' Donte said as they approached the grave.

Melissa's pace quickened. The two permanent vases were filled with fresh red roses and there was a huge card tied to her mother's headstone with the words 'Happy Anniversary' plastered across the front.

Heart beating wildly, Melissa snatched at the card.

To my darling, Carol
Gone but never forgotten
Until we meet again
Your Johnny xxx

'Mum, stop it! What are you doing?' Donte asked, as his mother started cursing out loud. There was an elderly couple walking towards them and they looked startled.

Melissa ripped the card into tiny pieces. 'How dare he? How fucking dare he! Roses, I'll give him poxy roses,' Melissa spat, ripping them out of the vases.

'Charming!' the elderly man exclaimed.

'Don't dither, Harold. Come on,' his wife ordered.

Melissa sank to her knees, ripping the petals off each rose. 'Cheating, lying bastard. I hate him.'

Jason Rampling downed the last of his drink and stood up. 'I need to be getting back now. I'll touch base with Deano when I've viewed the slaughters. But can you tell him not to come to the shop any more. I'll meet him elsewhere if need be.'

Craig grabbed Jason's arm. 'Not so fast. I need to talk to you about Darlene.'

'Why?'

'You know she's got breast cancer, right? The chemo's knocked her for six, could do with some cheering up, she could. I think a visit from you might be just the tonic she needs.'

Stunned, Jason sank back in the chair. He hadn't known Darlene was ill. 'Where's she living now?'

'Basildon. I'll give you the address.'

'I dunno, Craig. I'm not sure she'd want to see me after all these years.'

Craig scribbled on a piece of paper and handed it to Jason. 'Darlene's address and my new work number. In future you report to me, not Deano.'

Not knowing what else to say or do, Jason nodded. 'I really do have to go now.'

As Craig followed Jason out of the pub, neither spotted the two men watching them across the road in a green Fiat Uno.

'You're late,' Jason snapped as his brothers sauntered into the lounge as if they didn't have a care in the world. He'd been long overdue a chat with the pair of them, so had driven straight to the Mardyke from his shop.

'We lost track of time, was busy in the studio,' Elton replied.

'Sit down next to your sister,' Jason demanded.

He could tell the pair of them were stoned, could even smell the crap they smoked on their clothes.

'Best yous two liven yourselves up a bit,' he said. 'This silly gang bollocks and your behaviour lately isn't acceptable. I don't like the way you treat your sister, neither do I like the direction your lives are heading. You're going down a slippery slope and no way are you stopping here and leading Babs a dog's life. Up your game, stop smoking skunk, else I'll put you into care.'

'What da fuck!' Elton exclaimed.

'No way. Dat ain't happening,' Kyle added.

Seeing red, Jason leapt off the armchair and clumped both boys around the head. 'The word is pronounced that, not fucking dat. I mean it, boys. No more bunking off school or speaking to your sister like shit. You're lucky you've got her, else you'd be in care anyway. You stay away from Donte too, and Shay. I ain't bluffing. Pull your socks up or I'll physically remove you from this flat myself. Got that?'

Elton and Kyle glanced at one another.

'OK. Sorry,' Elton mumbled.

Kyle stared at his feet. 'Me too.'

Jason stared at the text message. It gave sod-all away, just read:

> I need to speak to you ASAP, in person. Please pop round. It's urgent.

Sighing, Jason tried to call her. What the hell did that bitch want now?

Debating whether to text her back, Jason quickly decided against it and instead drove towards her house. She wasn't to be trusted, therefore no way was he leaving any incriminating evidence for her to blackmail him with.

By the time he reached her gaff, Jason was in a foul mood. Just lately his life seemed more complicated than a five-thousand-piece jigsaw puzzle. He rapped on her door.

'Thanks for coming straight round. You'd better come inside.'

Barging inside the house, Jason stood in the middle of the lounge and glared at her. 'What do you want now? I said all I had to say to you the other day and you agreed to leave me the hell alone.'

Eyes brimming with tears, Tracey Thompson lowered her eyes like Lady Diana used to. Her mother had once told her she had that Lady Di look off to a T.

'I really don't know how to say this to you, Jason, so I'm just going to be blunt: I am pregnant, and the baby is yours.'

CHAPTER TWENTY-SIX

Jason fell back on to one of the armchairs as though he'd been poleaxed. He couldn't speak, could only sit there in stunned silence.

The night in question was blurry in parts, but he could also remember it as though it were yesterday. It was a Friday and he'd been on a golf day, a celebrity turnout with ex-footballers. The booze was flowing freely and when Simon left early to go on a date with his new girlfriend, he had ended up at a boozer in Brentwood with a crowd of lads. Worse for wear, he'd then gone to Palms, a nightclub along the A127, with a couple of blokes he barely knew.

'You OK, Jase?' Tracey asked.

'Not really, no. Get me a drink, will ya?' Jason put his head in his hands. He'd never been a fan of Tracey's, but that particular evening he'd needed a friendly ear to spew all his woes into. The day before he'd rung Melissa and she'd called him everything, before telling him she was going to speak to her solicitor about a divorce. He'd been hurt, upset, which was why he'd agreed to leave the club early and go back to Tracey's for a nightcap. He'd wanted to talk about Melissa, nothing more.

Tracey was a conniving cow, always had been, and Jason should've known better than to trust her. She hadn't long split up with Simon and had pretended she was upset too. The inevitable had happened an hour or so after they'd arrived home. For all Tracey's faults, she was a good-looking girl and that night she was wearing a low-cut black mini-dress that left little to the imagination. Jason hadn't had sex for months and when she'd leaned in for a kiss, he hadn't thought twice about Melissa. They'd literally fucked one another's brains out.

Tracey handed Jason a brandy. 'Not an ideal situation, is it?'

Jason glared at the bitch. He wasn't daft, knew she had always fancied him and was jealous of his marriage to Melissa. How could he have been so stupid? She'd entrapped him and he'd allowed that to happen. 'Does Mel know you're pregnant?'

'No. I only found out yesterday. Nobody else knows. I've been in shock myself.'

'You sure it's my kid?'

'I'm not a slag, Jason. I'm positive it's yours.'

Jason stood up and paced the room. 'Well, that's fucking great, isn't it? You're gonna have to get rid of it. I'll pay. I'll find you a private clinic so you don't have to see your own doctor. They just give you a pill these days, don't they? I mean, you're not that far gone, are you?'

'I'm not sure I want to "get rid of it", as you so eloquently put it. I'll be thirty soon and this might be my last chance of becoming a mother.'

Jason stared at Tracey with hatred. The sex between them had actually been good, which made him feel even guiltier. He'd never expected it to result in this, mind. 'Don't give me all that old flannel. If you'd have wanted to be a mother you wouldn't have aborted your dead husband's kid. And you told me you were on the pill, you lying cow. What happened? Gonna tell me now you forgot to take it, are ya?'

'Well, I must have done, or it didn't work. And don't you dare call me a liar. I never planned any of this. How the hell was I to know you'd be in Palms that night? You are just as much to blame as me. You were as up for it as I was.'

'So what do you plan on saying to Mel? Because I swear to you, Trace, if you tell her the kid is mine I will fucking kill you. She can't find out, not ever. It will break her heart. You're meant to be her best pal, for God's sake.'

'I know and I feel awful.'

'Well, get rid of it then. Surely that's the best solution?'

'I'm not making any rash decisions, Jason. It's my body, my baby, and I will decide what is best.'

Jason looked at Tracey with pleading eyes. 'Please don't do this to me. I've got enough on my plate as it is. I'll pay you money, a lump sum. If I give you, say, five grand, you can take yourself away on holiday or something. It'll do you good, a nice break in the sun.'

Unable to stop herself, Tracey leapt up and slapped Jason across the face. 'How dare you offer me money to abort my baby! Scum, you are. The lowest of the low. Get out of my house. Go on; piss off back to the Mardyke Estate where you belong.'

As Tracey tried to bundle him out the room, Jason grabbed both of her wrists. 'I swear, you breathe one word of this to Mel, Simon, or anybody else for that matter, you will live to regret it. Understand me?'

Tracey had known Jason wouldn't be happy, but she had never expected him to act as appallingly as this. The night they'd made love until the birds had started singing in the morning had been an amazing experience. The sex had been awesome, up there with the best she'd ever had. But now he was acting like a complete stranger, dishing out threats. 'Get out,' Tracey hissed, opening the front door.

Panicking, Jason grabbed Tracey by the neck and pushed her up against the porch. 'Not until you've answered my question. Do you fucking understand me?'

'Yes,' Tracey wept. 'Now please go.'

Jason ran to his vehicle and shot off at such speed, the silver Toyota Avalon that had been assigned to follow him had trouble keeping up.

Melissa had been unable to get hold of Jason all evening. She'd left numerous messages asking him to call her, so when the doorbell chimed she assumed it was him. 'Oh, hello, Simon. Long time no see. I thought you must be Jason. I've been trying to call him but his phone's switched off.'

'Ditto. He was meant to be meeting me in a restaurant earlier, but never showed up. Very unlike Jason. I thought he might be here.'

'Come in, Si. Jase told me he was definitely popping by later, so we might as well wait for him together. I hope he hasn't had an accident in the car. Shay doesn't know where he is either. She's at the flat. What can I get you? Tea, coffee, or do you fancy a beer?'

'A beer wouldn't go amiss thanks, Mel. So, how are you keeping? I'm pleased you and Jason are trying to patch things up. About bloody time.'

Melissa handed Simon a beer and made herself a coffee. She'd apologized to Donte for freaking out at the cemetery and promised him she was going to lay off the wine from now on. 'I'm OK, thanks. I have my up and down days still, but trying to move forward. Jason's moving in next weekend, has he told you?'

'Yeah. He's keen to move forward too. Shit happens in life, Mel. But you and Jason are good together. I'm sure, with a bit of effort, you'll make it work again. Time is a healer, as they say.'

'Hope so. How about you? I was sorry it didn't work out between you and Tracey. She might be my mate, but between you and me, she hasn't a clue what she wants out of life. Kieron's death knocked the stuffing out of her and I think she's afraid to get close to another man in case she gets hurt again.'

Simon smiled, his mischievous brown eyes twinkling behind his glasses. 'Please don't feel you have to explain, Mel. I've met plenty of Traceys in my time, trust me. In fact, I'll let you in on a little secret, if you promise not to tell her.'

'What?'

'I'd booked up to take another woman on that cruise with me – Suzie. But she decided at short notice that she was going back to her ex. I didn't fancy cruising alone, so to speak, so asked Tracey and changed the name over. We had a good time, to be fair, but I knew it wouldn't last once we got back home. I'm seeing somebody else now. Christine, her name is, and I think you two would get along great. You'll have to meet her. I met her online, but don't tell Jason that as I'll never hear the last of it. He ripped the piss out of me for even mentioning joining a dating site, so I told him I met Christine on a train,' Simon chuckled.

Melissa laughed. She'd always enjoyed Simon's company

and had barely seen him since Jason and she had separated. 'Your secret's safe with me, I promise. Right, will I call Jase again, or will you? Actually, you do it. He'll think I'm gagging for him to move back in if I keep bloody ringing.'

Simon scrolled to find his pal's number. 'Nope. Still not answering. Going straight to voicemail. Elusive bastard, eh? I wonder where he's got to?'

'Where have you been? I've had Melissa ring here three times and Simon twice. Why isn't your phone on?' Shay enquired. She knew her father well enough to immediately know something was wrong. His face said it all. 'What's up?'

'I'm not in the mood for being interrogated, Shay. I seriously have had the day from hell in more ways than one. Go round your mate's, eh? I could do with some space right now.'

'But I thought I was grounded?' Shay retaliated cheekily.

'You are. Were! Look, just sod off before I change my mind – and be home by nine at the latest. Make sure you get a cab an' all. I don't want you walking about in skimpy clothes in the dark,' Jason ordered, handing his daughter a twenty-pound note.

When Shay left, Jason punched the wall in despair. He'd ballsed up good and proper this time, that was for sure. Now he had to think sharpish. He hadn't meant to threaten Tracey, had just panicked. He wasn't a bully, especially where women were concerned. He'd handled things all wrong, but how could he correct the situation? He'd been as heartbroken as Melissa when Bobby had died, it still hurt now. No way could Tracey keep that baby.

Jason listened to his voicemail messages. Melissa

sounded worried and that made him feel guiltier than ever.

Taking the plunge, Jason dialled the house phone and took a deep breath. She answered within seconds, exclaiming, 'There you are! Where have you been? Simon's here. You were meant to meet him earlier.'

Blagging it as he usually did, Jason forced himself to sound cheerful. 'Sorry, babe. I've had the day from hell. Forgot to take me phone charger into work, so my battery went dead early doors. Then I had to shoot straight over the Mardyke. My brothers have been leading Babs a dog's life and I wanted to speak to 'em in person. I've told them I don't want them to have any more contact with Donte or Shay.'

'Good.'

'Apologize to Si for me. I couldn't find Elton and Kyle, hence why I never got to the restaurant. Tell him I'll bell him in the morning to rearrange, babe.'

'But he's here now. You're still coming round, aren't you? Simon is starving, so I've made us all supper. I made a chilli con carne. I've not boiled the rice yet though, we'll wait until you get here.'

Jason sighed. He fancied socializing as much as he fancied a bullet hole in the head, but what was a man to do? 'OK. I'm gonna have a quick shower, then I'll be round.'

Unable to look Mel in the eyes, Jason ate half of his supper, then pushed the plate away. His stomach was churning and, unusually for him, he was a bundle of nerves. Tracey was a ticking time bomb, she could blurt out the truth to Melissa any minute. He needed to pay her another visit to smooth things over. That was the only way to ensure she kept her trap shut, for now at least.

'Is it not as nice as normal, the chilli?' Melissa asked. Jason looked tired and wasn't his usual chirpy self.

'It was lovely, Mel, but I really don't feel too well. Got a headache, that's why I was going to skip coming round. I think it's taken its toll on me, me mum dying and her funeral.'

Simon studied his pal, finished his beer and stood up. 'I'm gonna make a move now, guys. Thanks for your hospitality, Mel. I got that form in the motor you need to sign, Jase. Do it now, eh? Then I'll post it tomorrow.'

Relieved to get away from the kitchen table, Jason followed his pal outside. 'What's really up?' Simon asked.

'Everything,' Jason sighed. 'I'll call you in the morning. We'll chat over a bit of lunch.'

Simon put a comforting hand on Jason's shoulder. 'If you need to borrow some dosh to tide you over, you've only got to ask, mate.'

Jason nodded, thanked his pal, then sank to his haunches as Simon drove off. The guilt was absolutely suffocating.

Tracey's heart beat wildly as she opened the front door. She'd known he'd return, but hadn't expected it be quite so soon. Neither had she expected chocolates and flowers.

'Nothing special, but only the garage was open. I had to apologize for the way I spoke to you earlier. I was bang out of order. Can I come in? I'll be rational, I swear.' Jason promised.

Secretly thrilled, but not wanting to show it, Tracey remained stony-faced as she nodded and opened the door wide.

Jason sat on the sofa and forced a half smile. 'What a messy situation we've got ourselves into, eh, girl?'

'I know. Mel rang me earlier and I couldn't even answer the call. How am I meant to face her now? I feel awful.'

'You're going to have to blag it. You can't avoid her, she'll know something's wrong. Tell her you've met a new fella on the internet that you like. That'll explain you being busy, and I'm moving back in at the weekend anyway.'

'You're still moving back? Even though I'm pregnant.'

'Case of having to. I've got cash-flow problems and I can't afford to keep the flat on any more.'

'How do you plan to support our baby then? I never realized you were skint.'

'I'm not. It's a temporary problem and if you decide to keep the child, of course I'll pay towards its keep. But, if that were to happen, then it's gonna have to be done in secret, not through the courts or my bank account. You're Mel's best friend, Trace, and I'm her husband. She can never know about this – nobody can, bar us. Remember how cut up Mel was over Bobby? She was mentally ill for a long time after his death, and I know in my heart she has never truly recovered from losing him and probably never will. If she were to ever find out about this, it would send her over the edge. I reckon she would take her own life. I can't have that on my conscience, and neither can you.'

'Whose baby am I meant to say it is then? Only, people are bound to be curious. Mel and I tell each other everything and she knows for a fact I haven't had a bloke on the scene these past couple of months. Not unless you include a couple of random dates I set up on the bloody internet.'

'The easiest way out of all this is to not have the baby. Do you honestly want to be a mum, Trace? Your life changes forever when you have a kid. It's a twenty-four-hour job, especially for the mother, and you really don't strike me as the maternal type.'

Tracey could not take her eyes off Jason this evening. He'd got changed from earlier, was now wearing faded Levi's and a black Lacoste T-shirt. He smelled fresh, of expensive cologne, and looked so bloody handsome. There was also a vulnerability about him, which was unusual, and that pleased Tracey no end. She held all the cards now, so she decided to lay them on the table.

'What you doing?' Jason asked nervously, as she moved seats, sat next to him and squeezed his left hand.

Tracey looked him in the eye. 'I don't want things to be awkward between us, Jason. Neither do I want to break Melissa's heart any more than you do. So, what I suggest we do is you see the baby on the quiet. Perhaps you can find me a house further afield and then you can stay over once a week, or even twice?'

Jason looked at the woman as though she were mental. He edged backwards, away from her. 'Let me get one thing straight, Trace. I have no interest in you or the baby. If I have to bung you a bit of dosh on the quiet, then so be it. But no way will I be playing happy families. You'll be bringing that kid up on your own, that's what I'm trying to drum into you.'

'Did that night we spent together mean nothing to you? We were at it all night. I know you like me, you must do. Men don't act the way you did otherwise.'

Holding his hands up, Jason shook his head in disbelief. 'Rein it in a bit, Trace. We were both shit-faced. It meant nothing other than the obvious – not to me, anyway.'

'How can you say that?' Tracey hissed. 'You were all over me like a rash,' she reminded him. Most days she would close her eyes and relive that special night again. His touch, smell, the things he'd said to her, and the look on his face each time he'd orgasmed. It had been more than just sex, she'd convinced herself of that.

Jason had always known Tracey secretly fancied him, but until recently he'd never had her down as a potential bunny-boiler. 'I dunno what you want me to say. When you invited me around for dinner after that night, surely it was obvious when I knocked you back that I wasn't interested? I am Melissa's husband and I have no intention of divorcing her. We've been through a lot together, as you well know. She needs me and I need her.'

'Are you and Mel going to try for another baby? Only it'll be awkward if you do, won't it? Say our kids look alike?'

'I have no idea what the future holds, but whatever Mel and I decide to do is our business, nobody else's. You need to concentrate on yourself, have a long, hard think about what you really want. Because, bar the financial support, I'm not going to be there for you or the kid. You're going to be a single mum, unless you find another geezer to play Daddy.'

Positive Jason was only being cold towards her because of Melissa, Tracey put her hand on his knee and leaned towards him. 'She will never find out, you know. I swear I won't breathe a word.'

When her lips zoomed towards his and her hand made a grab for his cock, Jason leapt off the sofa as though someone had shoved a firework up his backside. 'You've got to stop that, Trace; it really isn't fair on Mel. She's meant to be your best pal, or have you forgotten that?'

'I'm sorry,' Tracey mumbled.

Clocking she was near to tears, Jason crouched down in front of her. 'Look, you're a nice woman,' he lied. 'And I'm sure one day you'll meet the man of your dreams.

You've been through it too with Kieron. What happened to him was awful, and my heart goes out to you. But there is no me and you, and you need to get that into your head. What happened between us was a one-off. Not saying it wasn't enjoyable at the time, but it was a big mistake, one I will never make again. I just don't feel that way about you, Trace. I never have and never will. I'm sorry, love.'

Feeling ridiculously stupid that she'd read the signals wrong, Tracey angrily wiped away the lone tear dripping down her cheek. 'Just go, will ya. Go on. Fuck off.'

Knowing sleep wouldn't come easy after the day he'd had, Jason lay on the sofa, TV remote in hand. Dozing, he sat bolt upright as he heard Nick Ross mention a reconstruction of an armed robbery in a leafy Cotswolds village, and a Vincent van Gogh painting. 'Tonight viewers, we want *you* to help us catch these violent criminals,' Nick added.

Jason put his face in his hands. 'For fuck's sake. No. Please God no.'

Shay poked her head around the door. 'What's the matter?'

'Nothing.'

'What you watching?'

'*Crimewatch*. Go back to bed. You won't get up for school.'

Jason wound the recording forward to the part he needed to see. He then stared at the screen in horror as the intruders posed as workmen to gain access to the grounds before donning balaclavas and brutally terrorizing the elderly lady who lived there, and her staff.

'Oh, Jesus, no,' Jason stammered. That woman must be

in her seventies. She was already tied to a chair. What type of animal would batter her senseless with a baseball bat for no valid reason?

Aware that the woman's pet dogs were about to be shot, Jason turned the volume down and put his hands over his eyes. The violence used was all so unnecessary. The dogs were only poodles for Christ's sake.

A minute or so later, Jason peeped through his fingers and had his worst fear confirmed. There it was, flashing up on the screen. An image of the painting he'd bought via Mickey Two Wives.

As Photofits of four men were shown, Jason recognized the podgy one. He was the Irish gypsy he'd handed the money over to. 'Fuck, fuck, fuck,' he spat, slapping his forehead, appalled by his own greed and stupidity.

Grassing on them wasn't an option. Not only would he also be arrested, but every penny he had was tied up in that painting.

Bile reaching the back of his throat, Jason ran to the bathroom and vomited up the small amount of chilli he'd eaten. He knew in that instant that the life of crime wasn't for him any more. Once that painting was sold, he was walking away from it and going straight.

CHAPTER TWENTY-SEVEN

Jason felt ill as he drove towards the restaurant in Epping where he'd arranged to meet Simon. He'd been unable to get the images of those poor people being tortured out of his mind, had not been able to sleep.

He could remember the day clearly when Mickey Two Wives had bowled into his recently opened shop and asked if he wanted to buy a painting.

Mickey Two Wives must be in his sixties now and originally out of Rainham. An armed robber and bigamist, he had done time for both crimes and earned his nickname for the latter.

Jason had worked for Mickey Two Wives for a while as a kid, selling hooky stuff for him. He'd never particularly liked the bloke though. He was short-tempered, rude and very arrogant, so Jason's initial response was to say, 'Thanks, but no thanks.'

Mickey Two Wives had leaned across the counter. 'It's a Van Gogh. It's worth millions.'

That's when Jason's ears had pricked up. 'Is it stolen?' he stupidly asked.

'Of course it's fucking stolen! Van Gogh's been dead

for centuries. He didn't paint it last fucking week, did he?'

'Has it come out of a gallery?' Jason enquired.

'I don't fucking know, do I? I'm not a nosy bastard like you. A pal of mine has it. He only wants two fifty for it.'

'A quarter of a mil,' Jason stammered.

'Yes, of course. Not talking in fucking hundreds, am I, you clown. Look, I ain't got time to balls around. Take it or leave it – your call.'

Jason had a posh pal, Henry, who was an expert on art. He was also a dodgy bastard who would sell stolen stuff abroad. Jason had involved Henry, who'd nearly pissed his pants with excitement when verifying the painting was the real deal.

A meet had then been set up in Kent to do the exchange. Henry had accompanied Jason and both men had thought they were goners when four Irish gypsies turned up in a battered old horsebox. Evil-looking bastards they were, and they'd glared at Jason throughout while counting the money.

Jason pulled up outside the restaurant. He needed to confide in someone and he trusted Simon implicitly. He'd tell him about the situation he'd got himself in with Craig too. But he wouldn't mention Johnny Brooks or any of the robberies they'd done. Neither would he mention the predicament he'd got himself in with Tracey. A mate's ex was a no-go, and even though Simon had never actually lived with Tracey, Jason was sure his pal would still see it as a liberty-take. Simon had really liked her in the beginning, was smitten until he'd learned what a bitch she could be.

Jason entered the restaurant and spotted Simon immediately. 'All right, mate? Sorry I'm late. Traffic was bad.'

*

Finishing his rare T-bone steak, Jason pushed the plate away. Opening up to Simon had felt good. He'd needed advice and could not think of anybody better or more trustworthy to talk to. 'What am I going to do about Thurston? I really don't want him turning up unannounced at my shop any more.'

'Just stand your ground, Jase. Tell him you want out after this job. He made a hash of trying to top Johnny, so I doubt he's going to take a pop at you.'

'That weren't him, Si. Craig's no killer.' Jason quickly changed the subject: 'What about the painting? What should I do about that?'

Simon puffed his cheeks out. 'You're on your own with that one, I'm afraid. I can get hold of a few bob to put back into your bank before I do your accounts. I can make everything look legal and above board for you with the taxman. But the bloke I'll be involving will want ten per cent of anything that goes into the account on top of his dosh back. That's his going rate. Have you actually had this painting verified?'

'Yeah, course. It's sweet, and nobody knows where it's hidden, bar me. I've got a pal who is in the know. He's found me a buyer. But the geezer's currently banged up in a Dutch prison and isn't due for release until early next year. When I do sell it, I'm going to need assistance with the financial side of things. Some of the money I can hide myself, but I'll need a fair chunk laundered. Can you sort that for me?'

It was getting harder and harder to launder money these days, but Simon had some wonderful contacts, especially in Jersey. 'I'm sure I can sort something out. It'll cost you, though. The guys I use aren't cheap.'

'Whatever. Money's not exactly an issue when you've got your paws on a Van Gogh.'

Simon chuckled. 'I've met some chancers in my time and you're definitely up there with the Del Boys of this world.'

Immersed in bubbles, Tracey Thompson ran the hot tap again. A long soak in the bath always helped her think and she was more than happy with her plan now. Melissa would believe it, and Jason was bound to be infuriated by this latest turn of events. It served him right. A lesson not to go around using women in future.

Tracey dunked her head under the water. She knew she was shallow, but couldn't help that. It was part of who she was. Even at school, she'd had to be on the best-looking boy's arm. Who wanted to go out with or wake up next to some ugly bastard? She most certainly didn't. But she craved to live in a lovely home like Melissa, and now she was pregnant, there was an opportunity to make that happen. This was going to be her ticket to Repton Park.

Grinning at how clever she was, Tracey stepped out of the bath and wrapped a towel around herself. It was time to pay Melissa a visit and announce her life-changing news. She just hoped Jason would be there; otherwise she would wait for him to return. His expression was bound to be priceless and she couldn't wait to see it. Revenge at its finest.

With Craig turning the emotional screws on, Jason Rampling pulled up outside number twenty-three. If something were to happen to Darlene, he would never forgive himself had he not visited.

Picking the flowers and chocolates up, Jason felt quite nervous. It had been almost eight years since he'd last seen her and he'd missed her. Knocking on the door, he glanced at the nosy bastard who was pretending to wash his car over the road while watching him. It wasn't a council area. The houses looked quite nice, most of them new-builds.

'You Darlene's son?' the man over the road shouted out.

'No. A family friend.'

'She's not in. I saw a cab pick her up earlier. Probably gone to the hospital, I should imagine.'

Jason crossed the road. 'If I leave these flowers and chocolates with you, can you give them to her for me, please? I will pop a note through her door explaining you have them.'

The man dried his wet hands on his shorts. 'No problem. Who shall I say they're from?'

'No need to. As I said, I'll leave her a note.'

'There you are! I was beginning to think you were avoiding me,' Melissa joked.

'As if. I've had a lot on my plate, Mel, and needed some thinking time.'

'Why? What's the matter?'

'Put the kettle on and I'll explain all.'

Melissa sat opposite her friend. Her kitchen table was a huge wooden one and they'd had many a gossip there over the years. 'Spill the beans then. What you done now?'

Feeling a surge of excitement rush through her veins, Tracey squeezed her pal's hand. 'You have to promise me you won't say a word to Jason. Not until I'm sure in my own mind what I'm going to do.'

'I don't tell Jason sod-all these days, so don't worry about that.'

'I'm pregnant.'

Melissa felt her stomach lurch. Unlike herself, Tracey had never wanted children. 'Oh my God! No! Really?'

'Yep, really. That's obviously why I was chucking up. What am I going to do, Mel?'

'Who's the father?'

'Simon.'

'Jesus wept! He was only round here yesterday. I take it he doesn't know yet? How far gone are you then?'

'Must be three months. I can't remember the last time I slept with him exactly, but it was March time we got back off the cruise.'

'You going to keep it? I really don't think you should make a decision without consulting him first, Trace. He'd make a brilliant father. He's always wanted kids. But he's seeing someone else now, so it's awkward, eh?'

'Who's he seeing?'

'I've not met her but her name's Christine. He was chatting about her last night and I could sense he really likes her. I think she's quite career-minded, like him.'

'Well, I think I'm keeping the baby, so bollocks to Christine. I don't know how to tell Simon though. He's going to be shocked, isn't he?'

'You can say that again! Even I'm shocked. Surely you must've missed your period?'

'My periods have always been hit and miss. Don't you remember when I didn't have one for yonks and went to see that gynaecologist? She put it down to stress after losing Kieron.'

'Yeah, I remember you going somewhere. What made you decide to keep it? I thought you didn't want kids,' Melissa reminded her pal. She and Jason had found it upsetting and bemusing when Tracey had aborted her dead husband's child. They couldn't believe she had made such a decision when it would've been part of Kieron.

'Not getting no younger, am I? And even though I'm not in love with Simon, I think he's a nice person and will be a good dad and provider.'

Simon owned a beautiful home in Epping and certainly wasn't short of a few bob. Tracey had already dumped the man twice, so why did she now want his baby? Melissa thought. She knew her friend well enough to guess there was an ulterior motive. 'So, do you want to get back with Simon?'

'No. But neither do I want my child growing up in Collier Row. Perhaps Simon could rent us a place near him? Or buy us one?'

'Wow, Trace. That's a big ask.'

'Should've been more careful then, shouldn't he?'

The shrill ring of the house phone interrupted the conversation. 'Jason's on his way back and is bringing an Indian takeaway home. Do you fancy anything, Trace?' Melissa shouted out.

Tracey smiled. She could just imagine Jason squirming. 'Oooh, I'd love a chicken tikka, please.'

Five minutes later, Jason called the landline again. 'I'm so sorry, babe. Something's cropped up, family stuff. I've ordered the takeaway for you and Tracey to be delivered, and I'll be round tomorrow instead. Sorry to balls you about, Mel.'

'Who was that?' Tracey asked, knowing full well who it was.

'Jase. Something's happened with the motley Mardyke crew and he's not coming round now. Never mind. He's ordered our food and we can discuss the baby in more detail without him here. I still can't believe you're pregnant. It's not sunk in yet.'

Thinking what an absolute coward Jason Rampling was, Tracey smiled sweetly.

Jason did a U-turn at the Ardleigh Green traffic lights and headed back up the A127 towards Basildon. Hearing her voice again had seemed odd, yet comforting. 'Jase, it's me, Darlene. I got your note, the flowers and chocolates. Thanks,' she'd said.

Rather than share a takeaway with that conniving bitch, Jason had asked Darlene if he could pop back. She'd agreed, thankfully.

Driving in the fast lane at ninety miles per hour, Jason glanced in the interior mirror. Was he imagining things? Or was that burgundy Ford Granada following him? Only he'd noticed one pull into the garage behind him on the way back from Basildon, now this one had done a U-turn at the lights and was holding back, yet still keeping up with him at the same time.

Keeping an eye on the vehicle, Jason breathed a sigh of relief as he took the Basildon turn-off and the motor went sailing past. That was another reason he didn't want Craig Thurston turning up at his shop. If the Old Bill did choose to watch his gang and he was spotted with Craig, it could implicate him big time.

As he neared Darlene's house, Jason could not help but remember the good times. Their love-making had been incredible, especially after they'd argued. He'd never experienced sex like that, before or since. Wild yet loving, wrong yet so good. As a teenager, he could not get enough of her. She'd been to him like heroin was to the addicts on the estate – a drug he could not kick. She'd also been a mother figure. A friend and confidante who had welcomed him into her home and had treated him like a son.

Excited to see her again, Jason parked up. The front door was opened before he even reached it. Her long hair was gone. She was wearing a red headscarf, presumably to cover her baldness. He smiled at her. 'You all right, Dar?'

'I am now I've seen you. Hello, stranger.'

'I've been thinking,' Tracey said. 'You know you're dreading the first day Jase moves back as you're going to feel awkward and you think the kids will too.'

'Yeah.'

'What about if you invite me and Simon round? Obviously, say nothing to Jason, neither must you tell Simon I will be here. But you will have to tell him he can't bring his bird. Me breaking the news of the baby after dinner will be a bit of a diversion, take the pressure off you and Jase, eh? And I would much rather tell Si with my bestie by my side.'

'Oh, I don't know about that, Trace. Jason hates surprises, and I bet Simon does too. I don't think you should put it on him like that. Why don't you invite him round yours? Or out for lunch or something?'

'Because he is bound to say no. Why would he want to see me if he's all loved up with his new girlfriend? Please do this for me, Mel. I am so nervous about breaking the news to him. It will really help if you and Jase are there. Simon might get angry and blame me, for all we know.'

'Si's not like that. And if he didn't use a condom – which he obviously didn't – then how can he blame you?'

'Because he's a man and they're unpredictable. Please, Mel. I'd do it for you.'

Melissa rolled her eyes. Tracey had always been able to talk her round to doing what she wanted, ever since they were at school. 'OK. But, you can't say I already knew about the baby. Just announce it like I bloody don't. OK?'

Jason sipped his beer and studied Darlene as she told him about her treatment. She was mid forties now and the lines on her face showed her age. She was no longer a looker by any means, but would always be beautiful to him. Her striking green cat-like eyes were still the same, so was her sense of humour. 'Sorry about your wedding reception, by the way. Not the best idea ever, was it?' she joked.

'And I'm so sorry for not telling you about the wedding, Dar. I sort of got blackmailed into getting hitched by Johnny Brooks and didn't know how to break the news. He promised to buy us a house, you know, in our names. Then Melissa found out he was having an affair and knocked back his kind offer,' Jason laughed. 'It hasn't worked out too badly though. Me and Mel have had our ups and downs but she's a good person and was the mother figure I hoped she would be for Shay. I had to get Shay off the Mardyke, Dar. But I should've been straight with you at the time.'

Darlene smiled. 'Time's a healer, Jason, and I can't tell you how much it has cheered me up seeing you again. Craig said he was going to pay you a visit and get you to see me, but I never thought you would. Believe it or not, I'm also pleased Melissa turned out to be a good wife to you and mum to Shay. You deserve that.'

'Thanks, Dar.'

'Craig's a good person, you know. I'm glad you and

him are mates. This gaff belongs to him. He bought it and rented it out to me as he wanted to get me off the Mardyke. The Social pay the rent, and even if they'd refused to, Craig would've let me live here for nothing.'

'Are you shagging him?' Jason couldn't help but ask.

'No. He's extremely happy with his young wife and I'm happy for him. Just like I'm happy for you and Melissa. As for my son, I'm so disappointed in him, Jase. I was a good mum to him, wasn't I? He heard about me turning up at your reception and moved out. I don't hear from him at all now.'

'I knew he'd heard about my infamous blowjob as he rang me up, screaming abuse. I've never heard from him since.'

'Craig hunted him down recently and told him I was dying, yet he still hasn't been in touch.'

'Dying!' Jason spluttered.

'Yes. The doctors have given me a year, tops. Didn't Craig tell you that?'

Jason's eyes filled with tears. 'No, Dar. He didn't.'

CHAPTER TWENTY-EIGHT

'You all right, Jason? Only you seem very quiet. Not having second thoughts, are you? Because if so, say something now.'

Jason flopped on the sofa. He hadn't been sleeping well, could not stop thinking about that *Crimewatch* reconstruction, Darlene's plight, Tracey's baby, Craig Thurston, and how to shift the poxy painting. 'I'm just tired that's all.'

'Have a nap. I thought we'd get a takeaway later,' Melissa said. She'd yet to tell Jason that she had invited Tracey and Simon round. She had rung Simon herself and told him not to say anything as she wanted to surprise Jason on his first night back home. She'd also told him to come alone.

'OK.'

Melissa sat next to her husband and held his hand. She hated seeing him look so troubled. 'I want you to know that I'm here for you, and I intend to make our marriage work again. It's not going to be easy, I know, but I'm willing to give my all if you are.'

Feeling guiltier than ever that he'd slept with Tracey,

Jason held his wife's face in his hands and gently kissed her on the lips.

'What the hell you doing?' Donte asked, glaring at his mother around the door frame. He'd been earwigging outside.

'We're talking. What do you think we're doing? Have you tidied your room up like I told you to?'

'Yes. Can I go round Calvin's now?'

'As long as you walk. I'm having a day off of being your taxi driver.'

Jason stood up. 'I'll drop him off.'

Donte looked at Jason with hatred. 'No thanks. I'd rather walk than go anywhere with you.'

'Donte! Don't be so rude. Apologize immediately,' Melissa ordered.

When Donte flounced out the room, Jason stopped Mel from following him. 'Leave him be. He'll come round in time. So will Shay. Kids, eh? Pain in the butt.'

After trying on numerous outfits, Tracey Thompson decided on wearing her skinny white jeans, cerise silk baggy top and pink animal-print stiletto ankle boots which matched her outfit perfectly. Rifling through her jewellery box, she put on her Swarovski drop earrings with matching necklace. She no longer wore her wedding ring, but still wore the engagement ring Kieron had bought her. It was a massive rock, too good not to wear, so she'd swapped it over to her right hand.

She couldn't wait to wipe that self-assured smile off Jason's face later. By telling Simon it was his child she could have the best of both worlds. A lovely home, money in the bank, Melissa in her life, and revenge.

*

Simon Champion rang the Ramplings' bell and glanced at his watch. He'd purposely arrived early as he wanted to get away early. He'd promised to pick Christine up from Brentwood at eleven. She'd been out with friends all day at the races.

'All right, Si? Come in. Jason'll be back soon. He had to pop over to his sister. She's got a new job in a care home and he wanted to give her a card and present.'

Simon kissed Melissa on the cheek and handed her a bottle of wine and some flowers. 'I can't stay late. I need to leave about half ten to pick Christine up. Has Jason . . . ?' Simon's jaw dropped as he walked into the kitchen. 'Er, hello, Tracey. I didn't know you would be here. How are you keeping?' he stammered.

It had been a scorching July day and Simon was dressed in knee-length baggy beige shorts and a navy Hackett polo shirt; Tracey couldn't help but think how modern he looked for once. Even his slip-on brogues were pretty cool. Melissa was right, he did have a kind face and at six foot was a decent height. It was the glasses and beer belly that let him down mainly. He needed a decent haircut too. Tracey patted the chair next to her. 'I'm fine, thank you. How about yourself?'

Feeling incredibly awkward, Simon glanced at Melissa for clues. She knew full well he had met Christine and was happy, so why had she told him to come alone this evening and invited Tracey? It just didn't make sense.

Jason was surprised to see Simon's silver grey BMW X5 parked outside his house. His pal hadn't called him to say he was popping round. 'Gonna have to go now as I've just pulled up at home, sweetheart. If I don't get a chance to bell you tomorrow, I'll call you on Monday,'

Jason told Darlene, before switching off his pay-as-you-go mobile and hiding it in his glove compartment. He'd bought it after he'd got involved with Craig's firm, had thought it best not to use his own phone in case anything came on top.

'What's that dodgy accountant of mine doing 'ere, eh?' Jason shouted out as he strolled into the kitchen. His face fell and heartbeat increased as he saw Tracey sitting at his kitchen table. She had a sickly smile on her face. 'All right, Trace, Si? Yous two look cosy. Not back together, are ya?' he joked, hoping Melissa didn't cotton on to how awkward he felt. He hadn't contacted Tracey since he'd told her the score, was too scared to speak to her on the phone in case the vindictive bitch recorded him. She was that type and he wouldn't put anything past her.

'I invited Simon to join us for something to eat, Jase. I can tell you haven't been yourself these past few days and thought it might cheer you up. Tracey popped round on the off chance,' Melissa lied. 'So she's gonna have a take-away with us too. The more the merrier, eh? Just like old times.'

'Why haven't you been yourself, Jason? You worried about something?' Tracey asked innocently. He looked so hot tonight. His slicked-back blond hair glistened against his tanned skin and the blue polo shirt matched his eye colour.

'Only money. Right, who's having what to drink? Another beer, Si?' Jason asked, opening one for himself and taking a much-needed gulp. Tracey was toying with him, he knew that. Watching him squirm would give her immense satisfaction. What the hell had he been thinking when he fucked her? If only he hadn't been drunk; he'd never have gone there sober.

Feeling anxious, Melissa poured herself a glass of wine. 'Do you want a wine, Trace?' she asked her pal.

'Just a tiny glass. I'm being good.'

'You've changed. Thought I had shares in the vineyard on our cruise,' Simon chuckled. He had a strong sense of humour and laughing his way out of an uneasy situation was the only way he knew. She was a real looker, Tracey, had a bit of Kylie Minogue about her, and Simon had loved having her on his arm and in his bed. Intellectually, though, they were miles apart. Christine had more sense in her big toe than Tracey did in her whole body.

Determined to wipe the silly grin off Simon's face, Tracey announced, 'I only ever knock 'em back when I'm bored.'

Sensing an elephant in the room, Melissa said, 'Right, let's order some food. I don't know about you three, but I'm starving.'

'Actually, I've got an announcement to make first,' Tracey said, locking eyes with Jason, who quickly looked away.

'What's that then?' Melissa asked, hoping her voice didn't sound false.

Tracey turned to Simon and smiled. 'I'm pregnant. We're going to be parents.'

'You what!' Like a rabbit caught in the headlights, Simon glanced nervously at Melissa, then Jason, before turning back to Tracey. Was this some kind of a joke? Because nobody was laughing.

'Oh, wow, Trace! Really?' Melissa gushed, hoping she sounded shocked.

'Yes. I only found out earlier this week myself. I kept being sick, so did a pregnancy test. I was gobsmacked at first, wasn't sure if I wanted to be a mum, but now I've had time to digest the news, I have decided that it's meant to be.' Tracey couldn't remember the exact date when she had last slept with Simon as she had been inebriated most days on their cruise, but she guessed it was little more than a couple of weeks before she had slept with Jason. She intended to pretend the baby was overdue and was sure she could get away with the lie. Simon wouldn't be coming to her appointments with her; neither did she want him there when she gave birth. Mel could be her birthing partner, and the midwife and doctors would not be allowed to discuss her medical records with anybody, Simon included.

Jason was stunned, couldn't speak. Simon had always wanted to be a father. How could the bitch do this to him?

Simon held his head in the palm of his right hand. 'I don't know what to say. I have a new woman in my life now, Tracey, but obviously I will support my child and be there for you,' he muttered.

Melissa glanced at her husband. He looked shell-shocked and she knew why. It had brought Bobby's death back to him, just like it had her. She squeezed his hand. 'You OK, Jase?'

Knowing he had to pull himself together, Jason forced a smile, lifted his can of Stella in the air, and looked in turn at both Tracey and Simon. 'I'm made up for the pair of ya. Congrats, guys,' he said weakly.

Tracey grinned. 'Thank you, Jason. I know me and your pal Simon aren't an item, but I'm sure he'll make a wonderful daddy. Won't you, Si?'

Still flabbergasted, Simon lifted his arms and shrugged. 'Well, I'm forty next year and I've always wanted kids. So yeah, bring it on.'

*

Donte Brooks was not a happy lad. Furious with his mother for not telling him the truth, even though he genuinely needed the information for a school 'Family Tree' project, Donte had rung his grandfather. Unbeknown to his mum, he and Shay had visited Johnny in hospital after he'd been shot, and Donte had kept in touch with him on the phone ever since.

Feeling nervous, yet also incredibly excited, Donte clicked on to the internet site 'Friends Reunited'. He typed in 'Joel Wright' and lots of men popped up. Donte's heart beat wildly. Was one of them his dad?

His teacher had recently quoted, 'Every child has a right to know who their mother and father is,' and Sir was never wrong. His mum was bang out of order. No way would he forgive her for lying about his dad's surname. Not ever.

After another sleepless night, Jason was mentally drained. He had a busy day ahead and would have to pay that bitch another visit later. What the hell was she playing at? Was the kid his? Simon's? He would demand a DNA test when it was born before he shelled out any money, that was for sure.

Unaware he had been followed all morning by an array of vehicles, Jason drove to the small car park that was situated opposite the Camelot pub. He'd sorted the slaughters now, had the keys to both properties, and Craig had wanted to meet him in person.

First to arrive, Jason got out of his car and stretched his legs. His thoughts turned to Darlene. He was devastated she had terminal cancer, couldn't get it out of his mind. She might be a lot older than him, but she was the nearest to true love he had found. He'd rung her earlier and was taking her out for the day tomorrow. Melissa didn't know he was bunking off work, so she'd be none the wiser.

The screech of tyres made Jason jump. Craig pulled up beside him in a big flashy black jeep that was anything but inconspicuous. He jumped out. 'Let's walk.'

'Bit loud, that motor, ain't it? I take it you don't mind being spotted wherever you go?'

Craig opened the back door and two Rottweilers leapt out, nearly knocking Jason over. 'Don't bother me, being followed; I never get my hands dirty in the first place. Meet Ronnie and Reggie. Love a rabbit and a squirrel, they do. Reggie even killed a deer recently. A baby, it was – he ripped its throat clean out,' Craig laughed.

Noticing one of the dogs salivating at the mouth while giving him the evil eye, Jason averted his eyes from the creatures and fell into step beside Craig. 'The slaughters I rented are perfect, I think. One is in a block of flats not far from the Cross Keys in Dagenham; the other is in Barking, but on a busy road. Both are small blocks of privately owned flats. I viewed a few houses, but they were a bit iffy. One was on Scrattons Farm Estate and as soon as I pulled up I had a gang of kids hanging around asking me questions. Too much like the Mardyke, Scrattons is. Everybody knows everybody, and if you're a stranger you'll stand out a mile.'

'Yeah. I get that. What's the comings and goings like at the flats?'

'OK. Most people are at work all day, so my pal reckons. Probably better to get the lads to park away from the buildings, that would be my suggestion. There were no nosy bastards lurking about any time I pulled up there. I thought they had a good feel about 'em.'

'OK. I trust your judgement. Got the keys on you?'

Jason handed over an envelope.

'Good man.'

'Look, Craig, I can't keep doing this. I'm sorry. But it's making me ill. I'm not sleeping of a night.'

Craig grabbed Jason in a headlock and chuckled. 'Get some sleeping pills then, ya nutter. What am I gonna do with you, eh, mate? You're such a fucking pansy, you really are.'

Not knowing what else to say or do, Jason chuckled too. Little did he know at that point, his complicated life was about to get a whole lot worse.

Jason was just about to lock up the shop for the day when he heard the door open, and a distinctive voice. 'What do you want?' he snapped.

Mickey Two Wives picked up a DVD player. 'No need to be fucking rude, is there?'

'I need to be somewhere. Was just leaving.'

'Not before you've listened to what I've got to say, ya fucking don't. You got rid of it yet?'

Aware that Mickey meant the Van Gogh, instinct told Jason to say, 'Yes.' Those Irish gypsies were horrible bastards and he didn't want them turning up on his doorstep.

'See it on *Crimewatch*?'

'Yeah.'

'Well, I got a warning for ya. Those mushes don't mess about ya know. One whiff of you opening your fucking trap, they'll torture your wife and kids in front of ya, before chopping you up in segments.'

Finding it difficult to swallow all of a sudden, Jason nodded. 'I'm no snitch. As I said it's gone. Not even in the country any more.'

'Good. How much is this?' Mickey still had the DVD player in his hands.

'It's marked up at forty. Thirty to you, if you want it.'

Mickey Two Wives dropped the DVD player on to the floor, then obliterated it with the sole of his Dealer boot.

'What the hell are you doing?'

Mickey pointed at the mangled piece of equipment. 'If I find out you've lied to me, that'll be your fucking head.'

CHAPTER TWENTY-NINE

Jason Rampling drove towards Darlene's with the weight of the world on his shoulders. Melissa was refusing to speak to him this morning. She'd got paralytic drunk last night and demanded he sleep with her as she wanted another baby.

Jason sighed. It had been like shagging a floppy rag doll, but he'd done it to keep the peace. Now she was blaming him for taking advantage of her when drunk. He had never taken advantage of a woman in his life, would never dream of forcing a female into having sex. It had really pissed him off that his own wife should say such a vile thing, and what's the betting she would tell that bitch Tracey too.

When Jason had asked Darlene where she would most like to go for the day, her answer had been 'Margate'. She used to go there once a year on a beano with a crowd from the Silver Hall and said it reminded her of happier times.

Jason forgot his woes the second he pulled up outside Darlene's house. The July weather was scorching and she was standing on her doorstep looking a picture. She'd ditched the headscarf for what he presumed to be a long dark wig, and placed on top of that was a huge straw hat. She was dressed in denim jeans and waistcoat with a long mauve vest top and trainers. Jason got out the car. 'What you got in there?' he chuckled, as he spotted an ice box and woven basket.

'Food and drink. I made us a picnic,' she grinned.

Seeing the nosy bastard who'd been pretending to wash his car the other day peering out the window, Jason decided to give him something to look at. He put his arms around Darlene's waist and kissed her gently on the lips. 'You never fail to amaze me, Dar. When God made you he most certainly broke the mould, girl.'

'You come straight home from school, do you hear me?' Melissa Rampling shouted as her sulky son picked up his school bag. She'd caught Donte searching for his father yesterday, had smashed up his phone in temper and confiscated his computer.

'Lay off him, Mel. And where is my dad? I heard you two frolicking in bed last night like silly teenagers. It isn't going to work, you know. You're messed up in the head,' Shay smirked.

Ignoring Shay, Melissa yelled, 'Donte, I swear if you don't come straight home, I will pick you up from school every day until you break up for the summer holidays.'

Donte spun around and stuck his middle finger up. He hadn't known his mother and Jason had slept together last night. That made him despise her even more. 'Fuck you. And if you think smashing up my phone and hiding my computer is going to stop me searching for my father, you are very wrong. I'm going to find him and get away from you.'

*

'What do you want to do first?' Jason asked, holding Darlene's arm to steady her. She was very thin; he could feel her bones rubbing against him.

'Can we go to the amusement arcades? When I was growing up my aunt had a caravan in Great Yarmouth. I used to love the one-arm bandits, couldn't wait to visit her to play them again. I can't walk far now, so I thought after that we'd plot up on the beach for the afternoon. Are you expected home at a certain time?'

'Nope. I'm all yours.' Jason stopped outside a shop, picked up a hat with KISS ME QUICK written on the front and placed it on his head. 'Well?'

Laughing, Darlene stood on tiptoes and pecked the only man she had ever truly loved on his luscious lips. Jason Rampling was far more of a help to her illness than that bloody chemotherapy had been. He made her feel young and vibrant again.

'Oh, hello Si,' Melissa said. She was expecting a delivery and had thought it had arrived.

'I can't get hold of Jason. Don't know where he is, by any chance, do you? He isn't answering his phone and is not at the shop. I was passing, so thought I'd pop by on the off chance. I actually wanted to talk to you about the Tracey situation.'

'Come in, I'll put the kettle on. I've no idea where Jason is, I'm afraid. He went off in a huff this morning and it's all my fault. I feel terrible now.'

Simon sat down at the kitchen table. 'Do you want to talk about it?'

Without going into great detail, Melissa explained about Donte wanting to track his real father down. 'So last night, me being me, I downed two bottles of wine to forget the awful day I'd had, and Jason and I ended up in bed. I felt an idiot this morning, like a desperado, so I accused Jason of taking advantage of me. He looked horrified and now I feel dreadful. I've tried ringing him, but his phone's switched off.'

'Did you leave a message?'

'Yeah. I just said I was out of order and I didn't mean what I said. I find it so hard at times, Si, to forget what he did. I've been having horrible thoughts today. For all I know, he might be round at bloody Charlotte's house now. I want to trust him and I just hope that in time I do.'

'No way will he be with Charlotte, so get that out of your head. I'm his best mate, he tells me everything and I can assure you you're the only woman he has eyes for. He seriously wants to make another go of things, and is genuinely sorry for how he hurt you. If you give him a chance, he'll make it up to you, I promise.'

Putting two steaming mugs of coffee on the table, Melissa sat opposite Simon. 'What I want to know is why he is suddenly short of money. I've asked him and he's very vague. He said it's only a temporary blip, so has he got money owed to him?'

Simon shuffled uncomfortably in his seat. 'The one thing I can't discuss with you is his finances, Mel. I'm sorry, but as his accountant I'd be breaking the law. Jason trusts me and I'd never betray him.'

'I know. Sorry for putting you in an awkward position, but do you think his finances will improve in the long run?'

Thinking of the painting, Simon smiled. 'Yes, I think you'll be absolutely fine in the long run. But I can't say any more than that, OK?'

Relieved, Melissa smiled. 'Thanks for putting my mind at rest. So, when you seeing Tracey? She said you had to cancel going out for a meal.'

'I did. To be honest, I needed some time to get my head around the news. It was a bit of a shock, to say the least. Mel, if I ask you something could you please be truthful with me? Whatever you say, I will never repeat, I swear.'

'Of course.'

'You obviously know Tracey better than anyone else. I need to know if there is any chance this child might be another man's. I'm not thick; I know Trace wasn't that into me, so I wondered if she was seeing anybody else around the same time as me?'

'Absolutely not,' Melissa said confidently. 'Tracey tells me everything where men are involved and she's not slept with anyone else. No way did she cheat on you, she wouldn't be able to keep it secret, would have definitely told me.'

Simon breathed a sigh of relief. 'Thank you. Only Christine hasn't taken the news well at all. She isn't maternal and thinks we should call it a day. I've explained to her that I'm not interested in getting back with Tracey, but she's standing firm. She reckons a child would complicate things and I suppose she has a point. We haven't even been together that long. I am gutted though, I did really like her.'

'I know you did. What a shame. But there's plenty more fish in the sea and there's no point being with a woman who won't accept your child. I actually reckon when the baby's born you and Trace might get back together. Kids change everything.'

Simon shook his head. 'No way. Been there, done that,

got the T-shirt. She's a very pretty girl is Trace, but too much of an airhead for my liking,' Simon chuckled. 'Obviously, I will support her and the baby though. That kid will want for nothing. I'm gonna be a dad. I keep pinching myself to make sure I'm not dreaming.'

Melissa smiled. Simon had such a kind face and nature. 'You're going to make a fantastic father. I'm made up for you, and I mean that from the bottom of my heart.'

'Jesus, Dar. You've brought enough grub to feed the French Foreign Legion,' Jason mocked. Chicken legs, pork pies, quiche, French sticks, two big lumps of cheese, ham, pickles, tomatoes, cocktail sausages – she'd literally thought of everything.

'I fancy a cold beer. Want one?' Darlene asked.

'Does the Pope pray?' Jason laughed. He was thoroughly enjoying their day out. It was a welcome release from all the other shit going on in his life. He'd woken up in a cold sweat thanks to a nightmare, early hours of this morning. Mickey Two Wives and the Irish gypsies had him tied up in some barn and were torturing him.

'Take your T-shirt off. You can top up your colour. Not that you need to, you're as brown as a berry anyway. I often wondered when you were a kid if your dad was Spanish, as you used to go so brown. Don't get many blond Spaniards though, do you?'

'I inherited the dragon's hair colour. Shame I never knew my old man. I reckon he must have been a cool dude as I certainly never took after my mother. Then again, he must have had a screw loose to give her one. Either that, or he was blind drunk,' Jason chuckled.

'Stop it,' Darlene laughed. 'I can't eat any more, I'm full already. Poxy disease takes away your appetite. I barely ate anything when I was having the chemo. Everything tasted of metal to me.'

Jason took his T-shirt off, rolled up his faded jeans and propped his elbow up in the sand. 'Are you not having chemo now?'

'No. I can honestly say I have never felt so ill as when I was having that. It would've only prolonged my life for another six months or year anyway. Who wants to spend their last year or so on earth feeling like shit? And I lost all my hair. Broke my heart, that did. It's started to grow back now, but I look like something out of *Bad Girls*.'

Jason squeezed Darlene's hand. 'You look beautiful with or without hair, and anyone who tells you any different will have me to deal with.'

Darlene felt comforted by his hand holding hers. Jason was a beautiful man inside and out. His blond gelled-back hair glistened in the sun, and his eye colour matched the sea. 'I know I've already said this, but I truly am sorry for being such a bitch to you. Whatever must your wedding guests have thought?'

'It's forgotten, honest, Dar. And let's be honest, it was funny. Not often you see the groom getting a blowjob at the reception,' Jason winked.

Darlene chuckled. 'How is Mel? You getting on OK since you moved back in?'

Desperate to tell somebody his woes, Jason sat up and held both of Darlene's hands. The beach was busy and Jason could tell people were watching them, probably gossiping about the age gap. Jason was his own man, had never been bothered about other people. They must lead sad lives if all they had to do was stare at him and Darlene. 'I need your advice, Dar, in more than one area of my life. I know I can trust you and I don't know who else to turn to. You must never mention anything to Craig though. I know how close you and him are.'

'We're not that bloody close. Honestly, Jason, whatever you tell me I'll take to my grave with me.'

'I need to get out of the situation I've got myself in with Craig. I'm in over my head. I'm not a drug dealer, babe. I'm a Del Boy. I got roped in and it's started to keep me awake at night. Do you think you could have a word with Craig for me? You know full well I can be trusted. I don't know that much about what they're up to anyway, but I would never breathe a word about what I do know. I just wanna walk away, quietly like.'

Darlene stroked Jason's cheek. He had his dark shades on and looked so much like Don Johnson used to in *Miami Vice*. He had such a similar mouth and smile as Don. 'I will do my best. Craig does listen to me, but he can be an obstinate sod at times. I reckon I can get you a pardon though. Leave it with me.'

'You're a star,' Jason said, tenderly removing the lock of wig that had fallen over her eyes. 'I've also done something else even more fucking stupid.'

'What? You nutter,' Darlene laughed.

'Knocked up me wife's best mate, ain't I.'

Darlene gasped. 'Oh, Jason. You silly, silly boy. When will you ever learn?'

'Simon popped round earlier,' Melissa told Tracey as she sat at the kitchen table.

'And what did he have to say? I'm sure he is avoiding me.'

'He isn't, Trace. The news has only just sunk in, I think. He'll be ringing you later, wants to meet up with you tomorrow. He's ever so excited about the baby. His bird isn't though; I think she's ended it with him. Don't tell him I told you that, mind. Let him tell you himself.'

Tracey had a feeling of euphoria wash over her. She didn't want to be with Simon, but he would be far easier to exploit without his girlfriend sticking her oar in. 'So what's happened with you and Jase? You said you had an argument.'

Melissa told Tracey she'd caught Donte searching for his dad.

'Wow! Do you think Donte will track Joel down? Bet if he does, Joel won't want sod-all to do with him. Probably married with a family of his own now.'

'That's my point exactly. If I thought Joel was now a decent human being who would welcome Donte into his life and be a good influence, I would happily get in touch with him myself. My biggest fear is for Donte to be rejected by him. Imagine how he'd feel if he searched high and low for his father and then he didn't want to know him. It would break Donte's heart and mine. I worry about his studies. I really want him to do well in life and have a good career. If Joel messes with his head it's bound to affect him at school. His work went downhill when Jason and I split up, so I dread to think how this will affect him.'

'Donte's a sensible lad deep down, mate. I wouldn't worry too much. You were always unsure if Joel had given you his real surname anyway. Perhaps he won't even find him?'

'I hope not.'

'So is that what you and Jase rowed over?' Tracey pried. She was dying to know all the gossip.

'No. Oh, Trace, I've done something really stupid.'

Dying to find out what, Tracey struggled to sound casual. 'Don't keep me in suspense then, spill the beans,' she laughed.

'I slept with Jason.'

The silly big grin on Tracey's face literally evaporated within seconds.

Jason cracked open another two cans of lager and handed one to Darlene. 'Been a brilliant day, ain't it, babe? I could look at that sea for hours. It chills my bones.'

'I meant what I said, Jase. You really do need to find a way of telling Mel about you and Tracey. She's bound to hate you at first, but it's better than lying to her and Simon. A secret as big as that is always going to haunt you and come out in the long run. That Tracey sounds like a right wrong 'un to me.'

'She is, but I can't talk about her any more today. Even the mention of her name makes my skin crawl. The beach is clearing now, look. What shall we do next? I don't want to go home yet.'

'Neither do I, but we must. I'm happy, but shattered. And you must go home and make up with Mel. She'll be wondering where you are, seeing as you switched your phone off and left it in the car. You mustn't let her worry, Jason. She sounds like a nice person.'

'She is, but today is about us,' Jason kneeled in the sand, his eyes twinkling with devilment. 'How d'ya fancy staying down here the night? I'll find us a half-decent hotel or B & B.'

'No. We can't. We mustn't.'

'Why not? We never got to spend the whole night together in all the years I was seeing you, did we? You always used to chuck me out in case Andy came home,' Jason grinned.

Darlene smiled. If today was the day she took her last breath, she would die the happiest woman ever. 'It was always my dream to spend the whole night with you and wake up with you in the morning, Jason. But that was then and this is now. I'm knackered, old, dying, and you have a lovely wife waiting for you indoors.'

Jason's eyes stared into Darlene's. 'We haven't got to do anything, babe. I just want to be with you, that's all, and hold you in my arms.'

Grabbing Jason's head, Darlene planted a kiss on his forehead. 'OK, my love. Whatever you want.'

After getting over her initial shock that Melissa had slept with the man whose child she was carrying, Tracey was now doing her utmost to put a spanner in the works. 'No way should you be apologizing to him, mate. If you were that drunk and you can barely remember the sex, then he obviously took bloody advantage of you. If you were a nasty person, you could even ring the police and cry rape for such behaviour. Lots of women would.'

'Oh, don't be so daft, Trace. He isn't a rapist, he's my bloody husband. I remember banging on about wanting another baby. Chances are I dragged him off to bed to make one. I just felt such an idiot when I woke up naked and he was lying next to me. Talk about let him straight back into my bed! I was determined to hold out for at least a month or so, now I feel like a desperado. That's why I went on the turn with him.'

'Try his number again. Only, if Simon can't get hold of him and he isn't in the shop, you can bet your bottom dollar he's with a bird.'

Melissa's heart sank. 'Please don't say that. I've had a bad enough day as it is.'

*

The B & B was hardly the Ritz. It was a typical last-minute booking you would expect on a baking hot day in Margate.

Jason chuckled as he bounced on the bed. 'Jesus, Dar. This feels like concrete. You sure you don't want to go elsewhere?'

'It's fine. The company is the most important thing, not the room.'

Jason flicked through his iPod and stopped at the sultry sound of Bob Marley's 'Three Little Birds'. 'Reminds me of being round yours as a kid, this does. You were always playing Bob.'

Darlene sat on the bed next to Jason and squeezed his hand. 'I really think you should ring Melissa. She'll be worried sick if you don't go home.'

'Fuck her. Let her worry. Anyway, there's nowhere in the world I'd rather be at this precise moment than here with you.'

Darlene held his handsome face in her hands. 'I never stopped loving you, ya know. You'll always have that special place in my heart.'

Tears pricking his eyes, Jason wrapped his arms around her. 'Ditto, babe. I never stopped loving you either. You'll always be my girl.'

CHAPTER THIRTY

'Good morning, beautiful lady. Did you sleep OK? My neck's as stiff as a board. Worth it to wake up with you though,' Jason grinned. It had been a great day and evening. They'd reminisced and played music until the early hours. They'd kissed, cuddled, laughed and cried, but they hadn't made love. 'I don't want to complicate your life, Jason. I'd also rather you remember my body the way it was,' Darlene had insisted. She'd had a mastectomy and had slept in her clothes.

'I went out like a light. Hardly surprising though, that's the latest night I've had in ages.'

'I'm starving. I think I'll jump in the shower, then we'll grab a bit of breakfast before we head home. Would you like to use the bathroom first?'

'Yes, please. I have no appetite of a morning any more, but I'd love a strong coffee. Thanks so much for yesterday, Jase. It was brilliant. You really do know how to put the spring in the step of a decrepit old woman.'

Jason pecked her on the lips. 'None of that talk. You'll

never be old and decrepit in my eyes. You've either got it or you haven't, and you've always had it, Dar.'

Melissa woke up with a stonking headache. So much for turning over a new leaf and her diet. Two bottles of red she'd sunk when Jason hadn't come home.

Gingerly stepping out of the bed, Melissa was horrified to see it was gone ten o'clock. She'd stayed up until the early hours and wasn't sure what time she'd finally staggered off to bed. Checking Donte's room then Shay's, Melissa was relieved to see they'd taken themselves off to school. Donte still wasn't speaking to her, had even refused to come out of his bedroom to eat his dinner yesterday.

Melissa searched for her phone and found it in the kitchen. There was a missed call from Jason and her heart beat wildly as she pressed the call-back key. 'All right, it's me. I got your messages. Don't bother ringing me back as I got a bit of business to sort out this morning. I'll be home around lunchtime and we can talk properly then.'

Melissa burst into tears. She needed to get a grip on her life otherwise their marriage was never going to work. And what must the kids think of her? She always got up to make their breakfast and see them off to school.

Thinking of the conversation she'd had with Tracey the previous day, Melissa opened the remaining bottles of wine and poured the contents down the sink. Jason was right. Tracey was a bloody shit-stirrer. There had been no need for her to insist Jason was with another woman and if she hadn't got on the wine, she wouldn't have taken any notice of her friend's scare-mongering. Well, enough was enough. It was time for some major lifestyle changes.

Donte deserved better than having a lush as a mother, that was for sure.

As Melissa threw the empty bottles into the bin, she had no idea that her lifestyle would soon change in the most incredible way ever.

Having taken a couple of Alka-Seltzers to clear the fuzziness in her head, Melissa was mopping the kitchen floor when she heard the key in the front door. 'That you, Jason?' she shouted.

Jason sauntered into the kitchen. 'I don't want to argue, but you were bang out of order, Mel. I would never disrespect a woman sexually. You know me better than that, girl.'

'I know and I'm sorry. I felt embarrassed the next morning and took it out on you. I've decided to knock the drink on the head for good, Jase. It doesn't agree with me lately and I want to be the best wife and mother possible from now on.'

'You don't have to give it up; just don't be so greedy with it. It's only when you're really pissed you tend to go on the turn.'

'No. I've made my mind up. Where did you sleep last night?'

'At the shop,' Jason lied.

Tears stinging her eyes, Melissa asked, 'Can we start all over again? I do still love you and want to make us work.'

'Yeah. I don't see why not. Listen, I need to take this call. It's business,' Jason said, as Craig's number popped up on his personal phone again. He'd left his other phone in the glove box and knew this must be important as Craig never rang on this line as a rule.

'OK. I'll put the kettle on.'

Jason walked out into the garden and pressed Craig's number. 'Whassa matter?' he asked.

'Ring me on a different phone,' Craig barked, ending the call immediately.

Telling Melissa he'd left something in the car, Jason went out the front and rang Craig on his other phone.

'I need you to get hold of your estate agent mate and pick up a spare set of keys for the Dagenham gaff. The klutz who is running stuff there has lost his set. You got a pen and paper?'

'No. Why?'

'To take the geezer's number. Once you have the keys you can arrange to drop 'em off to him.'

'I ain't going nowhere near that flat, Craig. I'll meet you and you can drop 'em off to him.'

'I'm up in Liverpool at a funeral. Just drop 'em off for me, eh? Either that or my guy'll pick 'em up from your pal. Sort it and I'll make it worth your while, I promise.'

Not wanting to put his pal in a predicament, Jason reluctantly agreed to drop the keys off himself. He ended the call and sighed. The quicker Darlene spoke to Craig and got him out of this mess, the better.

'Cheers, Paul. Sorry about this,' Jason said, as his pal handed him the keys through his car window.

'No worries. I will have to send someone round to get the locks changed though. The owners are abroad and I'm acting landlord of the property.'

'No. Don't do that. I'll make sure the locks are changed and give you another set of keys. Don't go near the gaff, Paul, seriously.'

'OK. Not being funny, Jase, but I think I'll have to pull

out of this agreement of ours soon. My wife will chop my balls off if I get arrested, and it all sounds a bit too cloak and dagger for my liking.'

'No probs. I want out myself, between me and you. Nothing worse than constantly looking over your shoulder.'

'Too right. Drop the new keys in to me ASAP, Jase. Take care, mate. Look after yourself.'

Jason drove away from the rear of his pal's shop and stopped the car. With the untraceable phone, he rang the number Craig had given him. 'Hiya. Is that Smurf?'

'Yeah, man.'

'Your boss asked me to drop off some keys. Can you meet me at the Bull pub car park?'

'No can do. Here on my own at the moment.'

'I'll pull up nearby and you can run downstairs then.'

'I ain't got no key to get back in and no way am I leaving the door open. Anything goes wrong, it's my head on the chopping block.'

'OK. I'll come up the stairs.'

Vigilant on the journey, Jason was relieved when the motorbike he'd spotted behind him carried on down Church Elm Lane as he turned off. He took no notice of the Water Board van parked up near the flats. Neither did he get an inkling somebody was clicking away with a camera.

Simon Champion complimented Tracey on how glamorous she looked and held open the passenger door. 'I know you like fish, so I booked us a table at the restaurant adjoined to the Top Oak. The lobster's good there. I hope that's OK?'

'Yes, that's fine. How have you been? Has the news sunk in yet?' Tracey asked.

'It sure has. I'm extremely excited now, to be honest. A client of mine's wife is an interior designer and she's offered to turn one of my rooms into a nursery. I want the child to have sleepovers at mine – that's OK with you, isn't it?'

'Yes, of course. You can have weekend access, if you want. That will give me a break.'

'I would love that. I know it's too early yet, but are we going to find out the sex beforehand? Don't get me wrong; as long as our baby is healthy, I would be equally as happy with a boy or a girl. How about you?'

Thinking of Jason, Tracey replied, 'Boy.' Watching another man raise his son would be difficult for Jason and she knew it. Especially after Bobby's death. Once that kid was walking and talking he would truly regret the way he'd treated her. 'I'm not sure I want to know the sex beforehand, I'll think about that. There'll be lots of things to decide between us though. We'll need to discuss names, write a list and choose some we both like. I don't want to raise our child in Collier Row either, Simon. It's gone downhill since I first moved there. The kids near me are all little ragamuffins and I want better for ours.'

'I completely agree. I own a couple of flats in Loughton that I rent out, so I was going to suggest I put one of those on the market and buy a place for you and our child to live in. It won't be a mansion, but I can stretch to a two- or three-bedroom property. Obviously, our nipper will need a decent-sized garden for when he or she starts walking.'

'Will the property be in my name?' Tracey asked.

'Erm, no. We're not married, Tracey. We aren't even together. I will pay all the bills though, so you won't have to worry about that. Our child isn't going to want for anything. I will make damn sure of it.'

'OK, thanks. I would prefer a three-bedroomed to a two- though. Be nice to have a spare room for when our child is older and has friends over to stay. The estate Mel and Jason live on is nice, and you've got the security at the main gates for peace of mind.'

'Repton Park is way overpriced in my opinion, Tracey. I was thinking more Epping, Ongar or Abridge. You get some nice properties around those areas that are far more value for money than the ones on Repton Park.'

'OK. When can we start viewing some?'

'Not yet. I haven't even put my flats on the market yet, and I'll need to give the tenants notice. I actually think the contract is due up for renewal in September, so that would work perfectly. When is the baby due? Have they given you an exact date yet?'

'No. But my friend Kim said it's pointless taking any notice of their exact dates. It's quite common to be way overdue when it's your first – she was three weeks late with hers,' Tracey lied.

'Wow! That's a long time. I remember my sister was late with her first. My mum was having kittens, ringing me up every five minutes. I told you about my sister, didn't I? She emigrated to Australia.'

'Yes. I think so. Do you reckon you can buy me a new car as well, please? No way will a pram or pushchair fit in the boot of my Mini.'

'Yes. But I think we're getting a bit ahead of ourselves, Tracey. All in good time. We literally have months to sort all these things out before the baby arrives.'

When Tracey fell silent, Simon turned the music up. Jason had warned him that Tracey would try to extract every penny out of him she could, and he was right. Simon wasn't too bothered though. He could easily afford her demands and besides, she was carrying the one thing he'd always craved – his very own son or daughter.

Melissa and Jason were having a much-needed heart to heart. Not just about themselves, but about the kids too.

'You're being too tough on Donte, in my opinion, Mel, and you're achieving nothing by taking his computer away. You know how he loves playing all his games on it; he'll only hate you more if you stop him doing that.'

'But I don't want him tracking down Joel. That'll only make him feel worse. He's still a child, Jason.'

'He's old for his years, Mel, and if he is that desperate to look for his old man there is sod-all you can do to stop him. Computers are everywhere these days; taking his away isn't going to stop him searching for his father on somebody else's. You need to cut him some slack or you're gonna push the lad away for good. It's tough enough on him that I've moved back in,' Jason warned.

'Will you talk to him tomorrow? He's acting like he despises me – swearing at me as if he's some hooligan off the Mardyke Estate. I never expected that. He's always been polite until recently.'

'I can try, but I reckon you'd do better to sit him down and talk it over with him.'

Melissa squeezed Jason's hand. The more she thought about Tracey's pregnancy, the more desperate she was to become pregnant again herself. 'Wouldn't it be great if I got pregnant too? Our kid could be bezzie mates with Simon and Tracey's.'

'We need to be sure our relationship is sound before we bring a child into the equation, Mel. Not fair on the kid otherwise. There's no rush, is there? Why don't we give it a few months, see how things go?'

Secretly praying she was already pregnant as they'd used no contraception the other evening, Melissa yawned. 'I'm ready for bed. Will you be sleeping in Bobby's nursery or with me?'

'I'm gonna watch a film so will probably crash in Bobby's room. Night, babe. Sleep tight.'

CRASH, BANG, WALLOP – Melissa sat up in bed startled. She could hear men's voices, shouting, and was sure they were inside her house.

'Dad, Dad!' Shay screamed.

Leaping out of her bed, Melissa shrieked in terror as her bedroom door flew open. 'Don't move. Stay exactly where you are,' a man barked. He had a navy baseball hat on with the word POLICE written across the front and a thick protective vest underneath his clothing.

'Oh my God! Whatever's going on?' Melissa cried as Jason was marched into the room wearing only his boxer shorts and a set of handcuffs.

'Listen carefully, all of you,' another officer said as Donte and Shay were led into the room. 'I am arresting you all on suspicion of a conspiracy to supply Class A drugs. You do not have to say anything. But it may harm your defence if you do not mention when questioned something which you later rely on in court. Anything you do say may be given in evidence.'

'Is this some kind of joke?' Melissa spat.

'I'm afraid not, love,' an officer said, flashing a badge and piece of paper. 'DS Chatham, National Crime Squad – and this is a warrant to search your property. Smith, Singh, take the lady with you while you search each room. We don't want to be accused of anything untoward. Jacobs, you take the kids downstairs and make sure they don't tamper with any evidence. Anderson, Fletcher, you stay up here with me in case pretty boy plays up when we get him dressed. If he does, he can be interviewed at the station in his birthday suit.'

Totally shell-shocked, Melissa glared at Jason before urging Shay and Donte to follow the female officer who was beckoning them. She was dressed the same as the men, had the navy baseball cap on and a thick vest protecting her chest.

'Watch 'em like hawks, make sure they don't plant anything, babe,' Jason shouted after Mel. 'This is a big mistake, you'll see. Never taken or handled a drug in the whole of my fucking lifetime.'

CHAPTER THIRTY-ONE

Still in a state of shock, Melissa got inside the police vehicle with her children. Jason had been taken away in handcuffs in a separate unmarked van and hadn't even been allowed to speak to her and the kids before being dragged out the front door.

The neighbours were gathered, no doubt gossiping, and Melissa had never felt so humiliated in all her life as they were driven away. She had never broken a law in her life, so how could they arrest her and her children? It was beyond ridiculous. 'Donte, Shay, are you OK?' she enquired. As far as she was aware, nothing untoward had been found inside the house. The officers had certainly found no drugs, but had taken away a bag full of bits and bobs, including paperwork. They had also taken a mobile phone out of the glove compartment of Jason's car. That worried Mel, as she had never seen that particular phone before.

'Are we going to go to prison?' Shay asked, chewing at her fingernails.

'No. Your dad reckons there has been a mix-up. Hopefully, all will be fine,' Mel replied. She was trying to act brave in front of the children, but it wasn't easy as she was terrified herself.

'I bet my real dad wouldn't get us arrested,' Donte hissed. 'My teachers are bound to hear about this and I bet I get expelled.'

The female police officer turned and smiled at the children. 'You won't be going to prison or getting expelled from school. We just need to ask you some questions, that's all.'

'Where are you taking us then?' Shay asked.

'Barkingside police station. It's not far,' the officer replied.

'Will I be able to make a phone call when I get there?' Melissa asked.

'Not immediately. But later you will.'

Melissa had watched lots of police dramas on TV and knew she had rights. 'But I'm allowed one phone call. It's the law.' She planned to ring Simon. He would know what to do in a situation such as this, surely? She didn't even know the number of a decent solicitor and had no idea if Jason did either.

'Not if you're being held incommunicado, it isn't,' the male officer chirped up.

'And what the hell does incommunicado mean?' Melissa asked angrily. This was beyond a joke now.

'It means you aren't allowed to speak to anyone.'

'But why? I thought everybody who was arrested had the right to a phone call.'

'In a nutshell, your property wasn't the only one raided this morning. Your old man's cronies' homes have been turned over too. So until we know all your husband's pals are safely in our care, nobody gets to make any calls. Got it now?'

Melissa felt like crying. This sounded far more serious than she'd realized. Far more serious indeed.

Still in handcuffs and flanked by two officers, Jason watched miserably as the Old Bill raided his shop. He had lots of hooky stuff in there, items that he knew had been burgled or fallen off the back of a lorry, but he doubted they were interested in those. He'd covered his arse with false receipts for most of the clobber anyway.

'I need to use the toilet. I'm busting,' Jason said.

'Check the khazi, make sure there's no way out. Help him undress an' all. Do not take the handcuffs off,' Chatham ordered a colleague. 'He'll have to drip dry,' he added.

Jason stared miserably at his handcuffs. He'd thought when the Old Bill had smashed the door down in the ferocious way they had that they'd somehow got wind of the painting. Thank goodness they hadn't. That was well hidden elsewhere, along with any clues that might lead the police to it.

'I think we're done 'ere, guv,' said the officer who'd brought the two sniffer dogs in.

'You checked thoroughly out the back?' Chatham asked.

'Yeah. Nothing.'

'Right, let's get Rampling over to the station then, see what he's got to say for himself.'

Jason gave Chatham the evil eye. He was only in his early thirties, Jason reckoned. A cocky, bolshie type with a face only a mother could love. 'No comment, no comment, no comment,' Jason goaded. He was furious they'd taken Melissa and the kids in for questioning. There'd been no need for that whatsoever.

'Drag him up and chuck him in the van,' Chatham

grinned. 'He'll talk when he finds out what evidence we've got on him. Case of having to.'

Melissa had to wait a couple of hours before making her phone call, then couldn't get hold of Simon. So she agreed to let the duty solicitor sit in on the questioning, but refused to take his advice of replying, 'No comment.' She had nothing to hide and wanted to get home as quickly as possible. She had been told the children were free to leave provided a family member could collect them, but Melissa had asked if they could wait there for her. The police had agreed to this and to her request of bringing Donte and Shay sandwiches and drinks. The poor mites hadn't eaten since last night.

DI Parkes, the female office, was by far the nicer of the two asking the questions. Her colleague, DS Carling, was a gruff Scot and Melissa could barely understand him. His intense stare unnerved her too. Parkes had apologized for involving Shay and Donte, but had explained that it was a big operation and they'd had to bring all family members in who were present at this morning's raided addresses to ensure no word of the raids got out.

'Let's go back to your husband's finances, Melissa. Have you ever had a joint bank account since you got married?' Parkes asked.

'No. Jason gave me cards and I used those. He has always dealt with our finances.'

'Did you not enquire from time to time what your husband had in his accounts?' Carling asked.

'No. Occasionally Jason would tell me to rein in my spending if he was going through a bad patch, but so long as the business was doing well I could buy what I liked and all our bills were paid on time, so I had no need to ask. My dad always took care of my mother financially. She never used to worry about bills or money, so to me Jason looking after everything was normal.'

'Really? Even when you were separated?' Carling asked disbelievingly.

A short balding man in his late fifties, the duty solicitor reminded Melissa, 'Any question you aren't sure of the answer, it's wiser to say no comment, dear.'

Melissa nodded, then met Carling's stare. 'My husband is a generous man. Nothing changed financially when we separated. He's always kept me and our children. Paid the mortgage, the bills, and the school fees.'

'Can I ask you why you separated in the first place, Melissa?' Parkes enquired.

'Jason had an affair, but it wasn't all his fault. We'd been through a tough time. I gave birth to a stillborn son and neither of us dealt with it very well. I pushed him away and into the arms of another woman.'

'I'm very sorry to hear about your loss,' DI Parkes said sympathetically.

'Was that last question at all relevant?' the solicitor asked coldly. He hadn't expected to be working today, was meant to be taking his wife out for her birthday later, but because of the raids, the police had needed reinforcements.

'Yes. It was, actually,' Carling replied with more than a hint of sarcasm in his voice. He pushed a piece of paper towards Melissa. 'This is a copy of your husband's bank statement dating back to March this year – 2002, to clarify things for the tape. There is a £250,000 withdrawal made on March twenty-eighth. Have you any idea what your husband purchased with this money?'

Mouth wide open, Melissa shook her head.

'You need to speak up for the tape,' Carling urged.

'No. I don't know anything about the money. But I do know my husband. He isn't perfect – what man is? – but no way would he ever be involved in what you're insinuating. Jason is the most anti-drug person I know.'

'If that's the case, what else could Jason have used this cash for, Melissa?'

'I honestly don't know,' Melissa replied.

'My client needs to take a break now,' the duty solicitor insisted.

Parkes glanced at Carling and nodded. 'We are going to take a break. I am stopping the tape at 11.14 a.m.'

In another room at the same police station, Jason was being asked similar questions. Like Mel, he hadn't managed to get hold of Simon either and was being represented by a duty solicitor.

'If you don't want to spend months on end in prison awaiting your trial, you had better start talking, Jason. What did you need the two hundred and fifty grand for?' DS Chatham asked.

'No comment,' Jason said, for what felt like the hundredth time.

DI Singh leaned forward. 'You really aren't doing yourself any favours, Jason. Because if you cannot tell us what you used that cash for, we will assume that you are one of the ringleaders and used it to purchase the drugs that are now in our possession.'

'No comment.'

Singh picked up an envelope. 'For the benefit of the tape, I am about to show Mr Rampling two photographs. Who are these two women, Jason? Bear in mind, your wife is still being questioned and we could always ask her.'

Jason stared in horror at the two snaps. One had been taken in Margate the other day. He and Darlene were clearly holding hands on the beach. The other was even more troubling. He had a snarl on his face and a hand around Tracey's throat in her porch. 'No comment,' he stammered. All he could think of was thank God he hadn't got hold of Simon. Si had a pal who was a top solicitor and how would he have explained the Tracey photo if word got back to Si?

The solicitor whispered in Jason's ear and his client nodded dumbly. 'Mr Rampling and I would like to take a break now.'

Chatham grinned at Jason. 'While you're taking your break, have a good think. We have got quite a photo collection of you. Not sure Melissa would be impressed with any of 'em, to be honest.'

Singh winked at his prey. 'We are now going to take a break. I am stopping the tape at 11.42 a.m.'

Melissa and the kids arrived home shortly after 1 p.m. She still couldn't get her head around what had happened. She expected to wake up in a minute and realize it was all a bad dream.

The state of the house confirmed that it was no bloody nightmare. Everything had been left as it was after the police finished carrying out their search. Nothing was in the right place, even the furniture was all skew-whiff.

'Do you think they will let Dad come home soon too?' Shay asked.

Desperate for a glass of wine, Melissa remembered she'd poured it away, so instead put the kettle on. She needed a clear head anyway. She'd asked after Jason before leaving the station and was told he was still being questioned. 'I don't know, love. But your dad is no drug dealer, I know that much. I would be amazed if there isn't some mix-up, but who knows. The police must have something on your father to raid our bloody home.' She couldn't help but wonder where all that money had gone. Because he had never spent it on her.

'I'll get it, it might be Dad,' Shay said when the landline rang.

'Who is it?' Melissa asked as Shay handed her the phone.

'Simon.'

'All right, Mel? I was in a meeting and had missed calls from both you and Jase.'

'Oh, Si. Something terrible's happened, can you come round?'

'Erm, yeah, I suppose so. What's wrong?'

'The police raided the house this morning and arrested us all on conspiracy to supply a Class A drug. They've let me and the kids go without charge, but Jason's still being questioned. Do you know anyone who fits front doors too? Ours is ruined. They said they'd made it safe, but it isn't. It's an eyesore.'

'Holy shit! Don't panic, I'll sort it. I'm in Herongate at present. I'll be with you soon as I can.'

Back at Barkingside police station, Jason was in deep thought. If the police had been watching him, which they obviously had, chances were they'd have photographs of him and Craig together. Darlene would be the one to dig him out of that hole. He would say Craig has paid him a visit to tell him about Darlene's illness. He very much doubted the Old Bill had any evidence of him meeting Craig a second time. It was remote, that car park, and he certainly hadn't been followed that day as he remembered checking his mirrors as he turned right at Chigwell Row and there hadn't been a soul behind him.

The missing money was the big problem. He could hardly tell them about the stolen painting, so how the hell was he meant to explain two hundred and fifty grand being withdrawn from an account? It was from a bank in Jersey too, which made it look even more underhanded. He and Simon knew the bank manager in Jersey double well. They played golf with him. Gavin Rodgers was a shady bastard himself. He asked no questions and could somehow make large withdrawals or lump sums of cash going into the bank look perfectly respectable. He charged a hefty fee for his services, and Jason was sure he wasn't the type to spill his guts. Simon reckoned he had plenty of corrupt clients.

Resting his head in his hands, Jason sighed. He was short on readies, would have to sell his belongings to afford a decent solicitor. Pretending he was a heavy gambler seemed the best excuse. If he had to appear in court, which seemed likely, he could create a story about becoming addicted to gambling after he split up with Mel. A good pal of his owned greyhounds, he'd back him up.

Shutting his eyes, Jason said a silent prayer. The one thing he had no excuse for was dropping the key off at that flat in Dagenham. If the Old Bill had been watching him or the flat that day, he was in major trouble.

Melissa was running on autopilot until Simon arrived, then she broke down.

Simon awkwardly put his arms around his pal's wife. 'Don't get upset, Mel. Your Jason could talk his way out of a paper bag. Where are the kids? Are they OK?'

'They've been better. Shay's gone out and Donte's

upstairs in his room.' Melissa had felt so sorry for her son she'd given him his computer back. Donte searching for his father was the least of her problems right now.

'Sit down, Mel, and tell me exactly what happened. I'll make us a brew.'

Melissa explained everything in fine detail. 'It was awful watching the police ransack all our belongings. I don't think I've ever been so scared as when they barged into my bedroom. I thought we were being burgled at first. Jason talks to you, Si. Please tell me what he's involved in? You must know.'

Simon had already made his mind up to say as little as possible. He was a loyal friend and it was Jason's duty to tell his wife what he wanted her to know. 'He never told me he was up to no good, Mel. I'm as shocked by all this as you are,' Simon lied.

'You must know more than me, Si. You're his best pal, you must know something. When I asked you about Jase's money problems, you told me we'd be OK in the long run. Why did he take all that money out the bank? Only I'm now thinking he used it to buy the bloody drugs and he was banking on selling them to sort out our finances.'

'Jason has his finger in many pies, Mel. But I can assure you he would never buy drugs.'

'What has he bought then? You must bloody know.'

'That's for you and him to discuss, Mel. It isn't my place to say.'

'But it's definitely not drugs?'

'No. And you have my word on that.' Simon was actually a worried man. The police must have been watching Jason and if they knew about the withdrawal from his Jersey account, their investigation had gone way too deep for Simon's liking. Would their next step be to drag him in for questioning as well? The last thing he needed was the filth all over him. The majority of his clients were up to no good and he stood to lose them if word got about. 'The Old Bill didn't mention me, did they?' he asked.

'No. I didn't say anything wrong to them, did I?' Melissa asked worriedly. She had already told Simon the answers she'd given to all their questions.

Mel should have just stuck to 'No comment', but Simon didn't want to scare her. 'No. But I'll put you on to my solicitor in case they want to question you again. He's very good. If Jason has to go to court, Tim will represent him. Better the devil you know.'

'Thanks, Si. I wonder when they'll let him come home? Do you think if I ring the station they might give me an update?'

'I wouldn't ring just yet. Perhaps later this evening if you've heard no more. I play golf with a couple of coppers. Do you know the names of the ones who arrested you?'

'Erm, I think one was called Chatham, he raided the house. The two who interviewed me were Parkes and Carling. Parkes is a woman. They said they were from the National Crime Squad.'

Simon's heart sank. The National Crime Squad didn't mess about. They were the heavy mob.

Jason knew more about the law than most. He was street-wise, had been raised in an area where people were regularly nicked. He'd also had a tug or two himself, back in his teenage years, and both times he'd blagged his way out of it at the station.

This was different though. It was massive. But as much as Singh and Chatham poked, probed and threatened him, he wasn't about to crumble.

'How well do you know Craig Thurston, Jason?' Singh asked.

'No comment.'

Chatham leaned forward. 'We are trying to help you here, Jason. We've done our homework; we know you've only been on the scene recently. If you help us, we'll help you, lad.'

'No comment.'

Singh had seen the look of pure horror in Jason's eyes earlier when he had shown him the photographs. He'd been totally unprepared for that. Desperate for Jason to break, Singh took both photos out of the envelope again. 'For the tape, I am about to show Jason the same two photographs I showed him earlier.'

Not even bothering to look at the photos, Jason held Singh's gaze. 'No fucking comment.'

CHAPTER THIRTY-TWO

Having been advised by the solicitor that if he did not start talking he might be locked up until the trial, Jason was now answering some questions. He'd been at the police station for over forty-eight hours by this time and couldn't wait to go home, have a long soak in the bath and change into some clean clothes.

'Just to clarify for the tape, you are saying you had no idea that Craig Thurston and his cronies were involved in importing then distributing Class A drugs?' Singh asked.

'I didn't have a clue, I swear to you. Being a pawnbroker, I often get asked for bits and bobs. I'm no saint, I'll admit that, but I would never knowingly get involved with drugs. I was asked to supply half a dozen untraceable mobile phones. That's my only involvement. I haven't done sod-all else wrong and I wouldn't even have supplied the phones if I'd known it would've resulted in my front door being kicked in.'

'Who asked you for the phones, Jason?' Chatham enquired.

Not wanting to grass on his pal or anybody else for that matter, Jason shrugged. 'I'm not sure of the geezer's real name. I only know him as Woody. He's just a bloke who pops into the shop from time to time.'

'How well do you actually know Craig Thurston?' Chatham asked.

'I've known him for years, but only saw him again recently. He came to my shop enquiring about gold. He said he'd take as much off me as I can get.'

Singh chuckled. 'Pull the other one; it's got bells on, Jason. Gold! Really? I thought even you would come up with something more original than that.'

'It's true,' Jason insisted. No way was he snitching on Craig. Craig was bound to be refusing to answer questions and he would somehow get word to him of what he'd said so they could stick to the same story. That could be their get-out clause if the Old Bill had photographs of them together.

'Let's go back to that huge sum of money you drew out of your bank account. Where is it now, Jason?' Chatham asked.

'I already told you: I had a gambling problem and I spunked it all.'

'And you can prove that, can you?' Chatham replied.

'Not really. I don't tend to keep losing betting slips. Horses and dogs are my biggest downfall.'

'Can you remember the names of any of these dogs or horses you supposedly gambled on?' Chatham asked.

As luck would have it, a pal of Jason's owned a couple of racing greyhounds. 'Jimmy's Game and Beryl's Wrath are two I definitely remember putting a bundle on.'

'Who is your regular bookie?' Singh enquired.

'I don't use betting shops. I go to the tracks – the odds are better there.'

'What track did these dogs run on and what date?'

Chatham asked. He knew Jason was lying and was determined to catch him out.

'Romford and Catford, I think. I can't remember the exact dates, but it would have been end of March beginning of April time. That's when my addiction really took a hold of me.'

'Well, unless you can remember exact dates and we can check out your story and find some proof to back it up, you certainly won't be seeing your wife and kids any time soon. We'll be opposing bail,' Singh informed Jason.

Knowing their good cop/bad cop routine off by heart, Chatham leaned forward. 'We can only help you if you're honest with us, Jason. Be truthful with us and we'll have a word with the judge, get him to be more lenient with you. If you're lucky, you might even get bail.'

'You can't bang me up for something I haven't done. This whole drugs bust has sod-all to do with me, I already told you that.'

'We can bang you up, and if need be we will,' Singh explained. 'So I will ask you again, why did Craig Thurston come to your shop, Jason? What did he really want from you? And please do not say gold again. I don't take kindly to people who insult my intelligence. It makes me angry.'

Jason rested his forehead in his hands. He had a splitting headache. 'I need to take a break. I don't feel well.'

'How the hell am I meant to manage financially? I can't pay the fucking mortgage, can I?' Melissa screamed down the phone. It was two days since the police raid and this was the first time Jason had called her since.

'Let me talk to Dad. Please,' Shay begged.

Sitting at Mel's kitchen table, Tracey was all ears. 'Be

quiet, Shay. Melissa and your dad have important things to discuss,' she urged.

'Why didn't you let me talk to him? I asked you about ten times,' Shay cried, hands on hips when Melissa ended the call.

'Go to your room,' Melissa bellowed.

When Jason's daughter stormed out of the kitchen, Tracey said, 'Don't keep me in suspense. What did Jase say?' She had been stunned by the news. Could not believe she was carrying the baby of a drug smuggler.

Melissa poured herself another glass of the wine Tracey had brought round. Trying to give up the booze when you were married to Jason was proving impossible. 'He's being taken to court tomorrow to see if he can get bail. What am I going to do if he doesn't? I'll never be able to pay the mortgage, the kids' school fees and all the bills.'

Thinking she'd had a lucky escape by telling Simon he was the father of her child, Tracey squeezed Melissa's hand. She felt a bit guilty lately over her fling with Jason. Not terribly guilty, as all those years ago she had seen and liked Jase first and whenever she did feel bad, that's what she reminded herself of. 'You're a survivor, Mel. You'll be OK. Jason's bound to keep his shop open, isn't he? There will still be money coming in.'

'I don't know, and even if he does he'll have to pay somebody to run it full-time. We've not much money in the bank and our mortgage is ever so expensive. I'm scared and worried, Trace. I can't believe he could be so fucking stupid. I will never forgive him if we lose our home and I have to take Donte out of his school. I've got about ten grand in my savings account, but that won't go far.'

'What did you mean when you said to Jase he's hiding something?'

'He doesn't want me to go to court tomorrow for some reason. He said Simon's going and he or Simon will call me afterwards.'

'You should go. You're his wife. Bloody cheek! You don't reckon he's still seeing that Charlotte and she's going, do you? He's such a womanizer, I wouldn't put anything past him.'

'Thanks, Trace. Make me feel better, why don'tcha? I don't even know where the bail hearing is. He didn't say.'

'Well, we must be able to find out. I think you should just turn up. I'll come with you.'

'I'm not sure I want to be anywhere near him, Trace. I fucking hate him right now and I swear, if he doesn't get bail and I lose everything, that's me and him finished for good.'

The police decided to have one more crack at Jason. He was the only member of the gang who was talking. None of the others had said anything.

'My client has something to say,' the solicitor informed Singh and Chatham.

'I will tell you the truth why Craig came to my shop, on condition my wife doesn't find out,' Jason said. He hadn't really wanted to involve Darlene, but had little choice. No way did he want to spend another night cooped up in a cell. It was doing his head in.

'So you're admitting you lied about the gold, are you?' Singh asked.

'Yes, I did. But for a very good reason.'

'Well, providing we believe your reason and it checks out, there is no need for us to involve your wife.'

Jason took a deep breath. 'Craig came to the shop to tell me somebody very dear to my heart has terminal cancer.'

Chatham rolled his eyes. 'And you expect us to believe that?'

Jason slammed his fists against the table. 'It's true,' he bellowed. 'The lady I'm on the beach with in that photo you have, she's dying. She was like a mum to me when I was growing up, but then we lost contact. Craig is close to her too and paid me a visit asking me to visit her. She lives in Basildon now.'

'We know that. We followed you there,' Chatham informed Jason. 'So why don't you want your wife to find that out? Am I missing something here?'

'Darlene, her name is. Many years ago, she turned up at my wedding reception and created an awful scene. Melissa, my wife, was understandably upset and I had to promise her I would have nothing more to do with Darlene. But when Craig turned up at my shop and told me the news, I needed to see her.'

'Were you having an affair with her?' Chatham asked.

'You don't have to answer that question, Jason. It isn't relevant,' the solicitor advised.

'So if we pay your lady friend a visit, she will confirm what you've told us, will she?'

'Yes. It's the truth. Darlene knows Craig came to my shop to speak about her and give me her address. She might be a bit cagey at first, mind. Where we come from, you don't talk to the police. You might have to explain I'm in trouble to get her to open up.' The police had yet to ask him about his second meeting with Craig at the car park opposite the Camelot pub and, until they did, Jason wasn't mentioning it.

'Going back to your finances, why was the bulk of your money in a bank account in Jersey?' Singh enquired.

'Because I used to own flats in Jersey that I rented out.

When I sold them, I left the money out there,' Jason replied truthfully.

'Have you thought of a way yet to prove you gambled all your money away, Jason?' Singh asked. 'Only we are finding that particular story a tad far-fetched, to say the least.'

'I wasn't intending on frittering it away when I withdrew it. I just wanted to get it out my account so my wife couldn't get her hands on it. We'd split up at the time and she was threatening to take me for every penny I had. Temptation of having it close by proved too much for me though. My addiction got the better of me.'

'That doesn't answer my question, Jason. I asked if you had thought of a way to back up your version of events. Perhaps if you could remember the bookmaker you had placed these bets with we could speak to them. I doubt many bookies are going to forget some bloke placing fifty grand on a mutt running round Catford in a hurry, are they?'

'No. I weren't placing that much at a time. Five or ten grand per night I was doing. When you're gambling like I was, adrenaline kicks in and everything else is a blur. I can't remember any bookies off hand.'

With a bored expression on his face, Chatham slammed his fist against the table. 'Well, best you try thinking harder then. Because if you don't, you'll be on your way to prison very shortly.'

Having ignored Tracey's advice of turning up at court unannounced, Melissa instead waited anxiously by the phone the following day. Simon had called her late the previous night and told her she would be better off waiting at home for news.

'Jason wants to explain everything to you in person, Mel. Hopefully he'll get bail and will be home where he belongs. I'll go to the court and I'll call you as soon as the hearing is over,' Simon promised. He'd also informed her the hearing was being held at Snaresbrook and insisted the only reason Jason didn't want her to attend was because he didn't want to upset her any more than he already had.

Pouring herself a small glass of wine to take the edge off her nerves, Melissa continued to pace up and down her expensive wooden flooring like a woman possessed. The kids hadn't wanted to go to school today, but she had ordered them to. Company was the last thing she needed, which was why she had told Tracey not to come round either. Her friend sticking her oar in today of all days was something she just couldn't stomach. The fear of not knowing what the future held had kept her awake all last night and the constant churning in her stomach was making her feel sick.

The dreaded phone call finally came at 2.16 p.m. 'What's happening? Is he with you, Si?' Melissa gabbled.

'I'm so sorry, Mel, but he didn't get bail. I'm leaving the court now, will come straight round to you.'

Melissa's legs buckled and she sank to the floor on her knees. She would never manage financially. Jason had paid for everything since the day she'd first met him. He wasn't just her husband. He was also her bank.

By the time the kids arrived home from school, Melissa's shock had turned to anger and she blurted out the news without trying to soften the blow.

Shay's eyes filled with tears. She didn't remember her real mother and had no wish to ever trace her, having been left as a baby. Therefore, her father was the only real family she had, and he'd always bought and given her whatever she wanted. 'When can I visit him? Do you think he'll ring us tonight?'

'How the hell am I supposed to know that?' Melissa bellowed. 'He's going to prison. Hardly going to let him keep his mobile, are they?'

'Don't have a go at Shay. You've been drinking again, haven't you? I can smell it on you,' Donte spat accusingly.

'And so would you be turning to booze if you'd just found out your husband is a drug baron. How could he be so stupid? He must be guilty; I have no doubt about that now. They wouldn't be locking him up otherwise,' Melissa yelled.

'Let's go upstairs and do our homework,' Donte urged, grabbing Shay's arm.

'I wouldn't bother with your homework. You'll be going to new schools soon. Jason's bound to be mentioned in the newspapers. That'll look good, won't it? You'll be known as the drug baron's children. You'll probably be expelled, thanks to that bloody idiot. Not that I can afford to pay your fees anyway. It's not just my life he's ruined, it's yours too. What the hell are we meant to live on? Peanuts?'

Simon's arrival allowed Shay and Donte to escape. 'Mum's in a foul mood and she's been drinking,' Donte warned Simon as he opened the front door.

Bordering on hysterical, Melissa paced the room again. 'Well?' she yelled at Simon. 'And please don't tell me that bastard is innocent, because I wasn't born yesterday.'

'Sit down and calm down, Mel. Please,' Simon replied.

Melissa sank on to the sofa. 'What did the judge say? I wish I had come now. I feel like the silly wife who is always kept in the dark.'

Simon sat on the armchair opposite. He was gutted for Jason, truly gutted. 'The judge didn't give any of 'em bail. But believe me, Mel; Jason isn't involved like the others. The Old Bill obviously think because Jase drew out that lump sum from an account, he must have used it to purchase drugs, but I know for a fact he hasn't. He will explain all to you himself. Brixton, they're taking him to, so you can visit him there. Don't ask him any questions on the phone though. He won't be able to answer you on the blower in case the police are listening in.'

'Tell me what he used that money for. I need to know,' Melissa hissed.

'I can't tell you, but Jason will.'

'Another woman?'

'Oh, don't talk daft. There has only ever been one woman Jason chucks money at, Mel, and that's you. He's been a silly boy, I'm not denying it. But his only crime was to supply these geezers with mobile phones. Unfortunately, the Old Bill were following the gang and saw Jason meet up with one or two of them. That's the reason they've hauled him in.'

'Who are the other gang members? Do I know any of them?'

'I don't think so, but that's another question to ask Jason. I have got some more bad news unfortunately. Jason's had all his bank accounts frozen, they all have.'

'What do you mean? They can't do that, surely?'

'I'm afraid they can, Mel. They take out an application to freeze the assets. They see money in the bank as proceeds of crime until it can be proved otherwise.'

'But Jason's got his own business, and we haven't got a fortune in the bank anyway.'

Simon shrugged. 'I'm sorry, but that's the way it is, Mel.

All Jason's accounts are in his name only, same as your mortgage.'

'But I'm his wife. Am I meant to live on fresh air? I need that money to survive.'

'I can help you out temporarily, but not in the long run. I've promised to buy Tracey a place for her and the baby to live in and she wants a new car. Everything will be in my name, of course. Not saying I don't trust Tracey, but I won't allow anybody to take me for a ride. What about your dad? Does he still own properties in England? Only, your best option might be to touch base with him again. I know you two currently don't see eye to eye, but I doubt he'd see you on your uppers.'

Melissa's face contorted with fury. 'I would not ask that old pervert for a penny. He's dead to me.'

Over in Brixton prison, Jason Rampling lay on his uncomfortable bunk and stared at the dirty ceiling. He couldn't believe his luck.

Craig Thurston had glared at him throughout the hearing. A warning look to keep his trap shut, Jason surmised. Craig had been carted off to Wandsworth, thankfully. Two other members of the gang had been sent to Brixton with Jason and the rest scattered around other prisons. Jason didn't know the other two guys, but got the gist they'd been at the slaughter and been caught red-handed when the gaff had been raided.

'You OK, mate? Your first time inside, is it? My name's Nick, by the way,' said Jason's cellmate.

'Yeah, my first time. I'm OK. Just need time to get my head around things,' Jason replied. He wasn't in the mood for small talk, was worried about Melissa and the kids. Mel would be going ballistic, he knew that much, but surely she wouldn't take her anger out on Shay? His daughter had nowhere else to live, was totally reliant on Melissa right now and he would do everything in his power to ensure their family wasn't split in two. He needed to come clean to Mel about a lot of things before it was too late.

It was almost midnight when the doorbell chimed. Simon had left ages ago, Shay and Donte were in bed and Melissa was busy making a list of things to do, a trip to the Citizens Advice Bureau being at the very top.

Fully expecting to see Tracey on her doorstep, Melissa flung the door open and was stunned to see her father standing there. 'What you doing here? Who gave you my address?' she spat. He was much older and balder than she remembered, but had a deep tan and looked healthy.

'Can I come in, Melissa, please? Donte called me a couple of days ago. He's very worried about you, and so am I.'

Melissa poked her head outside and glanced around. 'You better not have brought that slapper to my home.'

'Shirley's in Spain. I got the first available flight. Let's talk inside, Mel, please. I know Jason's been banged up. Donte called me again earlier. I'm here to help you,' Johnny Brooks explained. He knew how much he'd hurt Melissa when he'd got back together with Shirley Stone after Carol died, but he'd had a second chance of happiness and had never regretted his decision. They had a nice life in Spain, were friends with lots of other ex-pats and lived a chilled existence these days.

Images of her beautiful mother popping up in her head, Melissa's eyes filled with tears. 'I want nothing from you. You can stick your help where the sun don't shine. I would rather beg on the streets than take a penny off you and that whore.'

Having heard voices, Donte came flying down the stairs. 'Granddad!'

'Get back upstairs. Granddad's just leaving.' Melissa still had her arm across the front door, blocking her father from entering.

'Please, let Granddad in, Mum. He's come all the way from Spain and wants to help us.'

Shay stood rooted in the middle of the stairs. She didn't want to butt in through fear of antagonizing Melissa and being sent to live on the Mardyke Estate.

'Let me see him. He's my granddad,' Donte shouted, trying to duck under his mother's arm.

'Get back to your room, now!' Melissa shrieked. 'You had no right giving out my address, just like that old bastard had no right telling you who your real dad was.'

When Donte burst into tears, Melissa swung around to face her father with a look of pure hatred. 'See what you've done? Get out! Go on; fuck off back to your slapper. I hate your guts and I never want to see you again.'

Johnny Brooks shook his head in dismay. He hadn't exactly expected the red-carpet treatment, but neither had he expected to find his daughter transformed into an overweight, drunken mess. 'Your mother would be turning in her grave at the state of you,' he mumbled.

Not caring that some of the neighbours had now opened their front doors to see what all the fuss was about, Melissa lunged at her dad, punching him with all her might. 'Don't you ever mention Mum's name again. I wish whoever shot you had actually killed you. Shame the bullet wasn't in your head.'

*

Three days after her father's unexpected visit, a sombre Melissa was driven to Brixton prison by Simon.

'How are the kids doing?' Simon enquired. Melissa had told both he and Tracey what had happened with her father.

'Donte still isn't talking to me. Well, apart from telling me he hates me.'

'He'll come round in time. What about Shay?'

'She's been quiet, but polite. I've got a meeting with the Citizens Advice tomorrow, with a woman called Janet.'

'Do you need any money to tide you over?'

'No. I'm fine thanks.'

'Jason called me yesterday. He's over the moon you agreed to visit him.'

'I bet he is,' Melissa spat. She had only agreed to visit Jason because she was desperate to learn the truth. What had he done with all that money?

'I'll wait here in the car for you,' Simon said, when they finally arrived at the prison. He was glad he'd had the sense to leave early as the traffic had been a nightmare. 'Try not to be too hard on him, eh? Listen to what he's got to say,' Simon urged.

Instead of replying, Melissa got out the car and slammed the passenger door.

Jason Rampling was a bundle of nerves as the visitors started piling in. He had visions of Mel changing her mind and not turning up. Rubbernecking, he spotted her and waved. She didn't wave back, then pushed him away when he stood up to hug her.

Melissa sat on the chair opposite the man who'd once been the love of her life. He was dressed in a grey tracksuit, black trainers and had a bright prison vest on.

'Thanks for coming, Mel. I'm so sorry about everything, I truly am.'

'You and me both,' Melissa hissed. 'Explain then – and don't you dare lie to me. I want to know everything.'

In a hushed tone, Jason told his wife of his involvement with the gang. She didn't interrupt, just listened to what he had to say. 'I've decided to use Simon's solicitor pal now. Si's said he'll foot the bill, if necessary,' Jason explained. He was no longer worried about the photo of him arguing with Tracey. He could explain that by saying he'd paid her a visit to order her to keep her nose out of his and Mel's marriage, and things got a bit heated. He wasn't too concerned about the Darlene photo either. He would tell Mel the truth, if need be: that Darlene was dying. That could be proved. All he cared about was being found not guilty, and to do that he needed the best solicitor available.

'So what did you do with all that money?' Melissa asked, her expression stony and lacking emotion.

Glancing around to make sure none of the screws were earwigging, Jason leaned closer to Mel. 'I bought a painting with it. A painting that is worth an absolute fortune. I've even got a buyer for it, but I can't flog it while I'm stuck in here, obviously.'

'Why didn't you tell the police that?' Melissa asked disbelievingly.

'Because it's stolen. I couldn't tell 'em because having that painting in my possession would carry a huge sentence. You gotta trust me on this one, Mel. When I get out this dump, we will be loaded.'

'Where is the painting?'

'Hidden, somewhere safe. Simon knows all about it; ask him if you don't believe me.'

'I will.'

'I promise I'll get us out of this mess. My shop's been shut since the raid, but my pal is going to open up again next week and keep things ticking over so you've got some income coming in. We're gonna register the shop in his name and split the profits fifty–fifty.'

'Will the police let you do that? I thought they'd frozen all your assets.'

'They have, but the shop's a rented premises anyway. Glenn'll just take over the lease. He's already spoken to the landlord.'

'What about the mortgage and school fees?'

'There's not gonna be enough money coming in to pay those, Mel. I'm sorry. The kids will have to go to different schools and you'll have to rent a smaller private property and let the Social pay for it.'

Melissa's lip wobbled. 'But I love my home. I don't want to live elsewhere.'

Jason shrugged. 'My hands are tied in here, babe. I can't pay the mortgage, can I? They are just gonna have to repossess it. We owe a fortune on it – the place is mortgaged up to the eyeballs.'

'But you put our money from our previous house into it.'

'I know, but we'll have to swallow that loss.' Jason glanced around and leaned forward again. 'I can get two million for the painting, maybe more. Stick by me and I'll buy you your dream home when I get out.'

Melissa was in turmoil. She didn't particularly want to stick by Jason after everything he'd put her through, but what choice did she have? If she agreed, she'd have some sort of income coming in and she could always end things with him when he got released if she couldn't forgive him.

Sensing her softening, Jason squeezed her hands. 'How're the kids?'

Melissa immediately snatched her hands away. 'How do you think? Their lives have been turned upside down. One thing you'll be pleased to know is I'm not pregnant. I got my period the other day,' she said bitterly. Tracey had started to show a baby bump now. It wasn't big, but she'd noticed it yesterday and it had upset her as it reminded her of being pregnant with Bobby.

'We can have more kids when I get out of here, Mel. We'll still be young enough.'

'I don't want your children now. We've fucked up the two we raised between us. Well, you have, anyway.'

'Simon told me your dad turned up. That must've been tough for you.'

'It was. I wish he was dead. Shame that bullet never killed him.'

Looking sheepish, Jason leaned forwards again. 'There's one more thing I need to tell ya that you're not going to like.'

'What?'

'The bloke who the police think is the ringleader of this firm is the same geezer you think shot your father.'

'Craig Thurston!' Melissa gasped. 'But you swore to me you had nothing to do with him any more.'

Jason put his finger over his lips. 'Shush.'

Absolutely stunned, Melissa sat open-mouthed. She had no words; there was nothing left to say.

'Where are you going?' Jason asked when Mel stood up, her chair screeching across the floor.

'Home. Best you make arrangements for Shay. I want no more to do with you or your family. You're a compulsive liar who cannot be trusted. Our marriage is over, Jason. This time for good.'

PART FOUR

'Heaven has no rage like love to hatred turned.
Nor hell a fury, like a woman scorned'

William Congreve

CHAPTER THIRTY-THREE

2008 – Six Years Later

Tracey Thompson tossed back her long blonde hair. She wasn't used to not getting her own way. 'Please can we go Club 195 instead, Mel?'

'No. We either go to the Prince Regent, or I'm not going out at all.'

'But why?' Tracey argued. 'The Regent is full of letchy old men. Gary Harvey and his mates are definitely going 195 tonight. I saw Gary yesterday and he made a point of asking me if I was going. I think he fancies me and we won't have to buy a drink with that lot. They're right villains, order champagne all night like it's going out of style.'

Applying her mascara, Melissa was determined to stick to her guns. 'I'm thirty-five, Trace. No way am I standing down Club 195 with a load of kids. At least they're our age down the Regent.'

'You're old before your bloody time, you. You look fantastic. You've lost all that weight. Why not flaunt it? We're not going to meet any decent blokes down the Regent.'

'I'm not going out to meet a bloke, Trace. I thought we were just having a girlie night out.'

'We are, but . . .'

Melissa chucked her mascara in her make-up bag and stood up. She doubted Tracey would bowl into Club 195 on her own and she had no other friends to ask. 'Do I get dressed? Or do I not? We go to the Prince Regent or I stay in. Your call.'

Face like a smacked arse, Tracey Thompson looked for potential prey in the Prince Regent. Unfortunately for her, there wasn't any. 'We can't stay here. It's shit,' she spat.

'The music's good,' Melissa reminded her pal. 'Let's dance.' Candi Staton's 'Young Hearts Run Free' was playing and Melissa loved that song. It reminded her of her marriage to Jason.

'No. Don't wanna dance. So how did you get on yesterday – visiting that wanker?'

'OK. He's up for parole soon. Reckons he'll be home in about six weeks.'

'You're not going to let him move back in with you, surely?'

Melissa shrugged. 'He doesn't have anywhere else to go.'

Tracey took a large mouthful of her vodka and tonic. 'You must be a raving loony even considering taking him back. You can do so much better.'

'I know, but he has money owed to him, lots of it.'

'What for?'

'I don't know. He never said,' Melissa lied. No way would she betray her promise to Jason and tell Tracey about the painting. Her so-called best friend couldn't be trusted and had a mouth the size of the Blackwall Tunnel.

'I bet he's lying. Probably got jack-shit owed to him,' Tracey hissed.

'I don't think he is lying. He's promised me the house of my dreams.'

'Yeah, right. And pigs might fly. You already had the house of your dreams until he lost that for you.'

'We'll see.'

'You don't still love him, surely? I mean, you haven't visited him much.'

Melissa shrugged. 'Not sure how I feel about him any more, to be honest. We've been through so much together though. Like being on a rollercoaster, being married to Jason.'

'Yeah, one you should have got off many years ago.'

Melissa grabbed her pal's arm. 'There's a bloke standing near the bar, to your right. Have a look in a minute, surreptitiously. He's well dishy and I'm sure it's you he can't take his eyes off.'

'There's no hotties in here, trust me,' Tracey mocked. She looked around and nearly fell over in shock as she locked eyes with one of the most handsome men she'd seen in years. She clutched Melissa's hand. 'Oh my fucking God! He smiled at me too. Get me another drink, Mel. I'm shaking.'

Not many men had ever had a nerve-racking effect on Tracey Thompson. She'd dated loads and only Jason Rampling, her deceased ex-husband and Barry Higgins – the crime lord – had ever had such an effect on her in the past.

Melissa nudged her friend. 'He's still looking over.'

'Does my make-up look all right? My false eyelashes aren't falling off, are they? What about my lipstick? It's not smudged, has it?' Tracey gabbled. Her heart was pumping away like a steam train.

'He's coming over,' Melissa hissed.

'Good evening, ladies – the prettiest two in here, may I add. Would you do me the honour of allowing me to buy you a drink?'

The man was even more gorgeous up close. Dressed in a dark suit, he had short dark-blond hair, bright blue eyes, thick lips, was a decent height and reminded Tracey of Brad Pitt. Tracey was unable to speak as she drank in his handsome features.

Aware that her friend was making a prat of herself, Melissa nudged her. 'A drink would be lovely, wouldn't it, Trace?'

Tracey nodded dumbly. He was far better-looking than Jason, Kieron or Barry bloody Higgins.

'Champagne OK? I'm Greg, by the way,' he said, fixing Tracey with his most penetrating gaze.

'Champagne's fine, thank you. I'm Tracey and this is my friend, Melissa.'

Greg winked at Tracey, his blue eyes twinkling with devilment. 'A joy to meet you. The first of many meetings, I hope.'

Not wanting to play gooseberry, Melissa was up dancing with a crowd of women. She knew one of them from the nail salon she went to, but couldn't remember her name.

'I can't believe how much weight you've lost, Mel,' the nail salon woman shouted in her ear.

Melissa grinned. For the first time in her life she was actually comfortable in her own body and didn't feel inferior to Tracey. If anything, Tracey looked tarty tonight in her short bright green mini-dress. Mutton done up as lamb, Melissa thought.

'I love your long hair too. How did you shift all your weight? If you don't mind me asking.'

'My hair is actually extensions,' Melissa chuckled. 'Look real though, don't they? I've always wanted long hair, but my hair is fine and would never grow that long. Got my personal trainer to thank for the weight loss. Roy Nixon, his name is. He's the best. I'll give you his number, if you like?' Melissa said, craning her neck to see how Tracey and Greg were getting on.

When the DJ played Gloria Gaynor's 'I Will Survive' Melissa whooped with delight. This song pretty well summed up the way she felt about that bastard she'd married.

When Greg headed off to the toilet, Melissa wandered over to Tracey. 'Well? How's it going?'

'He's gorgeous. I think I'm in love. He's asked to take me out for a meal tomorrow night,' Tracey slurred.

'He's certainly a looker. I'm pleased for you, mate. It's about time you had some luck with men.'

'I got you to thank for dragging me here. Sorry I was miserable earlier.'

'No worries. What does he do for a living?' Melissa asked. She knew full well how shallow Tracey was when it came to men. If they didn't have a high-paying job or a pile of ill-gotten gains from criminal activities, her friend wasn't interested.

'He reckons he's a property developer, but he might just be saying that. I think he looks a bit of a villain, don't you? He was very vague – at first he would only tell me that he "wheels and deals".'

'Shush. He's coming back,' Melissa warned.

Tracey squeezed Greg's hand. 'If you'll excuse me, I need to use the ladies' room now. Mel's my bezzie mate. Talk to her for a minute. She'll tell you all the terrible things we used to get up to at school. We were right cowbags, weren't we, Mel?' Tracey chuckled before walking away.

Greg smiled at Melissa. 'I think your friend likes me.'

Melissa smiled back. 'Yes. I think she does too.'

CHAPTER THIRTY-FOUR

Six Weeks Later

'Toby, don't squeeze the balloon like that, darling. It might burst and hurt you,' Melissa Rampling said, lifting the five-year-old in the air.

'Sorry,' Toby replied, hugging the woman he truly adored. Unlike his mum, Auntie Mel would play games with him for hours on end and he loved the sleepovers at her house because they were always so much fun.

Tracey Thompson ruffled her son's blond hair. 'Be a good boy. Thanks again for looking after him at such short notice, Mel. Dunno what I'd do without you at times.'

'My pleasure. You know how much I love spending time with him. Where's Greg taking you today? Anywhere special?'

'Yes. He's booked an overnight stay at some posh manor house in Surrey. Looked fabulous in the photos he showed me,' Tracey grinned. Meeting Greg Richardson had been a real stroke of luck. Though they'd only been dating six weeks, he was 'The One', Tracey was sure of it.

'Spill the beans then. How's it going?' Melissa laughed.

Given his striking resemblance to Brad Pitt, cheeky grin and bubbly personality, it was no wonder Tracey had fallen head over heels for Greg. He oozed charm.

'It's going well. But . . .' Tracey paused.

'But what?'

'Toby, go and play with your toys in the other room while Mummy talks to Auntie Mel,' Tracey ordered. Melissa was actually Toby's godmother, but for some strange reason her son insisted on calling her 'Auntie'.

'What's up?' Mel asked.

'Nothing bad. He's just a bit vague about things. Look, if I tell you something, you have to promise me you won't say anything to Simon or Jason.'

'Course I won't.'

'I'm positive he's a villain. Whenever I ask about his work, he changes the subject. He never talks about his friends either. I've not met a single one of them.'

'Well, he doesn't come from this area so that's why you haven't met his mates. Epsom is miles away. I spoke to him about his work and he told me he was looking for land around Essex to build flats on. I think you're being paranoid, Trace, I really do.'

'I'm not. There's something I can't put my finger on. And you're no bloody judge – you wouldn't know if Jason was hiding the crown jewels in the garage. Thing is, if Greg turns out to be a villain, I don't want Simon finding out. You know how he dotes on Toby. He won't allow Toby anywhere near him if he thinks he's dodgy.'

'Simon can talk. He's mates with bloody Jason and most of his clients are criminals. You're worrying over nothing, I'm telling ya. It's a long time since I've seen you this happy, so just enjoy it.'

Tracey grinned. 'Yeah, you're right. Listen, thanks again

for having Toby. I'll see you tomorrow . . .' She picked up her handbag, ready to go, but then paused midway. 'You excited about tomorrow? Six years is a long time. I still can't believe you're getting back with him, mind. You were adamant at one point you wouldn't.'

'I know,' Melissa sighed. 'Soft touch, me. It'll take time for Jase and me to get back on track but, fingers crossed, we can make it work. If we can't, then I suppose we'll call it a day. This is definitely his last chance.'

'Can I have a biscuit please, Auntie Mel?' Toby asked, poking his head around the door.

Glad of the interruption, Melissa scooped the boy into her arms. 'You can have whatever you want, my little ray of sunshine.'

'Bye, Mummy,' Toby waved.

Tracey blew a kiss. 'Bye you two. Have fun.'

'One more day eh, mate? Bet you can't wait to leave me,' said Jason's cellmate.

Jason chuckled. 'Not arf.' He'd spent the past few months at Ford Open Prison awaiting his release. 'Be your turn soon,' he added.

'What you looking forward to the most? Can't wait to get me leg over, me.'

'I'm looking forward to not listening to you banging one out any more,' Jason laughed. 'To be honest mate, I just want to make things right with Mel. I owe her big time for not only sticking by me, but also raising Shay as her own. Can't wait to spend some quality time with my nan and daughter as well.'

'What about your boy?'

'Sore subject. Gone off the rails. My fault. Lads need a father figure in their lives, don't they?'

'Too right. My old woman's been pulling her hair out with our Sam recently. Thirteen now, he is. Thinks he knows it all.'

'Same as Donte. Sixteen and sees himself as a big man. Knocking about with my brothers, he is. Mel's got no control over him at present. Need to sort that, I do.'

'I'm sure you will. I'm gonna have a wander, see where Big Dan is. Fancy a game of cards later?'

'Yeah. See you in a bit.'

When his pal left the cell, Jason lay back on his bunk with his hands behind his head. Six years, six long years would come to an end tomorrow and he'd finally be free as a bird again.

He'd been given a ten-stretch, which was light in comparison to what some of the other blokes got. One got a fifteen, another a twenty. Only one man had managed to walk free: Craig Thurston, of all people. He'd had a terrific QC who'd ripped the Old Bill to shreds. Even though Craig was the ringleader and the police knew it, they'd struggled to prove it. Nobody grassed, and he'd managed to get word to Craig before the trial to inform him of what he'd told the Old Bill in his interview. Darlene had backed the story up, God rest her soul. Jason's brief reckoned he would have got acquitted too, had he not been seen and photographed visiting the actual slaughter. It was the little mistakes that cost you in this life.

Jason had been gutted when he'd been refused permission to attend Darlene's funeral. He'd told the authorities she was like a mother to him, but they weren't having any of it. He'd seen her one last time, not long after the trial. Craig had driven her to the prison to visit him. It was very sad as he knew he would never see her again.

She looked really ill by then, could barely walk. She'd shuffled along like an elderly person.

Jason's thoughts turned to his own family. His nan had visited him regularly and was still as game as ever. Shay was doing well and had visited once a fortnight. Melissa hated prisons, so he'd only seen her once a month. But they'd spoken regularly on the phone.

Kyle and Elton were a particular worry for Jason. Elton was twenty-one now, Kyle nineteen. Both were still involved with a gang and had been in trouble with the law. Elton had done eight months in a young offenders' institution for mugging a bloke with a knife. They lived alone now in their mother's old flat, but had recently been threatened with eviction because of loud music and the noisy parties they regularly held. Babs didn't see a great deal of her brothers any more. They'd given her a torrid time of it, just like his mother had. Selfishness seemed to run in his family.

Thinking of his little sister, Jason sighed. Babs had a boyfriend and a year-old baby. Britney, the child's name was, and Jason reckoned the father must be an absolute dickhead. His name was Lee Britten and he'd chosen the kid's name. What sane person would choose to call their daughter Britney Britten? Babs had visited him a month or so ago and her demeanour told Jason she was having problems with Lee. She'd had a cut on her face, insisted she'd walked into a door. After some interrogation, Babs admitted that Lee didn't work, had no intention of getting a job and smoked far too much weed. Jason thought the world of his sister. She was still a big girl, wasn't a looker, but had a heart of bloody gold. He would be paying her and Lee a visit the day after his release, that was for sure. Babs had shown him a photo of Britney Britten's father and he'd loathed him on sight. A skinny little weasel with a massive nose and a scowl on his face. Jason had watched quite a lot of TV recently in open prison and Lee looked like a *Jeremy Kyle Show* regular.

Jason's thoughts turned to Mel. She looked good now, his wife. The best he'd ever seen her look. She'd cut down on the drink, was a fitness fanatic, a toned size 8 and her new hair extensions looked natural and really suited her. Jason had felt proud when some of the lads had said what a sort she was. He'd never really seen her as such until recently. She was a bit distant with him on her monthly visits, but Jason guessed she blamed him for everything that had happened – and she had every right to.

All that would change soon though. Once he sold that painting, Jason was determined to go straight and become the husband Melissa deserved. Not only did he owe the woman, it had taken a six-stretch to make him realize how much he needed her.

'Can we watch CBeebies, Auntie Mel? Igglepiggle, Igglepiggle, Igglepiggle,' Toby chanted, waving his favourite cuddly character in the air.

Melissa pressed play on the DVD and snuggled up to the child she had grown to love so very much. Toby was a gift sent from heaven, in every sense of the word. She felt ever so guilty now, looking back. As Tracey's bump had grown, she'd dreaded him being born.

Being Tracey's birthing partner had been an experience that brought sadness and joy. Simon had paid for Tracey to go private, but he'd had to wait anxiously outside. She was way overdue, and he was afraid something would go wrong. For Melissa, being in the delivery room brought memories of Bobby flooding back; she'd been totally dumbstruck when Tracey had given birth to a boy who was the spitting image of her Bobby. It was surely fate. The likeness was uncanny.

Simon was a great father. He worshipped the ground Toby walked on. Tracey wasn't what Mel would describe as a natural mother. She had little time for her son. Tracey had always been a selfish person and having a child hadn't altered that. She was forever dropping Toby off to either Mel or Simon whenever she fancied some 'me time', as she called it. Since meeting Greg, Tracey's demands for 'me time' had increased, but that didn't bother Mel. She was more than happy to oblige.

Hearing voices outside, Melissa craned her neck. It was Shay, talking to her friend who lived opposite. They lived on the Limes Farm Estate in Chigwell now. A council estate, which was a far cry from their old abode in Repton Park. Beggars couldn't be choosers though, and after Jason's pawn shop had closed down a few years ago, Melissa was just glad to have a roof over her head.

'All right, Mel? Hello, little man. What you doing here again?' Shay grinned, crouching to tickle Toby.

'How was work, love?' Mel asked. Her step-daughter was eighteen and had recently started her first job in a beauty salon. She attended college a couple of days a week, the salon were paying for her course and Mel was proud of the way she'd turned out. Ever since she'd chucked Shay out, then allowed her to move back in a fortnight later, their relationship had improved. Shay had never treated Mel with much respect beforehand, but after experiencing a couple of weeks living with Babs, Elton and Kyle on the Mardyke she soon changed her tune.

'Yeah, it was good. We had to practise our massages today and I did the best.'

'I picked the balloons and banners up earlier. We'll put them up in the morning. I still haven't heard from Donte though and I'm worried sick. Will you come over the Mardyke with me and show me where Elton and Kyle live? He could be dead in a ditch for all I bloody know.' Melissa sighed. Donte had started knocking about with a crowd of black lads from Hainault a couple of years ago. They'd hung out in Romford and that's where her son had bumped into Kyle and Elton again. She'd done everything to discourage the friendship with Jason's brothers, but Donte had got expelled from school earlier this year and had done as he pleased ever since. He regularly stayed out all night. She was at her wits' end, but unable to stop him. He'd never worked yet always seemed to have money, which was another concern.

'OK. Let me just have a quick shower first.'

Melissa got out of the lift and walked along the landing. She'd ordered Shay to lock the doors and wait in the car with Toby. She banged on the front door. There was loud music booming and, as she opened the letterbox, she could smell the sickly sweet odour of marijuana or something similar.

'Open the door. It's Melissa, Jason's wife,' she screamed through the letterbox. She could hear laughter and singing.

A neighbour came out. 'You from the council?'

'No. I'm looking for my son. I think he might be in there.'

The woman looked at Melissa in disgust. 'Scum, they are in there, the lot of 'em. I don't get no sleep any more. That racket goes on all night. It's a bastard liberty. I've been on to the council so many times, but they never do nothing about it. You should be ashamed of your lad.'

'I'm sorry,' Melissa said to the woman, before banging on the door again.

Finally it was answered by Elton. 'Yo, Mel. You OK?'

Melissa pushed past Jason's brother and marched into the lounge. There were a few girls, but mainly boys. Donte was lying on the floor in just a pair of shorts smoking a spliff with his arm around a blonde girl. 'Home, now!' Melissa ordered.

'Mummy's here, Posh Boy. Time to go home,' Kyle goaded. Even though it had been years since Donte went to a private school, the nickname for him had stuck.

Wanting the ground to open up and swallow him as all his pals laughed, Donte glared at his mother. 'I'm busy. I'll be home tomorrow, OK.'

Melissa marched up to her son and grabbed him by the arm. 'You're coming with me, now!'

Donte tore his arm away. 'No, I ain't. I'm not a kid any more. You can't tell me what to do.'

'I can while you still live under my roof. You either leave with me now, or I send the police round here to arrest you for taking drugs. Your choice.'

'Go, Posh Boy. See ya tomorrow,' Elton said.

'Five o'clock, man. Don't forget. That's if Mummy will let you out again,' Kyle chuckled.

'What a pussy, man,' one of the gang chuckled, clicking his fingers.

'I wouldn't say no to fucking that mother. I is a mother-fucka,' another joked.

Donte slammed the front door and pushed his mother in the chest. 'Why did ya have to fucking come round here? My pals are all laughing at me now, you stupid bitch.'

Melissa slapped her son across the face, hard. 'Get in that lift, you no-good little shit.'

The following morning, Melissa Rampling was up with the larks. She'd given Donte a stern talking to on the way home yesterday, but her words had fallen on deaf ears. Donte had stared out the car window, ignoring her, then had gone straight to bed when they'd got home.

Melissa opened Shay's bedroom door. 'Only me, love. I heard you mooching about. I'm just going to bath Toby, then we'll make a start on putting the banners and balloons up, shall we?'

'Yes, OK. I'm just sending me mate a message, then I'll go downstairs and make us a cup of tea.'

Melissa opened her son's bedroom door. 'Get up, Donte. I need your help decorating the house for your dad's party.'

When her son didn't respond, Melissa decided to shake him, but instead shook the pillows he'd put underneath his quilt.

Donte had gone out again and there was sod-all she could do about it.

'Jase, Jase! Over here, mate,' bellowed Simon Champion.

Jason grinned and walked towards his best pal. Simon was leaning against a black Audi Q7. 'You OK?' he asked, giving Jason a bear hug.

'I am now I'm out of there. New wheels?'

'Yeah. Bought this last year. Get in. Mel's proper excited to see you, so is Shay.'

'They both been OK?'

'Yeah, they're good. Toby's round at theirs. Tracey's out with the new bloke. Getting big now, my boy. Look,' Simon said, shoving his phone under Jason's nose.

'He's a cute kid, he really is. Can't wait to finally meet him,' Jason lied, trying to sound casual. He had very nearly crapped himself when Mel showed up one visiting time with a photo of Toby. 'He could be Bobby's double, couldn't he? It's an uncanny likeness,' she'd gushed.

For a split second, Jason had thought she'd cottoned on, but thankfully she hadn't. 'All babies look alike,' he'd insisted, and was relieved when she'd agreed.

'Bet you can't wait to flog the you-know-what, can you?' Simon chuckled.

Jason grinned at his pal. It was the thought of his prized possession and the life he would lead once he sold it that had got him through the dark days inside. He hadn't planned on telling a soul where he'd hidden it. But his prison sentence had forced him to tell Simon. The painting was hidden amongst a couple of dozen worthless paintings and some antiques in a storage unit in West London. The idea was, if the Van Gogh had come on top, Jason would've played dumb and said he'd bought a job lot off a geezer who'd come into the shop and had no idea of the worth. He'd even got a proper receipt printed out to cover his arse. He'd only paid a year's storage fee up front, so he'd had to involve Simon to keep up the payments. There was only one key though and nobody knew where that was, bar himself. 'I'll speak to my contact tomorrow, set the ball rolling.'

'Yeah. The quicker you get rid of it, the better. What you gonna do with the dosh? You can't go splashing the cash you know, putting stuff in your own name.'

'I know that. Listen, I appreciate all you've done, mate. I'd have been totally fucked without your help. I owe you a good drink out the proceeds.'

'I'm sure you'd do the same for me. That's what friends are for, Jase.'

'Does that look all right, Mel? Or does it look lopsided to you?' Shay asked. Mel had insisted on putting a massive WELCOME HOME JASON banner on the front of the house. She insisted word would get round the estate that Jason was a bloke coming home from a long stretch and that would hopefully keep all the louts away. Many a night they were woken up by cars screeching, arguments and fights, especially at the weekends.

'That'll do. It hasn't got to be perfect. It's the thought that counts.'

'OK,' Shay mumbled as she climbed down the ladder.

'You all right, love? You seem a bit quiet. I thought you'd be upbeat today, what with your dad coming home. Not worried we're going to argue again, are you?'

'No. If I tell you something, Mel, will you promise not to say anything to my dad?'

Hoping Shay wasn't pregnant, Melissa said, 'I promise.'

'You know I've recently joined Facebook?'

'Yes.'

'I met a bloke on here and we've been out a few times. He's ever so nice and he treats me well. His name's Luke and he works in finance.'

'So what's the problem?'

'He's older than me.'

'How much older?'

'He's thirty-four.'

'Oh, for Christ's sake, Shay. That's a big age gap, love. Don't be telling your father just yet. He'll go apeshit and will be back in prison before we know it.'

*

Tracey turning up was a welcome distraction for Melissa. She had guessed there was a lad on the scene by Shay's recent behaviour, but was shocked that it was a fully grown man. Perhaps with Jason inside, Shay had craved a father figure in her life. 'There's drinks in the kitchen, Trace, help yourself. Don't touch the food or champers yet though. We're saving that until Jason arrives. Where's Greg? Or should I say Brad?' Melissa grinned.

Tracey chuckled. 'Playing golf. He's coming later.'

Tracey crouched and ruffled her son's hair. 'How's my boy? Have you been good for your Auntie Mel?'

'Yes, Mummy.'

Melissa smiled. 'He's been a little angel, bless him. And he can't wait to finally meet his Uncle Jason, can you, Toby?'

Tracey couldn't help the rush of adrenaline. She had written to Jason in prison, sent photos of Toby, but the bastard hadn't even bothered to reply. Well, he could go fuck himself now. She had met the man of her dreams and Jason would have to stand by and watch Simon and Greg playing Daddy. She could not wait to see Jason's face when he was finally introduced to the kid. It was bound to be the ultimate picture. Her handsome boy was his father's little double.

'Where we going?' Jason asked.

Simon winked. 'I am under strict instructions not to get you home until three. So I booked a table at Beppe's. Thought I'd treat you to a slap-up lunch and we can talk business. I've got a couple of propositions for you.'

'What?'

'We'll discuss it over a drink. We're nearly there now.'

Simon shook hands with the waiter, who ushered himself

and Jason to a table in the far corner. 'Bring us a bottle of your finest bubbly, Dino. We're in no rush to order food. We want to have a chat first.'

Jason looked around the classy establishment. It felt weird being out of prison. He half expected a screw to bark an order at him any second. 'Not been here before, have I?'

'No. This is the restaurant I told you about. It opened not long after you first went inside. Family-run business. Nice people. I use it a lot. Was in here last night with a certain lucky lady.'

'Oh? You never mentioned you've got another bird on the firm,' Jason grinned.

'It's early days. I only met her a fortnight ago. Sally-Ann, her name is, but I think she might be a keeper. I haven't introduced her to Toby yet, as I don't want to confuse him.'

'How do you feel about Toby being around this new bloke of Tracey's? Greg, isn't it? Mel told me all about him last time she visited.'

'Toby hasn't been around Greg and I haven't met the bloke yet either. Mel says he's nice, but I don't reckon he's very child-friendly. He hasn't got any kids himself and whenever he sees Tracey they do stuff alone and either Mel or I babysit. That suits me though, to be honest. My son only needs one dad.'

The waiter brought over the champagne, poured two flutes and Simon raised one. 'Welcome home, mate.'

Jason chinked flutes. 'Cheers, pal. Seems surreal, sitting here with you. So, what are these business propositions then?'

'I've been thinking long and hard how to help you cover your tracks with the money you'll be getting and I've come up with a couple of solutions.'

'Tell me more,' Jason grinned.

'Well, as I said in the car, you can't be splashing the cash. You start buying big houses and flashy cars in your name, the Old Bill are gonna be bang on your case and you'll be back inside.'

'True. So how do I get round that?'

'I spoke to a good friend in Jersey. He's willing to invest the money for you and launder it over time. He wants two hundred and fifty grand for his services though. Reckons he's putting his neck on the line.'

'How's he going to make it look legal? I've not even got a job.'

'He never went into detail and neither did I. He knows nothing about the painting either. I just said we needed a favour and that was the deal he offered. We can arrange a meet with him soon, if you're interested.'

'A quarter of a mill is well steep. What's the other solution?' Jason enquired.

'Me helping you out. You and Mel are going to need somewhere decent to live. Once you've got the readies, I can put a property in my name for you. Nobody will bat an eyelid if it's me splashing the cash. I can get you a car the same way an' all. I don't know why you don't have a look at that gaff I've had refurbished in Upshire. It's nearly finished and will be going on the market soon. It's a real beauty. Nice and secluded too.'

'I think I would rather just deal with you than involve your friend in Jersey. Whatever we buy, we'd have to get something drawn up legally though, saying it actually belongs to me. You never know what's around the corner, do you? I might die or we have a fallout.'

'I'm not trying to shaft you, Jase, I can assure you of that. I'm only trying to help you. I can't see how else you are going to be able to spend your windfall. And you don't want to live like a poor man, do you? That's a rough estate Melissa's currently living on. A tidier-looking version of the Mardyke.'

'So what's in it for you?'

Simon grinned and refilled their flutes. 'You know me far too well. What's in it for me is seeing you and Mel happy again and fifty per cent of any sell-on profit. Property is going up all the time, so I view this as helping my pal and an investment for my future. I'll have something legal drawn up that covers us both if you're happy to go ahead. A document that states if one of us wants to sell the property, then it has to be sold and we split the profit equally between us.'

The bubbly had gone to Jason's head and he couldn't think straight. 'This all sounds good, Si, but I'm a bit all over the place today. Can I have a chat to Mel about it over the next couple of days and then we'll speak again?'

'Yeah. Of course. You've got to sell the painting first anyway, so there's no rush. Racked my brain over your situation, and these were the only two things I could come up with. I'll put my thinking cap back on, though; see if I can come up with another way.'

'OK, mate. Thanks. I really do appreciate your help.'

'Jesus wept! Please tell me this isn't what I think it is,' Jason said as he spotted the banner. He hated surprise parties and guessed that bunny-boiler Tracey would be there.

'Just go with it, mate. Mel wanted to do something special for you,' Simon urged.

Melissa opened the front door. 'Welcome home, Jason,'

she grinned, throwing her arms around her husband's neck.

'Welcome home, Dad,' Shay beamed.

Jason hugged his two favourite girls close to his chest. 'Well, this is a nice surprise, I must say,' he lied.

Seconds later, Tracey Thompson bowled over with his son in his arms. 'Toby, this is your Uncle Jason we've been telling you all about. Don't be shy. Say hello,' she said in a false sickly sweet voice.

Wanting the ground to open up and swallow him, Jason had no option but to hold the child in his arms. 'Hello, Toby. Nice to meet you,' he said awkwardly.

'Doesn't look like Simon, thankfully, does he?' Tracey said in a loud voice. She was already inebriated, had decided to knock the booze back when Greg had texted saying he couldn't make the party after all.

Simon chuckled. 'No. Luckily, he's a looker like his mother. But he's inherited his dad's clever brain, haven't you, boy?' Simon said, tickling Toby's chin.

Kissing the boy on the forehead, Jason put him on the floor. There was none of his family here. Apart from the obvious, he didn't recognize a soul. 'Where's Donte?' he asked his wife.

Melissa shrugged. 'Your guess is as good as mine.'

'Yo, Posh Boy. Want a toot?' asked Elton Rampling.

Donte wasn't a lover of cocaine. It made him hyper and he preferred being stoned. But he took the rolled-up ten-pound note and snorted the fat line anyway. The lads had been ribbing him all day about his mother turning up yesterday and he didn't want to look even more of a wuss in front of his girlfriend, Kayleigh.

Dressed in a dark Adidas hooded tracksuit, Kyle

Rampling stared out the window. They were holed up on the Hart's Lane estate in Barking today, waiting for a rival gang to show their ugly faces.

'I think we should go to Jason's party. Wasting our time 'ere when we could be drinking free booze,' Elton suggested.

'That bitch Mel won't even let me and you in, Bro. Anyway, I wanna sort these motherfuckers out. Nobody makes a pass at my woman and gets away with it,' Kyle hissed. He was dating the sister of Donte's girlfriend. Both girls lived with their mother on the Hart's Lane estate and members of another gang had been coming on to them.

'Don't call my mother a bitch,' Donte spat. That was another effect cocaine had on him. It made him braver than usual.

Kyle pushed Donte. 'I call your mother what I want. She is a bitch, turning up round ours threatening to grass us to the filth. She's a wrong 'un.'

'That's them. Well, some of 'em. That's Tyrone Dark in the red hoodie.' Kayleigh pointed to a group of black lads walking towards the flats. Dubzman, their pal, lived in the same block as her.

'Let's do this,' Kyle bellowed.

All the gang members flew down the stairs and as they ran out the front of the flats, the other gang, realizing they were outnumbered, scattered in different directions.

'Donte, dis way,' Kyle yelled.

Instead of following the rest of the gang, who were chasing the bulk of the other firm off the estate, Elton changed direction and followed his brother and Donte.

Tyrone Dark was only fifteen but was a tall lad. Running out of options to escape, he stopped dead in his tracks and produced a knife. 'Come on then,' he yelled.

Donte put his hand inside his tracksuit bottoms. He knew some of the other lads had sliced people up, but he hadn't been a member of the gang for long, therefore had not had a chance yet to prove his worth. Donte flicked the knife open. 'Kayleigh is my woman. You go near her again, I kill you.'

Elton rounded the side of the flats just in time to see Kyle grab Tyrone Dark in a headlock from behind. 'No,' he shouted as Donte lunged at the lad's stomach with the knife.

Kyle stared at Tyrone Dark as he fell backwards and landed with a thump on the pavement. His eyes were rolling backwards in his head.

'What da fuck,' Elton hissed.

Kyle turned to Donte, who was frozen to the spot. 'Why did ya do that? We said, no knives.'

Ordering Donte to pull the knife out of Tyrone's stomach, Elton had a good look around to check the coast was clear. 'Come on. We need to get out of here.'

CHAPTER THIRTY-FIVE

'Good morning. How's your head?'

Jason put his arms around Melissa and kissed her on the lips. 'Still attached to my shoulders, just.' He'd loathed the party. Melissa had invited her counsellor, fitness instructor and lots of their chavvy neighbours. Tracey Thompson had got slaughtered and showed herself up as per usual. The stupid bitch had even joked that Toby looked like him at one point. Thankfully Melissa and Simon hadn't heard her.

'I'll make us some breakfast. Did you sleep well?'

'Not bad. I'd have slept even better if I was lying next to you,' Jason replied wistfully. He had never seen Melissa look so good. She looked radiant and sexy.

Feeling her husband's erection rub against her, Melissa lifted his hands off her buttocks. 'I've already explained why I don't want to rush things, Jason. You've been away for a long time and I need to know you're not going to let me down again before we start sharing a bed. I can't go through any more trauma. I'm too long in the tooth for it.'

'I understand, but I won't let you down again. I love you. You're my rock.'

'I love you too.'

'Still no sign of Donte?' Jason asked.

'Nope. He never came home last night. Will you visit your brothers, Jase? Find out what they're up to. I'm sure Donte is taking drugs of some kind. His eyes look vacant.'

'Simon's picking me up at ten to collect his spare motor, so I'll shoot straight over to the Mardyke and find out what the hell they're up to.'

'What else you got to do today? I'll make a start on tidying up all this mess soon. State of the place. I wanted to give you a decent homecoming though.'

Jason smiled politely. Seeing Toby had been emotionally draining too. He was a lovely lad and it tugged at Jason's heartstrings that he could never be a proper father to him. 'I've got some running round to do. I'm gonna visit my nan and Babs to check out that loser she's with. I'm sure he's knocking her about. I need to make a few phone calls, set the ball rolling about selling the painting. I don't like this estate. The quicker I get us off of here, the better.'

'And how do you plan to do that? Simon said you can't start spending money willy-nilly. He reckons the police will be keeping an eye on you.'

'Si has come up with a couple of ideas. One being that he puts the property in his name and I give him the cash for it. He spoke about a gaff he's refurbished in Upshire. Did he mention it to you?'

'No. I've not seen much of Simon lately, to be honest. I think he's loved up again. Tell me more.'

Jason explained Simon's ideas in finer detail.

'I don't think you should involve the bloke in Jersey either. Why part with that kind of money if we don't have to? Simon is on the ball and trustworthy. He's also a shrewd businessman and you can guarantee if we sell the property in five years' time we will all make a tidy profit.'

'OK. I'll speak to him today. Perhaps we can drive to Upshire tomorrow and have a butcher's?'

'There's no point viewing anything, Jason. Not until you've got the cash. I can't build my hopes up only to have them dashed all over again. I'm past that.'

'All right, Nan?'

'I am now you're free. Give your old nan a cuddle then,' Peggy grinned.

Jason did as asked, then handed her a carrier bag. 'Two hundred fags in there and some Guinness.'

'She give you some money? Loony Lil?'

'No. Simon's lent me a couple of grand to tide me over. I need to get in the back of your cupboard an' all. I've still got five grand in there.'

'Not no more you ain't.'

'What do you mean?'

'There's only three there now. I had to borrow two. I can't go out thieving much now, what with me arthritis. Plays me up something chronic.'

Jason rolled his eyes. 'And how do you plan on paying it back?'

'Not thought that far ahead yet. You'll probably have to wait until I win the National,' Peggy laughed. 'So how's she been with ya?'

'All right. Laid on a homecoming party for me, which was shit.'

'Was that mate of hers there? The one you knocked up?'

Apart from Darlene, his nan was the only other person Jason had confided in over his biggest secret. 'Yeah. Cute kid. He looks like me.'

'Don't get all broody and knock Mel up, will ya? You don't want to lumber yourself with her in case you meet a nice girl.'

'Chance would be a fine thing. I slept in Donte's room 'cause she wants to take things slowly. There's one thing I can't work out though. Si paid for the booze and food for the party, but she's still having a personal trainer and getting herself pampered regularly. She's going for a massage today and they ain't cheap. She was pleading poverty every time she visited me in prison, so where's she getting the spare cash from?'

'Dunno, love. Ask her outright. Sly mare, she is. I wouldn't trust her as far as I could throw her.'

'Morning. I stopped off at that little sandwich bar near me, treated us to some lunch,' Tracey said, handing Melissa a white paper bag. Tracey and Toby lived in a lovely three-bedroom detached house not far from Simon in Epping. The house was in Simon's name but Tracey had decorated it to her taste and was happy there. It was quiet and the neighbours kept themselves to themselves.

'Good night, wasn't it? Do you remember stacking it? You went into the kitchen to get a plate of food and went flying across the lounge,' Melissa chuckled.

'Don't remind me. I only got drunk because I was pissed off with Greg. You don't reckon he's got a wife tucked away, do you? He's not answering his phone again this morning. I can't stand being messed around.'

'He's not married. You overthink things, that's your trouble. I think he's a lovely guy.'

As Jason approached the Mardyke Estate, thoughts of Darlene flooded his mind. He'd first become obsessed with her after watching Dustin Hoffman banging Mrs Robinson in *The Graduate*. She'd been so beautiful back then. He could picture her clearly, laughing in her kitchen in those faded denim dungarees she often wore. Craig had written to him in prison, told him that the funeral went well and where she was buried. Tomorrow he would visit her, take some flowers and say his own personal goodbye. He would never forget her, that was for sure.

'Long time no see. How's your mum doing?' asked old Mrs Talbot. She had dementia now, had forgotten what happened to Debbie.

Jason locked Simon's Land Rover. 'She's dead. How's your Frank?'

'He's dead too. And so will those brothers of yours be if they keep playing loud music until the bleedin' early hours. They've upset a lot of people round 'ere, Jason.'

'I'm sorry about that, Mrs Talbot. Leave it with me and I'll have a word.'

Jason walked inside the tower block and the familiar smell hit his nostrils. Nothing had changed. The Mardyke was a time warp. He took the lift and banged on the door of his old family home. 'Kyle, Elton, open up,' he bellowed. 'It's me, Jason.'

Kyle opened the door and glanced around outside. 'You alone?'

Jason marched inside the property. 'Of course I'm alone. Why? What you done wrong?'

The front room was a tip. There were turntables, big speakers and not a lot else other than a small TV, overflowing ashtrays, empty beer cans and takeaway wrappers. Donte and Elton were sitting on the ripped sofa looking sheepish. 'What's going on? Why didn't you come to the party?' Jason asked. All three lads were wearing Adidas tracksuits and Donte had the hood of his partially covering his face.

'Tell him. He'll help us,' Kyle ordered.

Elton stood up and paced the room. 'Donte's in trouble, Bro. Big trouble. He stabbed a lad in Barking last night and it's all over the news.'

Jason couldn't believe his luck. Melissa would go berserk.

Melissa was just clearing up the remains of the party when Shay came stomping down the stairs. 'Where's my dad?'

'Gone to see your nan and Babs. What's the matter?'

'I've decided to tell him about Luke. He's so lovely. I want you both to meet him.'

'Your dad won't see it that way, trust me. Why don't you wait until your relationship is serious? You've not been together long, have you?'

'No. But I think it is serious. I think I'm in love, Mel.'

'Oh, you found him then. Where was he? With your brothers?'

'Yeah. Go to your room, Donte,' Jason urged. 'Hungover, the three of them, but that all stops now,' Jason added, gently pushing the lad in the back to get him up the stairs. His brothers had told him exactly what had happened. There'd been little blood, they reckoned. But the incident was now plastered all over the local news. The police were appealing for witnesses. The lad who'd been stabbed was apparently fighting for his life in intensive care.

'He better not have been taking drugs,' Melissa bellowed, as her son bolted up the stairs without making eye contact with her.

Jason was no snitch. Neither did he want to see his brothers or Donte banged up. He had got rid of the knife on the way home. He'd cleaned it up and put it down a drain. He would do all he could to protect the lads. Mel wouldn't understand his way of thinking, though; women didn't.

'We've not heard a murmur from him and he's had nothing to eat,' Melissa said later that afternoon. 'I'm going to pop upstairs to check he's all right.' If her son had been drinking, she was petrified he might have choked on his own vomit. She'd shouted up to him his dinner was ready over an hour ago.

Jason grabbed Melissa's arm. 'He's fine, just leave him. If you want the truth, I gave him a good talking to on the way home and he's sulking. I've already told him he will no longer be knocking around with Elton and Kyle.'

'And what did he say to that? You never told me all of this when you got home,' Melissa snapped.

'Boys' talk, love. I'm telling you now, aren't I? I need to take this call. It's about you know what,' Jason said, jumping off the sofa as the phone Simon had got for him burst into life.

'Keep an eye on Toby,' Melissa replied, marching up the stairs.

Jason walked out into the garden. The call was from his art dealer pal, Henry. 'Well?' Jason asked.

'All sorted. Meet me tomorrow where we discussed and I'll give you the finer details.'

Jason grinned. 'Top man. See you soon.' There was two hundred grand in this deal for Henry. He would pay his pal a hundred grand and the buyer would pay him the same.

'You all right, lad?' Jason asked, sitting back down and ruffling Toby's hair.

Toby grinned at him and threw his little arms around his neck. 'I love you,' he declared.

Jason squeezed the child tightly. It was difficult to act normal around him in front of Melissa, but so far, he was managing to bluff it. Kissing Toby on the forehead, Jason looked him in the eyes for the first time. 'And I love you too, boy. Far more than you'll ever know.'

Later that evening when Elton tried to call him for the second time, Jason excused himself and took the call in the garden. 'What's up?' he hissed. 'I thought I told you not to call me from your personal phone.'

'You did, but we can't go out, can we? You seen the news?'

'No. We're watching a film.'

'He died.'

'Oh, Jesus fucking wept! You're just gonna have to sit tight and pray you haven't been spotted on any CCTV cameras near where the incident happened. You'll have to admit to being in Barking if questioned, but just say you always hang out there. You spoken to any of other lads?' Jason asked. There'd been nine of them all together. Five were black, four mixed-race, and they were all dressed quite similar. They'd all had their hoods up too.

'Yeah. Spoke to a couple of them. They reckon there's gonna be major repercussions. The lad that died is only fifteen and his cousin Dubzman runs the gang.'

'Deny everything, like I told you. If you all stick together and say you never did it, unless someone witnessed it or they have it on camera, they can't pin it on any one of you.'

'Their gang know we did it though, don't they? Say they grass? Or come round here trying to cut me and Kyle up?'

'Just stay indoors and be vigilant. I'll pop over tomorrow and bring you some food and drink. Watch what you say on the phone and delete any silly texts you've sent. You can never be too careful these days.'

'OK. We're scared, Bro.'

Jason bit his lip. He was scared too. If the Old Bill were to find out he'd disposed of the murder weapon, they'd lock him up and throw away the key.

'What time d'ya call this?' Jason joked, tapping his watch. His little girl wasn't so little any more. She'd turned into a beautiful young woman.

'I've had a wonderful evening,' Shay announced.

'Where have you been?' Jason enquired.

Melissa shot the girl a warning glance. It was obvious by the silly look on Shay's face that she'd been out with Luke.

Having indulged in a few glasses of champagne, Shay was feeling bold. 'I went to the Bluebell with my new boyfriend.'

'Go to bed now, Shay. You've got to be up early for work. Tell your dad another time,' Melissa urged.

Jason turned to Mel. 'You never said she had a new boyfriend.'

'I didn't know – until yesterday.'

Sensing an elephant in the room, Jason looked quizzically at Shay. 'What's a matter with the lad? Ain't got two heads, has he?'

Shay giggled. 'He has one head, a good job, and he's way nicer than all the silly little boys I've dated. Luke's a real man, like you, Dad.'

'How old is he?' Jason asked.

'Promise me you won't go mad if I tell you.'

'Off to bed, love. I'll talk to your dad first,' Melissa hissed. She knew what Jason's reaction would be.

'Just tell me,' Jason urged.

'He's thirty-four. But he doesn't look that old, he only looks about twenty-eight,' Shay said proudly.

'He's fucking what?' Jason leapt off the sofa and shook his daughter by her shoulders. 'Where's he live? Give me his phone number, now!'

'Stop it, Jason. You're hurting her,' Melissa ordered.

'I'll be hurting that dirty bastard when I get my hands on him an' all,' Jason retaliated. 'Did you know his age? Well, did ya?' Jason bellowed at Melissa.

'No. I already told you I didn't know he existed until yesterday.'

'I'm not putting up with this. I'm not a child. You can't tell me what to do,' Shay shrieked, the same fire in her eyes as her father's. 'Luke's lovely, and you won't stop me seeing him.'

'Won't I? We'll see about that,' Jason spat. 'Get back 'ere,' he ordered, as Shay ran up the stairs.

Melissa grabbed her husband's arm. 'Leave her, Jase. She's upset.'

'Not as fucking upset as I am, she ain't. Where's this geezer live? Where's he work? Where did she meet him?'

'I don't know where he works or lives. All she told me yesterday was she'd met him on Facebook.'

'What the fuck is Facebook?'

'A social networking site all the youngsters are joining. Look, calm down, for goodness' sake. I think she has only been out with him a handful of times.'

'It's a knocking shop, that's what it is. Filthy perverts

on there like him grooming young girls. He's old enough to be her fucking father, Mel.'

'Yes, but let's get a grip, shall we? When she told me yesterday, my first thought was she takes after you.'

'Whaddya mean by that?'

'Well, you liked them knocking on a bit, didn't you? If I remember rightly, Darlene was old enough to be your mother.'

'Oh, cheers. So it's all my fault is it?'

'It's nobody's fault, Jason. Just a case of like father, like daughter.'

CHAPTER THIRTY-SIX

'I'm off to the gym, Jase. Can you have another chat with Donte for me, please? He never touched his breakfast this morning and is acting very odd. He won't even look me in the eyes. I'm sure he's been up to no good. I'll call Shay later, make sure she's all right. Don't you ring her.'

Shay had stormed out late last night with her suitcase. 'I'm going to Natasha's and I won't be coming back,' she'd informed her father. Natasha was Shay's best friend.

'OK. How long you going to be? I need to be somewhere lunchtime.'

'I'll be hour and a half, tops. Whatever you do, don't leave Donte alone. I don't want him creeping back to your brothers' flat.'

'I won't. If I pop out, I'll drag him with me.'

'Thanks. Bye then.'

Jason ran up the stairs and burst into Donte's room. 'Bag up the clothes and trainers you had on the other night, even your underwear.'

Donte lifted the quilt from over his head. 'Is there any more news? What you gonna do with my stuff?'

'We're burning it. The lad died, Donte, so best you liven

yourself up in case the police come calling. Chop, chop, come on.'

Donte leapt out the bed. 'Do you think the police know I did it? You've not told my mum, have you?'

'No and no. If the Old Bill knew it was you they'd have smashed the door down by now, and if your mother knew it was you she'd have ripped your head off.'

Donte's lip wobbled as Jason threw his belongings in a black bin bag. He loved that bright blue Adidas tracksuit. It was new as well. 'I'm scared, Jase. I don't want to go to prison.'

'Too late for regrets, Donte. What is done is done. You got to man up and start acting normal though, else your mum is gonna cotton on. She already suspects something is amiss. Now get dressed, quick. You're coming with me to get rid of this lot and on the journey we'll go over what you are going to say if the Old Bill turn up.'

'Thanks for helping me, Dad.'

Jason grabbed the lad's head and stroked his cropped hair. This was the first time Donte had called him 'Dad' since his affair with Charlotte had come to light. Shame it wasn't under different circumstances, but it still meant the world to Jason nevertheless.

'Have I got some gossip for you!' Tracey exclaimed, marching past Melissa and inside her house. 'Is anyone in?'

'No. Donte's out with Jason and Shay's left home.' Melissa rolled her eyes. 'Don't ask, long story.'

'Did Simon pick Toby up earlier?'

'Yes. He picked him up first thing. Spill the gossip then. I can tell by your face it's juicy.'

'I was right all along,' Tracey grinned. 'Greg is a villain.

Told you, didn't I?' she bragged proudly. Not only did Tracey love being proved right, she also adored the glamour associated with the underworld. With her looks and figure, she had always envisaged herself as the ultimate gangster's moll. She'd actually dated a crime lord years ago, but he'd unfortunately chucked her a few weeks later after a reconciliation with his ex-wife.

'How do you know? Did he tell you?'

'Nope. I did some detective work when he left me with a sports bag of his belongings last night. He got a phone call about eight and told me he had to pop out urgently for a couple of hours. He then asked if he could leave the sports bag with me as he couldn't take it with him.'

'That sounds well dodgy.'

Clapping her hands excitedly, Tracey shrieked, 'Wait until you hear the rest. You haven't heard the half of it yet.'

'Go on. I'm dying to know.'

'You mustn't tell Simon or Jason any of this. Si would have a heart attack worrying about Toby,' Tracey insisted.

'I won't say a word. I promise.'

'So before Greg left he started to look a bit shifty, then he asked could he leave his sports bag inside my walk-in wardrobe. He told me not to look in it, said he had some important documents and stuff in there.'

'So you looked?'

'Course I did. You know me, Mel, I never could resist being nosy. You'll never guess what was inside.'

'What?'

'Guess.'

'Gold, jewels – I don't know. Don't keep me in suspense, you cowbag.'

'There was a black hooded tracksuit, a drawing that

looked like a plan of the inside of a building, a balaclava and . . . wait for it—'

'Wait for what?'

'A gun!' Tracey squealed.

Melissa put her hand over her mouth. 'Oh my God!'

'I reckon he's an armed robber planning a big inside job in Essex somewhere. That's why he doesn't want any photos taken when we're together.'

'I reckon you might be bloody right. I can't believe it. I honestly thought he was a property developer.'

'I knew that was a lie. Why is he living out of hotel rooms? You'd rent a place for six months if you were working round here, wouldn't you?'

'I suppose so, yeah. Trust you to meet a gangster,' Melissa laughed, knowing full well it had always been Tracey's dream to do so.

'I know! Only me. And I didn't fancy the Prince Regent that night we met him, did I?' Tracey laughed. 'I wanted to go Club 195, so you're getting the blame if I end up being arrested.'

'Whatever he's up to has sod-all to do with you, mate. If the police ever turn up at yours, just tell them what he told you. As far as you're concerned, he's a property developer. What happened when he got home? Did you manage to act normal?'

'Yep! Then I bonked his brains out. It's going ever so well now, Mel. The sex last night was awesome. He's talking about booking a romantic holiday abroad for us soon. He's definitely The One.'

Melissa chuckled. 'Bonnie and Clyde.'

'What area we in?' Donte asked Jason. They were driving down lots of country lanes.

'Never you mind,' Jason said, checking his interior mirror before swerving on to a dirt track. There was lots of rubbish on the left, burnt-out mattresses, a sofa and even an old TV. 'Give us the bin liner,' Jason urged.

'Who dumped all that stuff here?'

'Gypsies, I think. There's a site not far from here. Get the petrol can out the back.'

Donte grimaced as his dad poured petrol over his new Adidas jacket and Nike baseball boots. A hundred and twenty quid, those had set him back. Money he'd earned doing some cocaine drop-offs for Elton around the Mardyke.

'Give us your phone,' Jason ordered.

'I can't be without a phone,' Donte complained, but handed it over anyway.

Jason took the SIM card out and put it in his pocket. He'd get rid of that somewhere else. He chucked the phone on top of the fire and watched the plastic melt. 'I'll get you a new phone soon, but you're never to call Elton, Kyle or any of them gang members on it. Understand?'

Donte nodded sadly. Being part of a gang was the first time he'd felt he truly belonged somewhere. They were more like brothers, always watching each other's backs.

Satisfied there was no incriminating evidence left, Jason put his arm around Donte's shoulders. 'Come on. Let's go. And whatever happens, you must never tell your mother or the Old Bill I helped you. That's our secret.'

Donte's big brown puppy dog eyes looked into his father's bright blue ones. 'I won't, Dad. I promise. Thank you for helping me. I'll never forget it.'

After dropping Donte off, Jason went to meet Henry. He shook hands with his art dealer pal, then grinned like a

Cheshire cat as he listened to what he had to say. Finally, the sale of his painting was going ahead and he could not wait to get his hands on the cash and start afresh. That's what had got him through his prison sentence, the thought of his future being bright.

'I will accompany you to meet Hans, obviously. I have dealt with him in the past and cannot foresee any problems. I think it is in our best interests to hire a newish van.'

Jason had first met Henry at an auction house around nine years ago and they'd hit it off immediately. They were chalk and cheese. Henry was an ex-public schoolboy, who'd been born with a silver spoon in his mouth, but they shared a similar sense of humour and both loved to sail close to the wind when it came to business. 'Yeah, good idea. Is Hans flying the helicopter himself or bringing an entourage with him?' Henry had informed him Hans would be arriving in his own helicopter and they would be meeting him on private land belonging to a farmer in Great Dunmow.

'Hans has a pilot. I should imagine his business partner will accompany him also. I have dealt with his partner in the past too. He's a jolly nice chap.'

'Cool. Shall I sort the van and meet you at the usual spot, say eleven thirty?'

'Perfect. I take it you will have the painting with you when we meet?'

'Sure will.'

Henry grinned. 'Tomorrow it is then. I have my eye on a red Aston Martin. I think I'll treat myself to it out of my cut.'

Jason winked. 'As Del Boy used to say, "This time next year . . . "'

*

'Police, open up,' boomed a loud voice.

Kyle looked at Elton in horror. Both were extremely stoned as their pal had turned up earlier with some emergency supplies.

'Don't open it,' Kyle urged when his brother stood up.

'We have to. Makes us seem guilty if we don't. Besides, we can't escape, can we – 'less you fancy jumpin' out a tenth-floor window? Better we open it than have them booting it down. Anyway, we done nothing wrong. Remember what Jase told us to say, OK?'

As Elton opened the door, two coppers grabbed him and another two ran inside the flat and grabbed hold of Kyle.

'Elton Rampling, Kyle Rampling, I am arresting you both on suspicion of the murder of Tyrone Dark. You do not have to say anything. But it may harm your defence if you do not mention when questioned something which you later rely on in court. Anything you do say may be given in evidence. We also have a warrant to search these premises. All understood?'

Kyle glared at the officer who'd handcuffed him. Apart from a small amount of weed, there was nothing incriminating to be found. Elton never kept the cocaine he sold at home, he hid that elsewhere. 'You got the wrong lads. We ain't done nothing, man.'

Grabbing Kyle by the shoulders, the fat copper pushed him on to the sofa. 'We'll be the judge of that, Sonny Jim.'

Jason stared at Darlene's grave. She hadn't wanted to be buried in Rainham, so had been laid to rest in Pitsea.

The photo on the front of her headstone was a beauty. It looked as though it must have been taken when she was in her late thirties; she looked so radiant and pretty.

Jason kissed his hand and rested it on the image of her. 'So sorry I couldn't make your funeral, Dar. It wasn't through lack of trying,' he said. 'I still think about you, ya know. Lots. I drove past your old flat on the Mardyke yesterday and all I could think of was you bopping around in those baggy denim dungarees, singing away to Bob Marley with a spliff on. Those were the days, eh?'

The grave was well kept and Jason wondered if that was down to Craig. She had been one of the loves of his life too. Putting the flowers he'd brought in the plastic vase, Jason filled it with water. 'I gotta go now. My sister's having grief with her boyfriend and I'm gonna sort it. I'll be back soon though, sweetheart. I can come and visit you regularly now. Love you. You'll always be my girl.'

A lone tear running down his cheek, Jason took one last look at Darlene's grave before walking away. He still couldn't believe she was gone.

By the time he arrived at his sister's flat, Jason had cheered up a bit. Melissa was right, it was bound to fizzle out with Shay and the Sugar Daddy and, when it did, he'd find the nonce and give him the hiding of his life. Visiting Darlene had comforted him somewhat. It had been freaky when he'd switched on the Land Rover stereo and the O'Jays' 'Use Ta Be My Girl' was playing. He'd always loved that tune and so had Darlene. It was definitely a sign she was still with him.

Armed with gifts for young Britney, Jason took the stairs two at a time. He'd treated Babs to a pair of gold hoop earrings too. He'd been well chuffed when he'd found out Babs had been allocated a low-rise flat in Ongar Way. He would have hated her to have been given a high-rise on the Mardyke.

'Hiya. Come in. Look who's come to visit us, Britney. It's Uncle Jason,' Babs beamed.

'Nice gaff, Sis,' Jason said as he poked his head around the bathroom and bedroom doors. It was very basic, but tidy and clean with some nice little touches. Unlike his sloth of a mother, Barbara had always had the qualities of a homemaker.

'Lee, this is my brother, Jason.'

Glued to the TV screen, Xbox controls in his hands, Lee grunted, 'Let me just finish this game first.'

Jason picked Britney up and tickled her until she giggled. She was a pretty little thing, had tiny Afro ponytails, big eyes and an infectious smile. 'Did your daddy's mum never teach him any manners, Brit?'

When Lee turned around snarling, Babs started to panic. She'd been desperate for her brother and boyfriend to get off to a good start, even though she knew deep down Lee would not be Jason's type. Her boyfriend could be an idiot at times. However, she was a big girl, and no other lad had ever taken an interest in her, so for that she was grateful to Lee. He'd also given her the most precious gift ever, her beautiful daughter. 'Stand up and say hello properly to Jason, please Lee,' she said bravely. She knew full well she'd probably get a clump for speaking out later, as Lee often lost his temper if she said the wrong thing.

Lee stood up and in a sarcastic tone drawled, 'Hello Jason. A pleasure to meet you.'

Jason weighed up the skinny big-nosed weasel. He looked even worse than he had in his photo, one of life's no-hopers without a doubt. His face was spotty and he looked like he could do with a good soak in the bath.

'Tea, coffee, biscuits anybody?' Babs gabbled. She could sense this wasn't going well.

'Got any beer?' Jason asked, hoping she didn't.

'No. Lee drank the last two yesterday.'

Jason put his hand in his pocket and handed Babs a tenner. 'Pop to the shop, sweetheart, and get some beers for me and Lee. Men bond better over a lager than tea. Take the little 'un with you. Kids like the fresh air.'

'OK. But please don't argue yous two, will you?'

'Course not,' Jason grinned, slapping Lee on the back.

Suddenly realizing Jason was a lot taller than him and looked a bit of a handful, Lee stared at his Admiral trainers. 'Get carried away with Xbox sometimes. Sorry about that.'

As soon as the front door closed, Jason grabbed Lee by the neck and pushed him against the wall. 'You might've got away with treating my sister like shit while I was away, but things are very different now I'm out, sunshine. Babs ain't said nothing. For some strange reason, she's very protective of you. But I've clocked lots of cuts and bruises on her. Nobody walks into doors that frequently, do they now?'

Lee's eyes bulged with terror as Jason lifted his feet off the floor by his neck. 'I haven't laid a finger on Babs, honest I ain't,' he lied, before starting to choke.

'Glad to hear it. Only if I ever find out different, I won't just be squeezing your neck, I will break it in two. Now, do we understand one another?'

Absolutely petrified, Lee croaked, 'Yes.'

Jason let go of the lad and watched as Lee fell to the carpet, gasping and spluttering. 'Oh, and not a word to Babs about our little chat, eh?'

Lee nodded fearfully.

'Right, get up and man up then. Show us your Xbox game or something. Babs'll be back soon and it's very important to her to see us getting along.'

When Babs returned a few minutes later she was amazed and totally thrilled to see the two men she loved playing Xbox together. 'I got Foster's, is that OK?' she beamed. She knew Lee preferred Stella, but he sometimes got nasty when he drank that.

'Foster's is fine thanks, babe,' Lee replied.

Babs was taken aback but elated at the same time. It had been a long time since Lee had called her 'babe'.

Jason smirked as he cracked open a can. His next mission would be to force lazy Lee to get a job. You have kids, you support them, was Jason's take on life. He wouldn't mention that today though, doubted the lad would survive another shock.

'That your phone ringing?' Jason asked his sister.

Babs took the call. 'Oh no. When? OK. Thanks for letting me know. Jason's here with me. I'll tell him.'

'What's up?' Jason enquired.

'That was Debbie Lane. Her brother reckons Elton and Kyle have been arrested. He saw them being taken in handcuffs about an hour ago.'

'Shit!' Jason stood up. 'I gotta go. There's presents in those two bin liners in the hallway. I'll pop round again soon.'

The last thing Jason heard as he bolted out the flat was Lee shouting, 'Bye, Jason. Nice to meet you, mate.'

Fearing for Donte's welfare, Jason headed towards home. On the journey he rang Simon. 'I don't suppose you could drop that key off to me at some point today rather than me coming to you, could ya? I've just been informed my brothers have been arrested.' Unbeknown to Simon, the key Jason had told him to keep in his safe was the key to his safety-deposit box in Hatton Garden. Inside the safety-deposit box was the key to the storage unit where the painting was stored.

'Yeah, no probs. I'll drop it round this evening. What your brothers been arrested for? Drugs?'

'No idea, mate,' Jason lied. With a bit of luck it was drugs, but surely it was too much of a coincidence that they'd been hauled in today of all days.

Nervously putting his key in the door, Jason was relieved when Melissa cheerfully called out to him. He had wanted her badly when he'd been banished to the sofa again last night, was half tempted to go upstairs and climb into bed next to her. But he didn't want to chance his luck, so had satisfied himself with a wank in the bathroom instead. Six years was a long time without sex, and if Mel didn't succumb to his charms soon he might have to visit a brass. To say he was gagging for it was an understatement.

'You all right, love?' Jason asked, pecking Melissa on the lips. 'Where's Donte?'

'Upstairs, but he seems better today. More cheerful. We had a nice chat earlier and he's eating again.'

'Great stuff. Told you he'd be OK, didn't I?'

When the doorbell rang, Jason's heart sank. 'I'll get it,' he said, praying it wasn't the police.

'All right, Jason? I heard you were out. How you doing?'

Unable to believe Craig Thurston had the brass neck to knock on Melissa's door after everything that had happened, Jason hissed, 'Mel will go apeshit she sees you here. Wait round the corner and give me five minutes.'

Busy cleaning the kitchen, Mel turned to Jason with the mop in her hand. 'Who was it?'

'Some dickhead from the Labour Party. Do you need anything from the shop? I got a real urge for a cigar. Not had one in years.'

'Get us some Diet Coke, Jase. Two bottles, please.'

Jason left the house and walked around the corner. Craig's brand spanking new Range Rover Sport stood out a mile on this estate and he was aware of a group of lads nearby admiring it. He got in the passenger seat. 'Drive,' he ordered.

'You OK?' Craig asked, putting his foot on the accelerator.

'You got some fucking front, turning up 'ere. And no, I'm not all right. I've just done a six-stretch for a crime I did not cunting-well commit.'

'Yeah, sorry about that. This is for you,' Craig said, chucking the duffle bag at Jason.

Jason looked inside. It was full of money.

'Hundred grand in there. A goodwill gesture for your trouble. Cheers for keeping your trap shut an' all.'

Jason debated whether to tell Craig to shove his money where the sun doesn't shine, but he quickly decided against it. The geezer did owe him and as much as he wanted to hate Craig, he couldn't. He had some decent qualities which included being very good to Darlene in the past. 'Thanks. This'll come in handy.'

Craig pulled up outside a pub. 'Let me buy you a drink.'

'I gotta get back. I told Mel I was only popping to the shop.'

'Let's have a swift one. You're not under lock and key now, ya know.'

'Go on then.'

Craig ordered two brandy chasers and two pints of lager. He sat at a table and knocked the brandy back in one. 'What's your plans? Gonna open another pawn shop?'

'Not sure yet. Got a few ideas that need checking out. I went to Dar's grave today. You did her proud. How was she? You know, at the end?'

'Do you want the truth?'

'Yeah.'

'She went really downhill the last couple of weeks, was unrecognizable. The cancer was in her bones and everywhere by then. Bastard disease. She wasn't alone though. She spent her last three weeks in a hospice and I visited her every day. I don't think she even knew I was there the last couple of days, but I still chatted away to her while holding her hand.'

'Thanks, Craig, for what you did. It comforts me to know you were there for her. Heartbroken, I was, when the guvnor refused me permission to go to the funeral.'

'She truly loved you, ya know.'

'She thought the world of you too,' Jason replied.

'Yeah, but not in the same way. I always loved her, but she never wanted me. Her heart belonged to you.'

Jason's eyes welled up. 'I'll never forget her. She was my saviour.'

CHAPTER THIRTY-SEVEN

Jason was awake early. Today was the big day and he prayed everything would go smoothly. He had no back-up plan, so if this Dutch geezer had him over, he was well and truly in shit street.

Jason's thoughts turned to his brothers. He hadn't heard a dickie bird from them, so guessed they were still being questioned. They knew a decent solicitor, one who'd represented Elton in the past, so Jason assumed they'd called him.

Understandably, Donte was still panicking. Jason had had a long chat with him last night and did his best to calm the lad's fears. 'If the police knew it were you, they'd have been round here hammering on the door by now. Just act as normal as you can so your mother doesn't get suspicious, and pray to God you've got away with it.'

Shay was still refusing to have anything more to do with him. Melissa had called her yesterday. She was staying round her mate's house and had told Mel she would pick the rest of her things up when he was out. He would visit her soon, apologise for flying off the handle.

Jason jumped in the shower, got dressed and wandered

downstairs. 'Morning, sweetheart. Did you sleep well?' He walked up behind Melissa, put his arms around her waist and nuzzled his face into her neck. She flinched. 'What's a matter?' he asked. He was getting a bit sick of her coldness.

'I'm cleaning, Jason. These worktops don't tidy themselves, you know. What time are you meeting your friend?'

'Half eleven.' Jason leaned against the fridge. 'Are you sure your heart is in this marriage? Only if it isn't, now's the time to tell me. I won't see you short. You can still have half of what I've got coming.'

Melissa put her cloth down and dried her hands on the tea towel. She walked over to Jason and draped her arms around his neck. 'You know how much I love you. I would never have stuck by you had I not wanted our marriage to work.'

'Well, you've got a funny way of showing it. I thought it weird you invited that posh counsellor tart to my party. What was that all about? You've not been having sessions with her, have you? Only, how you affording that? She was charging you a bullseye a session before I went away, so fuck knows what she charges now.'

Melissa removed her arms from Jason's neck. 'Oh, don't talk so stupid. I barely have enough money to put fuel in the car most days, let alone pay for counselling sessions. Eleanor trains at the same gym as me and we've become friends. Sorry, I should have mentioned that.'

'How you been affording your gym membership? And your massages? And Roy, your personal trainer you seem so fucking friendly with? I bet those hair extensions weren't cheap either. And who bought the kids computers?' Jason asked suspiciously. 'You haven't been reefing around Steve the mechanic again, have you?'

'No, I bloody well haven't. And what is this, twenty questions? If you must know, my dad bought the kids their computers. He also put five hundred quid in my bank account each month because Donte told him how much we were struggling. I paid for my gym membership, personal trainer, massages and extensions out of that. Anything else you want to know?'

'You talking to your dad again then?'

'No. Donte keeps in touch with him though. Listen, Jason, beggars can't be choosers. I despise my father, but I needed that money to put food on the table. You left us with nothing.'

'I know and I'm sorry. Fingers crossed, that all changes today though, eh?'

'Exactly. Good luck. What time do you expect to be home later? You're not bringing that money back here with you, are you?'

'No. Simon's gonna put some in his safe and I'll stash the rest. Not here, mind. I ain't that stupid. Please God all goes to plan, we'll go look at that property tomorrow. I shouldn't be late back. Around teatime, I reckon.'

'I thought we might celebrate. There's tons of booze left over from the party. Why don't you invite Simon and his new lady friend over and I'll invite Tracey and Greg. Simon and Greg have to get to know one another for Toby's sake, so tonight can be a bit of an ice-breaker. I won't cook. We'll get a takeaway.'

'Si's probably busy, babe, and I can do without an evening in Tracey's company. She does my head in. Why don't the two of us go out to celebrate? I'll book us a table somewhere special.'

'We can celebrate alone after we've looked at the house tomorrow. Please, Jase. Do this for me. I worry about

Toby. Tracey isn't the best mother in the world. She tries, but she's not a natural like me. She's really serious about Greg and if they are going to start spending all their time together, I want to make sure he's OK around Toby. If he isn't, then Simon can intervene.'

Jason sighed. 'OK. But on one condition.'

'What?'

'Once we move home, I want us to try for a baby of our own. Seeing how you are with Toby makes me all maternal. Is a man allowed to say that?'

'You big softie,' Melissa laughed.

Jason took his wife in his arms and rocked her to and fro. 'Is that a yes then?'

Melissa grinned. 'You bet it is.'

Jason kissed her. 'I love you.'

'Love you too.'

The journey to Hatton Garden to collect the key for the storage unit took Jason an hour and twenty minutes. He then headed to West London, glancing in his mirrors all the way to ensure he wasn't being followed, to collect the painting from the storage unit. It was already wrapped. He'd protected the finish with plastic, then sealed it in Styrofoam and put it inside a cardboard box. Henry had told him what to do, said it was the safest way to avoid any damage.

Manoeuvring the painting inside the van, Jason made his way to Herongate to pick up Henry. The adrenaline was kicking in now, he was buzzing with anticipation.

'Good afternoon. Beautiful day, isn't it?' Henry said as he leapt into the passenger seat with a racket and sports bag.

The July weather was scorching and Jason couldn't help

but laugh at his pal's outfit. 'What you done up like you've just come off Centre Court in Wimbledon for?'

'Because it will throw any undesirables off the scent. Put your visor on. Suits you,' Henry grinned, as he placed a visor on Jason's head. 'We will not be pulled up or searched looking like this, I can assure you.'

'Mental, you are,' Jason chuckled.

'Don't go that way. Do a right here. We'll go the back route. Quieter roads where you barely see a soul,' Henry said.

'Good thinking.'

The journey took about half an hour and as they neared their destination, Jason's mouth dried up and so did the conversation. He was edgy now, paranoid something might go wrong. He had waited all his life for what he referred to as 'The Biggie' to come off. And this was it. There'd be no more life of crime for him afterwards. He could not wait to go straight.

'Take this left, there's a dirt track fifty yards or so down on the right. Drive to the bottom of that, Jason.'

Jason was glad he had Henry with him as no way would he have found this place alone. It was in the middle of bloody nowhere. 'What do we do now?' he asked, as they approached a padlocked metal gate.

'We wait. The other side of that gate there is an enormous field. That is where Hans will be landing.'

Jason looked at his watch. They were early. He took a deep breath. His heart could not beat any faster. It was thumping against his chest like the clappers.

Melissa tapped on her son's bedroom door. She was on edge, knowing Jason would either arrive home rich, or he would remain bloody poor. She had waited a long time for this moment. Her husband owed her. To while away the time, Melissa had called Tracey. Greg couldn't make tonight, so she'd arranged for Tracey to bring him around tomorrow. Same with Simon. She'd spoken to him earlier too, and he and his new lady friend were both free the following evening.

'Donte, you OK, love?'

'Yeah. Come in.' The last thing Donte wanted or needed was a conversation with his mother, but he had to take his dad's advice and try to act normal.

'It's a beautiful day. Not like you to be holed up in your bedroom. Why don't we go for a drive? We can put some flowers on Nanny and Bobby's graves, then I'll treat you to some lunch.'

Having just murdered someone in cold blood, the last place Donte wanted to go was a graveyard. 'Nah, you're all right, Mum. It makes me sad seeing Bobby's grave and I'm not that hungry at the moment. I've been eating crisps all morning,' Donte lied. He'd actually thrown his breakfast in the bin when his mother had turned her back earlier. His stomach was constantly churning at the thought of being locked up and he was struggling to eat a morsel.

'What about bowling? Do you fancy that? We've not been for years.'

'Not really.'

'I know: Monopoly. You used to love a game of Monopoly. How about I take the coffee table out in the garden and we'll play it out there? I'll let you have a cold can of lager as well, if you like? I don't want you drinking behind my back any more, but I know you're not a little kid either.'

Remembering Jason's advice, Donte forced a smile. 'OK. Monopoly and lager it is.'

*

Watching the helicopter land was one of the most exhilarating yet nerve-racking moments of Jason Rampling's life. Not because it was the first time he'd seen one land up close; it was the two million quid on board that set his pulse racing.

'Come on,' Henry said, climbing over the fence.

Jason followed suit and watched two men clamber out the helicopter. One was about fifty, grey and very distinguished-looking. The other was shorter, plump and reminded Jason of Danny DeVito.

Henry strutted towards the men with a grin on his face. 'Jason, this is Hans,' he said, gesturing toward the grey-haired bloke. 'And this is Raphael, Hans' partner.'

'Nice to meet you,' Jason said, shaking both men's hands. They had firm handshakes and Jason saw that as a good sign. 'Never trust a man with a limp handshake, boy,' his nan had always told him.

Henry and Hans spoke briefly about the journey, then Hans asked where the painting was.

'This way,' Henry said.

Starting to panic, Jason grabbed Henry by the arm. 'Where's the money?' he whispered.

'Stop worrying,' Henry mouthed silently.

The men unwrapped the painting and checked it over meticulously. Raphael then pulled out a magnifying glass and began mumbling something in Dutch.

Jason prodded Henry. 'What's he saying?'

Henry put his finger to his lips to urge Jason to be quiet.

After what seemed like ten hours, but was in fact only ten minutes, Hans turned around and smiled. 'It seems we have a deal. Raphael, bring the money so the gentlemen can count it.'

The adrenaline that surged through Jason's veins when the two suitcases were opened was the biggest high of his life. He stared at the bundles of fifty-pound notes, could barely believe his luck. Finally, he'd cracked it. He'd pulled 'The Biggie' off thanks to, of all people, that tosser Mickey Two Wives.

'And this is for you, Henry,' Hans said, handing Henry an extremely large brown envelope. 'Thank you once again for thinking of me.'

'You're very welcome,' Henry replied, checking his own cash, then flicking through the bundles in the cases. 'It's all there,' he assured Jason.

'We will be going now then. Raphael, grab the other end of the painting.'

Raphael was busy wrapping the painting up, so Jason held out his hand to Hans. He still could not believe his good fortune. It would take a while to sink in.

Raphael turned around and shook both Henry and Jason's hands. 'A pleasure doing business with you, gentlemen.'

Jason could not wipe the soppy grin off his face. 'Likewise, lads. Likewise.'

'You cheat. I wanted to buy Mayfair. How comes you always snap up all the good ones?' Melissa chuckled. It was hard to concentrate on Monopoly when she was willing her mobile phone to ring to find out if she was a rich woman, but she was trying her damn hardest.

When the call finally came, Melissa could barely breathe, she felt so nervous. 'Well?'

Jason's response – 'Sweet as a nut, babe' – filled Melissa with a joy she thought she'd never feel again. She wanted to dance around the garden, such was her elation, but

Donte knew nothing about the painting, so she sat back down and instead bought Fleet Street.

'Who was that, Mum?' Donte asked suspiciously. His mother had a silly grin on her face.

'Only your father. He said he'll be home around teatime.'

'I need to use the toilet. Won't be a minute.'

When Donte went inside the house, Melissa clapped her hands with glee. Very soon she would have everything she had ever dreamed of. Good things come to those who wait, and she'd waited long enough. Bad things came to those who'd wronged people in life, so she felt no guilt.

Having received a phone call from Jason to say he was on his way, Simon greeted him on the driveway with a big smile on his face. 'Well done, mate. I knew you'd pull it off. A millionaire, eh? How's it feel, Del Boy?' Simon laughed, grabbing Jason in a playful headlock.

Jason could not wipe the grin off his face as he hugged then slapped his pal on the back. 'I can't believe it came off. Even up to the last minute I was expecting something to go wrong. Over the fucking moon, I am. My shit run of luck has finally changed. I'm buzzing.'

'I bet you bloody are. Come inside and we'll sort the money out. So chuffed for you and Mel. You both deserve this after all you've been through.'

Jason carried both briefcases inside Simon's house and clicked one open on the sofa. He counted the bundles of fifty-pound notes and handed Simon two hundred and fifty thousand. 'That's my solicitor's fees, money I've borrowed, money you've given Mel, and the rest is a drink for you.'

'You sure?' Simon asked. 'I wasn't expecting that much. Take some back.'

Jason shook his head. 'No. I insist. Without your help, I don't know what I'd have done. I really appreciate it.'

'I'm sure you'd do the same for me.'

'Course. Right, let's get down to business. How much do you want for the house in Upshire? I know we haven't viewed it yet, but Mel has already fallen in love with it in those photos you emailed us.'

'I was going to put in on the market for eight hundred grand, but if you and Mel want it, it's yours for seven fifty.'

Jason clicked the suitcase shut and handed it to Simon. 'Stick that in your safe then for now. Seven hundred and fifty in there. We'll view the property tomorrow and I'm ninety-nine per cent sure we will take it. I'll stash the rest of the dosh somewhere safe after I've taken some spending money out. I had to give Henry a hundred grand, so I've got nine hundred left to carve my future out with. Exciting times.'

'What do you want to do about a motor? You still want me to put one in my name for you?'

Jason took another fifty thousand out of the second case. 'Put that with the other. That'll buy me and Mel a decent motor each. Put both in your name.'

'Where you going to put it? Whatever you do, don't leave it indoors.'

'I won't. That safety-deposit box you kept up the payments for while I was away – I'm going to stash it in there.'

'Wise move.'

'If Mel and I view the house tomorrow, how quickly can we move in?'

'The builders will be finished there in a couple of days.

They're just applying the final touches. There were a couple of issues, nothing major. You can probably move in as early as Saturday if you want? It still needs a bit of decorating though.'

Jason grinned. 'We'll sort that ourselves. I find painting rather therapeutic, believe it or not. Mel and I had a chat earlier. Gonna try for another baby once we've moved. Seeing you with Toby has made me want to be a dad again.'

'Great stuff. It's a brilliant feeling, as you well know. Can't beat it, fatherhood.'

'I was only a kid myself when Shay was born. I'm sure I would appreciate it even more now.'

'Course you would. And you and Mel will make brilliant parents.'

'Your solicitor pal – can he draw up something legal, sharpish, to say I own the property if we agree to it tomorrow?'

'Yeah. Same goes for the cars when you purchase them.' Simon took two keys off his keyring and handed them to Jason. 'As soon as you and Mel have viewed it, let me know if you want it and I'll have the solicitor draw up the necessary. Don't get me wrong – anything should happen to you, God forbid, I would put the property in Mel's name anyway. But it's better to have it in black and white. We all know where we stand then.'

'Sweet. Right, I best make a move now. I don't want to hit Hatton Garden in rush hour. Cheers again, Si, for everything.'

'My pleasure, mate. Speak tomorrow.'

*

'Whatever's wrong now?' Melissa asked, as she opened the front door. Tracey Thompson looked a mess. She was holding a bottle of wine, her hair was all over the place and all her mascara had run down her cheeks.

'I can't stand it no more. He's messing me about too much, Mel. I reckon I ballsed it up when I gave him a door key and said he was welcome to turn up any time he wanted. He must have thought I was a right desperado,' Tracey wept.

'You didn't drive here in this state, did you?' Melissa asked.

'No. I've already had a bottle of wine, so I got a cab. I rung you about ten times, but you weren't answering your bloody phone.'

'I've been busy, Trace. My phone is on charge in the kitchen. What's Greg done now?'

'Blew me out after I'd got ready tonight. Yesterday, when I asked to see him, he says he was busy. Then this morning he rings, tells me how much he's missing me and to get glammed up because he's picking me up at seven and taking me somewhere special. Then at six, I get a text – not even a fucking phone call – saying something's cropped up and he can't make it after all. Sick of being messed around, I am. I don't know where I stand with him at all. He must have a wife or girlfriend tucked away somewhere, I'm telling you. You might not have clocked it with Jason, but I'm not totally stupid.'

As Melissa turned her back to pour her friend a drink, she couldn't help but smirk. Her wonderful mother had always told her, 'Your mate Tracey is not a very nice person, love. One day karma will bite her on the bum.'

*

The Farthings lived in a stunning five-bedroom property in Loughton. It was set in a few acres, had its own indoor swimming pool, games and cinema rooms and gym.

Leaning out of the Land Rover window, Jason pressed the buzzer. The journey to and from Hatton Garden hadn't taken as long as expected and his windfall was now safely hidden.

'Hello. Who is it?' asked an Eastern European-sounding woman's voice.

'Is Felicity or David around?' Jason enquired.

'No. They are away. Who is asking?'

'Shay Rampling's father. She's staying here and I need to speak to her urgently.'

'Ah, OK. Shay and Natasha are sunbathing in the garden. Drive up to the house.'

Jason pulled up, leapt out of the motor and was met at the door by the housekeeper. 'Sorry. Your daughter informs me she doesn't want to see you.'

'Tough luck,' Jason replied, strutting inside the property. 'And you want to be careful who you buzz in, ya know. I could've been anybody.'

Shay and Natasha had been firm friends since the age of eleven, so Jason knew the layout of the house well. He marched in the garden. 'Shay. We need to talk.'

Dressed in a skimpy white bikini, Shay leapt off the rattan furniture, her eyes glinting with anger. 'I have nothing to say to you. Fuck off.'

Jason locked eyes with his defiant daughter. She'd only been a kid when he'd got banged up, but was now a beautiful young woman. She looked like a model – not the type who flashed their tits, the catwalk type. 'Please, Shay. Come out to the car with me.'

Shay put her hands on her hips. 'What's the point?

Unless you've decided to give Luke a chance. Nat's met him, haven't you, mate? Tell my sergeant major of a father how nice he is. Go on.'

'He is a nice bloke, Jason. You would like him. He's ever so good to Shay. Only takes her to classy places.'

'I bet he does,' Jason mumbled, under his breath. He held Shay's gaze. 'All I want is the best for you and for you to be happy in life, sweetheart. That's all I've ever wanted. Sixteen years is a hell of an age gap. He's only six years off of forty. The same fucking age as me, love. I would never dream of having a relationship with a girl your age. It's not right. It's wrong.'

'No, it's not,' Shay bellowed. 'And you can talk. You dated that old woman.'

'Look, I'm not going to argue with you. But I want you to think about what I'm saying. When you're thirty, Luke will be nearing fifty. Will your kids really want some balding, beer-bellied old bastard picking 'em up from school? I doubt it very much.'

'Why do you always have to look into the future? Like I'm going to get married or have kids any time soon. I know what you're trying to do, Dad. I'm not bloody stupid.'

'I'm only saying what I see. You and some pensioner, pushing a spotted pram. Look, why don't you come home. There'll be no more arguing, I promise. I miss you, have barely seen you in years.'

'Not yet. I promised Nat I'd stay here until her parents came home. Anyway, we're having fun.'

'Fair enough. Am I allowed to phone you?'

Shay shrugged miserably. Her father's words had actually given her food for thought, but she'd never admit it. Because she hadn't seen her dad for years, she'd forgotten how old he was. It felt weird that her boyfriend was the same age. 'I'll phone you,' she said.

'Do I get a hug?' Jason smiled.

'No.'

'Oh well, I'll be off then. Enjoy yourselves, girls. I love you, Shay. Never forget that.'

'I won't. Bye then.'

CHAPTER THIRTY-EIGHT

Upshire was a beautiful area and Jason could not help but laugh at Melissa's enthusiasm as he drove towards the property that was destined to become their new home.

'Oh my God! Look at that gigantic house over there. I bloody love this area. It's amazing! I shall feel like the lady of the manor, living around here.'

'I'll be lord of the manor then,' Jason chuckled. 'According to my sat nav, we're nearly there now.'

The property Simon had had refurbished was set in an acre of land. It had previously belonged to an elderly couple who had lived there for years, letting the place go to rack and ruin, hence the amount of work that had needed doing.

The driveway was barely visible as it was hidden by trees and bushes. As Jason pulled in, Melissa gasped with delight. 'Oh, Jase. It's gorgeous. I love it.'

Melissa's happiness was infectious and Jason felt like a million dollars as he stepped out of the vehicle. 'It's proper, ain't it? Let's look inside.'

The rooms were bare and reeked of fresh paint.

'Open the windows, Jase. That smell's choking me,'

Melissa complained, before checking out the bedrooms. 'Look at the en suite. It's been done up beautifully.'

Jason put his arms around Melissa's waist. 'We're gonna be so happy here. Having seen it, I think we've got ourselves a bargain an' all. I'd have said this is worth a million all day long at today's prices.'

'I don't like the colour on the walls, that'll have to be changed.'

'We can do what we like with it. I want to get some gates put on the front with a buzzer. Be nice and secure for you and the kids when I'm out and about.'

'Good idea. Let's look at the garden,' Melissa said, grabbing Jason by the hand.

The garden was stunning, with newly planted shrubs and flowers. It also had a wishing well and a quaint wooden bridge that gnomes sat on.

'Oh, Jase. This is the nicest garden I have ever seen. Ours in Repton Park was shit in comparison to this.'

Jason slung his arm around his wife's shoulders and studied the breathtaking view. Simon had told him the garden had been like a jungle and he'd hired a landscape firm to redesign it. 'Perfect for a kiddie to play in, isn't it?'

Thinking of Toby, Melissa smiled. 'Yes. It is.'

After dropping Melissa off and ringing Simon to tell him they'd take the house, Jason drove to the Mardyke Estate. Elton had sensibly said very little on the phone, just that he and Kyle had been released on bail.

Every time Jason stepped in the lifts in his old block, it took him back to his awful childhood, so instead he used the stairs. He'd only been a nipper when he'd first got stuck in the lift alone, and he'd been terrified. Every time he was naughty after that, his bitch of a mother used to march him on the landing, shove him in the lift and press 'ground floor'.

Kyle answered the door. 'We got a flat full,' he informed his brother.

Jason walked into the lounge. It was smoky, stank of weed, and there were six lads lounging on the furniture and floor. 'Nice. I feel high just walking in 'ere. I wanna word, Elton. Outside.'

Wearing a white Nike tracksuit, Elton put his hood up and followed his brother on to the landing.

'You must be bloody sweltering in that clobber. Why don't you open some windows in there? The fire brigade'll be called otherwise. Someone'll think the place is burnin' down.'

'The window in the lounge is jammed, Bro.'

'So what happened then? Good lad for not saying anything on the phone, by the way. I've taught you well.'

'The Old Bill say they know we were chasing the other gang. They kept asking who the other lad with us was. They know Donte was wearing a bright blue tracksuit. I told him not to wear bright colours.' Elton kissed his teeth. 'Now we're all in the shit.'

'That the rest of your gang?' Jason asked, gesturing his head towards the lounge.

'Yeah. They ain't happy.'

'Nobody has mentioned Donte, have they?'

'No. But Clayton told his ma and she's threatened to tell the Old Bill.'

'Why did he tell his fucking mother? Which one's Clayton?'

Elton grabbed Jason's arm to stop him marching back inside the flat. 'Leave it, Bro. You'll only make matters worse. Clayton is very close to his ma. She goes to church, believes in God and stuff. She made him tell her.'

'Well, that's bloody great that is, innit? You better make sure he untells her, Elton. Because if you don't, I fucking will.'

Adrenaline pumping through her veins at the thought of showing Greg off in front of Jason, Tracey Thompson took extra care getting ready for the evening ahead. She always looked glamorous, but tonight she was determined to wear something tight-fitting and sexy. She'd clocked Jason looking at her a couple of times at his party and even though she was happy with Greg now, Tracey held grudges and would never forgive or forget. Jason had knocked her back, twice. He was the only man to have ever done that, and his rejection had left a sour taste in her mouth.

Pink was currently in fashion, so after trying on numerous outfits, Tracey decided to wear the slinky bright pink dress she'd bought recently from a designer boutique in Chigwell. It was sleeveless, calf-length and clung to her perfect curves. It was also low-cut and showed off her ample breasts.

Unable to get hold of Greg earlier, Tracey decided to ring him again. When they'd first met he was forever texting and calling her, but these past few days she'd barely spoken to him and when she had he'd said he was busy. She guessed it was to do with those plans she'd found in his sports bag and had been listening to the news in case they mentioned an armed robbery had taken place locally.

Greg didn't answer, so once again Tracey left a message on his voicemail telling him to pick her up at 6.45 p.m. A minute later she received a text.

Got a lot on. You go ahead. Will meet you round your mate's house.

Peeved that Greg would not be accompanying her and worried as he hadn't even put as much as a solitary kiss on the end of his text, Tracey tried to call him again. Annoyingly for her, Greg didn't answer.

Melissa felt elated as she zipped her new skin-tight faded jeans up without a struggle. She hadn't been able to fit into a size 8 since her early teenage years. She was still having regular sessions with her personal trainer, Roy Nixon, and her hard graft was certainly paying off.

'What we got for dinner, Mum?' Donte shouted out. Jason had spoken to him late last night and told him Elton and Kyle had been released without charge. He was still edgy though, only felt safe in the comfort of his bedroom.

Melissa walked into her son's room. 'Simon and Tracey are coming round, so we're getting a takeaway. You going to eat with us?'

'Are Simon and Tracey back together?'

'No chance of that,' Melissa laughed. 'Simon is bringing his new girlfriend and Tracey is bringing her boyfriend, Greg.'

'Oh. Can I have chips, curry sauce, a pancake roll and special chow mein, please? I'll eat it up here though. Tracey's voice does my head in.' Donte's appetite had finally returned, so he was making up for lost eating time.

Melissa sat on Donte's bed, put an arm around her son and kissed him on the forehead. 'Why don't you give Calvin a ring, see what he's up to these days? You two were so close at school, I'm sure he'd love to hear from you.'

'Nah. Not seen Calvin in ages and I doubt I'd have

much in common with him now anyway. He was always a bit of a sap.'

'You can't stay holed up in your bedroom like a hermit for ever more, Donte. Are you sure there's nothing troubling you?' Melissa asked. She had no idea that Elton and Kyle had been arrested on suspicion of murder. Jason had told her they'd been caught with some weed.

Donte forced a smile. 'I'm fine, Mum. I swear, I am.'

'I'm early. Am I the first to arrive?' Tracey asked, feeling flustered.

'Yes. Jason's not even home yet. I've no idea where he's got to. He isn't answering his phone. Where's Greg?'

'Snap! No idea where Greg is, and he isn't answering his bloody phone either.'

'He is still coming, isn't he?' Melissa enquired.

'Yeah. He said he'll meet me here. What am I gonna do, Mel? I think he's going off me. We've not had a proper conversation since he left mine the other night and he didn't put any kisses on the end of his last text. You don't think he knows I looked in that bag, do you? Perhaps he left it as a test, to see if I could be trusted.'

'Oh, don't be so daft. I swear I've never known anyone with such an overactive imagination as yours, Trace.'

'Well, why has he gone cold on me then?' Tracey asked, opening the bottle of wine she'd brought with her.

'He's obviously busy. Probably robbing a bank,' Melissa chuckled.

'Auntie Mel, can I have some orange juice, please?'

Melissa picked up Toby and planted kisses all over his handsome face. 'You, my little soldier, can have whatever you want.'

*

'What's this?' Peggy Rampling felt the carrier bag. 'Ain't you bought me no fags or Guinness?'

Jason rolled his eyes. 'Just open the bloody thing, will you, Nan.'

'Money. Lots of it. Want me to hide it for ya?'

'Nope. It's all for you,' Jason grinned.

'Really? Aww, bless you, boy. How much?'

'Eight grand. Was going to give you ten out my little windfall, but seeing as you borrowed two while I was inside, you got eight,' Jason laughed.

'Cheeky bugger,' Peggy chuckled. 'What you done, robbed a bank?'

'As good as. I finally sold that painting. Bought a house today an' all. You wanna see it. Set in an acre of land. The bollocks, it is, Nan. Moving in at the weekend.'

'She moving in it with you? Loony Lil.'

'Yeah. We've decided to give our marriage another go.'

'I bet she wants to give it another go now you've come into money. The woman is a fucking vulture.'

'She ain't all bad. I really want another kid now myself, so we've chatted about it and we're gonna try for one.'

Peggy pursed her lips. 'You want your brains tested, impregnating that one. She'll never be happy while she's got a hole in her arse. Fact.'

Tracey Thompson slung her phone across the room in temper. 'Bastard!' she shrieked. 'Who does he think he is, keep blanking my texts and calls? I'm going to get some money together, hire a private detective and have him followed. No way is he mugging me off any more. And I want my spare key back. Waste of time him having it if I hardly ever see him.'

'I doubt he's mugging you off, mate. If he said he'll be

here, he'll be here. He's probably just in the middle of something.'

'Yeah. Like shagging his wife. Probably got kids an' all, knowing my luck. I blame you for this, Mel, I really do. If you hadn't dragged me up the Prince Regent that night, I'd never have met the no-good arsehole.'

'Give us your glass. I'll pour you another drink. Jason's just pulled up outside and I'm sure Greg will soon too. Be patient. This is part and parcel of the life, Trace, take it from somebody who's lived it.'

Jason was horrified to see Tracey already looking slightly inebriated.

'Hello, Uncle Jason,' Toby said, holding his arms out.

Tracey smirked. 'Give him a cuddle then, Uncle Jason. He likes you, although I have no idea why.'

'Where you been? I rang you five times,' Melissa informed her husband.

'Sorry, love. My battery went dead. I popped round to see Babs again after I left my nan's. I really don't like that prick she's lumbered herself with and wanted to check she was OK after the little talking to I gave him the other day.'

'And is she?'

'Yeah. My threat to break his neck seems to have done the trick, for now at least. Come upstairs a tick, babe. I wanna show you something.'

'Oi, oi. Get a room you two,' Tracey shouted out.

Once out of earshot, Jason turned to Mel. 'Is she pissed already? What time did she get here – and where's Greg?'

'She's had three drinks, that's all. She got here at half six and she doesn't know where Greg is. He said he'll meet her here, but he hasn't been answering his phone, apparently.'

'Brilliant!' Jason exclaimed sarcastically. 'He better fucking turn up or she's bound to make a scene in front of Simon's girlfriend. Don't let her drink no more until after we've eaten.' Tracey was so unpredictable, Jason was actually worried she'd blurt something out about him too if she was stood up.

'Tracey's a grown woman, Jase. I can't tell her what to do. If you're that worried, then you bloody tell her to lay off the vino.'

The doorbell chiming ended the conversation and Melissa ran downstairs. 'Hello. Do come in. You must be Sally-Ann. I've heard lots about you – all good, might I add. Simon and my husband are best friends. Actually, joined at the hip might be a better description,' Melissa laughed.

'Simon has told me all about you and your husband too. It's lovely to meet you,' Sally-Ann replied, kissing Melissa then Jason on both cheeks.

'Hello. I'm Toby.'

Simon scooped his son in his arms. He had only told Sally-Ann that she would be meeting Toby yesterday. 'Give the lady a kiss then, boy,' he urged, tilting Toby forward.

Sally-Ann tried to hide her awkwardness. She wasn't great with kids, had none of her own.

'What would you like to drink, Sally-Ann?' Jason asked. She wasn't Simon's usual type. Nice figure, but her nose was too big for her face, and she was dressed very formally. He usually went for the dolly bird sort.

'I'd love a red wine, please,' Sally-Ann replied, following Melissa into the kitchen.

Simon put his arm around his girlfriend. 'This is Tracey, Toby's mum. Tracey, this is Sally-Ann.'

'All right,' Tracey said, shaking the woman's hand. She looked like a man in drag, Tracey thought smugly.

'Tracey's boyfriend will be joining us soon,' Jason said. He could sense Sally-Ann's discomfort.

'Ah, OK.' Sally-Ann was gobsmacked. Simon hadn't mentioned his ex would be having dinner with them. Neither had he told her Tracey looked like a glamour model.

'You all right?' Simon asked, handing Sally-Ann her wine.

Sally-Ann nodded. She liked Simon but couldn't help think that this was all a bit too much too soon. They barely knew one another. Talk about throw her in at the deep end.

'Sorry about the furniture. I've had to push two tables together and use some garden chairs. There's little room to manoeuvre I'm afraid, but it will have to do until we move.'

'Do you know where you're moving to yet?' Sally-Ann asked politely.

'Yes. Upshire,' Melissa replied.

Tracey choked on the mouthful of wine she was about to swallow. 'Sorry. Wrong hole,' she apologized, waving her hands erratically before composing herself once again. 'Upshire's well expensive, Mel. Unless you've won the lottery, I doubt you'll be moving there, mate.'

Simon had ordered both Melissa and Jason not to breathe a word of his involvement in the property to Tracey or anybody else. He told Jase that the taxman would come down on him like a ton of bricks as he had no intention of declaring the house as sold. Tracey also knew nothing of his finances, had no idea he'd even purchased the house in the first place. 'Give your bloke a ring, Trace. We're going to be ordering food soon,' Simon urged.

'Will do.' Tracey picked up her handbag and walked into the hallway. Greg had better answer; else she would look a complete fool.

'Well?' Melissa asked, when Tracey returned.

'He must be busy. Just order the food anyway. I don't wait around for no man, me,' Tracey snapped.

Watching Tracey pour herself another large glass of wine, Jason looked at Simon and rolled his eyes. Some night this was turning out to be.

By nine o'clock Tracey was performing, her voice having gone up a decibel. 'So, where did you and Simon meet then?' she asked Sally-Ann. She was distraught she still hadn't heard from Greg, but was determined not to show it.

'Erm, online actually. I joined a professional dating website and Simon sent me a message.'

'I bet you would never have put me and Si together, would you?' Tracey chuckled.

Sally-Ann was feeling uncomfortable. She liked Melissa, but thought Tracey was awful. Everything about her was fake. Her hair extensions, nails, breasts, and even her smile. A typical bimbo, and Sally-Ann was extremely disappointed that Simon had dated such a woman. Perhaps he wasn't the man she'd first thought he was. 'My ex is the total opposite of me,' Sally-Ann replied courteously.

Tracey leaned towards Simon and put a drunken arm around his shoulder. 'He's all right, is Si. No oil painting, but he's got a good heart, ain't ya, mate?'

'Shut it, Trace. No need to be insulting, is there? No wonder your geezer's blown you out. He's probably had a gutful of you already,' Jason hissed. He didn't want to antagonize her, but somebody needed to shut her up.

'Saint Jason has spoken, everyone,' Tracey mocked. 'Mel wants a medal for giving you chance after chance, if you want my opinion,' Tracey retaliated, her eyes glinting dangerously. She had already decided to give him a wake-up call next week. She wanted maintenance money off the bastard. If he could afford a house in Upshire then he could afford to give her twelve hundred quid a month to help with Toby's upkeep.

'Right, I'll wash up if everyone has finished eating,' Melissa said. 'I can't wait to own a dishwasher again, Jason. Roll on Saturday,' she added.

'You ordered a dishwasher for in here? Where you going to put it?' Tracey enquired.

Ignoring Jason's warning look, Melissa said, 'Not for in here. We're moving into our new home on Saturday.'

Tracey was stunned. 'What new home? Where you moving to?'

'Upshire. I already told you,' Melissa replied.

'You didn't say you were moving this weekend. What you done, rented a place?' Tracey asked.

'No. We've bought one. Jason had some money owed to him,' Melissa informed her friend.

'I'm no expert, but houses don't go through that bloody quick,' Tracey responded.

'I know. That's why it's a good job Jason set the ball rolling while he was still inside, isn't it, love?' Melissa said, smiling at her husband.

Knowing what a jealous bitch Tracey was, Jason replied, 'Yeah,' then immediately changed the subject.

'Who wants another drink?' Melissa asked.

'Sally-Ann and I will have one please, Mel,' Simon said.

Sally-Ann sighed. She wasn't enjoying herself at all and wanted to go home.

Simon squeezed his girlfriend's hand, then stood up. 'I'm just going to check on Toby. Won't be a tick.' Toby had been tucked up in bed by Melissa an hour or so ago.

Melissa took two tablets out the drawer. 'I've still got that headache, Jase. Paint always does this to me. You're going to have to decorate that place on your own and open all the windows to allow the smell to drift away before I move in. Makes me feel nauseous.'

Tracey grinned as she received a text message. 'It's Greg,' she said.

Her expression soon turned to one of anger and disbelief as she read what Greg had to say.

'Is he coming round?' Melissa asked.

'No. He fucking ain't,' Tracey spat, bolting into the hallway. She was crying now, tears of anger, and didn't want anyone to clock her heartache.

'What's the matter?' Simon asked, as he came down the stairs.

'Nothing that concerns you,' Tracey hissed, calling Greg's number.

Melissa followed Tracey into the hallway. 'What's up, mate? What did Greg say?'

'That he's got to go away for a while and won't be able to speak on the phone. He said he'll make it up to me when he gets back. I just tried him again and he won't answer,' Tracey wept.

Melissa put her arms around Tracey. 'He's obviously up to you-know-what. I bet he comes back loaded and spoils you something rotten.'

'Do you think so? Or you just saying that to make me feel better? I hate not knowing where I stand, Mel. I really like him an' all.' Tracey wept. 'We had such a lovely evening last Monday. I even let him shag me up the arse, and you know I'm not a fan of that.'

'I swear I'm not saying it just to make you feel better. Greg's really into you, I can tell. You need to be patient and play it cool. This is the type of life you're going to have to get used to now you've bagged yourself a gangster, Trace.'

'Jason ain't a gangster,' Tracey reminded her pal.

'I know that. Jason's just a chancer,' Melissa chuckled. 'Now dry your eyes and come back in the kitchen. I'll pour you another wine. It'll make you feel better.'

By ten o'clock, Tracey was dancing around the lounge to the tunes on Melissa's iPod. 'Always reminded me of you, this song, Jase,' she cackled, singing along to Richard 'Dimples' Fields' 'I've Got To Learn To Say No!' The song was about a man who had women dotted about all over the place.

Jason grabbed Melissa's arm and led her into the kitchen. 'She's a bastard nuisance, your mate. Call her a cab. I don't know what Simon's girlfriend must think. It hardly looks good on us, does it? That lush being your best pal.'

Having allowed herself a rare couple of Proseccos, Melissa was thoroughly enjoying herself. 'Don't be such a fuddy-duddy. You seem to be forgetting, Simon was the one who got Tracey pregnant. If his bore of a girlfriend doesn't like our company, so be it. We don't look bad.'

'Keep your voice down, Sally-Ann'll hear you,' Jason hissed. He was truly having the night from hell. Only a few minutes ago that stupid bitch Tracey had asked out loud, 'Toby looks nothing like Simon, does he, Jase?' She was that drunk now she was liable to blurt out anything.

Melissa draped her arms around Jason's neck. 'Tracey's upset because Greg's gone on the missing list. I said she could stay here tonight.'

'What did you say that for? Where's she going to sleep? There's no room.'

'She can sleep in my bed with me and Toby. It's only one night, Jase. Trace was a good friend to me while you were inside. She even gave me her car.'

'Only because Simon bought her a new one. She ain't your mate, Mel. She's a jealous vindictive bitch, always has been. Did you see her face earlier when you said we were moving? Envy etched all over it.'

'Taking about me, are ya?' Tracey laughed, appearing at the kitchen door.

'We're talking about our new home. Let me get you another drink. Where's your glass?' Melissa asked.

Relieved to have Simon to herself for a minute, Sally-Ann asked. 'Can we go now, please? I cannot believe you brought me here with that awful woman. I don't mean to sound disrespectful, but whatever were you thinking? She had the cheek to ask me if I had ever considered having a nose job. How rude is that?'

'I love this song,' Tracey shrieked, darting back into the lounge. Singing loudly to Viola Wills's 'Gonna Get Along Without You Now' she grabbed Simon by the hand while thinking of Greg. 'Dance, Si,' she ordered.

Simon smiled. 'No. You know I'm not much of a dancer, Trace.'

'Oh, go on. Your bird won't mind. You don't mind me dancing with Si, do you, Sal?' Tracey slurred. 'I can assure you I don't fancy him. Never did, to be honest,' she laughed.

Sally-Ann stood up and grabbed her handbag. 'A bird

is something that flies in the sky, my dear. I want to go home, Simon. This very minute.'

'All right. Keep your hair on,' Tracey cackled.

Simon stood up and put his hands on Sally-Ann's shoulders. 'Trace don't mean no harm. She's just very drunk.'

'If you won't take me home, I'll get a taxi,' Sally-Ann snapped, her face contorted with rage.

'I'll take you.' Simon walked into the kitchen. 'Sally-Ann wants to go, so I'm going to make a move now,' he told Melissa and Jason. 'Thanks for inviting us over.'

'Jase, come and dance with me. Another record that reminds me of you. 'Cause you know it all, don'tcha?' Tracey laughed.

Hearing the opening chords of Stevie Wonder's 'He's Misstra Know-It-All', Jason grabbed his keys off the kitchen counter.

'Where you going?' Melissa asked.

'Simon's. Your notright friend – you fucking entertain her. I've had enough.'

CHAPTER THIRTY-NINE

Melissa Rampling swung her legs over the edge of the bed. She'd been unable to sleep at all last night, but didn't feel too tired. Today was the day all the furniture she'd ordered online would be delivered to her lovely new home. The beginning of her new life.

Switching her phone on, Melissa sighed as the messages started to bleep. She didn't usually turn it off, but Tracey had been driving her mad ever since she'd stayed at hers the other evening. She still hadn't spoken to Greg and wanted to talk about him constantly. Was he in love with her? Was he married? Was he robbing a bank? Melissa had played along with the conversation for as long as she could and had then lost the will to live. Tracey thought she was clever, but in reality was as thick as two short planks.

Melissa jumped as her phone rang. It was Jason, so she answered it. 'You all right? How's the decorating coming along? Did you sleep well?' she gabbled. She'd driven over to the house yesterday, had taken a blow-up bed, quilt, plus boxes of their personal belongings.

'I've only painted the lounge and kitchen so far. I might ring around today; see if I can get a pal to help me.'

'No, don't,' Melissa snapped. 'Just paint our bedroom and the kids'. We can do the rest another time. I just want to get in there now.'

'OK. Was comfortable, that bed you brought over. I slept like a log. Thanks.'

'Looks like we'll both be sleeping on that. Our headboard's arriving today, but we've got to wait until next week for the actual bed and mattress.'

'As long as I'm snuggled up next to you, babe, I'm happy,' Jason replied honestly. He'd had the right hump the other evening when he'd stormed off to Simon's house. It had seemed to him that Melissa had encouraged Tracey's ridiculous behaviour rather than putting a stop to it. They'd made up the following day though and Mel had promised him that Tracey wouldn't turn up at their new home whenever the mood took her fancy. 'This move is a fresh start for us. No visitors unless invited,' she'd assured him.

'Any deliveries arrived yet? The kitchen table and chairs are coming this afternoon, but all the other stuff I ordered could be there at any time.'

Jason chuckled. 'It's only just gone seven. I know you're excited, but I'm not sure delivery drivers start this early.'

'They do. When I ordered our garden furniture at Repton Park, it turned up about half seven. Make sure you don't have the music on too loud in case you don't hear the doorbell.'

'I left the front door open all day yesterday to get rid of the smell of paint for you. I'll do the same today. There's sod-all to nick and we're tucked away from the rest of the world.'

Melissa smiled. 'Perfect.'

*

Tracey Thompson was in a terrible mood. She had taken Melissa's advice to play it cool with Greg, but the uncertainty of where he was, what he was up to and the not knowing if they were still a couple or not was driving her insane.

Toby entered his mother's bedroom and held his arms out for a cuddle.

'Go and play with your toys,' Tracey snapped.

'Can we see Auntie Mel today, Mummy?' Toby asked.

'No. Your father's picking you up soon. Now go and play with your toys until he gets here,' Tracey shouted. That was another thing she was thoroughly pissed off about. She'd driven to Melissa and Jason's new house the other day. Not only was it much bigger and nicer than hers, she couldn't see how the hell they could afford it when Jason had only just come out of prison. Mel had met her there and shown her the inside. It was stunning, and it really grated on her that, no matter what went wrong in Mel's life, she always seemed to come up smelling of bloody roses. It just wasn't fair. She never had that type of luck.

Deciding she'd played it cool for far too long, Tracey picked up her mobile. Greg shouldn't toy with her emotions the way he had. She needed to ask him outright if their relationship was over, would rather hear the worst than be led up the garden path any longer. Anything was preferable to wasting another day drinking wine and daydreaming of Greg being holed up in an underground vault with some other blokes, tunnelling his way towards hidden treasures.

Debating what she was going to say, Tracey took the plunge. She was horrified by the words that greeted her ears: 'You have dialled an incorrect number.'

*

Imagining the future, Melissa was lounging on a sun bed catching some rays. Donte was tired, was still in bed, so she'd brought her iPod and headphones out in the garden for company. Singing away to Maria Muldaur's 'Midnight at the Oasis', Melissa didn't hear her neighbour Ann calling her at first.

'Mel, Mel,' Ann yelled again.

Spotting Ann waving her arms, Melissa sat up and took her headphones off. 'You OK, Ann?'

'Yes. But the police are knocking on your door, love. Four of them, there are. What you been up to?'

Melissa felt ice run through her veins. Surely nothing had gone wrong? Not now. She dashed inside the house to be met by her son, who was standing at the top of the stairs partially dressed. 'Don't open it. Please don't open it, Mum,' Donte begged.

'Open up,' Melissa heard a voice bellow. She looked up at Donte. 'Why? What have you done?'

'Nothing.'

'If you don't open the door, we'll break it down,' another voice boomed.

'No, Mum. Noooo,' Donte shrieked. Panicking, he bolted barefoot into the garden.

Four policemen burst into the house and as Donte tried to climb over the fence, he was grabbed by the ankles and landed on the grass with a thump.

'Whatever's going on? Leave him alone. He's only a child,' Melissa yelled, pushing one of the policemen in the chest.

An officer handcuffed Donte and rolled him on to his front. 'Donte Brooks, I am arresting you on suspicion of the murder of Tyrone Dark. You do not have to say anything. But it may harm your defence if you do not mention when questioned something which you later rely on in court. Anything you do say may be given in evidence.'

Melissa was stunned. 'Murder! Who is Tyrone Dark?' she mumbled. This couldn't be happening. Especially today of all days. There must be some mistake.

'It weren't me, man. I didn't do nothing,' Donte sobbed. He was scared now, petrified. Had one of the others grassed on him? he wondered.

An officer turned to Melissa. 'Seeing as, in the eyes of the law, your son is still classed as a minor, would you like to accompany him to the station?'

Melissa didn't know if she was coming or going. This was her baby, the boy she had given birth to. How could he be a murderer? This was beyond ridiculous. 'Erm, yes. Let me put some clothes on. You've got this all wrong, you know. My boy wouldn't hurt a fly.'

One of the officers laughed. 'No disrespect, love. But if I had a pound for every mother who'd said that to me, I'd be rich by now.'

Singing away at the top of his voice while painting the ceiling, Jason never heard the doorbell chime.

'Excuse me, mate. Delivery,' a bloke said, knocking on the bedroom door.

Jason clambered down off the ladder and paused the music. 'Sorry, pal. I was miles away. What you got for us?' he asked, following the guy down the stairs.

The delivery driver looked at his worksheet. 'Erm, a chest of drawers and a bedside cabinet. Where do you want them?'

'Just shove 'em in the lounge for now, please. That's already been painted. Mind the door frame though. It might still be a bit wet.'

When the driver left, Jason decided to open all the boxes that had already been delivered. He smiled when he saw the child's outdoor swing. Mel had obviously ordered it for when Toby stayed over, but hopefully one day in the not too distant future, their own child would enjoy playing with it.

The interview room at Barkingside police station reminded Melissa of that awful time when Jason was arrested. She'd never believed she would one day come back here for something even more terrifying, but that was the situation she currently found herself in. She had known Donte hadn't been himself of late, but not even in her worst nightmares would it have occurred to her that he'd be capable of taking another lad's life. He was a good boy at heart, or so she'd stupidly thought.

'Where is the blue tracksuit and the knife, Donte?' DI Travis asked again.

'I left the tracksuit at my mate's and I dunno nothing about no knife,' Donte lied. His heart was beating wildly and he wished Jason was here with him. He would know what to say and do. His mother was useless. The silly cow kept urging him to tell the truth.

Knowing full well her son was lying, Melissa hissed, 'Tell the man the truth, Donte. The police know you were there – they have you on CCTV, running away.'

Donte glared at his mother. 'Why don't you shut the fuck up? You know nothing, woman.'

Wondering what on earth she had given birth to, Melissa punched her son in the arm. 'Show some respect, you little arsehole,' she hissed.

Instead of using the phone call she was offered to call Jason, Melissa had rung Simon. She knew he'd get Donte a decent solicitor, but Simon hadn't answered so she'd had to leave a message.

'What mate's house did you leave your tracksuit at, Donte?' Travis asked.

'I dunno. I was with friends at a party somewhere in Dagenham. I was drunk and got in bed with some girl. When I woke up, my tracksuit had gone. It was new. Someone nicked it,' Donte fibbed.

'What address was the party held at?' Travis was going through the motions. It was clear the lad was lying and would hopefully trip himself up soon. He certainly wasn't the brightest spark ever to be interviewed.

'I was drunk. It was a flat in a big block. I don't know the address 'cause I've never been there before. He was a black lad who lived there.'

'You said it was a house a minute ago. Make your mind up, lad. Was it a house or a flat?' Travis spat.

'A flat. It was definitely a flat.'

The duty solicitor leaned towards Donte and whispered something in his ear.

'So this flat you supposedly went to fully dressed only to leave naked, who invited you there?' Travis asked.

'No comment.'

'What were the names of the friends you went to the party with?' Travis pressed.

'No comment.'

'Can I talk to Donte for five minutes alone, please?' Melissa asked.

The two interviewing officers glanced at one another and one nodded. 'Interview suspended at 11.17 a.m. to allow the suspect's mother, Melissa Rampling, to talk to the suspect, Donte Brooks, in private,' Travis said.

'The tape has been sealed in a bag that Melissa Rampling

and Donte Brooks will now sign for,' said Travis's colleague, DS Charlton, pushing the bag towards Mel, then Donte.

'I will stay with you. We need to discuss one or two—'

Melissa stopped the solicitor in his tracks. 'No. You go outside. I need to speak with my son alone.'

Donte stared at his hands. They were shaking, just like his legs.

Melissa scraped her chair along the floor to be as close to Donte as possible. 'You're not doing yourself any favours, you know. Where is the tracksuit?' she whispered.

'Where is Dad? I want Dad here with me, not you.'

'Why's that then? Jason know about this, does he?'

'No. There's nothing to know,' Donte hissed.

'Don't fucking lie to me, boy.' Melissa grabbed her son by his shoulders. 'Look me in the eyes,' she ordered.

As Donte did so, his eyes filled with tears. 'The tracksuit's been burnt, but you can't tell them that 'cause they will think I'm guilty and bang me up,' he warned.

'Where was the tracksuit burned? Tell me, Donte. I cannot help you unless you're honest with me.'

'Don't know.'

'Don't lie. It was you, wasn't it? You stabbed that lad, didn't you?'

'So what if I did? He had a knife too. What was I meant to do? Let him stab me?'

'So you did do it?'

Donte shrugged. 'Didn't mean for him to die, did I?'

'We need to tell the police that. Did Tyrone pull out his knife first?'

'Yeah.'

'Well, it wasn't your fault then, was it? You were acting in self-defence. A judge will be far more lenient with you if you tell the truth. It was an accident. Where is the tracksuit?'

Donte bowed his head. 'I dunno the road. It got burned in a field where gypsies dump stuff.'

'And what about the knife?'

'I dunno where that is, I swear I don't.'

'Who disposed of it for you?'

'I dunno,' Donte lied.

Unable to stop herself, Melissa slapped her son hard across the face. 'If you don't tell me who disposed of it, I will tell the police everything you've said,' she threatened.

'It was Dad,' Donte spat. 'But don't have a go at him; he was only trying to help me.'

Melissa's face twisted with rage. Jason never failed to disappoint her.

Singing along with the Sugarhill Gang's 'Rapper's Delight', Jason thought back to his childhood. This song reminded him of a happy time living on the Mardyke Estate. He'd only been about five or six when 'Rapper's Delight' first came out. His mother had loved the song and taught him all the words. That was probably the only thing she had ever taught him in his lifetime, but he could remember one particular day clearly. It was extremely hot, summer time, and his mother was sitting on the grass at the front of the flats smoking joints and drinking cider with the neighbours. Someone had a big stereo, one of those ones black guys used to prop on their shoulders back in the day, and Jason could recall his mother urging him to stand up and rap. He'd been word-perfect and all the neighbours had cheered and clapped him. He'd felt loved and special for a split second that day. But it wasn't to last. Later that evening, he'd wet himself and his mother had shoved him in the lift as a punishment.

Engrossed in his music and reminiscing, Jason never heard anybody walk up the stairs.

Suddenly catching a glimpse of dark clothing out the corner of his eye, Jason spun around. 'All right? You got a delivery for me?'

Clad in leathers and a helmet, the biker lifted the face shield up. 'Sure have.'

Jason gasped and dropped his roller. 'Jesus! Long time no see. What the hell you doing here?'

The man took a gun out of the inside of his jacket and pointed it at Jason's head. 'Why don't you have a little guess.'

Melissa shut her eyes and leaned against the back seat of the taxi. She'd just left the police station and was still in a daze. Her son, the murderer. She couldn't take it in. In her eyes, Donte was still a child himself.

'Bad day, love?' the taxi driver asked.

'You could say that,' Melissa replied, her eyes welling up again. Thankfully, Donte had taken her advice and admitted he'd acted in self-defence. He would have crumbled under pressure in the end anyway. He hadn't implicated Jason though, still insisted he had no idea where the tracksuit or knife was. He had told the police he'd only meant to scare Tyrone Dark, not kill him. 'On my life, it was an accident,' he'd sworn.

Melissa believed her son's version of events, but it didn't make the situation any easier. In the eyes of the law, her son had taken another lad's life and Melissa couldn't begin to imagine what Tyrone Dark's mother and family were going through. The solicitor had followed her outside the police station and had a quiet word in her ear. 'I'm going to advise Donte to plead not guilty to murder, but accept the lesser charge of manslaughter. It carries a much lesser sentence,' he'd told her.

Wanting to weep, but knowing full well she had to hold herself together, Melissa switched her phone on. Message alerts began bleeping and Mel pressed the voicemail button. Two were from Jason.

'*Hi, babe – I've been opening all your parcels. Some chairs have arrived, but no table yet. Oh, and I love the kiddie swing. Best we start making babies, I say, so it don't go to waste*,' Jason chuckled. '*Right, I'm gonna get back to me decorating now. Just had a coffee break. Ring you later. Love you.*'

'*Hi, Mel – where are ya? Some pots, pans and cutlery just been delivered. Gissa bell when you get this message, girl. Laters.*'

The other messages were from Tracey, and Melissa could tell by the third she was pissed.

'*Mel, that bastard's only had his phone cut off. Fuming, I am. What am I gonna do if he doesn't get in touch? Ring me.*'

'*It's me again. I ain't putting up with this. Nobody takes me for a mug, and I mean nobody. Ring me back ASAP.*'

'*Where the fuck are you, Mel? You're not avoiding me an' all, are ya? I need to talk to you. I swear to God, if he don't get in touch, I will go to the Old Bill and grass the tosser up. That'll teach him to fuck with me, won't it?*' Tracey had slurred.

Composing herself, Melissa called Jason's phone. It rang, then connected to voicemail. 'Give me a ring ASAP, Jase. Donte's been arrested and I've only just got out the police station. I'm in a cab now, so can't talk properly. I'll explain all when we speak later. Love you lots . . .'

CHAPTER FORTY

'I'm gonna ring Simon again. Jason still isn't answering,' Melissa informed Tracey and her neighbour, Ann.

'Perhaps he's gone to the pub. Or he's round some old slapper's house,' Tracey replied nastily.

'That's not a very nice thing to say about your friend's husband,' Ann remarked. She lived next door to Melissa and liked her very much. She was no fan of her mate though; had always thought Tracey was a trappy mare when she'd overheard her loud high-pitched voice squealing in the garden. It was clear she rated herself extremely highly too. One of those types who thought she was Miss World and better than everybody else.

'You don't know Jason like we do,' Tracey snapped, wishing Ann would sod off back to her own house. She wanted to talk about Greg, but couldn't speak freely in front of her.

'Si, it's me again. Sorry to be a pest. Tracey told me you'd taken Toby to the zoo for the day. I still can't get hold of Jase and I'm starting to worry. It's so unlike him not to get back to me. I've rung him four or five times now. He isn't with you and has forgotten his phone, has he? Ring me as soon as you get this message please, mate.'

'I had better get back to my brood. They have no idea how to use an oven, so are probably all starving. I'm so sorry about your Donte, lovey. If there's anything I can do, you just give me a shout, OK?' Ann said.

'Thanks, Ann,' Melissa replied, giving the woman a hug. She had fallen into Ann's arms sobbing after arriving home from the police station. If only she could've got Donte away from this area sooner. It was all Jason's brothers' fault. They had introduced him to gang warfare and turned him into a boy she didn't bloody recognize any more.

'Thank God she's gone. State of the fat cow. Needs to go to Weight Watchers, her,' Tracey piped up, as the front door closed. She could tell Ann didn't like her and the feeling was mutual. The woman had tattoos, rotten teeth and dressed in the most unflattering tracksuits.

'She's nice is Ann. I like her, anyway.'

'You've lowered your standards since you moved here, that's your trouble. So why do you reckon Greg's changed his number then? I'm livid, Mel. Wouldn't you be?'

Melissa looked at Tracey with hatred. Her son had just been charged with murder and all she was concerned about was Greg and taking a swipe at the neighbour. Her mum had been right about Tracey all along. She was a selfish, horrible person who cared for nobody but herself. 'I haven't got time to talk about Greg at this precise moment,' she said, turning away.

'Who you ringing now?' Tracey enquired.

'Shay. Jase might be with her. And if he isn't, I need to tell her about Donte anyway.'

'You got any wine here, mate? I'll pour us both a drink.'

'In the cupboard. I don't want one, but you help yourself.'

Shay didn't answer her phone so Melissa left a message asking if she knew where her father was, and told her to call back ASAP. She then rang Barkingside police station to find out if Donte was still there and was informed he would be appearing in court the following morning. 'Will he be able to come home and wait for his actual trial?' she asked hopefully.

The officer told Mel that was up to the judge.

'Has my husband been at the station at all? Only, I can't seem to get hold of him and I wondered if he'd heard what has happened to Donte through the grapevine. Jason Rampling, his name is.'

'Well?' Tracey asked, when the call ended.

Melissa's eyes filled with tears. 'Donte's appearing via video link at Snaresbrook Crown Court tomorrow morning. He must be so scared. He's still at the police station, locked in a cell.'

'What about Jason?'

'They haven't seen him.'

Shay arrived at the house on Limes Farm Estate an hour later and wrapped her arms around Melissa. 'I'm so sorry. How could Donte be so stupid?' Her step-mum had explained on the phone what had happened and she was shell-shocked and upset. Her brother wasn't a bad lad, he was just easily bloody led.

'Don't cry, Shay. You'll start me off again. I can't believe how silly he's been. He had so much going for him when he was younger. I blame myself. I should have done more to keep him away from the likes of Elton and Kyle. I knew they were trouble and leading him up the garden path. But apart from giving him the odd talking to, I did sod-all.'

'It isn't your fault, Mel. You mustn't blame yourself. Donte is headstrong and we both tried to warn him on numerous occasions. He wouldn't listen though. To be fair, he'd fallen in with a bad crowd way before he started hanging out with Elton and Kyle. I thought he was just going through a bit of a rebellious stage and would grow out of it, like I did.'

'You heard from your dad, Shay?' Tracey asked. Melissa had no interest in Greg disappearing and changing his phone number, and she would secretly laugh her head off if Jason had done the same to her.

'No. Has Dad still not been in touch?' Shay asked Melissa.

Melissa jumped as her phone rang. It was Simon. 'OK, Si. Shay's here and Tracey. See you in a bit.'

'Is Jase with him?' Tracey enquired.

'No. Si's been trying to get hold of him too. He and Toby are just leaving the restaurant. They're coming straight here.'

'Perhaps we should drive over to the house, see if Jason's there?' Tracey suggested.

'He's decorating, Trace. Not like him to blank my calls, but I'm sure he'll be fine. It's Donte I'm more worried about. You know, my son who has just been charged with murder,' Melissa responded, her voice laden with sarcasm.

Tracey topped her glass up. 'All right. Sorry. Keep your hair on. Not being funny, Mel, but Donte dressed and acted like something out of So Solid Crew.'

'And what is that supposed to mean?' Melissa hissed.

'Do I have to spell it out? He walked around with his arse hanging out of his jeans.'

Glaring at Tracey, Melissa dragged Shay upstairs.

'I dunno how you suffer that unfeeling bitch,' Shay whispered. 'I hate her.'

'With difficulty. She's been acting really weird ever since she arrived. Keeps talking about your father all the time. I'm sure she's obsessed with him. You don't think she knows where he is, do you?'

'She fancies Dad. I've seen the way she looks at him. That's why she's always trying to stick her oar in your marriage. Jealous cow, she is. Dad wouldn't touch her with a bargepole.'

'I know he wouldn't, love. Will you come to court with me tomorrow? I'm sure they'll let us in to watch the video link. Perhaps if the judge sees Donte comes from a good family, they might allow him to come home until his trial.'

Shay doubted very much that Donte would be allowed to walk the streets any time soon, but didn't voice her thoughts. She squeezed Mel's hand. 'Of course I'll come with you. He's my brother.'

By the time Simon pulled up outside, Tracey was mangled. 'Fucking bastard. How dare he treat me like this?' she slurred, taking a mouthful of red wine and spilling the bulk down her white Gucci T-shirt.

'Who is she talking about?' Shay whispered to Mel.

'Your father probably. Who knows? Answer the door for me, love. I'll put the kettle on.'

'Look what I got,' Toby shrieked, running straight past his mother and into the arms of his Auntie Mel.

'Oh, I don't like snakes. That's very scary. Take it away from me,' Mel said playfully. The snake was made of rubber, but looked very lifelike.

Toby couldn't stop giggling. 'His name is Peter.'

Simon locked eyes with Melissa. 'You OK? So sorry

about Donte, mate. That brief who will represent him is top drawer though. If anyone can get him off a murder charge, it's him.' Simon had spoken to his solicitor pal on the way home, and he'd already agreed to handle the case.

'I still can't believe it. It hasn't sunk in. Thanks for your help though, Si. You got hold of Jason yet?'

'No. I've rung him half a dozen times and left three messages. Perhaps he popped to the local pub, left his phone at home, then ended up staying for a few beers?'

Shay was concerned. She still hadn't completely forgiven her father for kicking off about Luke, but she regretted being so horrible to him when he'd visited her round Natasha's. 'Dad isn't a pub person and he always has his phone with him.'

'Probably with some old scrubber,' Tracey slurred.

Shay turned to face Tracey, her eyes blazing. 'Shut up, you. You've done nothing but have a dig at my dad since I arrived. You got a thing for him, or something?'

'Oh, don't be so daft. I'm not that desperate,' Tracey spluttered.

'I don't know why you don't go home. We don't want you here. You're drunk and you've hardly said a good word about Donte. It's obvious you don't give a shit about him or anybody else other than your vain self.'

'Who does she think she's talking to, Mel? You want me here, don't ya?'

'Not really, Trace. Not tonight. You've had far too much to drink, mate, and I just need to be alone right now. I've got to go to court in the morning.'

'Ring me a cab then. Don't bring Toby back too early tomorrow, Si. I'll give you a bell when I get up. Men, you're all bastards. I hate the lot of you,' Tracey rambled.

The cab arrived quickly and Melissa helped Tracey get in the back. She could barely walk, she was that inebriated.

'Is Mummy ill?' Toby asked when Melissa shut the front door.

Mel picked Toby up and stroked his soft blond hair. 'No, darling. She's just tired.'

'Can I stay with you tonight?'

'Not tonight. You're staying at Daddy's. You can stay here tomorrow though, if you like?'

Toby smiled. 'Thank you.'

'I was just saying to Simon, Mel, I'm a bit worried about Dad. Shall we drive over to your new house and make sure he's all right. I won't sleep otherwise.'

'Perhaps he can't get a signal?' Mel suggested.

'His phone wouldn't be ringing if that were the case,' Shay replied. 'Let's go now. How long does it take to get there?'

'Simon'll drive over there. I'll go with him,' Mel said.

'But I need to talk to Dad,' Shay argued.

'Why don't you stay here with Toby, Shay? Let me drive Mel over there. It's silly us all going, and Toby'll crash out soon. He's been hyper all day.'

'No. I want to go,' Shay insisted, picking up her bag and marching out the front door.

Simon squeezed Melissa's hand. 'You stay here with Toby. See you in a bit.'

Munching on a Penguin biscuit, Toby watched Mel with interest. 'What you doing with my toys?' he asked.

'Nothing, darling. Just looking for something I dropped earlier in your toy box. You carry on watching CBeebies. There's a good boy,' Melissa replied, shoving a fluffy toy dog up her top.

Melissa walked out into the garden. The police had searched the house earlier under Ann's watchful eye. They'd concentrated mainly on Donte's bedroom, Ann had informed her. Obviously looking for evidence to connect her son to Tyrone Dark's murder. They had taken some items away in a bag, including Donte's computer.

Putting her hand inside the toy dog, Melissa pulled out the key and folded-up paperwork. Thank God Jason had agreed to her looking after both. He hadn't told her where the safety-deposit box actually was and she had no reason to ask. Incriminating evidence was all she'd been worried about. The police could have tugged Jason at any time and she would have been beside herself had he gone back in prison.

It was beginning to get dark now, so Melissa had a good look around to make sure none of the neighbours were watching. Satisfied they weren't, she took a lighter out of her pocket, held the paperwork over a plant pot and promptly set fire to it.

'Wow! This is nice. It's much bigger than our Repton Park house,' Shay gushed.

'It's nice and secluded too. I don't think your dad's here, love. I can't see any lights on.'

'Well, he can't have gone far. Mel's got your Land Rover, so unless Dad got a cab he must be within walking distance.'

Simon took the spare key out of his pocket. He'd had to stop off at his house on the way to get it.

'The door isn't shut properly,' Simon said, pushing it open.

'Dad, Dad!' Shay yelled.

Simon switched the hallway light on. 'Jase. You about, mate?' he shouted.

As Shay went to dart past him, Simon put his arm out to stop her. 'You wait in the car while I have a look around, just in case, love.'

'In case of what? There's nothing to burgle,' Shay replied, ignoring Simon's advice and running up the stairs.

'He's not down here,' Simon shouted out. Seconds later he heard a bloodcurdling scream.

Simon ran up the stairs. Jason was lying on the floor of the main bedroom with a big gaping hole in the front of his head, and a pool of blood surrounding him. 'Oh no. God, no,' he mumbled.

'Dad, Dad! Wake up. Please wake up,' Shay shrieked. She fell to her knees next to the man she had always been able to rely on and put her arms around his waist. 'Please wake up, Dad. I'm sorry I was horrible to you the other day. I didn't mean it. I love you.'

Tears rolled down Simon's cheeks. He'd always liked Shay, she was a good kid. He lifted her off Jason. 'You can't touch him, love. This is a crime scene. We need to ring the police.'

Shay looked at Simon with confused eyes. 'What about an ambulance? Dad can't be dead, Si. He can't leave me.'

Simon bent down and checked Jason's pulse. Standing up, he held Shay close to his chest. 'I'm so sorry, Shay. I truly am. But your dad has already left us, sweetheart.'

Unable to relax, Melissa was busying herself by packing some more personal belongings. She didn't want to take any of the furniture or ornaments with her. They would always remind her of bad times. She wanted a completely fresh start.

'My friend has got a real dog. Can I have one too?' Toby asked, out of the blue.

Melissa sat beside the boy and stroked his beautiful face. No way would he ever end up like Donte had, she wouldn't allow it. The boy deserved so much better than having Tracey as a mother. She wasn't fit to look after a dog, her. 'Dogs need lots of walks and care. We'll ask Daddy when he gets home, shall we?'

'Can I call it Peter?'

As stressed as she felt, Melissa smiled. When she was with Toby she always felt happy, no matter what.

Glancing at the clock, Mel scrolled down her phone and found Simon's number. He and Shay must be at the house by now. The call went to voicemail. 'Si, it's me. Is Jase there? I've tried ringing him again, but his phone's switched off now. Call me. I'm ever so worried. It's getting late.'

Simon drove back to Melissa's house in silence. Shay was lying on the back seat, whimpering like an injured animal and her obvious distress was heartbreaking to witness.

'I feel so guilty. I never even hugged him when he came round Nat's. He told me he loved me and I wouldn't say it back. But I did love him, more than anything,' Shay wept.

'You mustn't beat yourself up, Shay. Your dad knew how much you loved him and the feeling was mutual.'

'He was so nice, and funny. Who would want to hurt him, Si?'

'I have no idea, Shay, but the police will get to the bottom of it. Poor Mel. She's going to be devastated too. Donte getting charged with murder this morning and now this. I'm gonna miss him so much, ya know. Your dad was my best mate by a long shot.'

'I know he was. Are the police still behind us?'

'Yeah.' The police had turned up swiftly and cordoned the house and driveway off with tape. Two of the officers were now following them back to the house to ask some questions. Simon had insisted on taking Shay home ASAP and being the one who told Melissa the news. He'd explained he was Jason's accountant, best pal and a close family friend.

'What am I going to do without him? I'm an orphan now. I've got no one,' Shay cried.

'Yes, you have. You've got me and Mel. We'll be there for you, darling. Always.'

Staring out the window, Melissa's thoughts turned to Donte. Were they treating him OK? Had he been fed? Where would they place him after his court appearance if he didn't get bail? Jason's brother had been sent to Feltham when he'd got into trouble. Would they send Donte there too?

Melissa sighed. She hadn't even told her father the horrific news yet, would have to call him tomorrow. Bound to go ballistic, he was. A month or so ago he'd pleaded with Donte to go and live with him in Spain for a while. Her son hadn't wanted to and Melissa hadn't pushed the subject. How she wished she had now. Donte's behaviour of late was always going to end in tears, one way or another.

When she spotted Simon's Range Rover pulling up outside, Melissa's heart began to beat wildly. The police were right behind him; they parked outside Ann's house.

Melissa yanked open the front door. 'Did you find Jason? What are the police doing here? Is it about Donte?' she shrieked at Simon.

Shay got out the Range Rover and clung to Melissa like a limpet. 'Whatever's wrong? Where's your father?' Mel asked her step-daughter.

Gesturing to the police to follow him inside the house, Simon held Mel's arm and led her into the lounge. 'Sit down, lovey,' he ordered.

'No. Why? What's going on? Is it Donte? It is, isn't it? Please don't tell me he's topped himself,' Melissa cried.

Simon took a deep breath to compose himself. 'I'm so sorry, Mel, but there's no easy way to say this. Jason is dead.'

'Dead! Don't be so stupid. He can't be. I only spoke to him this morning.'

Simon grabbed Melissa's hand and led her to the sofa. He looked her in the eyes. 'I'm so sorry, mate. Someone shot Jase. The police are at the house now. They will catch whoever did this.'

'It's true, Mel,' Shay sobbed. 'There was loads of blood and Dad had a big hole in his head.'

Melissa stood up and promptly fell to her knees. 'No. Not my Jason. He can't leave me. We're moving home. No, nooo, nooooo.'

CHAPTER FORTY-ONE

Melissa dabbed her eyes with a tissue, then blew her nose. She could hear Shay crying again and that had set her off. If only she'd insisted on going to the house with Simon instead of letting Shay go. No child should have to witness their parent with a bullet in the head, and Mel just hoped in time the girl would be able to move on with her life.

Deciding to wear a black dress as a mark of respect, Melissa got showered. How she appeared in court was important to her son's welfare and surely if she told the judge her husband had been murdered the previous day, he would take pity on herself and Donte? He'd have to be a hard-hearted bastard not to.

Thoughts turning to the impending police visit, Melissa applied some mascara. Simon had answered most of their questions last night after she'd informed them she was in shock and in no fit state to talk or even think straight. Simon had finally left about three in the morning and had promised to pop back later today. The police wanted to question him again also. They were going to his house first.

When the landline rang, Melissa ignored the call. It was Tracey again and she really couldn't be dealing with telling her about Jason's death just yet. That no-good selfish cow would find out soon enough anyway.

'Mr Champion, I'm DI Noakes and this is my colleague, DS Fenton. Is it convenient to ask you some questions now?' asked Noakes.

'Yes, fine. Come in and make yourselves a cuppa. I'm just getting my son dressed. I'll be with you in a tick. The kitchen's through there,' Simon pointed.

Fenton looked around and whistled. 'Nice gaff. Must've cost a few bob. Obviously pays well, having villains as clients.' He had done his homework on Simon late last night at the station.

'Keep your voice down,' Noakes urged. 'And don't be mentioning any of his other clients. We need him on side to help crack this case.'

Minutes later, Simon entered the kitchen with Toby in his arms. 'Go and play in the garden, boy, while Daddy has a chat with the policemen.'

Toby stopped in his tracks and pointed at the two men. 'Why they not got policemen hats on, Daddy?'

'Because it's hot,' Simon fibbed, unlocking the back door. 'Now out you go. There's a good lad.'

'Cute kid,' Fenton grinned. 'He looks roughly the same age as my youngest.'

'Did you want a cuppa?' Simon asked, flicking the kettle switch. He'd had a crap night's sleep and needed a strong coffee to liven himself up a bit.

'No, we've not long had one, thanks,' Noakes took a notepad out of his pocket. 'We'd like to ask you some more questions about Jason. You mentioned to a colleague yesterday that he'd been in prison up until recently and I've done a bit of digging. Craig Thurston, had Jason heard from or seen him recently?'

'No. Not to my knowledge.'

'What about any of the other men who Jason was sentenced with? Do you know if he'd been warned or threatened by anybody?'

'Jason got banged up for something he wasn't part of, yet he still kept his trap shut throughout the trial and in prison. He was a bit of a wide boy, but he certainly wasn't a grass. So there's no valid reason for any of the other lads to have any beef with him, in my opinion,' Simon replied honestly.

'Would Jason discuss such problems with you?' Fenton enquired.

'Yeah, always. We were very close. I knew him better than he knew himself at times. He was like a brother to me. Jase was a very popular guy and I'm baffled by what's happened, to be honest. I didn't sleep at all last night. It just doesn't make sense.'

Noakes cleared his throat. 'I know this must be difficult for you, but you're doing great. The property that Jason was decorating belongs to you, and Jason and Melissa were going to move in at the weekend, is that correct?'

Simon nodded. 'I bought the property as an investment. It previously belonged to an elderly couple, had been left to rot. So I had it all done up and Jason and Mel were to be my tenants. Better the devil you know when you're renting out a property, eh?'

'I suppose it is,' Noakes replied. 'Any idea how Jason would have afforded the rent?'

'Jase was skint, but he's a go-getter. It wouldn't have taken him long to get back on his feet. I planned to let him have the gaff rent-free for the first few months as a coming home present. He was trustworthy and so is Mel. She looks after my son quite a lot, helps out with childcare and stuff.'

'How do you think Jason would've got back on his feet, so to speak?' Fenton probed.

'Pawn. Not as in tits and fanny. As in pawning jewellery and valuables. Jase had already asked me if I'd lend him a bit of dosh so he could open another shop and I'd agreed. He knew the business like the back of his hand and, as I've already stated, was thoroughly reliable. I'd have got my money back, plus a decent drink on top. That was Jase all over. A gentleman.'

'When did you last see Jason alive?' Fenton asked.

'The day before yesterday. He popped over to mine to discuss in more detail his plans to open another shop. We discussed areas and possible locations. He always trusted my advice. Then we popped out and grabbed a bit of lunch in a local pub. I also saw him a couple of nights before that. Melissa arranged a small dinner party and I took my new lady friend, Sally-Ann, along. That didn't end too well though, to be honest. The mother of my son was there and she started kicking off. She was drunk; upset Sally-Ann and Jason. He was fuming, stormed out and stayed at mine. He'd calmed down a lot by the next morning, mind.'

'So, was Jason involved in an actual argument?' asked Fenton.

'Well, yeah. Sort of. It was nothing major though. Tracey, the mother of my boy, is Melissa's best pal. She can be a bit of a handful and a bitch at times, between me and you. Jason always said she had it in for him since day dot. They'd known one another way before I came on the scene; Mel and Tracey were knocking around together when Mel first met Jase.'

'What started the argument? Can you remember what was said?' Noakes probed.

Simon paused. 'Erm, I think it was when Melissa mentioned she and Jason were moving to Upshire that Tracey started to go on the turn.'

Fenton furiously scribbled away in his notebook. 'Can you remember what was said?'

'I didn't hear all of it. Jase had a go at Mel for inviting Tracey and Tracey overheard it. Sally-Ann insisted I take her home immediately after Trace had laid into her, so I took her out to the motor, then ran back for my jacket. Melissa was restraining Tracey from following Jason outside. He'd stormed out behind Sally-Ann. "Tell your mate he'll fucking regret speaking about me like that. He'll get his comeuppance," were Tracey's parting words as I left, but that's to be taken with a pinch of salt. As I said earlier, Tracey was very drunk.'

Noakes glanced at Fenton. Something had been found at the house. Evidence that could prove to be crucial. 'What is Tracey's surname?'

'Thompson. Tracey Thompson. But listen, she ain't no murderer. She's a pain in the arse, but also the mother of my son.'

Eyes brimming with tears and dressed in black, Melissa Rampling marched into Barkingside police station with Shay by her side. 'I need to speak to my son, Donte Brooks, in private,' she told the duty sergeant.

The duty sergeant stared at his computer. 'No. Sorry, but that won't be possible.'

'His dad has just been shot in the head,' Shay shouted.

'And our mum needs to tell him before he hears it through the grapevine.'

The duty sergeant picked up his phone. He spoke to a colleague, then told Melissa, 'OK. Someone will be here to take you to him soon. Sit back down in the meantime, please.'

As Melissa and Shay did so, then clung to each other, there were no step-mother/daughter barriers any more. They were the real deal.

Donte Brooks strutted up and down his cell. The lad in the next cell was laughing. He'd overheard the Old Bill saying his mother and sister needed to see him and Donte felt a right mug. He was only pleading guilty because his stupid mum had forced him to. His dad wouldn't have done that. Jason was cool, but unfortunately he hadn't been there when he'd needed him the most.

'What do you want now?' Donte spat, as his mother and Shay appeared, flanked by two officers.

Melissa urged her son to sit down.

'Just do one, will ya? Leave me alone,' Donte shouted, determined to be the big man.

'Stop acting like a prick,' Shay yelled. 'Dad's dead. He's been murdered.'

Donte stared at Shay. 'Don't talk shit, you stupid cow. She told you to say this, has she?' he asked, pointing to his mother.

Tears were streaming down Melissa's cheeks. 'Your sister isn't lying. I'm so sorry, son. Your dad got shot, yesterday. I know it's a shock, but when you go to court, you need to show the judge how upset you are. I have told your solicitor to tell him what's happened. They will give you bail then. You'll be able to come home with us.'

'You stupid cunt. Can't you see what you've done? You forced me to confess and now Tyrone Dark's gang have murdered Dad. I fucking hate you!'

'Don't talk to Mel like that,' Shay wept. Her beloved dad, she hadn't slept at all last night. She could not believe she would never see or speak to him ever again. Each time she'd closed her eyes she'd visualized him, so she'd got up and sat downstairs in the armchair.

'I very much doubt it had anything to do with Tyrone's gang,' Melissa said. 'It happened at our new house in Upshire. They wouldn't have known your dad was there, would they?'

His face like thunder, Donte leapt up and pummelled his fists against the bars that were separating him from his thick mother. 'They know everything, you dumb motherfucker. Why do you think I wanted to say nothing in the first place? Fuck off. Go on; get the hell away from me. You got Dad's blood all over your hands. I fucking hate you and I never wanna see your face again.'

'Sit down, Peggy. You'll wear the carpet out, pet,' said Irish Ted.

Peggy peered out of the window again. She knew her grandson like the back of her hand. He always returned her calls, would never leave her in limbo, worrying about him. 'Something's happened, Ted, I'm telling you. Frantic, I am. So unlike my Jason.'

'Can't you ring Melissa?'

'Not got the new landline number, nor her mobile.'

'What about Shay?'

'Not got her number either. Never had much to do with his family, have I? He's my world though, that boy.'

Irish Ted stood up and put a comforting arm around

Peggy's shoulder. 'Shame they took my driving licence away. I'll tell you what we'll do. If you've not heard from Jason by this afternoon, I'll work out the bus route and we'll go over to his house.'

Peggy treated Ted to a look of pure distaste. 'I'm not getting on bus after bus with my bleedin' arthritis. You can fork out for a cab, you tight old bastard.'

Melissa Rampling had her heart in her mouth as she waited for the all-important verdict. Surprisingly but rather pleasingly for Melissa, the judge turned out to be a woman. Surely she would show some compassion? Mel prayed.

Donte hadn't done himself any favours on the video link. Instead of sitting up straight, he'd been slouched in a chair and when asked to confirm his name, had stared defiantly at the camera rather than looking regretful, scared or upset. He actually had a look of hatred on his face and Melissa was sure that was aimed at her.

The judge had a thin pair of glasses perched on the end of her nose and was staring at some paperwork. Donte was no longer looking at the camera, was staring at his hands. Melissa could barely breathe. Donte needed to be at home, where he belonged.

'After careful consideration, bail has been rejected,' the judge barked, her voice sounding stuffy and lacking any real emotion.

Melissa stood up in the gallery. 'No. Please. He's only a little boy. He has to come home,' she shrieked. 'He has just lost his daddy.'

The judge eyed Melissa over the rim of her spectacles. Donte wasn't a little boy in her eyes. He was an unruly teenager, a gang member, who had taken another's life. 'I am very sorry for your loss, but my mind will not be changed. Bail application rejected.'

After leaving the court, Shay borrowed Melissa's Mini and drove towards Rainham. Somebody had to tell her relations the news and it was better coming from her. No way did she want Melissa blurting it out over the phone.

Barbara Rampling opened the door with Britney in her arms. 'Hello, Shay. What a lovely surprise,' she beamed. She'd thought it was Lee. He had gone to the shop ages ago. She had got her money off the Social this morning and he'd borrowed some to buy cans of lager and cigarettes. She knew he'd come back with weed too and she wouldn't get her money back, but she didn't mind. Lee had been so nice to her since Jason had got out of prison, had even promised to look for a job soon.

Shay burst into tears the second she stepped into the hallway.

Babs put Britney down, fear immediately flowing through her veins. 'Whatever's the matter?'

'It's Jason,' Shay stuttered.

'Has he been arrested again?'

Shay put her hands over her face and shook it from side to side. 'Worse.'

Alarmed, Babs asked,'Where is Jase? What's happened?'

Mascara streaking down her pretty face, Shay let out a huge sob. 'Jase is dead, Babs. Some bastard murdered him.'

As the reality of Shay's words hit home, Babs screamed so loudly and manically, the whole street could hear her.

Noakes and Fenton stepped out of the unmarked vehicle and introduced themselves. Both were in plain clothes and it was Noakes who asked Melissa if it was convenient to ask some questions.

Melissa agreed and invited the officers inside the house. 'I don't know how much help I'll be to you. My son was refused bail and I don't know if I'm coming or going. I'm totally lost without Jason. He was my rock.'

'I'm so sorry for your loss. But believe me, we are determined to catch whoever did this to your husband,' Noakes promised.

'Thank you.'

Noakes and Fenton asked Melissa similar questions to the ones they'd asked Simon earlier and were not surprised to receive very similar replies. Mel didn't mention any arguments at the dinner party though, just said Jason had the hump and had gone home with Simon that evening.

'Why was your husband in a mood? Had you had words?' Fenton pried.

'No. Well, not really. Jason and my best friend don't get on. They've always clashed and he wasn't happy I invited her. Tracey, my pal, said some stuff to Jason and he took the bait. She was out of order, but she's always like that when drunk. She had a dig at our friend Simon's girlfriend too.'

'Was there any particular reason why Jason and Tracey didn't get along?' Noakes enquired. 'Had they once been in a relationship? Or fallen out over something in particular?'

'Goodness, no. They'd never got on since I first met Jase. Tracey set her sights on him first, you see. He worked on Dagenham Market at the time and Tracey wasn't amused when it was me Jase asked out. If I remember rightly, she didn't talk to me for days afterwards. We were only teenagers back then though. It was donkey's years ago. Why are you asking about Tracey? Surely you don't think she had anything to do with what happened to Jase?' Melissa asked, dabbing her eyes.

'We have to explore every avenue. It's our job to,' Fenton explained.

'Have you seen your friend Tracey since the police broke the news to you yesterday?' Noakes enquired.

'No. She's called the landline and left a couple of messages, but I can't be doing with her at the moment. I only want to be around family, people who loved Jason like I did. Tracey isn't nice-natured. She'll probably be secretly pleased Jase is dead. I haven't even told her the news yet. I can't bring myself to.'

Fenton scribbled something down in his notebook, then asked what time Tracey had arrived and left.

'I didn't get home until after two, so Tracey must have arrived about three. My neighbour Ann was here with me at the time – she'd come over earlier, while the police raided my house, and stayed with me. She shut Tracey up for saying something nasty about Jason, then left.'

'What exactly did Tracey say?' Fenton asked.

'Something about Jason being with another woman. She reckoned that's why he wasn't answering his phone. Some years ago, Jason and I lost a son, Bobby. He was stillborn,' Melissa explained, tears rolling down her cheeks. 'I was overcome by grief, pushed Jase away and he ended up having an affair. I slung him out for six months, but I was still in love with him and forgave him. Tracey didn't though. She would never let the subject go. She would always bring it up, so that's what she was probably referring to yesterday.'

'To your knowledge, was that the only affair Jason had, Melissa? I know these are upsetting questions, but we need to build a picture of Jason and his lifestyle,' Noakes said, apologetically.

'Yes. That was the only affair and Jase was genuinely sorry. It was horrible at the time, but if anything, it made our marriage stronger. We spoke about going abroad to renew our wedding vows only last week, and we planned to try for another baby soon,' Melissa wept. 'I cannot get my head around the fact he's dead. I keep expecting him to walk through the front door and give me a big hug like he always did.'

Noakes laid a see-through plastic bag on the coffee table. It contained a large gold-coloured earring. 'Does this belong to you, Melissa?'

'No. I don't wear dangly earrings, only hoops or studs.'

'Have you any idea who it might belong to? Could it be Shay's?' Fenton enquired.

'I doubt it, but I can't say for certain. It's not really Shay's style. She goes for the rock-chick look.'

'Could it be Tracey's, do you think?' Fenton probed.

'Erm, I suppose so. She always wears big dangly earrings. Jase used to say she was trying to give Pat Butcher a run for her money. He was so funny, bless him. Why do you ask? Where did you find it?'

The two officers glanced at one another, but said nothing. It was too early to jump to conclusions.

Elton Rampling answered the front door. 'All right?'

'Can I come in?' Shay asked.

'Whatever you wanna say ain't gonna take long, is it? Only me and Kyle gotta be somewhere soon,' Elton replied, surreptitiously glancing around the front door. There'd been no word from the other gang yet, but Elton was still expecting some kind of retribution. Donte was part of their gang, therefore revenge would be sought at some point. They couldn't stay holed up for ever though, had to brave it and be seen not to be scared. As Jason had always said, 'What will be will be.'

Babs had been inconsolable, so much so, she'd collapsed holding her chest and Shay had been forced to call an ambulance. Shay hadn't wanted to leave her, but was too grief-stricken herself to face sitting up a hospital. Lee had stayed at home to look after Britney and Shay would visit Babs later if she ended up being admitted.

'Whassa matter?' Kyle asked, as tears poured down Shay's face.

Shay perched herself on the edge of the filthy sofa. 'It's Jason. He's been murdered.'

'No way, man.' Elton gasped. 'Where? When?'

'Yesterday. He was at a property in Upshire. I was the one who found him. Someone shot him in the head.'

Kyle's face drained of colour and he stared knowingly at his brother. 'Fuck, man. They gonna get it big time now.'

Elton booted the door. 'Motherfuckers. No way, not Jase.' This was the exact kind of retribution they'd been expecting.

Melissa opened the front door and was horrified to see Jason's nan standing there. 'Oh hi, Peggy,' she said awkwardly.

'Where is he?' Peggy barked.

'Erm, you'd better come in. I take it you haven't already spoken to Shay?'

Peggy marched inside the hallway. 'No. Spit it out then. What's happened? Been nicked again, has he?'

'Come in the lounge and sit down, please.'

'Just cut the crap, will ya? We've got a cab waiting outside.'

Melissa took a deep breath, then burst into tears. 'He's dead, Peggy. I'm so sorry.'

'Dead! Don't talk such bollocks. I saw him only the other day and he was fine. Full of the joys of spring, if anything.'

'If this is some kind of wind-up, it isn't very funny,' Irish Ted warned.

Melissa glared at the man. 'I would hardly be joking about my husband dying. Jason was my world. I loved him dearly.'

The colour drained from Peggy's face. 'When? How?'

'Yesterday. He was shot. Some bastard murdered him. I'm in bits and so is Shay. She was the one who found him, bless her.'

'He got shot here?'

'No. He was in Upshire.'

Peggy eyed Melissa with suspicion. 'Where was you?'

'At the police station with Donte. He had a fight, stabbed a lad and has been charged with murder,' Melissa wept.

'Where's the money?' Peggy snarled.

'What money?'

'The money from that painting.'

Completely thrown that Peggy even knew about the painting, Melissa grabbed the door frame for support. 'I don't know. Not being funny, but the last thing on my mind at the moment is bloody money. We were going to renew our marriage vows, try for another baby. We had our whole future mapped out, and now he's gone.'

Peggy pushed Melissa hard in the chest. 'Your crocodile tears don't fool me, you gold-digging tramp. Come on, Ted. Let's go.'

'How dare you speak to me like that,' Melissa yelled.

Peggy turned around and pointed a finger. 'I've got your number, don't you worry. I'll be speaking to the police me fucking self.'

Depressed and inebriated, Tracey Thompson flicked through the Sky channels. 'Fucking good luck to her. I'd do the same given the chance,' she said out loud, as she clocked the title of the documentary she'd found: *I Murdered My Boyfriend.*

Thoughts of Greg tormenting her mind, Tracey started to weep. She had convinced herself earlier that Greg was genuine and would be in touch as soon as he could, but deep down she knew the longer she didn't hear from him, the less chance there was of that happening. Perhaps he'd been caught carrying out his big job? was the latest story Tracey had invented in her overactive mind. She'd already planned to stand by Greg if the sentence wasn't too long and even visualized their reunion in prison. He would get down on one knee in front of the other inmates and proclaim his undying love to her.

The thumping on the door startled Tracey. It was obvious Mel was avoiding her. Her mobile was switched off and she hadn't answered her phone all day, so it couldn't be her. Nobody ever visited this time of night apart from Greg so, wondering if it were him, Tracey quickly put some lipstick on and, full of optimism, yanked open the front door.

'What the hell! What do you think you're doing?' Tracey yelled, as a horde of policemen barged inside her property. There were dogs as well, two of them, and she hated dogs, they scared her. 'Get them beasts away from me. I don't want them in my lovely home,' she screamed hysterically.

Noakes grabbed hold of Tracey and marched her into the lounge. He waved a piece of paper in her face. 'This is a warrant to search your property. Sit down and be quiet, otherwise I will have to handcuff you.'

'Greg's not here. I haven't seen him, I don't know where he is,' Tracey shrieked.

'Clock the programme,' Fenton grinned.

Noakes glanced at the television screen. 'Very apt,' he mumbled.

'Guv – up here,' one of the team yelled within minutes.

'Watch her,' Noakes ordered Fenton. He could hear the dogs going ballistic.

'Not very well hidden. Found under a loose floorboard in the walk-in wardrobe,' an officer said, triumphantly patting his canine companions who'd led him straight to the haul.

Gloves already on, Noakes peered inside the black dustbin sack. It contained a gun, blood-splattered clothes and shoes. He turned to his colleague and grinned. 'Bingo.'

CHAPTER FORTY-TWO

Melissa was in bed, dozing, when she heard the doorbell chime. She'd lain awake most of the night, worrying.

'I'll get it,' Shay shouted out. She hadn't slept either. Every time she shut her eyes all she could see was her father with a gaping hole in his head. 'Mel, it's the police,' Shay bellowed.

Melissa put on her dressing gown and glanced in the mirror. She looked awful, every inch the grieving widow.

'We think it would be best if you sit down, Mel. You too, Shay,' Fenton urged. This was bound to come as a big shock to both women, Melissa especially.

Melissa's heart pounded against her chest as she sat on the sofa. 'What's happened?'

Noakes sat on the armchair opposite the two women. 'Late last night, we charged somebody with Jason's murder. They are denying any wrongdoing, but we have ample evidence and are confident of a positive outcome.'

'Who is it? Who killed my dad?' Shay cried.

'I'm so sorry to have to inform you of this, but the person we've arrested is Tracey Thompson. We found what we believe to be the murder weapon hidden inside her house, along with other incriminating evidence. The evidence is currently with forensics and we are hoping to have some answers by the end of tomorrow at the latest. We have marked our findings as extremely urgent.'

'Tracey! No. But why?' Melissa asked, her voice tinged with bewilderment.

'This is all your fault. She was your mate. I never liked her in the first place,' Shay screamed at Melissa.

'I know this is an awful shock, but we will need to take statements from both of you as soon as possible. The more evidence we gather, the less chance Tracey's defence will have,' Noakes explained.

'Well, she can't be innocent if you've found the gun, can she?' Shay spluttered. 'And she was acting weird round here the other day. That was the afternoon of the day Dad was found. She kept going on and on about him, the murderous evil slag. I'll fucking kill her. If I ever see her again, I'll throttle her with my bare hands.'

'I can't believe it,' Melissa wept. 'We've been best friends since school. I knew she had a nasty streak, but this! Jason didn't like Tracey, but he never stopped her coming into our home and being part of my life. I'm even godmother to her child. Poor Toby. How do you tell an innocent child that his mother has committed a murder? Has Simon been told the news yet? Only, he'll have to take full parental responsibility for that poor little mite now. How could she do such a thing? I've always been there for her, always.'

Tracey Thompson lay in her cell in Chelmsford police station, her mind running amok. Jason was dead, so the police reckoned, and they'd had the audacity to charge her with his murder. It was ridiculous, beyond ridiculous in fact, and she could not wait to make them look like the stupid arseholes they were by proving her innocence.

Last night had been awful. She'd just finished her second bottle of wine when the police had turned up. Apart from going ballistic when they'd handcuffed her, she could remember very little. Had they marched her upstairs and shown her a gun? Tracey mused. Or, had she dreamt that bit? It was all a blur, but she could recall kicking out at a dog and the officer who'd handcuffed her.

Visualizing Jason, Tracey shut her eyes. She didn't believe for a minute he was dead. If anything, he'd probably faked his own death and run off with another woman. It wouldn't even surprise her if he'd tried to implicate her in some way before doing so. He looked at her with hatred. She'd seen the way he looked at Toby too. What's the betting he couldn't handle being around his son, so had done a moonlight flit? She wouldn't put anything past Jason Rampling.

When her cell was unlocked, Tracey sat bolt upright. She couldn't remember being questioned last night, had been thrown straight in this cell if her memory served her correctly. 'About bloody time. You found Jason? Can I go home now?'

Having been warned she was a violent one, the officer handcuffed Tracey. 'The way it's looking, you won't be going anywhere for a long time, love.'

Simon Champion shook his head in disbelief. Two officers he'd not met before had come to tell him the news. 'Nah, that can't be right. Tracey's a fantasist, makes stories up. She's no psycho though. I dated her twice.'

When Dennings, the male officer, explained they'd found incriminating evidence at Tracey's house, including what they believed to be the murder weapon, Simon flopped back on to the chair with a thud. 'That house belongs to me. I bought it especially for Tracey and Toby to live in. She can't be guilty. She wouldn't murder Jase. She was always round his place, eating his food and drinking his wine. Why the hell would she want to kill him? I know she was always jealous of his and Mel's marriage, but that was only because she couldn't find happiness herself. She was married once, her husband died in a collision on his motorbike. I think it was because of that she was very bitter towards others.'

'Have you got a key for Tracey's property, Mr Champion?' asked Simms, the female officer.

'No. Tracey asked me for the spare key a while ago and never gave it back. She preferred me to pick the little 'un up away from the house. She's all about appearances, is Tracey. I never matched up to the Brad Pitt criteria she saw herself with. I bumped into one of Tracey's neighbours recently and the woman had no idea I was Toby's father. Tracey had told the woman his father was a gangster serving a long sentence for smuggling diamonds. This is what I mean when I say fantasist. I would never have her down as a murderer though. What am I meant to tell our son? Will she get bail?'

'I think that's highly unlikely, considering the circumstances, Mr Champion,' Dennings said. 'We will need to take a statement from you. Seeing as you own the property Jason was found in, and also the property where the evidence was found. You'll need to confirm your whereabouts on Wednesday as well – not that you're a suspect or anything.'

'I was at Colchester Zoo most of the day with Toby, a pal of mine and his son, Peter. We stopped at a restaurant for something to eat on the way home, then I drove straight to Mel's. She'd left messages on my phone earlier in the day saying she was trying to get hold of Jase, but I'd purposely left my phone in the car. A couple of my clients had been driving me mad the past few days and I needed a break. I returned Melissa's calls while I was in the restaurant and could tell she and Shay were worried. That's why I drove straight there. Tracey had not long left, by all accounts, had been drunk and acting weird, Shay told me.'

'And you and Shay drove straight to the property in Upshire, did you?' Dennings asked.

'Yes, that's right. Jason can be a bit of a fly-by-night, so I wasn't unduly worried. I only started to panic when I realized the front door had been left open. All the lights were off and it was getting dark by then. I urged Shay to wait in the car, but she's headstrong, like Jason. She ran upstairs and found Jase laying there, the poor bastard.'

'Have you a spare key for the Upshire property?' enquired the female officer.

'Yes. It's in the safe at my office. I keep all my sets of spare keys there.'

'Is there any way Tracey could have got her hands on that key?'

'Well, yes, I suppose so. I gave her the code after Toby was born. She took money out a few times while I was away on business. But she would always ask me first. As far as I'm aware, she has never been to my office without my knowledge.'

The two officers glanced at each other. The key that had been found among other evidence was the key to the property in Upshire.

*

Tracey Thompson stared at the evidence that was lying on the table in front of her very eyes. It was a gun, very similar to the one she'd found in Greg's sports bag. Not that she'd know one gun from another, but it was the same size. 'And?' Tracey said nonchalantly.

Noakes pushed the sealed see-through bag towards her. 'For the benefit of the tape, I am showing Miss Thompson exhibit A, the gun that was found under her floorboards inside her walk-in wardrobe.'

'No way!' Tracey spat. 'That isn't mine. I've never seen it before.' She was angry now, wanted to get out of this dump so she could visit Melissa. Jason wasn't dead. He couldn't be and only Mel would tell her the truth. Assuming she knew it, of course.

'We believe this gun is the weapon that was used to kill Jason Rampling. It was found in your house, Miss Thompson, and has your fingerprints all over it. How do you explain that, if you've never seen it before?' Noakes probed.

Tracey smashed her fists against the table. This was beyond a joke now, was becoming scarier by the second. 'You're lying! You never found that in my house, neither is Jason dead. Prove to me he's dead. Go on, prove it.'

Fenton grinned. He had hated Tracey Thompson on sight and didn't believe in the dumb blonde act she was putting on. She actually reminded him of his ex-fiancée, Laura. She'd been a lying bitch too. 'For the benefit of the tape and Miss Thompson's lack of belief in what the police force tell her, she is being shown a photo of the deceased, Jason Rampling.'

Tracey flinched as her eyes focused on the photo in front of her. A man who looked very much like Jason was lying on the ground, his eyes closed and a gaping hole in his head. 'Oh my God! That isn't him, is it? Please tell me it isn't Jason. It can't be him,' she screamed.

Shay opened the door to Simon, her eyes red and puffy. 'Mel's in the kitchen. What you brought him round here for? That's her son. The slut who murdered my dad,' Shay hissed. She was so angry, hated the world right now and everybody in it.

'What matter, Shay?' Toby asked, perplexed by the unusual greeting. Shay normally gave him kisses and cuddles.

'Go see your wonderful Auntie Mel. She's in the kitchen,' Shay barked, without even looking at the child.

When his son scuttled off, Simon turned to Shay with hurt in his eyes. 'Tobes is an innocent child, Shay. I know you're upset, and you've every right to be. But it isn't Toby's fault what happened, or mine, or Mel's. None of us could have foreseen this coming.' Melissa had told him on the phone earlier that Shay was blaming her.

'I don't want to look at her kid, OK? I'm going to my room,' Shay growled, stomping up the stairs like a naughty schoolchild.

Melissa rolled her eyes as Simon entered the kitchen. 'Leave her be. She's in shock; bless her, like we all are.' Mel picked Toby up and smothered him in kisses. She would always be there for her favourite little boy, no matter what.

'Swimming pool,' Toby grinned, pointing towards the garden. The rain they'd had the past couple of days had stopped now. It was bright and sunny again.

'Go put your trunks on first then. You know where they are,' Melissa said, lowering the child to the ground and playfully tapping him on the bottom.

'You heard from Donte yet?' Simon asked.

'No. He has broken my heart, Simon. He hates me.'

'No, he doesn't. He'll come round.'

'Do you fancy a coffee?'

'It's too hot for coffee. I'd love a beer though, if you've got one.'

Melissa opened the fridge and handed Simon a cold can of Foster's. 'I still can't believe Jase is dead, can you? I didn't sleep at all last night. I miss him so much; keep expecting him to walk through the door. I can't believe the police have charged Tracey. What could possess her to want to kill Jason? It doesn't make any sense, does it?'

Simon cracked open the can. 'The woman is obviously a fucking psychopath, she must be. I can't get me head round what's happened either. It's madness, just doesn't seem real. Shall we sit in the garden and talk? We can watch Toby play. It's sweltering in here.'

Melissa smiled. 'OK.'

Simon winked. 'After you.'

Tracey Thompson was no longer brazen. She was scared witless, the reality of the situation she'd gotten herself into having now hit home with one almighty bump. The duty solicitor was useless, had advised her to not comment on the accusations, but Tracey was determined to prove her innocence. 'I swear on my son's life, I am telling the truth. Ask Melissa, if you don't believe me. I told her all about finding Greg's sports bag with the gun inside. That's how my fingerprints must've got on it. Mel knew I touched the gun, I told her that too. Ask her, go on, ring her up or something.'

Noakes looked at Fenton and raised his eyebrows. Tracey was certainly a fantasist. She acted as though she truly believed in what she was saying. 'For the benefit of the tape, I am now showing Miss Thompson exhibit B, a bloodstained pink Dolce and Gabbana T-shirt. Does this Dolce and Gabbana T-shirt belong to you, Miss Thompson?'

Tracey was open-mouthed. 'No. Well, yes. But I only bought it a couple of weeks ago. I've only worn it once. That's not my blood on it, or Jason's. It can't be,' she shrieked.

'We'll see about that when the forensics results are in. This really isn't looking favourable for you, Tracey,' Fenton said. 'Why don't you just admit the truth and tell us why you killed Jason? Were you having an affair with him? Was that the reason? Only, your friend Melissa is in bits, deserves to know the truth, don't you think?'

Tracey felt sick to the stomach as Greg's handsome face flashed through her mind. He'd set her up, he must have done. But why? No wonder he'd had his phone cut off, the evil conniving bastard. 'I swear to almighty God that I am innocent. You have to believe me,' Tracey wept. If circumstances had been different, she would've been inclined to blurt out the truth. That she'd always secretly been in love with Jason, Toby was his son, and she'd have run off with him tomorrow, given half a chance, but she couldn't say that now. The police would see that as an incentive for murder, would think she was some bunny-boiler who'd flipped, and nothing could be further from the truth. 'Speak to Melissa, please,' she begged. 'I swear she will tell you all about Greg and the gun. There was paperwork too, a plan of a building and a balaclava. I thought he was an armed robber. Mel's met him. We were out together at the Prince Regent the night I first set eyes on him. He looked like Brad Pitt. Ask her. She'll back up my story, I promise you she will,' Tracey sobbed.

Realizing Tracey was in no fit state to continue the interview, her solicitor asked to take a break.

Noakes said he was stopping the tape, sealed it in a bag, then asked Tracey and her solicitor to sign for it.

Overcome by the enormity of Jason's death, the accusation aimed at her and Greg's ultimate betrayal, Tracey fell in a heap at Noakes's feet and clung to his ankles. She looked up at him, sobbing. 'Please go and see Mel. I beg you.'

Noakes gestured for Fenton to follow him. 'Don't worry, we'll check out your story. I hope for your sake you're telling the truth, love. Because if your mate tells us any different, chances are, you're doomed.'

Toby Champion stared forlornly at his toy truck as Shay stepped over it completely ignoring him again. As far as he knew, he hadn't done anything wrong.

Melissa was fuming, had had enough of Shay's childish behaviour. She stomped into the kitchen after her stepdaughter and slammed the door. 'I thought better of you, d'ya know that. I was proud of you yesterday when you told me you'd visited Babs and Jason's brothers to tell them the news in person, and your father would've been proud of you too. But this, today, is playground behaviour. That poor little sod asked me earlier if he'd been naughty. He hasn't a clue what is going on. You're not the only one who is hurting, Shay. I've lost my son and husband in the space of two days. And my best friend, so to speak. How the fuck do you think I am feeling?'

Shay's eyes welled up as the truth hit home. 'I'm sorry. I know it's not your fault, or Si's, or Toby's. It's that nutty slag's fault, nobody else's.'

Melissa walked over to Shay and enveloped her in her arms. 'Let all them tears out, sweetheart. Don't bottle 'em up. I'll always be here for you, ya know. You're the daughter I never had.'

'And you're the mum I never had,' Shay replied sincerely.

'Go and give Toby a cuddle, eh? None of us have eaten all day. Shall we order a takeaway in a bit?'

'Mel, the police are back again,' Simon shouted out. He opened the front door and invited Noakes and Fenton inside.

'Sorry to bother you again, Melissa,' Noakes apologized. 'But I have some more questions regarding Tracey. She was insistent I visited you.'

Melissa sat on the arm of the sofa. 'Would you take Toby upstairs and bath him, Simon?' she asked. 'The little 'un is staying here tonight. Simon hasn't told him anything yet,' Mel explained to the officers.

Noakes sat on the armchair and took out a notebook. 'Tracey informs us she's recently been dating a man named Greg Richardson whom she met on a night out with you. Can you verify that for us?'

'Erm, I wouldn't exactly call it dating. She met a guy called Greg when we last went up the Prince Regent, but as far as I know, he took her out a couple of times, then she never heard from him again.'

'Tracey also informed us that Greg left a sports bag at her house that had a gun inside. She proclaims she handled the gun and told you all about her find.'

'No,' Melissa lied. 'First I've heard about a gun or sports bag. I don't think Greg ever stepped foot inside her house. She would've told me had things gone that far. She really did like him though, kept on droning on about him all the time. She's like that with every man she meets, mind.

Becomes obsessed very quickly and I think that's what drives them away.'

Noakes glanced at Fenton. Both were thinking the same thing. A positive DNA result was all they needed now and they could celebrate.

'I'm going with Simon to pick up the takeaway, Shay. It's so stuffy in here, I need some fresh air. Do you want anything else brought back?' Melissa asked.

'A bottle of Coke. I'm not even hungry, but I know I should try and eat something.'

'Yes, you must. We'll start planning your dad's funeral tomorrow, give him the send-off he deserves. Have a think about what music you want played. I won't be long. Keep your eyes peeled in case Toby wakes up, won't you?'

Melissa followed Simon outside and got in the passenger seat of his Range Rover. 'You OK?' she enquired.

Simon put his forefinger to his lips and drove towards a spot he knew was secluded. You could never be too careful. He very much doubted the police were treating himself or Melissa as suspects, but he'd learned from an early age, it was better to be safe than sorry.

Peggy Rampling marched into Dagenham police station with Irish Ted by her side. There was a queue of people waiting and none of them looked English. 'I need to go before you lot,' Peggy said in a very slow manner, hoping they would understand her. 'My problem is very important,' she added pointing at herself.

'So is mine,' said a Muslim-looking chap with a cockney accent.

'Your grandson been fucking murdered by his wife an' all then, has he?' Peggy hollered.

'Keep your voice down, pet. You don't want to get arrested yourself,' Irish Ted warned.

'Why don't you sod off down the Paddy club with all your Paddy mates. You're a bastard hindrance, not a help.' Peggy's heart was literally broken, but she was determined not to let her emotions get the better of her. It was too much of a coincidence that Jason had been murdered right after receiving a huge windfall and Peggy wanted to make sure a certain woman got her just desserts. Only after that would she grieve, in private. Her Jason had always been there for her, God rest his kind soul, and Peggy was determined to be there for him. It was the least she could do. She had known from the start that marriage would end badly, but never in her wildest dreams had she envisaged this.

As somebody walked out the reception area, much to the displeasure of the others waiting, Peggy barged in there.

'Were you next in the queue?' the duty sergeant asked.

'That doesn't matter.' Peggy banged her fists on the counter. 'I want to report a serious crime. My grandson's wife had him murdered.'

Simon reached his destination, leapt out the motor and opened the passenger door.

Melissa fell into Simon's arms. 'Did you get the money?' she whispered. She had given Simon the key to Jason's safety-deposit box.

'I sure did,' he grinned. 'The world's our oyster now, babe. Well, it will be once the trial is over.'

'I wouldn't be so sure about that. Jason's nan knows about the painting.'

'Shit! He never told me he'd told her.'

'Nor me. She turned up at mine today, all but accusing me of murdering him. She said she was going to the police.'

Simon rolled his eyes and stared into Melissa's. 'Try not to worry. She's known to the police for shoplifting and no one on earth would suspect us as long as we stick to our story and plan. Did you get rid of the contract for the house?'

'Yes. I burned it.'

'Good girl.'

'Do you honestly think we've got away with it?'

'Without a doubt. More chance of hell freezing over than Tracey getting off.'

'I did feel sorry for Shay though, finding Jason like that.'

'Unavoidable, unfortunately. She was adamant on accompanying me to the house. Would've looked fishy had we stopped her.'

'I know.'

Simon moved a lock of Melissa's hair away from her face. 'Any regrets re Jason or Tracey?'

Melissa looked into the kind eyes of her husband's best friend. 'None whatsoever. What goes around comes around.'

Squeezing Melissa's buttocks against his rock-hard penis, Simon smiled. 'That's my girl. I love you.'

Melissa felt a wave of happiness wash over her. All she had ever wanted in life was a man she could trust, who loved her unconditionally and who wanted the same things as she did. It was just a damn shame she'd had to go to such lengths to achieve it.

CHAPTER FORTY-THREE

2009 – Eight Months Later

Melissa Rampling clambered inside the black taxi, put her seatbelt on and closed her eyes. She was dreading today even more than she'd dreaded Jason's funeral and giving evidence, couldn't wait for it to be over with.

'Why didn't Simon travel with us?' Shay enquired. She had no idea her step-mum and Simon were deeply in love.

Melissa opened her eyes. 'Because he had to drop Toby off at his sister's house first. He'll meet us at the court.'

'How long does a jury usually take to reach a decision?'

'It varies. Not being rude, Shay, but I really don't feel like talking. I had no sleep again last night and can barely think straight. Why don't you put your headphones on, listen to some music.'

When Shay attached her Beats to her ears, Melissa shut her eyes again. Giving evidence had been one of the worst experiences of her life. Tracey had understandably looked at her with hatred throughout, as she'd told lie after lie. 'You absolute fucking wrong 'un. I thought you was my friend, you evil bitch. I've been set up. She knew all about

Greg and the gun. Tell 'em. Go on, tell 'em the truth,' Tracey had screamed at her at the top of her voice, before being carted away to calm down.

'How could you do this to me, Mel? I loved you, like a sister. My DNA was only inside that property because you asked me to meet you there and you showed me around. Why are you lying? Tell them the truth, I beg you. Please,' Tracey had sobbed on another occasion. Melissa had run out the court that day, hadn't been able to handle it.

Jason's nan had been another thorn in Melissa's side. 'You've got the wrong person in the dock. It should be her on trial, Jason's wife,' Peggy had pointed out. 'She's the one who had him topped, you thick bastards.'

Another time, Peggy had mentioned the painting. 'He'd just come into a lot of money, my Jason. He'd sold a very expensive painting. That's why his wife had him murdered. Ask her where the money is. Go on, ask the evil conniving gold-digging whore,' Peggy had screamed at the jury. Thankfully for Melissa, the judge had slung Peggy out that day and told her not to come back.

Melissa wished there had been another way, but there hadn't. Under no circumstances would Jason have allowed her and Simon to set up home together, raising his son. He would have demanded a DNA test, then made sure she and Simon never saw Toby again. Tracey would've sided with Jason too, especially if he was fucking her occasionally. Knowing Jason as well as she did, he might've even moved in with the deceitful slapper as some kind of sadistic payback. Jason was jealous-natured and would have hated her to be happy with another man, especially Simon.

The moment Toby had been born, Melissa had known.

The likeness to Bobby was uncanny, eerie in fact. Desperate for her fears not to be true, she had tried to push her suspicions to the back of her mind. But the more Toby began to develop, the more she could see Jason in him, so she'd visited her husband in prison, swiped a plastic cup he'd drunk out of, and sent it, along with a swab out of Toby's mouth, for a DNA test. The test confirmed her very worst nightmare and Melissa had cried herself to sleep for weeks afterwards. She'd been unable to get the vision of her husband and Tracey fornicating out of her mind. How long had they been seeing each other? Had he been fucking Tracey when he married her? Did he love Tracey? All sorts of questions tainted Melissa's thoughts and that's when the hatred had started to fester. She'd been a good wife to Jason, loyal, had even raised his daughter. She deserved better, much better, so she'd hatched a plan to get her hands on his money. Many a time she'd wanted to tell the no-good bastard and her so-called best friend that she knew their sordid little secret, but that would've blown her plan to smithereens. So she'd bided her time, polished her sweetness-and-light act, while secretly planning her revenge.

Acting normally around Tracey wasn't easy, but as time went by, Melissa actually quite enjoyed pulling the wool over her treacherous friend's eyes. By then, she and Simon were in cahoots. Having always valued Simon as a family friend, Melissa could not keep such an awful secret from him, so after some deliberation had told him the truth about Toby. Simon had been devastated beyond belief, would have throttled Jason with his bare hands had he not been in prison. But Melissa had urged him not to do or say anything rash. 'Between us, we can con him out of that money he gets for the painting, Si. He owes us both big time, so let's hurt him where it'll hurt him the most, in his pocket,' she'd suggested.

As she and Simon plotted and planned, feelings they never knew they'd had for each other began to develop. Learning Toby was Jason's flesh and blood made no difference to the way either of them felt about him. Toby was a beautiful boy with a soul to match. Nobody would ever replace Bobby, but Melissa cherished Toby as though he were her own, as did Simon. That would never change, no matter what.

Shay's voice snapped Melissa out of her daydream. 'See those flats, Mel? They look exactly the same as the one me and Dad lived in. In Buckhurst Hill,' Shay pointed out miserably. She missed her father terribly. Throughout those years he'd spent in prison, they'd written, spoken on the phone regularly and she'd been able to visit him. Now all she had to visit was his grave, and she hated going there. The thought of her handsome, strapping father's corpse lying in that coffin was too much for Shay to bear.

Also being driven to the court was Tracey Thompson. She'd spent the past eight months residing in Holloway Prison and had hated every single second of it. A gang of black women regularly picked on her, bar one, a fat lesbian who insisted on being called Beyoncé. She looked nothing like bloody Beyoncé and Tracey was more scared of her frequent heavy-handed advances than the actual bullies.

Chewing furiously at what was left of her fingernails, Tracey thought about Melissa. She hated her one-time best pal with an absolute passion now, and if she could have smuggled a knife into court today, she would've stabbed the lying bitch through the heart.

What Mel had done to her was beyond despicable. She'd sworn on the bible, then lied through her teeth while giving evidence. Simon had also lied. He hadn't known about the sports bag or the gun, neither had he known much about her relationship with Greg. But he had known full well she did not know the code to the safe in his office. She hated him now too, but nowhere near as much as she despised Melissa. Tracey had trusted her like a sister; even let the sad bitch play mother to her son, and this was how she'd repaid her.

There was no doubt in Tracey's mind that she'd been set up and Greg was the bait. She had genuinely thought he'd liked her, could be 'The One', and now felt incredibly stupid at being conned. She'd even let the no-good bastard shag her up the arse. Tracey had told her solicitor all about Greg and had demanded DNA and fingerprints be taken from her house to catch him. Unfortunately for her, there had been no match on the police database with anybody called Greg Richardson, and Tracey now doubted that was his real name. He was probably called Charlie or Tom, or knowing her fucking luck, Brad. No wonder he had been so vague all the time, giving nothing away about his life. She didn't have a clue who the hell he was and kicked herself all day every day for being so bloody gullible.

As the meat wagon slowed down, Tracey concentrated on what she did know. The only reason she could think of for Melissa betraying her in such a cruel manner was Mel wanted her son. No way could she be involved in Jason's murder. Melissa was weak, gutless and wouldn't be able to live with herself. It must've been Simon who'd ordered the hit on Jason. He'd found out that Jason was Toby's father and told Mel. That had to be it. There was no other viable explanation, none whatsoever.

*

Outside the Old Bailey, Johnny Brooks greeted his daughter with a comforting hug. 'Not long now and it will all be over,' he reassured her.

Melissa was now on very good terms with her father. They'd built bridges while Jason was in prison. She'd never told Jason, because it was sod-all to do with him, but she'd finally forgiven her dad for all his wrongdoings. Shirley Stone was actually a very nice lady. Melissa had spent a lot of time in her company these past few months, and they got on extremely well. Her father and Shirley were the only other people who knew she and Simon were in love, and she and Si now spent a lot of time over in Llafranc on the Costa Brava where her dad and Shirley lived. They would travel separately on different days to avoid any unwanted suspicion. Simon would even fly to a different airport, then travel to Llafranc by car. It was the only place they could be a proper couple and both of them had fallen in love with the pretty costal town. Unlike a lot of the Costa Brava it wasn't overrun with tourists. It was an idyllic location for them to blend in.

Greg's real name was Duncan Pierce. Her father had met the handsome, charismatic con man in Spain. Duncan lived on the Costa Brava, not far from where Johnny was based. Melissa knew Tracey's taste in men to a T and the second she'd clapped eyes on Duncan at a secret meeting arranged by her father, she had known her pal would fall hook, line and sinker for him, providing he played his cards right. 'Tracey has always seen herself as a gangster's moll. You need to have an air of mystery about you to keep her interest. You also need to flash the cash. She is extremely money-orientated,' Melissa had informed Duncan.

The night at the Prince Regent had been all planned

out. Then at the last minute Melissa had been totally thrown off balance when Tracey suddenly insisted they should go to Club 195 instead. As long as she could remember, Melissa had gone along with whatever Tracey wanted. But that night she'd stuck to her guns. Thankfully, Tracey had agreed.

Duncan had been brilliant in schmoozing Tracey, gaining her trust, and hoodwinking her. It had been his idea to set up a tiny camera in Tracey's walk-in-wardrobe after Melissa had told him Tracey wouldn't be able to stop herself from looking inside the sports bag. The camera had since been disposed of, along with the video evidence of Tracey handling the gun with her bare hands. Melissa and Simon had been shown the webcam footage and chuckled over it for days afterwards.

It hadn't been Duncan who had carried out the actual hit on Jason though. An associate of his had been responsible for that. Whoever it was wished to remain anonymous, and that suited Mel and Simon. They had no desire to know his name, as long as the job had been carried out properly.

Thick Tracey had entrusted Greg with her spare key, therefore it was Duncan who planted the blood-splattered clothes, shoes and gun inside Tracey's house. The whole operation had cost Simon a hundred grand plus expenses, but seeing Toby's happy face on a regular basis, Melissa knew it was money well spent. Toby knew nothing of his birth mother's predicament. She and Simon planned to sit him down after the trial to explain in a way a child would understand. Toby barely mentioned Tracey these days anyway. All he'd been told was that Mummy had gone on a long holiday, and he seemed happy with that. He hadn't even asked when she was coming back.

'You OK, love? You're miles away.' Johnny Brooks nudged Melissa's arm.

'Yeah – well no, not really. Say she gets away with it, Dad. What then?'

'She won't get away with it. She'll go down for life, you mark my words.' His Carol had loathed Tracey Thompson from the first day their daughter had brought her home. 'She's trouble that one. A bad apple. Let's hope Mel's friendship with her fizzles out quickly,' were Carol's exact words.

Melissa thought back to all the witness statements. She'd invited certain people to Jason's homecoming knowing they would stand up in court if need be. She'd also plied Tracey with alcohol, knowing full well it would lead to her slagging off Jason.

Eleanor Collins-Hythe had stood in the witness box and told the jury, 'In my opinion, Tracey Thompson had an unhealthy interest in Jason Rampling. She would not stop talking about him that evening at the party. She even told me about an affair he'd once had with a woman called Charlotte. I told her she was wrong to be discussing her friend's business behind her back, but she just carried on regardless.'

Knowing what a nosy cow Eleanor was, Melissa had wanted to laugh. She wasn't a bad person though, unlike Tracey.

Another witness had been Melissa's personal trainer, Roy Nixon. He'd also heard Tracey slagging off Jason and had seen her follow him out into the garden, where an argument seemed to occur.

Ann, Melissa's neighbour, had been fantastic in court. She pulled no punches, did Ann. She'd stood there as bold as brass in her Primark tracksuit and told the jury, 'Tracey

Thompson is a bunny-boiler. You ever watched that film *Fatal Attraction*? Well, that's how she was over Jason. The woman is a complete and utter fruitcake.'

The only witness who hadn't come across well was Simon's supposed ex-girlfriend, Sally-Ann. She hadn't wanted to take the stand and had spent the whole time glaring at Simon. Melissa remembered the evening well when Simon had showed her the woman he'd chosen off the dating site. They'd needed a decoy in case anyone suspected their relationship. 'Jesus, Si. She's got a nose like Concorde. You could have picked a better-looking one,' Melissa had laughed.

'Morning, Melissa. No word re the jury yet, but my instinct tells me we'll have a verdict by the end of the day. Don't hold me to that, mind,' DI Noakes said. He was in an extremely buoyant mood this morning, 99 per cent certain the decision would go their way.

Feeling jittery, Melissa forced a smile. She hadn't wanted to attend court today, could not face looking Tracey or the jury in the eyes again. Say the jury had worked out she'd lied? They might send her to prison instead. She'd started to freak out last night and it was Simon who'd insisted she must attend. 'It'll look bad if you're not there. One more day, babe, and it'll all be over, for good,' he'd told her.

When Simon appeared minutes later, Melissa said a casual 'Hello' then excused herself to use the toilet. What if Tracey started shrieking what was very near the truth out loud again? Had the jury believed her version of events? Tracey obviously had no idea that her and Simon were an item, as Melissa knew without a doubt she'd have screamed that out too.

Splashing her face with cold water, Melissa stared at

her reflection in the mirror while giving herself a good talking to. She couldn't crumble now, she'd come too far.

Tracey Thompson paced her cell like a woman possessed. 'Fucking bitch, lying slag, evil whore,' she shrieked as Melissa's face popped into her thoughts.

The jury were still deliberating, which was a good sign according to her solicitor. Surely they would see through all the lies? As if she'd be stupid enough to hide the murder weapon and evidence in her own home had she committed such a crime! It was ridiculous to even suggest such a thing.

Wondering how Toby was, tears poured down Tracey's cheeks. He'd be getting big now, and must miss her terribly. If only her own stupid mother hadn't sodded off to Turkey, she could have looked after Toby.

Convincing herself the verdict would be a positive one, Tracey allowed herself a wry smile. Once she was set free, she would hire a solicitor and tell the truth about who Toby's father really was. That would give her total control, and she would ensure Melissa and Simon never saw her son again. That would teach the lying bastards not to mess with her.

Not in the mood to join in with Simon and her father's conversation, Melissa sat outside the court alone and thought back to all the evil things Tracey had done to her. It made her sick to the stomach to think what a fool her so-called best friend and Jason must've thought she was. They'd always acted like they loathed one another in front of her, when in reality they were fucking one another's brains out. How they must have laughed at her in private, made jokes about how thick she was. Well, not any more. Jason had paid the ultimate price for underestimating her and, hopefully by the end of today, Tracey would too.

Melissa's mind drifted back to her schooldays. Tracey had been a bully, always picking on less popular girls in the playground. Truth be known, Melissa had only started knocking around with her in the first place because she was scared of Tracey. She was the type of girl that you were better having on side than not.

Melissa was snapped out of her reminiscing by the sound of Simon's voice. 'The jury are back. They've reached a decision.'

Stony-faced, Tracey Thompson stood in the dock glaring at Melissa. The bitch wouldn't look back at her, which was hardly surprising, considering the wicked lies she'd told.

The judge cleared his throat. 'Will the foreman of the jury please stand up?'

Melissa was sitting between her father and Shay. She clenched her father's right hand and Shay's left. 'Please God, let her be found guilty. Please, please, please,' she mumbled, staring into her lap.

'Have you reached a decision on which you all agree?' the judge asked the foreman.

'Yes, your honour.'

'Defendant, please stand,' the judge barked.

Tracey stood up and clung to the dock, her hands trembling. They had to find her innocent, she had done nothing wrong.

'On the count of murder, do you find the defendant, Tracey Louise Thompson, guilty or not guilty?'

Melissa's heart was in her mouth. She could barely breathe.

'Guilty, your honour.'

'Yes!' Shay yelled, leaping up in triumph. 'Rot in hell, bitch.'

Tracey's knees buckled from under her. 'Noooo. You can't do this to me. I'm innocent. I've done nothing wrong. I would never hurt Jason,' she sobbed.

Thoroughly drained, Melissa clung to her father for dear life.

Eyes blazing with fury, Tracey turned to the jury. 'You stupid cunts! She's a liar. I told the truth. Jason is the father of my child, you morons. I loved him. I've always loved him.'

As two prison officers made a grab for her, Tracey began wriggling like an eel. She kicked one, spat at the other, then turned to Melissa and pointed. 'This ain't over, you lying slag. I'll have you for this; you won't get away with it. Over my dead body will you bring up my son, you conniving two-faced fucker.'

Judges in English courts rarely used gavels any more, but Judge Sutton was old school. Banging away, he glared at Tracey over the rim of his glasses. 'Get her out of my sight,' he bellowed. 'Take her down.'

CHAPTER FORTY-FOUR

2010 – One Year Later

Listening to the waves lap against the shore, Melissa smiled. She loved living in Llafranc. The pace of life was so much slower; it was a different world from Chigwell.

'Would you like to order some food, madam?' asked the waiter.

'No. Not yet. I'm waiting for the others to arrive. They'll be here soon.'

Melissa rarely thought back to the past these days, had trained her mind not to, but today she couldn't help herself. She had learned only yesterday that Tracey was appealing against the life sentence she'd been given, which Melissa found unsettling.

Simon had urged her not to worry. 'So what if she proves Jason was Toby's real father? It's my name on Tobe's birth certificate, nobody can take him away from us,' he'd insisted.

Melissa prayed Simon was right. It was common knowledge they were a couple now and living together on the Costa Brava. Shay had been none too impressed at first, had thought it was too soon after her father's death, but Melissa and Simon had stuck to the same story. Their relationship had started approximately a year after Jason's death, grief having played a part in bringing them together.

Tracey had been told she must serve a minimum of fifteen years for Jason's murder. When sentencing her, the judge described her as: 'A callous woman, a fantasist who had shown no remorse.' Simon was right about one thing. Even if Tracey was to prove Toby wasn't his, no way could she pin Jason's murder on them. There was too much evidence against Tracey for her to walk free.

Donte was still a thorn in Melissa's side. He had been sentenced to seven years for manslaughter, but had then got into even more trouble in Feltham. He'd hooked up with some bad lads, a newcomer had been stabbed, and an extra three years had been added to Donte's sentence. He was no longer at Feltham, had been carted off to Ashfield Prison in Pucklechurch near Bristol after his latest misdemeanour.

Melissa was so disappointed in the way Donte had turned out. He was sullen, cocky, rude and showed no remorse for his actions. His real father, Joel Wright, had been a bad apple, so Melissa surmised it was in the genes. She would never give up on him though; he was still her flesh and blood, no matter what he did. Every month she and her father would travel back to the UK just to visit him.

Melissa still kept in contact with Shay, would always class her as her step-daughter, and Shay had promised to visit her in the Costa Brava later this year. Soon after Jason's death, Shay had ended her relationship with Luke, insisting it's what her father would have wanted. She'd settled down now, was living with a lad called Grant in a flat that Simon owned. Melissa had yet to meet Grant, but he sounded very nice and obviously treated Shay well.

Mel had no contact with the rest of Jason's family but heard snippets via Shay. Peggy Rampling was still adamant Melissa had taken out a hit on Jason, but thankfully neither Shay nor the police believed her. Having got herself chucked out of the actual trial, Peggy had been waiting outside the court after the verdict. She had attacked Melissa, hit her over the head with Irish Ted's walking stick, and the police had carted her off. Peggy often popped up in Melissa's nightmares even now. She was too close to the truth for comfort.

Babs was no longer with Lee. That relationship had ended badly. Lee had regularly knocked Babs about, by all accounts, and he'd ended up pushing her down the stairs in the flats they lived in. Poor Babs had wound up in intensive care with a fractured skull. She now lived with her daughter at a secret address and had taken out an injunction against Lee. He was forbidden any contact with Babs or her daughter, Britney.

Jason's brothers hadn't changed, were still a waste of space. Elton had got a five-stretch for dealing in cocaine and Kyle had been sentenced to three years for robbing an Indian shopkeeper. Melissa rued the day Donte had ever got involved with those two. They'd certainly played a huge part in her son spiralling out of control.

Melissa's reminiscing was ended by her father and Shirley Stone's arrival. 'Christ, Dad. Couldn't you have worn a louder shirt? Good job I have my sunglasses with me,' Melissa joked.

Johnny Brooks looked down at his latest Hawaiian number. 'Sod-all wrong with it. Shirley said the same as you. Got no bleedin' taste, you women, that's your problem.'

Shirley hugged Melissa. They were good friends now, often went shopping at the local market and visited the beauty salon together. 'I did try to tell him, Mel, but you know what an obstinate man he can be,' Shirley chuckled.

'You told him yet then?' Johnny asked.

Melissa pointed to the box on the table. 'No. I thought I'd wait until we were all together. I've given him all his other presents though.'

'Has he got an inkling, do you reckon?' Shirley asked.

Melissa grinned. 'None whatsoever.'

'Excuse me a tick. I'm desperate to use the ladies' room,' said Shirley Stone.

As soon as Shirley walked away, Melissa leaned closer to her father. 'What do you think about Tracey's appeal? Did you speak to Simon earlier? I'm worried, Dad. Very worried.'

'Stop worrying. Everything will be fine. Tracey hasn't got a leg to stand on, trust me.' Johnny Brooks put his arms around his daughter's shoulders.

'I so hope you're right. It's always there in the back of my mind, you know. I had the most horrendous nightmare early hours of this morning.'

'You got to look to the future now, Mel. That's what your mum would want you to do. The past is the past. Sod-all we can do to change it.'

'Yeah, you're right. Did Duncan ever say if it was quick, Dad? You know, Jason's death.'

'It was an in-and-out job. These hitmen don't mess about,' Johnny lied, squeezing his daughter's hand. 'You have a wonderful man now and a brilliant future ahead of you. I don't want to hear any more talk about the past, OK?'

'OK.'

'Mummy, Mummy.' Melissa's thoughts returned to the present as Toby ran towards her, arms outstretched.

'Sorry we're late. But, because it's my birthday, Tobes decided it must be Dolly's birthday too and I've been dragged around the pet shop, looking for a present for her,' Simon explained, jovially rolling his eyes.

Melissa chuckled. Dolly was the stray dog who had turned up at their apartment as a puppy. Toby had fallen in love with her cute foxy appearance and had insisted she was his. She was now, had cost Simon a fortune in vet bills, toys and accessories. Spoilt rotten, the bloody mutt was.

'Look what I made for Daddy.'

Melissa gushed as she studied the front of the homemade card. It had been she who had sat Toby down and told him, 'Mummy did a bad thing and the police have sent her away for a very long time. But you're not to worry as Daddy and Auntie Mel will take good care of you, we promise.'

Having not seen Tracey for months anyway, Toby had been totally unfazed. 'If my mummy has gone away, can I call you Mummy now?' he'd asked. Melissa had agreed of course. He was like a son to her anyway.

Shirley Stone walked back over to the table. 'Happy birthday, Simon. Your present's in the car. We'll give it to you later.'

'Cheers, Shirl. You all ready to order? I'm bloody starving,' Simon grinned.

Melissa pushed a square box towards him. 'Open this first.'

'Not more presents. How lucky am I?' Simon chuckled.

Inside the box was a white envelope with a bow tied around it. Simon undid the bow, ripped open the envelope, then gasped as he clocked the content. 'Oh my God! Really? You're kidding me!'

Melissa beamed from ear to ear as Simon studied the scan of the baby that would be arriving in five months' time. It had been so hard keeping the news a secret from him, but not only had she wanted to get past the three-month stage, she'd also wanted it to be the best birthday present ever.

Simon grabbed hold of Melissa and hugged her. 'I can't believe it. I thought you'd put on weight.'

'Cheeky!' Melissa chuckled.

'What is it?' Toby asked, jumping up and down. He could sense it was something exciting.

'A bottle of your finest champagne over here please, Roberto,' Johnny Brooks bellowed. He stood up and shook Simon's hand. 'Shirley and me already knew, but Mel was determined to surprise you on your birthday. So chuffed for you both. Brilliant news.'

'Cheers, Johnny.'

Simon picked Toby up and spun him around in the air. 'How do you fancy having a little brother or sister?'

Toby turned his nose up. 'Don't like girls.'

Watching the joyous scene, Melissa finally knew she'd done the right thing. Taking a hit out on Jason had been her idea, and it wasn't an easy decision. It was the right decision though. Fuck Jason and Tracey. She wasn't the weak, simple woman they'd taken her for.

As the old saying goes, 'Hell hath no fury like a woman scorned.'

EPILOGUE

The moment he lifts the shield on the helmet, I know I'm in big trouble. 'Long time no see. What the hell you doing here?' I stammer.

When he points the gun at me, urging me to guess, I know my minutes left on this earth are numbered. I think of Shay, my nan, Babs and Donte. The four people who rely on me the most. Then I think of my wife. 'Does Melissa know you're here?' I ask him.

'No. But she certainly knows your life is about to come to an end. It was Melissa who ordered the hit on you.'

I am gobsmacked at that point. 'You what! But why?' I stupidly ask.

Johnny Brooks laughs out loud. 'Did you honestly think she hadn't cottoned on that Toby was your son? You thick piece of shit. I reckon what swung it though was when I told her it was you who took a pop at me that time outside my home. You and that dickhead mate of yours, Craig Thurston.'

I know there is no point in lying. 'I'm so sorry, Johnny. It wasn't me who pulled the trigger. I couldn't go through with it and begged Craig not to either,' I admit.

'I know. I heard you. Story of your life, eh? Unlike myself, you were never truly cut out for a life of crime, Rampling. I thought you were at the beginning – it was one of the reasons I encouraged my Melissa to marry you. But I soon realized I'd judged you wrong. You were never going to be an asset to me in the heists my gang pulled off. It was all a front, my builders' merchants, you know. I've taken part in some of the biggest robberies this country has ever witnessed.'

'Why are you telling me this?'

'Because I want you to know everything before you die. I'll tell you something that will really shock you now, shall I? Bet you didn't know Melissa and your mucker Simon were in love. They've been planning a new life together with your money from that painting. Gotta give you credit for that one, lad,' Johnny chuckles.

My legs buckle. I fall backwards against the wall and slide down it. 'How long?' I ask, putting my stupid head in my hands.

'How long is what? A piece of string?' Johnny taunts.

'Simon. How long! How long has it been going on?' It's all beginning to make sense now.

'Their affair started while you were in prison. Nobody knows apart from me and Shirley. Oh, and Greg Richardson. That's not his real name though. I hired him to set up Tracey Thompson. She's the one who'll be going down for your murder,' Johnny laughs. 'What goes around comes around, son.'

I am stunned. What type of woman did I marry? I'd always thought Melissa was a good person, and Simon. But all along the pair of no-good bastards have been plotting behind my back.

I am not going to beg, I'm far too proud for that. But

I make one desperate attempt to save my life. 'Think of the kids, Johnny. Shay and Donte both adore me. I'll get out of the way, go abroad, you'll never see me again, I swear.'

'Too late, sunshine. Taking a pop-shot at me – that I could deal with. But not upsetting my girl. I warned you when you married her that I would kill you if you ever hurt her. Unlike yourself, I'm a man of my word.'

As I see Johnny's hand go to squeeze the trigger, I decide I have nothing to lose by making a lunge at him.

I fail miserably and the bullet enters my head. I try to fight death, but then I see her. She looks radiant, not like when she had the cancer, and she is holding her hand out, urging me to follow her.

I take my final breath, then fall into the arms of Darlene Michaels. My one and only true love.